# SCENT OF THE ROSES

## ANNOTATED EDITION

## PG FORTE

"Long, long be my heart with such memories fill'd!
Like the vase in which roses have once been distill'd
You may break, you may shatter the vase if you will,
But the scent of the roses will hang round it still."
(Thomas Moore — Irish Melodies)


"Absence diminishes commonplace passions and increases great ones, as the
wind extinguishes candles and kindles fires."
(Duc de la Rochfoucauld)

# INTRODUCTION

*"Scout Patterson had been running away from home for twenty years."*

That was the line that started it all. The "gift" that popped into my head one sunny, Sunday afternoon. It's the opening line of the very first book of my very first series. And today, it's truer than ever before.

It was in 2003 that I attended my very first writers' conference. As luck would have it, I was seated at lunch next to the owner/editor-in-chief of a small, independent publisher who had come to the conference looking for something very specific: Big books in a long series with a magical element. In other words, the next Harry Potter.

I was there pitching the first four books in the Oberon series. Big books? Check. Long series? Check. Magical element? Check!

Oberon met her criteria, her contract met with my-brother-the-lawyer's approval, and six months later, book one, Scent of the Roses, was released. It didn't exactly set the publishing world on fire, but it did launch my author career and it's always held a special place in my heart.

But times change and publishers close their doors and when I first got the rights back to the series, a few years ago, I wasn't quite sure what I wanted to do with them.

My first thought was that they needed updating. So I planned go through each of the books and figure out how to make them more contemporary. But so much had changed!

Advances in technology have altered how we relate to and communicate with each other. Changes in social mores mean that some of the characters' actions hit differently now than they did when the books were written and/or first released.

When I was writing the series, I felt like I was writing a love letter to my adopted home state of California. Oberon encompasses everything I loved about California. It's sort of a modern day Camelot.

That's Camelot from the Broadway musical of the same name, by the way. Which is NOT necessarily the same as the Camelot from the ancient Arthurian legends.

But reading the books now, I realize they were love letters to the time, as well; and to the life I was living in the late 90s – early 00s . Raising my kids; socializing with friends; docenting at a couple of local nature centers; hanging out in restaurants and cafés, at wineries and breweries, in kennels and wildlife rescue centers. And the idea of ripping that apart to create something new and different kind of hurt my soul.

Plus, there were a few dedicated readers who'd read and loved the books when they were new and who'd deemed them "comfort reads"...well, maybe not books seven and eight, those can be a little dark, but as a whole.

I felt a sense of responsibility to those readers. I figure the world needs all the comfort it can get, at this point. And if traveling back in time a little, teensy bit, can do that for people, I'm all for it.

But that didn't help me with the problem I faced. I couldn't get away with calling a book "contemporary" when there are pay phones on every corner and landlines in every home. Where nothing is ever stored in the cloud—because the cloud doesn't exist yet. Where marijuana is illegal everywhere and the term marriage equality hasn't even been coined—to say nothing of #MeToo and "Own voices".

Y'see, Oberon is a progressive kind of place. In one of my earliest rejections, a NY editor informed my then-agent that the series was "too far left of center" for them to consider.

She wasn't entirely wrong. And that's kind of been true of me, as well. So I feel confident in saying that a lot of the changes we've seen over the years are ones that would have been celebrated and embraced by most of Oberon's residents. If I moved the series fully into the twenty-first century, I couldn't ignore those changes. But incorporating all of that into the series would have been a massive undertaking. With—potentially—far reaching consequences for the characters. It would have changed so many things in so many ways that, in the end, I just couldn't do it.

I don't recall how or when I first hit upon the idea of annotating the books as a quasi-solution, but I'm so glad I did.

Delving back into the stories, noticing the "march of progress" (so to speak) making small changes and celebrating a place and time that I lived in and loved has been an absolute joy for me. And I hope the result is something that readers of the series, both new and old, can find pleasure in as well.

Welcome (back) to Oberon. I hope you enjoy your stay.

PG Forte

# PLAYLIST

I listened to A LOT of music while I wrote this book and I thought it would be fun to share some of it with readers. But, as often happens, once I started I found it hard to stop. So, here's a link to nearly 100 songs—just under six hours of music—to (hopefully) enhance your reading pleasure. Enjoy!

https://tinyurl.com/Scent-of-the-Roses-Playlist

# CAST OF CHARACTERS
## IN ORDER OF APPEARANCE

**Scout Patterson:** Banished from her home as a teenager, her return will have far-reaching consequences for the other inhabitants of Oberon.

**Gil Patterson:** Scout's father—the celebrated, much married artist whose tragic death resulted in Scout's being forced to leave town.

**Caroline Larson:** Scout's stepmother. Twenty years ago, she sent Scout away. Now, her death, and the unexpected terms of her will, draws Scout home again.

**Larry Mitchell:** Scout's agent.

**Marsha Quinn:** Once one of Scout's best friends, this 'born-again Pagan' has an unfortunate penchant for 'fixing' other people's lives. Her teashop, The Crone's Nest, is a popular local meeting place.

**Celeste Greene:** One of Marsha's closest friends. Her tarot card readings prove to be very unsettling.

**Lucy Greco Cavanaugh:** Loyal to a fault, and capable of holding a formidable grudge, Lucy has never forgiven Scout for the mess she made when they were all in high school together.

**Heather Finch and Ginny Hartman:** Also friends of Marsha's, these relative new comers to Oberon, own the local bookstore.

**Jasmine Quinn:** Marsha's daughter—she's bound for college in the fall.

**Robyn Smith:** A student at the local college, she has been renting rooms from Caroline for the past two years.

**Glenn Gilchrist:** Lisa's high school sweetheart, now a lawyer for the firm handling Caroline's estate.

**Lisa Larson:** Caroline's daughter and Scout's stepsister. The mystery surrounding her disappearance has never been solved.

**Dan Cavanaugh:** Lucy's husband. He runs the local nursery where Robyn works.

**Nick Greco:** Lucy's cousin and a local police officer. Twenty years ago, he was Scout's 'mystery boyfriend' but was it really nothing more than a 'lovely fantasy'?

**Seth Cavanaugh:** Lucy and Dan's fifteen-year old son.

**Mandy (Amanda) Cavanaugh:** Lucy and Dan's daughter.

**Kate Greco:** Nick's daughter. She and Mandy are inseparable.

**Paige Delaney:** The local reporter is sure there's a story behind Nick's obsession with Scout.

# 1

---

*S*cout Patterson had been running away from home for twenty years.[1] But her home was in quirky, idyllic Oberon, California. And Oberon was not an easy place to leave behind.

There's something magical about the place—that's the one thing everyone could always agree upon. Something that transcends explanation and defies description.

To the Native Americans who'd originally settled the area around Mt. Totawka, Oberon was sacred ground, a natural focus for spiritual power. Or, to frame it another way; things happen there that could happen nowhere else.

But magic is just one part of the Oberon mystique. People are also drawn there because of the hot springs, the artist colony, the annual hot air balloon fest; to any one of a half dozen local harvest festivals – almond, artichoke, strawberry, olive, garlic, grape; and to the widely publicized, public observance of every solstice, equinox and sabbat celebration on the solar calendar. [2]

So, despite its being the smallest of small towns, located along a particularly remote stretch of Central California coastline, Oberon had always attracted more than its fair share of tourists. And so it had often seemed to Scout that someone she knew was always either just about to go there or had only recently returned.

For twenty years she'd viewed the snapshots they'd taken; she'd admired their acquisitions – the artwork, the wine, the occasional tan. And she'd listened to the stories they'd brought back from their trips with the same unwilling fascination that causes drivers to slow to a crawl as they pass the scene of an accident. Part fear and loathing, part morbid curiosity.

Now, after all those years of knowing she could never return, Scout Patterson was going home.

*Home. Now there's a concept!* Scout thought, as her car sped along the very roads she'd spent years avoiding.

For most of her childhood, the idea of 'home' had held very little meaning. She was still an infant when her parents separated and her mother had taken off for parts unknown, leaving Scout's father to bring her up as best he could.

And he *had* done his best, she supposed. But Gil Patterson had been an artist—first and foremost—and that role would always take precedence over almost everything else. His main focus had been his work. And he'd funneled most of his remaining passion into his love life, diving headfirst into one disastrous relationship after another, often moving them from city to city in the process. No one had ever argued that Scout's upbringing had been ideal. Certainly Scout had never felt inclined to defend it.

Oberon had been the only place that ever even came close to meeting her expectations of what home should be. She'd passed most of her adolescence in the little town, experiencing more warmth and security than she'd ever known. Until, without warning, a brief, bewildering confluence of events swept through her young life. And, in the space of a few short weeks, she lost everything she held dear.

Shortly after her sixteenth birthday, Scout found herself bound for Florida to live with a grandfather she hadn't seen since she was three years old. It had not been her idea to leave Oberon, but by the time she'd boarded that plane she was long past caring about much of anything.

Her charmingly eccentric father was dead. Her beautiful step-sister had disappeared. And she had betrayed, or been betrayed by, most of her friends and everyone she loved.

So Scout would go where she was sent, do as she was told, answer whatever questions were asked her; and generally try to live life as best she could with her heart dull and dead within her.

*But for how long?* The thought welled up out of nowhere. Scout lunged for the radio, flicking it on and rapidly punching buttons in a vain attempt to find something worth listening to. But the barren stretch of highway that extends north from Los Angeles is not known for its plethora of alternative rock stations. Muttering a curse, she gave up the search and resigned herself to being captive to her own sorry thoughts.

*How long? Well, it's been twenty years so far. Twenty years and counting...*

Scout's goal during those years had been simple: to steer clear of emotional entanglements. The income from her father's estate had made her independent and allowed her to indulge her own dreams of being an artist. She had traveled. She had wandered restlessly. Like a shark who must always keep swimming – even during sleep — or die.

For the last few years, she'd been living in Los Angeles, home of the professional dilettante, where she had dabbled in various forms of artistic expression. Including a de rigueur, extremely short-lived career as a film actress. Most recently she'd begun to receive recognition for her work as a sculptor.

If it sometimes struck her that the life that she'd created was just the slightest bit empty, just a little too aimless, boring and bland, well, it sure beat the alternative.

The ringing of her cell phone called her thoughts back to the present. Grateful for the distraction, she fished it out of her handbag without taking her eyes from the road.

"Scout! Where the hell are you?" Her agent's voice crackled through the phone. "I got a message here saying you're going out of town for awhile. *Awhile* is not a time frame I can work with, Princess.

You're not eloping with one of those yummy boy-toys you're always flaunting at me, are you?"

Scout smiled. "No such luck, Larry." Larry Mitchell, her agent and sometimes friend, had developed a hopelessly over-inflated picture of Scout's love life – of just about everyone's love life – since the departure of his most recent partner, Ronnie. "The boy-toys are all yours. I'm on my way to Oberon." [3]

"Ooh, lucky girl. What're you going up there for? It's June so…oh! I know; the Midsummer Festival—is that it? Gonna dance naked around the bonfire?"

Scout couldn't help but laugh at Larry's enthusiasm. "It's called a *balefire*, Larry. And yep, that's just exactly what I had in mind to do. I'll be back in a week or two."

"*Weeks*?" Larry's screech was sharp enough to cut glass. "What is it you're not telling me? I know there's gotta be a man in this somewhere. But even so, Midsummer's a two-day affair, darling. Three at best."

Scout gripped the phone against her shoulder as she swerved around a slow-moving truck. "Relax, Larry. It's nothing exciting, I assure you. Just some family business I need to take care of."

Larry was silent for so long that Scout began to think she'd lost the connection. "I didn't know you had family in Oberon," he said at last, his tone subdued.

*Of course, you didn't.* Scout bit back her response. There was a reason why she never discussed her family, or her past, with anyone. She could almost hear the wheels turning in Larry's mind as he scented a possible intrigue. With any luck, he'd have forgotten all about it by the time she got back to LA. And if not? Well, then perhaps it was time for her to think about getting a new agent.

She sighed. "I don't have any family there, Larry. Not anymore."

It was just over a week since she'd received the letter from the executors of her stepmother's estate, informing her of Caroline's death and acquainting her with the terms of her will. She'd immediately recognized the opportunity for what it was.

It was a chance to redeem herself, to redress a few wrongs. A chance, perhaps, to – ever so slightly – even the score. Possibly the last chance she was ever going to get.

It hadn't taken more than a couple of days to set things in order. She lived alone; worked for, and by herself; and had studiously avoided acquiring anything that would need even the most minimal amounts of maintenance—such as a goldfish, or even a houseplant. It had been several months since her last relationship had withered quietly away from neglect and disinterest, and there was no one to whom she owed an explanation for her decision to return to Oberon. Least of all her nosy, soon-to-be-ex-agent!

There was no one who would even think to wonder whether it was justice she was after, or revenge. But then again, no one had wondered about that twenty years ago, either.

Back then, she'd wanted revenge. Pure and simple. She'd gotten it, too. But the train of events she'd set in motion had run her over right along with everyone else. And ever since then, she'd been living with the guilt of what her revenge had cost.

After promising Larry she'd stay in touch, a promise she had every intention of ignoring, Scout hung up the phone and threw it back into her bag. Damn him anyway. She was fond of Larry, but she did not need *anyone* hovering over her like a mother hen.

She pressed down harder on the gas and the Mustang surged forward. The long strands of her hair, loose beneath the bandana she had tied around her head, snapped in the wind. Tears stung the corners of her eyes, and she gripped the steering wheel a little more tightly.

She had no illusions about what she was returning to. Or, at least, not many. Twenty years was a hell of a long time to be away from a place. It was quite possible there wasn't anyone left in Oberon who would still remember her, or care about those long-ago events. But if there was, they had best understand one thing; she was through with taking the blame for everything. What had happened back then hadn't *all* been her fault! There was more than enough guilt to go around. And she was more than willing to share.

THE MORNING WAS PERFECT. June. Sunny. A gentle breeze. There was not the slightest glimmer anywhere along the horizon to suggest that disaster was, even now, speeding towards Oberon; not the faintest tang in the air to warn of the storm that was brewing.

On the terrace of the little teashop she owned on Oberon's Main Street, Marsha Quinn sat and visited with a group of friends. It was her favorite place in the world, and she was conscious of a deep thrill of satisfaction as she looked at the women seated around the table with her. They were an unlikely mix, but each of them dear to her heart.[4]

She and Lucy had grown up together, right here in Oberon, and had been permanent fixtures in each other's lives for as long as either of them could remember. Being friends with Lucy Greco Cavanaugh, Marsha had reflected on more than one occasion, was a lot like being a member of a street gang. Once you were in, you were in for life. The commitment was total. Getting out, if you ever really could, would require an act of treachery so huge it might very conceivably end your life.

It was Lucy who had designed and created the terrace. Knowing that Marsha was short of money at the time, she had bullied her husband, Dan, into providing most of the plants for it free of charge. And then cajoled him into helping her plant them, as well.

The terrace was as perfect as the morning. Sunlight glinted off red and yellow sandstone pavers surrounding a large fountain, set amid a planting of nasturtiums and Mexican sage. The cool plash of water within the terracotta basin provided a soothing counterpoint to the wind chimes that hung from the branches of the surrounding trees. Corsican mint and dwarf thyme grew in low, wooly patches between the tiles. Their pungent scents, heady and intoxicating, rose from leaves bruised by careless footfalls.

A rose covered arbor, and several brightly colored beds of hibiscus, lavender, lantana and ornamental grasses further divided the space into a series of cozy, intimate nooks set about with mosaic topped tables. It was around one of these tables that the women were seated. They sipped mocha lattes and drank herbal tea and talked about whatever came to mind. Business and family. Life and love. Health, wealth, and happiness. Serious and inconsequential matters, alike. While the others conversed, Celeste idly flipped tarot cards. Her murmured commentary blended with the chatter.

"*A new beginning,*" Celeste intoned quietly.

Marsha watched her friend lay down another card. There was something especially mesmerizing about her performance this morning. Sunlight flashed from Celeste's bejeweled fingers and little rainbow-colored shimmers of light danced over the tabletop.

Marsha had been barely twenty years old, struggling to deal with both a new baby and the sudden emergence of psychic powers she could neither control nor understand, when Celeste appeared in her life. Serene and compassionate, Celeste was possessed of a wisdom that far exceeded her years. She had been the answer to all Marsha's prayers, providing guidance and encouragement, as well as free child-care for her daughter, Jasmine.

"*Re-evaluating a belief system.*"

The cards were a recent obsession, and so far, Celeste's readings with them had been wildly inaccurate. Which, considering that they had also been unremittingly alarming and grim, was not necessarily a bad thing.

"*The need for greater attunement.*"

Despite being a life-long practitioner of Wicca, Celeste was surprisingly diffident about her own abilities. She'd always been unquestioningly enthusiastic about Marsha's, however. And Marsha was all too happy to return the favor now. If Celeste felt she needed to spend all her spare time practicing with the tarot instead of going with her real strength, which was reading tea leaves, she'd get no complaint from her.

"*Nurturing. A deep and total love.*"

The other two women at the table were relative newcomers to the town. Ginny Hartman and Heather Finch ran the local bookstore. As fellow small business owners, they and Marsha often found themselves on the same side of the many debates that seemed to spring up with tiresome regularity during City Council meetings. But there was more than business or politics that drew them together. Heather had a wry wit that resonated with Marsha's own appreciation for life's little absurdities. And Ginny's warm, comforting presence was a balm for any emotional ache she might have.

*"A rite of passage."*

"Is Jasmine excited about her bike trip?" Heather inquired, vigorously stirring several spoonfuls of sugar into her latte. "When do they leave again? It's soon, right?"

"Monday morning," Marsha groaned, vainly attempting to suppress the feeling of panic that gripped her every time the subject of her eighteen-year-old daughter's cross-country bike trip was mentioned. "And you would not *believe* the amount of gear she has to have."

Ginny's brown eyes were warm with understanding. She reached across the table to squeeze her hand. "She'll be okay, Marsha. And so will you."

*"Unresolved issues."*

"Oh, I know," Marsha agreed. "It's ridiculous for me to feel this way. The boys are spending the entire summer in England with Alex, and I'm handling that okay. But this thing with Jasmine is really throwing me."

"It's probably because she's never really been away from home before," Lucy suggested reasonably. "You just need time to adjust."

*"Roots in the distant past."*

"Well, I guess I'd better hurry up and do that then, hadn't I? Since she's leaving for college in September."

*"A mysterious disappearance. Or, possibly, a reappearance?"*

Ginny turned to Lucy. "Speaking of trips, did your cousin ever get things straightened out about the camping trip next week?"

Lucy ran a piece of lemon rind around the edge of her at her espresso cup and scowled. "Of course not. His ex-wife just 'happened to forget' that it was his week to have Kate when she arranged to take her to visit her folks. Mandy was so upset that I—"

"*An unexpected death.*"

Silence descended around the table. Celeste looked up, seemingly surprised to find the others staring at her. "What?"

"Really, Cee?" Lucy snapped. "An unexpected *death*? Care to elaborate on that?"

Celeste just smiled. "Lucy, you know I'm not that good at this yet. It's all just impressions."

This remark was met with silence. Lucy continued to glare at her.

"Very vague impressions."

More silence. More glaring.

Celeste sighed. "Okay, fine. Let me see what else I can get."

Hooking a stray strand of silver-blond hair back behind her ear, she turned over a few more cards and studied them earnestly. "Hmm. Well okay, see, there are several women. Or possibly just female archetypes. I believe this one here is an especially young woman, maybe still a girl. But, basically, all the cards seem to point to a transition of some sort. I suppose it doesn't have to be an actual death, but some form of ending or transformation is definitely indicated."

She looked up and eyed them all solemnly. "Where it gets confusing is here. See this?" She pointed, first at one of the cards, and then at another. "It's still mostly in the future, but there's definitely a link to similar events that have occurred in the past."

Marsha shifted restlessly as a sudden awareness made her skin crawl. All week long she'd had this nagging sense of incompletion, and now—

"What is it?" Lucy's eyes narrowed. "You've got that 'oh, shit' look in your eyes again. Does this mean something to you?" [5]

"No, not really." Marsha shook her head slowly. "I think it just reminded me of a dream I had last night. But don't ask me what it was about, because I can't remember. I really ought to be more consistent about writing them down."

"You always say that, Marsha." Lucy smiled wryly. "But then you never do. All right, Celeste, let's see those cards again."

While her friends pored over the cards on the table, Marsha lapsed into thought. She could not account for the sense of unease that had been hounding her these last few days. It didn't seem to be connected to her children. True, her sons were spending the summer with their dad, but no matter how she felt about that situation, she knew the boys would be fine. Just as she knew there wasn't any real reason to be worried about Jasmine.

And it was unlikely her teashop was the source of the problem. Business was good. She looked around her, noting with satisfaction that most of the tables on the terrace were filled. Business was *very* good. She had taken a gamble opening this place four years ago with the money she'd received as part of her divorce settlement. Alex had hit the roof when he'd first learned about it. But then, the divorce had been his idea. He should have figured his resistance would only make her more determined to go forward with her plans.

In any event, the gamble had paid off. The Crone's Nest had become a Mecca for the legions of tired shoppers who trekked along Oberon's Main Street, asking for nothing more than a quaint place to stop for coffee or afternoon tea, or even just a chance to rest their feet.

More than a tearoom, the shop was also gaining a well-deserved reputation for carrying the very best in crystals and incense, ceremonial robes, jewelry, amulets, statues, books—basically anything that fell roughly into the category that Marsha had chosen to term 'Wicca-ware'.

Or, as Alex preferred to phrase it: weird, bloody overpriced, new-age magic crap.

Marsha and Celeste handled the day-to-day running of the business, as well as giving tea-leaf readings on request. Lucy provided most of the herbs, scented oils, soaps and candles they sold. Marsha loved the symbolism inherent in their triumvirate. They were like the three fates. Or the three witches in Macbeth. Or, even more importantly, the three aspects of the Goddess. Maiden, Mother and Crone.

But if it wasn't her family, her business or her friends she was worried about, what was at the root of this recurring frisson of unease?

"Who are you sending over to the nursery tomorrow to help Robyn harvest the herbs for the festival?" Lucy leaned across the table to ask, interrupting Marsha's thoughts.

"I was thinking of sending Maya," she replied, transferring her attention back to her friend with some difficulty. "She doesn't have a lot of experience, but I know she and Robyn are friends. So...unless Celeste wants to go?"

Celeste carefully slipped her cards into their little red velvet bag. "Oh, I don't care, sweetie. Whatever you decide is fine with me. Right now, however, I see that we're getting busy. So, if you ladies will excuse me, I need to go to work."

"Speaking of Robyn," Ginny said, turning to Lucy. "How is she doing these days? She's still out in that big house all by herself now, isn't she? That must be so hard for her."

Lucy shrugged in response. "Yeah well, I don't suppose coming home and finding your landlady dead could ever be easy. And I know that she and Caroline had gotten close—so I'm sure that made it worse. But she seems to be handling it okay. It's just too bad the other kids who share the house had already left for summer break."

"Not really by herself though, is she?" Heather grumbled. "She's got all those damn animals to take care of. I hear that place has turned into a real zoo." [6]

"But she has no other *people* out there with her," Ginny insisted, quietly. "It makes a big difference, Heather, you know it does. Anyway, I'm glad the new owner will be here soon. It will be nice for Robyn to have some real company."

With her teacup midway to her lips, Marsha froze. A cold, coiling sensation twisted knots in her stomach. Out of the corner of her eye she saw Lucy lean toward Ginny, an apprehensive expression darkening her gaze.

"What new owner?" she asked, in a voice that was ominously soft.

"Caroline's stepdaughter," Ginny replied, oblivious to the spiking tension Marsha could sense, flaring like an electrical storm through Lucy's aura. "At least, that's what I heard."

Lucy's voice was barely audible. "No. Way."

Ginny glanced at her in surprise. "Why, yes, dear. I think so." She turned to Heather. "Who was telling me about it? Heather, do you remember?"

"Nope. Your sources are always a mystery to me."

"Apparently, she's coming up from LA this week to deal with the estate. As I understand it, the plan is for her to stay in the house while she's here."

Marsha studied Lucy's sullen expression. "Are you okay?"

"What do you think?" Lucy snapped, a dangerous light gleaming in her eyes. "You know what this means."

"Yeah." Marsha knew her smile held little humor. "I know. Scout's coming home."

"Whoa, what's this now?" Heather demanded. "Who're you guys talking about?"

Marsha sighed and took a sip of tea. Finding it cold, she got the attention of a passing waitress, and ordered a fresh pot of jasmine tea before she answered Heather's questions. "We're talking about Caroline's stepdaughter. Scout Patterson. I assume that's who Ginny's referring to. Lucy and I went to school with her. We were friends."

Heather's flint blue eyes narrowed suspiciously. "Were you? So then, why is it that neither of you are looking all that friendly at the moment?"

"Really Heather," Ginny admonished. "If they don't want to talk about it—"

"Oh, hey, you know, it's not like it was a big deal or anything," Lucy muttered sarcastically. "Just because Marsha and I ended up getting expelled from high school thanks to our *friend*."

Heather's eyebrows rose. "Oh, I see. So, with friends like that, et cetera, et cetera, huh?"

"Look," Marsha felt obliged to point out, "if we're going to be honest, it wasn't *all* Scout's fault. We weren't exactly angels either. What Lucy conveniently neglected to mention is the reason *why* we were expelled. But as my mother never tires of reminding me, we're still the only students in the history of Our Lady of the Angels High School to ever be expelled for cheating."

"Well, I know I'm shocked."

Marsha grinned at Heather. "Yeah, you look it. It was pretty damn useless trying to explain that we hadn't exactly thought of it as cheating, you know? It was just supposed to have been an experiment with hypnosis."

"An experiment? Oh, I can't wait to hear this."

Marsha's mood turned serious as she remembered. "No, really. Scout was a great subject for hypnosis. She'd go into a deep trance almost instantaneously. And while she was under, she seemed to be able to access all sorts of psychic abilities. Things like astral projection, time travel, precognition; you name it, she could do it. It was wild."

"Yeah, but what was really important," Lucy cut in, a trace of her usual good humor resurfacing for just an instant, "Was that while she was in a trance, she'd also give us the answers to our math tests. For a while, we even got her to do our homework for us."

"Well, that sounds tres manipulative," Ginny murmured. "Weren't you even the slightest bit concerned about the repercussions?"

Lucy's smile disappeared again. "Aw, hell Ginny, we were teenagers. And good Catholic schoolgirls, at that. What did we know about the law of threefold return? Plus, it was *math*."

Heather chuckled. "Oh, right. Stupid of us. All's fair in love and war—and math. Obviously."

Marsha couldn't help laughing. "Something like that."

"So, what went wrong?" Heather asked as she lifted her cup to her lips. "I mean, questionable ethics aside, it sounds like you guys had it made in the shade, as they say."

Marsha sighed. "You don't know how many times I've asked myself that same question. But shortly after Scout found out what we were up to, the information we were receiving from her started to get faulty."

"What she's trying to say is that Scout lied," Lucy snapped. "Which really shouldn't have surprised any of us who knew her."

"Bullshit. You can't lie under hypnosis." Heather was emphatic. "Everyone knows that."

"Actually, I'm not so sure." Ginny shook her head. "It seems to me I was reading something recently that suggested that's not always the case. Of course, it would probably take a strong motivation."

"Or a really good imagination," Marsha added. "And Scout certainly had that."

Lucy scowled. "Imagination my ass. Stop prettying things up. That girl was a compulsive liar, and you know it."

"And now she's coming back." Ginny's tone was pensive as she fidgeted with the empty cup she'd picked up from the table.

"Jeez. Some fun reunion you guys are gonna have, huh?" Heather shook her head. "It'll be an interesting time, that's for sure."

Lucy sighed. "Interesting. Yeah. Not quite the word I had in mind. But hey, isn't there a Chinese proverb about that? *May you live in interesting times*, or something?"

"Yes, exactly," Heather replied. "Only it's not a proverb, hon. It's a curse." She jumped as Ginny dropped the cup she had been holding. "Although, I guess no use crying over spilt milk would be more apropos," she said, turning to her partner with a wry smile.

"Sorry about that Marsha," Ginny said, her voice subdued, more clipped than usual.

Marsha smiled reassuringly. "Not a problem. No use crying over spilled tea leaves, either." But she felt another frisson sizzle along her nerves. She glanced around uneasily.

"A curse. How perfect," Lucy muttered.

"Now, that's not like breaking a mirror, is it?" Heather teased Ginny. "You know, seven years of bad luck?"

"No," Ginny said firmly. "In fact, I think it's the reverse."

"Well, I certainly hope so," Marsha replied, trying to shake off the vague anxiety that nagged at the edges of her mind. "Because I have a feeling that we're gonna need all the good luck we can get."

---

1. This is the sentence that started it all. It literally popped into my head one Sunday afternoon as I was driving along the 580 on my way home to Berkeley (from San Rafael, if memory serves). I spent the next several years writing nine

long-ass books (and a handful of novellas) all to answer the questions, who is Scout Patterson and why is she running.

2. There is no one town upon which Oberon is based. I modeled it on quite a few small (and not so small) towns that can be found all along California's coast. But almost everything that you might find in Oberon can also be found (in some form or another) elsewhere in California. And all the things that draw people to Oberon are the same things that draw people to California in general.

3. Larry ended up being more of a minor character than I expected. He does show up toward the end of book two, but that was it UNTIL I wrote a short, Christmas story—I'll be Home for Christmas in which he plays another small but pivotal part. I might expand that story, at some point, but you can check the Oberon Christmas page on my website for more info.

4. At the time I started writing this series, I used to meet, on a more or less regular basis, with a group of women—usually for coffee, but sometimes for breakfast, or lunch, or...wine.

   There was one particular café we frequented and whose terrace provided the inspiration for The Crone's Nest. Just as our conversations (which were frequently about some of the various inexplicable experiences we'd all had) provided the inspiration for a lot of the psychic goings-on that occur within the series.

   Across the street from the café was a nursery/gardening center. It was pretty easy to combine the two in my head to come up with the perfect outdoor eatery.

5. Marsha's "Oh, shit" expression is something that Sam picks up in book two, and continues to reference throughout the rest of the series.

   One of my favorite things about getting to know these characters was seeing how all their little traits continue to wind their way from one book to another.

6. Fun Fact. Speaking of zoos, I'd just like to note that, at the time this book was written my family and I shared our home with six cats, five chickens, four lizards, three frogs, two turtles, one spider, a fish tank and a dog. So Caroline's house (and Lucy's as well) was definitely a case of art imitating life.

# 2

_____

*W*hen Scout left Los Angeles late that morning, she'd headed North, taking Route Five over the Grapevine and up through the San Joaquin Valley. She'd turned off the Five an hour or so past Bakersfield, and headed southwest on one of the leisurely winding roads that snake through part of the Los Padres National Forest. Then north again when she hit Route One, California's Pacific Coast Highway.

Now, as the sun was sinking into the waters of San Bartolo Bay, she left the coast road at Milagro Beach and headed east.

Her heart was beating just a little more quickly than usual as she took in the once familiar sights, glowing like molten gold in the evening sun. Fields lush with artichokes, garlic and strawberries segued into elegant vineyards where ancient-seeming stone buildings rose majestically above acres of carefully tended vines.

Softly rolling hills covered in tall yellow grass and dotted with dark, mysteriously twisted live oaks gradually replaced the Monterey cypresses that clung to the verdant coastal cliffs. And were then replaced, in their turn, by narrow, winding streets where quaint Arts and Crafts cottages and Mediterranean bungalows half buried in bougainvillea stood side by side with elegant Victorians and sprawling ranch-style houses.

Before her memories had a chance to emerge, her mind – with an ease born of long years of habit – adroitly steered itself away. Bypassing any connection that might trigger the grief and guilt that had once nearly overwhelmed her. Detouring around any thought that could lead to those areas of her heart where loss and loneliness still crouched like a wounded child.

Twilight had just begun to gather in pools of amethyst as she drove through the streets of her old neighborhood and pulled, at long last, into the elegant, circular drive.

*Someone's taken my spot.*

Annoyance flashed through her as she parked the Mustang behind the shiny black Montero [1]arrogantly angled below the front steps. She quickly suppressed her reaction. It was ridiculous, after all. Even when she'd lived here she hadn't had a designated parking spot. She'd had to share – both the space, and the silver Honda Civic she'd driven – with Lisa.

*Lisa?*

For an instant, she felt an irrational surge of something very like hope, but she suppressed that, as well. She knew better than to give in to anything so treacherous. Whoever the SUV belonged to, it almost certainly wasn't her stepsister.

She sat for a few moments, quietly reacquainting herself with every detail of the imposing yellow Victorian she had once called home. Her gaze caressed the lovingly preserved wood siding and gingerbread trim, the little round tower room rising above the gray-slate roof, the front porch, the bow windows, the white picket fence overgrown with wild Wood's roses.

*Caroline's house.*

It had changed so little since the day that she and her father had moved into it. She had to fight back the sensation that she could just walk through the front door and find the intervening years had been erased.

With a sigh, Scout wrenched her eyes away from the house and reached for her bag. The envelope Caroline's lawyer had sent her contained a set of keys, directions, even a map.

As though she would ever need directions to find her way back here!

Why, for the last few years she'd felt like one of those migrating birds – the ones with the little magnetic particles in their heads. No matter where she traveled, she had always known exactly where she was in the world in relation to Oberon.

Or maybe she was more like a salmon. She could probably have driven here today blindfolded, navigating by scent alone.

Heart thundering in her ears, hands shaking, Scout let herself into the house. The elegant foyer with its black and white marble floor and wide, sweeping staircase was just as she remembered it. She put her bags down on the floor and paused for a moment. There was no earthly reason why she should be out of breath; it was silly, really. But she was, just the same.

Faint rustles of sound coming from the back of the house alerted her to the fact that she wasn't alone. Twin phantom blades of hope and fear twisted in her heart, then dissipated under the weight of logic. Not Lisa, and most likely not an intruder either Caroline's lawyer had mentioned that at least one of the students who rented rooms in the house would be staying through the summer.

"Hello?" she called loudly. "Is anyone here?"

Rapid footsteps answered her call. Moments later, a tall, excitable looking young woman appeared in the hallway. "Oh good, you're here. He said you would be, but—Omigod!" she broke off with a quick intake of her breath. "Oh, wow, I never realized. Of course. You're *her*."

The last was said with a hand thrown out to gesture, dramatically and compellingly, at the wall next to the front door.

Scout should have known what to expect. Had she been thinking, she might not have turned just then. Might not have chosen that moment to confront the larger-than-life portrait that many critics considered one of her father's finest works.

A searing sense of loss hit her at the sight of it, followed quickly by wonder. How on earth had the girl recognized her from *that*? She'd been fifteen when she sat for that painting, and Lisa sixteen, less than a year before they'd both left Oberon behind.

Looking at it now, she could see no resemblance to the face that looked back at her from her mirror these days. Those smiling girls with their sunburned faces and windblown hair, with their arms thrown casually around each other's shoulders, were both long gone.

"I'm Scout," she said, turning her back to the portrait and extending her hand. "Scout Patterson."

"Right. And I'm Robyn Smith. One of your housemates."

It was not exactly how she would have put it. Even assuming she did decide to stay here permanently, which was not a possibility she envisioned, Scout was very sure she wouldn't need, or want a house-mate. But there was no point in going into that right now. She merely smiled politely.

As she shook Robyn's hand, her glance fell on the dog, an uncertain mix of mostly greyhound, white with reddish brown ears,[2] who had accompanied Robyn to the door.

"Nice to meet you, Robyn. And your dog."

"Oh, but she's not mine!" Robyn appeared shocked by the idea. "Come to think of it, I guess she's yours. She doesn't have a name yet, in case you're wondering. But I guess you can take care of that now that you're here."

Scout stared in surprise. Caroline's lawyer had said nothing about a dog. "She's *mine*? No, I don't think so."

"Well...sure. Just like everything else here, right?"

"Well," Scout began to disagree, but quickly decided against discussing the terms of Caroline's will. "I guess," she ended lamely.

And just what in the hell was she supposed to do with a dog?

As if in answer to her unspoken question, the dog began to growl softly, turning its head to stare back down the hallway. An instant later, Scout heard it, too. Another set of footsteps approaching.

She didn't recognize the man, but he smiled as he came toward her as if they were old friends. He was tall, maybe six-three, with hair the color of tarnished brass. Something about his smile did seem vaguely familiar, but his eyes were those of a stranger. His eyes were like blue beach glass – cool, opaque, unfathomable.

"Hey, there Scout," he murmured. "Been a long time."

"*Glenn*?" Scout gasped at the wrench of recognition in her gut. "What the fuck are *you* doing here?"

He laughed, and his smile grew even wider, but she couldn't help noticing that the expression still stopped just short of his eyes. "Hello to you, too, sweetheart."

*Sweetheart? Oh, hell, no.* Scout fell back a step as he reached out to grasp her shoulders, not sure what to do, or what to think as he bent and kissed her on the cheek. Expecting a reaction, she was surprised when she felt nothing—and thank God for that.

It was good to know that whatever had passed between the all those years ago had apparently left no lingering memory in her body's cells. Still, the foyer seemed suddenly to have shrunk to the size of a closet around them. Her heart tripped over itself for several beats.

"I need a drink." Her voice emerged squeaky and breathless. She wanted to bite her tongue when she heard herself ask, "I brought some wine with me, would either of you like some?"

*Now, why did I say that?*

She really wasn't looking for company, but, on the other hand, she could definitely use a drink. The whole week had been a regular stress-fest. Coming face to face with Glenn Gilchrist was just so much icing on the Goddamned cake.

Glenn smiled complacently. "Sure, that sounds great."

She could hear the confident amusement in his tone. An unpleasant flare of some emotion she didn't want to identify flicked across her nerves. Turning she led the way into the kitchen. As she uncorked the Merlot,[3] Scout tried to get her bearings. Item one on her agenda was puzzling out Glenn.

"So, Glenn—seriously—what in the world are you doing here?"

He shrugged one big shoulder nonchalantly. "Well, word around the office was that you were arriving today, so I thought I'd stop by."

Scout splashed some wine into the fragile balloon glasses Robyn had taken from the cupboard, and sneaked a surreptitious glance at Glenn. He'd always been tall, but now he seemed absolutely massive. "The office?"

"Donahue and Connelly. I'm practically a partner, you know."

She couldn't help but gape. "You're a *lawyer*?"

"You don't have to sound so surprised." He took the glass she offered him, allowing his fingers to graze slowly across hers as he did so. Then he leaned casually back against the counter. A small smile hovered on his lips as he watched her.

"I'm not surprised. Exactly." Scout felt herself flush. Okay, so maybe she had sounded the teensiest bit condescending. She hadn't meant to. Not really. There was just something about Glenn that always brought out the absolute worst in her. Suddenly chilly, she rubbed her hands up and down her bare arms. "It's just— I don't know, I guess I always imagined that you'd do something more athletic, or something." *Something less cerebral.* "I mean, you were always so good at sports, and physical stuff, that I—"

She broke off abruptly as it occurred to her how he might choose to interpret any remark she made about his physical prowess. *Damn.*

"Uh-huh." Glenn smiled. His eyes probed deeply into hers. The seconds ticked silently away.

Scout knew what he was up to and it was really pissing her off. She hadn't fallen for his act twenty years ago – although she could hardly blame him for thinking she had – she sure as hell wasn't falling for it now. Still, as the pain and frustration that had been building inside her for days began to mutate into something even more dangerous, more volatile, she had to fight back a sudden urge to accept the challenge he was presenting. To take him on and beat him at his own game.

She'd learned to play quite a few games over the last twenty years. She was very good at them, in fact. But she didn't want to play anything with Glenn. Been there, done that. So no fucking way was she making *that* mistake again. Once had been more than enough.

*Keep your temper*, she admonished herself, firmly. *Just find out what he wants and then get rid of him.* "You still haven't answered my question."

He smiled charmingly. "Why am I here? Maybe I just wanted to see you again. It's been a long time, but I've never forgotten you."

"Aw, gee, Glenn," she simpered, as her determination to remain civil dissolved again. "That is sooo sweet. But, well, here I am; and I really am tired from the drive. So now that you've seen me, perhaps you should go?"

Emotions flashed across his face. Too many to name, too quickly to count; in an instant they had all been replaced by another wide grin. "Same old Scout," he chuckled, though she'd swear he hadn't found her remarks amusing. "You always did have a mouth on you. I remember how much Lisa used to hate that. That, and how smart you were."

"Yeah, well. Not that smart as it turns out." Certainly not smart enough to have kept from walking right into that one. Lisa. The one subject she *really* didn't want to discuss with Glenn.

"Oh? You mean you're not a rocket scientist like everyone always thought you'd be?"

Scout sighed. "These days, I'm mostly into ceramics."

"Huh?" The look of sheer incomprehension on Glenn's face was almost comical. Well, that was Glenn for you, wasn't it? Always one hell of an athlete, but never the sharpest knife, even in a drawer full of mostly spoons.[4]

"Ceramics. You know, like pottery? Clay? I make bowls, pots, coffee mugs. Things like that," she improvised. Imagining what Larry's reaction would be to this description of the work he was currently representing in several major art galleries; it was all she could do to suppress a smile.

"Oh, yeah? Is there any money in that?"

She shrugged. "I do all right."

"Well, see? Something else we have in common. We both enjoy doing the opposite of what people expect us to."

"Is that why I can't get an answer to my question, Glory?" Glenn's old nickname tripped too easily off her tongue. "Because you think I expect one?" She took a sip of wine. And watched him. And waited.

Irritation flashed in Glenn's eyes. "Okay, look, I heard you were maybe a little upset about your stepmother's will. Donahue's an old fart, but I thought perhaps I could help."

*A little upset? Maybe? There's an understatement!* "How could you help?"

"Well, I don't know yet. Why don't you tell me what's bothering you."

Trust Glenn? Scout studied him for a long, silent moment. She wasn't sure she could. She was even less sure she wanted to. "How familiar are you with Caroline's will?" she asked at last.

"I, uh, I had a look at it before I came here," he admitted. She was unexpectedly diverted. "Is that legal?"

Glenn shrugged. "Do you really care?" he asked with a small smile that she couldn't help returning.

"Not really. No." She shook her head to clear it. "Okay. So then, you know the terms, right? Lisa and I share everything unless Lisa is dead. In which case I get it all. Only, as I'm apparently the last to learn, nobody seems to know where Lisa is."

"Is *that* the problem?" Glenn's smile widened into one of those charming, confident expressions he'd always done so well. "Because there are a number of ways to deal with that," he continued, leaning nonchalantly against the counter. "I'm sure Donahue—"

"The *problem,*" Scout interrupted, "is that until your office contacted me last week, I had no idea that Lisa was still missing! I mean, can you believe Caroline kept that little piece of information a secret from me all these years? The few times I saw her, or talked to her – idiot that I was, I just assumed she'd chosen Lisa over me. But that wasn't the case at all, was it?"

She knew she was ranting but couldn't seem to stop. "She just didn't want me around. After everything that happened, she didn't want me getting anywhere within miles of Oberon, ever again. And now— How the hell can I allow Donahue to have Lisa declared legally dead? Why not just come right out and say I killed her! It's the same thing, as far as I'm concerned."

Glenn looked stunned. "But...no. That's ridiculous. What are you saying? That it was Caroline's intention to hurt you? I'm sure that wasn't the case."

"Oh, no?"

"Look, Scout... I think we all have to accept that Lisa's dead. I mean, after all this time? She must be, right?"

*No!* Scout pushed the anguish to the back of her mind and scowled. "I'm sure that's easy for *you* to say. Nobody's ever blamed you for what happened to her."

"Scout, I—"

"Caroline blamed me for all of it—right from the start. And now you expect me to believe she'd simply changed her mind, at some point? And left me *everything*? Why would she do that?"

"Omigod, are you serious?"

Scout jumped at the sound of Robyn's voice. *Damn, I forgot she was even here.*

"Who else would she leave her stuff to? You're her *daughter*!"

"Stepdaughter." Scout and Glenn corrected automatically, at the same time.

Robyn rolled her eyes. "Yeah, yeah; whatever. The point I'm trying to make is that whatever else might have happened, you two were *family*. Caroline *loved* you."

"Oh, please." Scout shrugged dismissively. "Family? Love? What could you possibly know about that?"

Robyn flushed bright red. "Oh! That— that's harsh. How could you? I don't know what you think you know about me, but just because I was adopted it doesn't mean I don't have a family." Her voice shook with emotion. "Just because I didn't go home for the summer doesn't mean that I *can't*. Or that—" She stopped suddenly, tears gleaming in her eyes.

Scout was mortified. "Oh, hell. Robyn, I didn't mean that. Look, I'm sorry. I wasn't talking about you, honest. I was talking about Caroline and me. And you couldn't possibly know anything about that."

Robyn wiped at her eyes. "Oh, no?"

"No. Our relationship was weird, okay? To be honest, I'm not sure myself how things were between us. And I don't know why Caroline left things the way she did, but trust me, everything is not what it seems."

"Maybe. But I lived with Caroline for almost two years, you know. We talked a lot. She told me all sorts of stuff about you and your step-sister. I bet I know more than you think I do."

"Is that so?" Scout poured herself another glass of wine. Her hands were shaking again, and even the dog was watching her with a worried look on its face. "You know, Robyn, I hate to burst your pretty little bubble, but believe me, Caroline wasn't always as warm and fuzzy as you're making her out to be. She talked to you, did she? Well, I'd love to hear how she explained kicking me out of her house when I was just sixteen. And less than a week after my dad died, at that. She *loved* me? How can you say that?"

As old aches stirred to life, Scout glared at the other woman. "For twenty years, we hardly spoke. If she cared so much, then why didn't she ever invite me to come back – not even for one little visit?"

"Well, probably because she was afraid something might happen to you, right?" Robyn explained carefully, as if she was speaking to a small child. "You know, because of that guy and all."

Scout looked at Glenn and felt an unexpected surge of empathy. She was sure her face wore a look of blank confusion that was identical to his.

"Uh, Robyn? Exactly what guy would that be?" she prompted.

"The *guy,*" Robyn repeated, as though she'd just realized that the small child was also not too terribly bright. "You know. *The one who was after you*? I think she was afraid he might have been the same guy who'd kidnapped Lisa."

Once again, Scout found herself exchanging puzzled looks with Glenn. This time, she let him give voice to the thoughts they were both thinking.

"Lisa wasn't kidnapped. She ran away." His voice was as flat as his gaze. "And, just for the record, this is the first I'm hearing about anyone being 'after' Scout."

For an instant, in the face of Glenn's surety, Robyn's confidence faltered. But only for an instant. "Well, maybe...maybe Caroline just didn't tell you about it. You ever think of that? Maybe she didn't want to scare you."

"Scare me with what?" Scout replied. "There *was* no guy. No one was *after* anybody. There was nothing to be scared *of!*"

"Well, Caroline thought there was," Robyn insisted stubbornly. "She said people had been murdered. I think she was afraid that you and Lisa had somehow gotten mixed up in it."

This time, when Scout turned to look at Glenn, she was startled by the thoughtful, almost speculative look on his face.

"Don't tell me you're listening to this?" she demanded.

"There were rumors at the time," he said slowly, his attention seemingly focused on the glass in his hand. "Not that I paid any attention to them, of course."

"Rumors? About me and Lisa being murderers?"

"No, of course not. Nothing like that. About some...well...some unsavory activities that might or might not have been going on at your school. Devil worship. Blood sacrifices. Ritual killings. Stuff like that."

"Oh, please," Scout scoffed. "And I was involved in this, *how* exactly?"

Glenn sighed. "Not you, Scout. The rumors were about some of your friends."

---

1. Ah, the Montero. The Yuppy Status Car. It was a nice looking vehicle. Unfortunately, Mitsubishi stopped making then in 2006.

2. In Celtic Mythology, the Cwn Annwn, or Hell Hounds, are a pack of spectral dogs—white with red ears—that accompany the Lord of the Underworld as he rides through the skies from during the winter months. I'm not saying Scout's dog is a literal hell hound, but given all the trouble I knew she'd be getting into, I figured she could use a little supernatural security. You can read more about Annwn in my book IRON, in which the Lord of the Underworld goes in search of a wife.

3. Merlot was actually very popular at the time Scent of the Roses was first published. Which was a year before the movie Sideways was released. I think if it had been published even a couple of years later, I would have had to given Scout a different wine to drink.

    No Monteros, no merlot. We lost so much in the 00s. ;)

4. Like this line? You can thank my sister for it. lol!

# 3

*How many times have I dreamed this?* Scout thought, as she roamed restlessly through the old house that had once been home. She slid her fingers gently down the aged oak of a doorframe as she passed through it. Ran a hand lightly across the back of an old leather chair in the library. Paused again in front of the fireplace to admire the play of light upon the red marble hearthstones.[1]

They were not just dreams and memories now, but the things themselves, fresh and real and right there in front of her. Full of details she'd half forgotten. Like the cracked varnish on the roll top desk, the missing crystal knob on the dining room breakfront, or the clouded glass of the mirror in the downstairs bathroom.

As she made her way from room to room, she ignored the eyes that followed every move she made. Eyes with all the color and compassion of beaten gold. They glared balefully at her from every angle. From the top of the china cabinet. From the landing in the hall. Beneath the dining room table. Behind the piano. Caroline's cats. All from the same litter, she'd been told. All with the same hard, reproachful, yellow eyes.

"Wait a minute," she'd demanded of Robyn, when the subject had come up earlier in the evening. "*How many* cats are we talking about?"

"Eight." Robyn's brow creased as she thought about it. "No, nine if you count the mother cat, but to tell you the truth, I'm not even sure which one she is. They were already here when I moved in. She was a stray and I guess already pregnant when she turned up."

"Some stray cat had her kittens here and Caroline couldn't be bothered to find homes for them—is that what you're telling me? And now *I'm* supposed to figure out what to do with them?"

Robyn looked surprised. "Well... I mean, you know what she was like, right? Caroline was always taking in strays. And she was way too softhearted to turn them over to Animal Control. You wouldn't have expected her to just...get rid of them, would you?"

"Oh, no, of course not. Whatever was I thinking?" Scout resisted the impulse to mention that Caroline hadn't been so softhearted when it had come to getting rid of *her*.

Of course, to be fair, Caroline must have been devastated by the loss of her daughter. And believing it to have been Scout's fault? Having to endure her presence must have been unbearable. But what Scout had never been able to forgive, or even understand, was that Caroline blamed her, not just for what happened to Lisa, but for her father's death, as well.

The night before her father's funeral Caroline had marched into Scout's room and ordered her to start packing...

"I've made arrangements for you to stay with your grandfather," she'd told her, in a voice that brooked no argument. "You have a flight out the day after tomorrow."

*What?* For an instant Scout had been too stunned to respond. *No!* "But...I don't want to go away. Why can't I stay here?"

"Please don't make this more difficult than it already is," Caroline said quietly. Her face betrayed no emotion, she held herself rigidly erect. Only her hands, twisting restlessly together at her waist, gave any sign of her inner agitation. "You just can't stay here anymore, Scout. That's all there is to it."

"Why are you doing this? This is my home."

"There have been far too many problems with you, lately. So much has gone wrong. It's not safe having you here. After your father's death I realized—"

"But what does...*that*...have to do with me?"

"Because it should have been you," Caroline hissed, her icy control slipping suddenly. "Don't you understand that? It was *your* car. *You* were the one who ought to have been driving it, who should have died that night— Not Gil. *You!*"

Her voice broke, and she hurried from the room leaving Scout to stare after her in dismay. Far down the hall, she could hear the slam of Caroline's door closing behind her. She felt an echo, deep in the recesses of her heart. As though another, internal door had slammed shut, as well. Up until that moment, she'd always believed Caroline loved her.

A high-pitched keening split the silence, snapping Scout's mind back to the present. She shivered. Somewhere, a window had been left open. The damp night air pushed its way into the house. Heavy, moist and loamy, it carried the scent of roses in from the garden, along with the fretful, seesaw whine of myriad night insects.[2]

Somewhere, two cats challenged each other. Their eerie cries abraded Scout's over-worked nerves like nails on a blackboard.

*Caroline's cats*, Scout thought as she teetered on the brink of panic. *Caroline's cats. Caroline's roses. Caroline's garden. Caroline's dog. Caroline's house. All mine now.*

A wave of guilt washed through her. *Mine and Lisa's.* If Lisa was still alive. And if she could be found. A foghorn sounded in the distance, low and mournful. Scout shivered once again.

Lisa had been seventeen when she ran away, following an argument between them. Scout had always taken it for granted that Lisa had been found, or that she'd returned on her own. After all, what purpose had her banishment been meant to serve, if not to bring Lisa back?

In a letter mailed to Lucy a few days after her disappearance, Lisa made it clear that she blamed Scout for everything that had gone wrong in her life recently. She was not the only one. Practically everyone Scout knew seemed to feel that, with the sole, possible exception of her math teacher's murder, Scout was the one at fault for everything.

*Well, okay,* she'd told herself. *If that's how it's gonna be. I'll just find a way to live with it.*

It was mostly true, after all. Not the part about her father's death —she refused to accept the blame for that. And not the part about her having seduced Lisa's boyfriend away from her, either.

No seduction had been necessary. Glenn had jumped at the chance to go to bed with her. Just as Scout had known he would.

She sank wearily down on the couch in front of the fireplace and considered some of the choices she'd made back then. Sleeping with Glenn Gilchrist had definitely *not* been one of her brighter ideas. Blond, blue-eyed, with the face of an angel and a surfer's tan, Glenn had looked like the quintessential California beach boy.

It had seemed that every teenage girl in Oberon had been half in love with him. And, at first, Scout had been no exception. But Glenn had been Lisa's boyfriend for almost a year; and Scout had seen how he treated her. Under normal circumstances, he was one of the last people she would have chosen to go to bed with. But circumstances that spring were anything but normal.

In a town the size of Oberon, it's hard to keep a secret for very long, even a small one. And as far as secrets went, Scout's was pretty big. Her friends had already begun to suspect she was involved with someone, but no one had a clue who that someone might be. Scout had done what she had to do to keep things that way, even though it meant lying to everyone – including her myste-rious new boyfriend, who had no idea the girl he was seeing had only just turned sixteen.

Nick Greco was exciting and dangerous, devastatingly attractive and totally unobtainable, with unruly, thick, brown waves of hair and eyes the color of warm honey. Eyes that were even more unsettling than the mirrored sunglasses he was seldom without.

At twenty-two, he should have been completely off-limits, but Scout had been ready to test every limit she could find that spring.

The fact that he was also Lucy's cousin, and a cop, only made him more desirable, as far as Scout was concerned.

If pretending to sneak around with Glenn would keep everyone from finding out about Nick, then that's what she would do. And if sleeping with Glenn was necessary? Well, even that would be worth it.

*God, I was so young back then.* Young and stupid. She'd thought she could get away with anything. She'd never imagined how much her fun was going to cost, or how many people would end up having to pay for it. She'd learned about that the hard way.

And she'd had the last twenty years to reflect on all the careless, life-changing, devastating mistakes she'd made in one six-week period in the spring of her seventeenth year.

The sound of the front door opening startled Scout out of her reverie. She looked up as Robyn peeked into the living room.

"You're still awake?"

Robyn appeared greatly astonished by this. Scout suppressed a groan. *I bet she's always astonished.* Astonished or gleeful or some other unbearably perky emotion. Scout found her quite astonishingly tiring. *Small wonder Caroline had a stroke. If I stay here much longer, I might have one, as well.*

She forced her mouth to form a polite smile. "I never sleep very much," she lied. "Don't seem to need it somehow." *No, not much.*

"Oh. Well, okay then. Thanks for letting me borrow the dog. I really like taking her along when I have to be out late at night. She's such excellent protection, you know."

"Yeah, sure, but listen," Scout insisted—ignoring the absurdity of anyone's needing protection *here*. "It's like I told you. If you want her, she's yours. I honestly don't know what I'm going to do with a dog, anyway."

"Oh, no!" Robyn replied, looking as if she were on the verge of a cardiac arrest. "No, I couldn't *possibly* do that! I know Caroline would have wanted *you* to have her!"

Scout shook her head in resignation. What Caroline might or might not have wanted for her was not something she was willing to think about, at present. It was not even something she was sure she *should* care about.

"Well, I'll see you in the morning," Robyn announced brightly as she headed off to bed. There were four bedrooms on the second floor, all of them currently vacant. Caroline had apparently encouraged Robyn to sleep downstairs, in a room that had previously functioned as a rec. room.

Scout remembered it well. A large, sunny room, with a view of the gardens visible through French doors that opened onto the patio, it had been decorated with the most hideously garish flowered wallpaper, flowered upholstery and drapes, and Caroline's collection of antique floral prints.

The relentless insistence of the flower motif – flowers everywhere, both inside and outside the room – suddenly struck Scout as being wildly ironic. She was shocked to find herself giggling hysterically as she wondered if the decor had in any way contributed to her decision to allow Glenn to deflower her there?

*Oh, fuck, no.* Scout pulled herself together with an effort, as the memories she'd evoked set her skin to crawling. *What in the hell is wrong with me tonight?* She hated that term. She never, ever used it. And she had never, except in her most paranoid moments, ever questioned her motives for that afternoon with Glenn.

*It's the lack of sleep. That's all it is.* For days now, ever since she had heard from Caroline's lawyer, in fact, she'd found it impossible to sleep for more than a couple of hours at a time. She refused to even consider any kind of medication. She'd always feared the resultant loss of control so much more than she did the loss of clarity and common sense that accompanied chronic sleep deprivation. But she had tried almost everything else she could think of. Long walks, herb tea, hot baths, warm milk, dull books, strong drinks – nothing had helped. And now, she was obviously well on her way to losing her mind.

Her giggling had gotten the dog's attention. The creature ambled over and nudged Scout's hand with her wet nose. She was a very sweet dog. But Scout had no use for dogs, or for pets of any kind.

Didn't like them. Didn't need them. Didn't want the complications and responsibilities that went with having them. Her life was simple. Peaceful. It was perfect just the way it was.

So, okay. Maybe it was also the slightest bit empty and dull, but she could stand that. Couldn't she?

"Don't even think about it, dog!" she murmured, reluctantly tickling her behind one velvety ear. "I don't do relationships, see? I'm too much my father's daughter."

Living with her father, Scout had been able to observe firsthand exactly the types of behavior least likely to contribute to a healthy relationship. Unfortunately, whoever said children learn what they live was not entirely wrong. Over the course of her thirty-six years, she had put together a depressingly impressive record of broken relationships and failed friendships.

*Or do I mean impressively depressing?* she wondered, as another wave of irrational hysteria hit her. And really, when she thought about it, wasn't it all just an advanced type of performance art, anyway? Just another art form for her to exploit. Just one more piece of the genetic legacy she'd inherited from her artist father.

It had been her father's art that had brought them to Oberon in the first place. His work – always very much in the plein air style–[3]was just beginning to gain popularity, at the time. And Oberon, with its thriving artist's colony and exquisite natural beauty, seemed like the ideal location for Gil Patterson to base himself.

Her father had been creative and charming, witty and – upon occasion – surprisingly perceptive. When she announced, at the age of ten, that she was changing her name to Scout, after the heroine of *To Kill A Mockingbird,* her father had encouraged her. Although he did draw the line at her suggestion that he change his own name to Atticus so that they'd match.

The truth was, she needed to be Scout, a girl who knew who she was and wasn't afraid to fight for what she believed in, rather than Jen.

Jen Patterson was a girl who – more often than not – wasn't sure who she was, or where she belonged. A girl whose own mother hadn't wanted her. Scout didn't have a mother either, but she seemed to get along just fine without one.

Most of the time, however, her father had been amazingly obtuse. He seemed genuinely incapable of understanding why Scout might be less than thrilled when he presented her with yet another new set of stepsisters or brothers. Or how they, in turn, might fail to be completely enamored of her.

By the time her father had married for the fifth and final time, Scout had the drill down pat. She figured she could handle anything this new stepfamily threw at her. She couldn't have been more wrong. Caroline turned out to be the closest thing to a mother she would ever know, and Scout couldn't help but love her. She'd even grown to love beautiful, blond, cool-eyed Lisa, although the relationship between them had never been an easy one.

She thought again about that portrait of the two of them in the foyer – she could still remember the joy that had been behind the brilliant smiles her father had captured all too well. She closed her eyes against the pain her memories brought her. It didn't do any good to go on living in the past like this, except...there didn't seem to be anyplace else for her to go.

For almost twenty years she'd tried to run away from her past, only to end up here. Right back where she'd started.

Her dad was dead, and Caroline was dead, and Lisa was who-knows-where. Probably dead as well. And Scout was back where she had no business being. Home at last.

---

1. The red-marble hearthstones here are a nod to the ones in my grandparents' house. Caroline's house itself is based on the house of a friend of mine from high school. It was a *great* house!
2. Yeah, I said it. Nowadays, I know a lot of readers don't care for the word moist, but back then it was a perfectly respectable word. Still is in my opinion.
3. Plein Air Painting is a fancy way of describing painting that is done outside. I studied art in school and my mother and grandfather were artists, so I thought this was a commonly used phrase. Until people kept asking me about it. So, IYKYK, and if you didn't—now you do.

# 4

―――――――――

"*S*cout? Can you hear me? Come back, now." Marsha's voice called her out of the thick, groggy darkness that had obscured her sight.

As her vision cleared, Scout's heart began to pound. *What. Is. Happening?* Only an instant earlier, or so it seemed, she'd been in study hall, her mind doing its best to drift away from the history text she was supposed to be reading. Now she was here, on a couch in the nurse's office.

The familiar, sharp-sweet scent of antiseptic made her stomach flutter. Desperate to make sense of things, she tried but failed to pierce the darkness that stretched within her mind, wide and impenetrable, between now and a moment ago.

A very long moment, to be certain, but just the same –

"Scout!" Marsha repeated, more urgently, her freckled forehead creased with worry.

"Marsha? Wh-what's going on? How'd I get here?"

Marsha shrugged and looked away. "Well, uh, you sorta passed out. Tell me, what's the last thing you remember?"

Scout dragged her thoughts back through what suddenly seemed like a thousand years of blankness. "I don't know. I think I was trying to study. But then Claire and Amy started arguing about some stupid old song, but I don't— No, wait. I *do* remember that part. It was *Mandy*. Claire was claiming it was about some girl named—"

"Okay, okay," Marsha waved a hand to silence her. "Stop. That's enough. I got it. Damn. I was afraid it was something like that." She chewed on her lip for a moment before continuing. "Okay, listen. Don't worry, all right? Everything's going to be fine. I promise. It's just that... Well, the nuns kinda think you might be on drugs, or something."

*The nuns?* A faint alarm began to ring in Scout's mind. *No. That's wrong. I don't belong here. I need to leave—now.* She shifted on the couch, squirming beneath the intolerable, warm heaviness that had settled in the region of her heart. There was something horribly familiar, yet still not quite right about this conversation.

"Drugs? Just because I fainted? Come on, Marsha, that's stupid!"

"I agree. But, you see, you didn't exactly lose consciousness. At least— Look, I'll explain everything later, okay? Just for now, if anyone asks, tell them you were sick. Or, no, wait, I've got a better idea. Tell them you were asleep. And you were, like, sleepwalking or something. You can do that, right?"

*Sleep? I am asleep. I have to be. Because it's been years since high school. This has to be a dream.*

But even knowing that, Scout still couldn't pull herself away. The dream continued...

"What are you talking about?" she demanded. "What's going on?"

The arrival of Sister Mary Francis, the school's tall, grim faced vice-principal forced them to cut their conversation short.

"Miss Quinn. You have someplace else to be, I presume?"

"Yes, Sister." Marsha's voice exuded polite innocence. "I was just so worried about Scout."

"Yes. So are we all. You may go now." The nun turned frosty eyes toward Scout. "Miss Patterson, your stepmother is here to take you home."

*Caroline?*

Scout's eyes flew open. She all but sprang off the couch. Her sudden movement dislodged the cat who'd been sleeping on her chest. She recognized where she was now. *Home.*

No, *not* home, she reminded herself sternly, merely back in Oberon. *And it's happening all over again.*

That was no dream she'd just had; it was a flashback. A memory. One long suppressed and best forgotten, like so much of that year. But, once upon a time, the whole sorry scene had actually taken place. She closed her eyes and concentrated on her breathing – in and out, deep and slow – until the bitter tide of betrayal began to subside. Until her thoughts grew quiet, and her mind clear.

As the last tattered shreds faded from her consciousness, her heart shuddered back into a slow, leaden rhythm. Sighing, she opened her eyes and looked around, once more. Sunlight streamed into the living room. It was morning. *Thank God.* The big orange cat whose nap she'd disturbed licked at one paw, and then glared at her from the coffee table. [1] Several more felines had arranged themselves around the room, in various attitudes of watchfulness. They were all but motionless, except for the hypnotically regular flicking of their tails, and the occasional blink.

The dog lay on the floor beside the couch, eyeing the cats with an anxious look on her narrow face, and every now and again venting her unease in a sporadic whimper. Suddenly, apparently in response to some sound Scout couldn't hear, all six cats jumped to their feet and left the room. She got up more slowly, as did the dog, and together they stumbled after the cats.

In the kitchen, Robyn was busy getting ready for work – the summer intern position at a local nursery which Scout had heard all about, at great length, the night before.

"Oh! Hi, there. Good morning. Care for some coffee?" She smiled brightly at Scout as she spooned cat food into a collection of plastic bowls. The cats twined impatiently around her ankles.

Scout had found Robyn's perkiness hard enough to take the

previous evening. First thing in the morning, after a too-short, too restless night, it was unbearable. *Somebody is going to kill this woman, for sure. I just hope it isn't me.* She cringed as the bowls hit the floor with a series of thuds. *But no promises; it just might be...*

A look of concern crossed Robyn's face. "Ooh, do you have a headache? There's some feverfew tea on the shelf over the sink if you want some. It always helps me. I didn't wake you, did I? Or are you just not a morning person? Mornings I'm always in a rush, and I never notice how noisy I'm being until I've gone and woken everyone up."

Robyn reminded Scout of her own younger self; except she was pretty sure she had never been so perky. Not by miles. Still, they were about the same height and build, with nearly identical hair color. In fact, Scout realized with an eerie shock, Robyn bore an uncanny resemblance to the portrait hanging in the foyer.

*She looks more like teenage me than I do.*

Scout shook her head. "I was getting up anyway," she lied, as she poured herself a cup of coffee. It looked way too weak. She collapsed at the table and studied Robyn as she continued to putter around the kitchen.

"Well, okay," Robyn said, as she tossed her dishes in the sink and began washing them vigorously. "But, you know, it's probably quieter upstairs. I mean, if you *did* want to sleep in and all. At least that's what Caroline always said. But I guess you'd know that, wouldn't you? I mean, since you lived here before. You've probably thought about that already, huh?"

Scout nodded absently. She sipped her coffee. Damn. It *was* too weak. She couldn't help but wonder whether the physical similarities between her and Robyn were all in her own overwrought imagination, or whether Caroline could have noticed it, as well.

*How did that make her feel?* Had Robyn's relentless cheerfulness begun to make her think better of Scout? Was that what led to her being included in Caroline's will? Or had she something else in mind?

"So, it looks like I'm going to be late again tonight. And we're almost out of cat food." Robyn's remarks snapped Scout out of her reverie. "So, do you think maybe…?"

"Oh. Right." Picking up the cue in Robyn's tone, Scout smiled. "Sure, no problem. Why don't I pick some up while I'm in town today?"

"They're pretty fussy." Robyn looked suddenly doubtful. "But I'll leave an empty can out by the door, so you'll know what brand to get.They'll eat fish, chicken, liver and beef, but not turkey. Oh, and nothing shredded or sliced."

*Huh?* "Oh, uh, right. Sure. Got it."

"Okay then. Cool." Robyn grabbed her things and all but skipped to the door. "Well, I'll see you later." And she was gone. Leaving Scout to the silent stares of the cats.

*Nothing shredded or sliced? Gimme a break.* Never mind the dog, whatever was she going to do with all these friggin' cats?

"When do you think she'll show?" Lucy asked, a little too casually.

Marsha regarded her friend with a wry smile. Lucy had been fidgeting ever since she got here this morning. It didn't take a psychic to figure out who she was talking about. "Scout, d'you mean? Well, Ginny said sometime this week. And today's Friday, so soon, I guess."

"It's not like there's any reason that we *have* to see her though, right?" Lucy brightened at the thought. "I mean, not if we don't want to. It's not like Oberon is *that* small a place, or anything."

"Lies and malicious falsehoods." Celeste slid into the seat next to Lucy. "Who says Oberon's not small? Of course, it is. That's a big part of its charm."

Lucy sighed. "All I meant was, it's not so small that you can't avoid running into someone if you don't want to see them."

"Oh." Celeste thought about this for a moment. "So, who is it that don't you want to see?"

"Nobody," Lucy insisted. "Nobody at all. I was just making a point."

"Lucy's in a very philosophical mood this morning." Marsha couldn't resist teasing. "Why don't you give her a reading, Celeste? Maybe it'll cheer her up."

Celeste's face brightened. She took out her cards and began to shuffle them.

"Yeah, that's just what I need." Lucy glared at Marsha and resumed tapping her fingers on the edge of the table. "Thanks, Marsh. You're a real pal."

"Not a prob, Luce. Anytime." Hiding her smile, Marsha glanced idly out at the street, searching with her mind for the source of the restlessness she was once again feeling. She was aware of the conversations eddying around her, but she tuned them out with practiced ease.

She took a deep breath and let her eyes unfocus. The energy patterns that revealed themselves told her nothing. Everything appeared just as it should be. Suddenly she stiffened. Had there been a flicker of awareness just then? Rather like a car, whose motion you barely detect as it disappears into a blind spot.

She searched again. And once again, she encountered a curious blankness. It was like being on the wrong end of a two-way mirror, she was sure there was something there, she just couldn't see it. She snapped her attention back to normal, but she could still see nothing that would explain the curious sensation she had just experienced.

A slight breeze ruffled the sage in the planters and set the nasturtiums nodding on their stems. A few cars drove slowly along Main Street. People moved up and down the block. A middle-aged couple, obviously tourists, paused in front of an art gallery. A young mother dragged a reluctant child along behind her. Two women examined antiques in the shop window across the way. A huddle of teenagers, out of school for the summer, sauntered down one side of the street, seeming to take no notice of a second group of teens on the opposite sidewalk. A tall, strikingly blond woman walked her dog.

*She looks like Diana, Goddess of the Hunt, with one of her hounds,* Marsha thought, watching the way the woman's head turned from side to side, as though she were testing the wind for the scent of prey. She smiled in amusement, *all that's missing is her bow, and a quiver full of arrows.*

A belated shock of recognition went through her, and she gasped. She knew that lithe, loping stride, the alert twisting motion of the head. The streaked mane of hair might be a little shorter than she remembered it, but she would have bet anything that behind those sunglasses, a familiar pair of bright hazel eyes was coolly scanning the streets they hadn't seen in twenty years.

"Well, holy shit," Marsha whispered softly. "Speak of the devil."

SCOUT STALKED ALONG THE SIDEWALK, trying not to notice the irritating way the dog stuck to her side. Like she'd been glued there. It was a perfect morning, she thought. Sunny and warm, but not too warm. With just the slightest gossamer hint of a breeze. Much nicer than she'd expected for June.

Summer, as she well remembered, was not necessarily the warmest season here along the coast. More often than not, it was cooler and foggier than either spring or fall. Still, she had always been able to tell when it finally arrived. There was a peculiarly summer scent given off by the vegetation. Or perhaps by the earth itself, after it had steeped in sunshine for enough hours at a time. A musky, faintly dusty, dried-honey fragrance hung in the air. Scout breathed it in and a wave of nostalgia hit her so hard, she had to actually stop for a moment and catch her breath.

Across the street, she saw a shop whose adjoining terrace was set with umbrella-covered tables. According to the sign hanging over the door, the place was called The Crone's Nest. That didn't exactly scream restaurant, but Scout could smell breakfast on the breeze, and she steered herself toward it. She was in desperate need of something a good deal stronger than that brown bath water Robyn had brewed. It would take some serious caffeine to get her brain in gear today.

*The Crone's Nest? Sheesh. Only in Oberon.* Nowhere else, she was sure, would you find a place with a name like that. Just as she reached for it, the door of the shop burst open. Scout found herself enveloped by a cloud of sandalwood scent, quantities of emerald-green silk, a profusion of clinking bangles, all topped by masses of red-brown hair that could only belong to one person in all of Oberon.

"Marsha? Is that you?"

"Of course, it's me," Marsha chuckled, as she pulled away. "But you! Here, let me look at you." She ran her hands through her heavy hair, holding it out of her face, and Scout couldn't help but notice that her short nails were painted a deep, iridescent blue that glinted in the sunlight.

Marsha gazed at her intently for a long moment. Just as the scrutiny was beginning to make Scout uneasy, Marsha shook herself, in a way that brought to mind a small and impatient dog. Grabbing Scout by the wrist she began to pull her into the shop. "I only heard yesterday that you were coming. It's so good to see you! C'mon, we gotta talk. What do you want, coffee? Some tea? Chai maybe? No, wait. I know. A latte, right? I see you have your hound with you," she giggled, seeming almost as giddy as Robyn. "Don't worry, you can bring the dog in. Have you named her yet?"

"Uh, no," Scout answered, a little startled by the reception. "And yeah, a latte sounds great." *When the hell did Marsha become so manic?* The Marsha she remembered had been a lot more chill.

"Oh, yeah, normally I'm much calmer than this," Marsha said, reassuringly. "But I'm just so excited to see you!"

Scout stared; she knew she hadn't spoken aloud. *How...?*

"Oh." A sheepish grin appeared on Marsha's freckled face. "Yeah.

Um, don't worry about that either, 'kay? They tell me you get used to it."

Deciding the whole conversation had become way too cryptic, Scout let it drop. "Whatever," she muttered as she looked around. Her gaze skittered over a long counter where several people were waiting to place their orders; then a glass display case full of pastries; a refrigerated cooler holding fresh juices and a variety of energy drinks. There were several tables scattered throughout the space, as well, but that's where all resemblance to a cafe ended.

Tall shelves lined two of the walls. They were crammed with books, and with green mason jars, the latter of which were filled with roots and herbs and a variety of teas. There were vats of incense, bottles of oil, baskets of beads, and rows of statues set out on low counters. Two large, lighted display cases held beautifully crafted cups, knives, jewelry, and crystals of every conceivable size, shape and color. Towards the back of the store were racks that held what looked like cloaks and gowns and long flowing robes.

"Uh, Marsha? What is this place?"

"This?" Marsha's shrug was determinedly nonchalant, but it could not disguise the pride she so obviously felt. "Oh, it's just my store. C'mon, we're out in the garden."

As they passed the counter, she called to one of the young women working there to bring out a latte and another pot of tea. Then she led the way out to the terrace Scout had noticed from the street.

Scout breathed in the intriguing mixture of scents – coffee and lavender and fresh baked bread, rose, sage, cinnamon and thyme – as she followed Marsha towards a table where two women sat watching their approach. Some long-buried emotion tried to surface as she recognized one of the women. Lucy Greco. Scout dropkicked whatever she'd been about to feel back into its closet and slammed the door shut.

Judging from the look in her dark brown eyes, Lucy wasn't happy to see her. *Fair enough. I'm not exactly thrilled about it, myself.*

Marsha looked from Lucy to Scout and back again, then groaned. "Oh, come on you guys! It's been years. Get over it already!" She pulled out a chair and practically pushed Scout into it. "Don't you know holding grudges is bad for the soul?"

Lucy made a face at her. "I'm Italian, Marsha. My soul can handle the occasional vendetta just fine, thanks."

Marsha brushed that aside. "Oh, be quiet, you Strega. Scout this is Celeste Greene. She and Lucy are my partners in the store."

Celeste was a petite, waifish blonde with large lavender eyes. Scout knew a moment of disorientation as she gazed into them. That color was impossible, wasn't it? *Colored contacts*, she finally decided, as she extended her hand.

"Very junior partners," Celeste corrected, with a small shake of her head. "Marsha was the one with the initial vision. We're just along for the ride." Her voice was low and musical and the hand she placed in Scout's was small and narrow, with unusually long fingers and a cool firm grip. "Scout. It's a pleasure."

"Yeah, me too," Scout answered, not really meaning it. As she sank into her seat, she almost tripped over the dog who had chosen to settle herself directly beneath her feet.

"Scout *used to live here*," Marsha told Celeste with an odd emphasis—just as though there was a significance to what she was saying that Scout wasn't grasping. "She's *just reappeared*. Somewhat *unexpectedly*. And as you've probably figured out by now, she and Lucy have some *unresolved issues*."

"Oh?" Celeste looked at Scout speculatively. "Interesting. I guess that would fit, wouldn't it?"

"Excuse me," Scout said, annoyed at the unexpected drama. "What are you two talking about?"

It was Lucy who answered. "Tarot cards. Celeste predicted you'd show up. Or, anyway, I assume that's the consensus." A flash of enjoyment suddenly illuminated her eyes as she added "I'm not sure if you're also supposed to be connected with a sudden death. But I seem to recall that was also part of the prediction."

*Oh, really?* Scout took a deep breath. Drawing on all her acting skills, she answered as coolly as possible, "Well, I don't know if I would call it sudden. I believe she'd been ill for a while." Now it was

45

Scout's turn to enjoy Lucy's discomfort. She raised one eyebrow at her and continued. "Or hadn't you heard about Caroline?"

Marsha shook her head. "Of course, we've heard. And we're all very sorry about Caroline, Scout. But this death hasn't happened yet." She made a face at Lucy. "If it's even *death* we're talking about. You know the cards aren't always clear on things like that. But whatever it is, it's still in the future. If you want, Scout, we could check out your tea leaves, they tend to be a little more specific."

*Not a chance.* Scout turned to glare at Marsha. "Tea leaves. Tarot cards. Why am I not surprised? You guys haven't changed a bit." A sudden surge of unease raced along Scout's nerves. She folded her arms protectively across her chest. "You know, I'm not so sure I want that coffee, after all."

What she wanted was to not pass go, screw the two hundred gees, and get the hell out of Oberon. For good.

"Oh, relax, Scout." Marsha's mouth curled up in a crooked smile. "It's just one little latte. And I swear, I can't read steamed milk for shit. If it makes you feel any better, we won't even *drink* tea while you're here."

Marsha's eyes flicked over her once, and then once again, a little more intently. Scout felt a hard jolt as if some internal switch had been thrown. Her heart slammed against her chest. She gritted her teeth, stilling the impulse to bolt from her seat.

A worried expression replaced the gleam of amusement in Marsha's eyes. "Come on, Scout," she continued, sounding suddenly a lot less self-assured. "Stay awhile. We haven't seen you in years. I promise we won't do anything that makes you uncomfortable. It's not our fault that the cards knew you'd be here."

"It was Robyn who knew she'd be here," Lucy snapped. Her gaze bounced from one to the other of them, and then settled on Scout. She scowled. "And then she told Ginny. I'm still not convinced about the cards. And, anyway, I believe Celeste said something about a *very young* woman?"

"There was more than one woman indicated, if you recall." A

smile hovered on Celeste's lips, "Although, really, age is such a relative thing."

"Look," Scout interrupted. "I really have no interest in any of this. I was just on my way downtown and I thought I'd stop and get some coffee. I'd ask what you've been up to Marsha, but I think I get the picture." And it was definitely not anything she'd want to take home and hang on her wall. She looked around and grimaced slightly. "Nice garden, though."

For some reason, that appeared to amuse Marsha. A smile flickered on the edges of her mouth. "Yes, isn't it? Oh, thanks Vanessa," she added, as the waitress deposited Scout's coffee, a large teapot, and several cups and saucers on the table.

Lucy handed her empty cup back to the waitress. "Vanessa, I'll have an espresso, when you get a chance. Make it a double, please. And maybe a couple of the anisette biscotti?" She leaned back in her chair, folded her arms and stared once more at Scout. "So, you like my garden?"

"Yeah, I do." Scout looked around appreciatively. Then Lucy's words sunk in. "Wait. *Your* garden?"

"Lucy is very talented at landscape design." Marsha smiled at her friend fondly. "Among other things. We were one of her very first projects. The whole terrace is her baby. See? I knew you two could find something in common to talk about."

"I'm not exactly sure it qualifies as being something we have in common," Scout answered dryly. "But it's certainly a beautiful place."

"It has a very peaceful, relaxing atmosphere," Celeste said. "Ordinarily, that is. Are you sure I can't pour either of you some tea?"

"No, thank you," Scout and Lucy muttered simultaneously.

Scout didn't miss the look that passed between the two women as Marsha handed her cup to Celeste. But there was no time to try and decipher it. "Oh, come on Scout," Marsha said with a sudden show of impatience. "I'm dying of curiosity. What's been happening with you? Where have you been all this time? What are you up to now? C'mon, girl, talk!"

Scout grimaced. *Oh, goody. The past. My favorite subject.* "There's not all that much to tell. After Caroline kicked me out, I went to live with my grandfather in Florida. I stayed there until I finished high school. By then he had died, so...I moved around a lot. I lived in New York for a short time. Bummed around Europe for several years. I was living in LA when I got word about Caroline. And now I'm here. End of story."

"Now you're here?" Lucy repeated. "What does that mean? You're not staying, are you?"

Scout stuck out her chin. "Any reason I shouldn't?"

"No. Are you kidding? That'd be great," Marsha interrupted, quickly. "It'd give us all a chance to get to know each other again."

"I'm not sure that's such a good idea," Scout said, feeling suddenly very weary.

"Uh, yeah," Lucy muttered. "Me, neither."

Celeste laughed. "Well, Marsha I can see what you mean. They do seem to have a lot in common, don't they?"

"They always did." Marsha sighed and sipped at her tea.

"Maybe it was the stuff we had in common that caused all the trouble in the first place," Scout suggested quietly.

"Excuse me?" Lucy leaned towards Scout, her eyes glittering with anger. "As I recall, *all the trouble* was caused by you opening your big mouth. Right before you skipped town."

"Oh, like *skipping town* was my choice?" Scout snapped back at her. "Take my word for it, Lucy. Moving to Florida wasn't exactly my idea of a good time." [2]

Lucy's voice was ominously soft. "Right. While we, on the other hand, were having a big ol' party, dealing with the mess you'd left behind. Tell me, Scout, was there a particular reason you had to rat us out like you did? Or were you just showing off in front of my cousin?"

THERE WAS a sudden chill in the atmosphere. Marsha felt as though she'd been wrapped in a cold, dank mist. She glanced at Scout. There was no noticeable change in her expression, but her eyes had turned oddly blank.

"Lucy," Marsha said urgently. "It was a long time ago. Let it drop."

Lucy subsided, sulking, just as Vanessa returned with her espresso.

"No, Marsha, it's okay." Scout's voice sounded eerily conversational, strangely unemotional. "Let her talk." Marsha shuddered at Scout's icy, slick politeness. *What in God's name is wrong with the woman*, she wondered, uneasily.

"That's one of the reasons I'm here, after all," Scout continued, "to find out what happened to Lisa. So, I'll need to know what went on after I left town."

"What happened to Lisa?" Lucy stared at her. "You know damn well what happened. She ran away. You screwed us over and she couldn't take it, so she left."

"Yeah, yeah, I got that already. But if it was just me that she was pissed off at, why didn't she come back? I was run out of town less than two weeks later! How come no one was ever able to find her since then? And besides, I notice *you two* didn't go missing. Does that mean it wasn't too much for you?"

Marsha stared unseeing into her cup, remembering her last encounter with Lisa – the one she'd never told anyone about. "It was twenty years ago. I don't imagine anyone will ever know what really happened." She sighed and added, "So, what *do* you plan on doing?"

Scout shrugged. "I don't know, exactly; try and track her down, or something. I mean, I know Caroline spent a lot of time and money over the years. With minimal results, according to her lawyer. But he also told me she was in contact with someone about ten years ago who claimed to have some information on her whereabouts."

"What? Are you saying there's someone out there who claims to know where Lisa is now? That's impossible."

Scout flashed her a curious look. "Why'd you say that? Do you know something I don't?"

Celeste laughed suddenly. A bright, tinkling sound, like a small silver bell, it broke the tension Marsha had felt building around the table.

"Well, doesn't she usually know things before the rest of us do?"

Celeste looked at Scout with amused expectancy. Scout returned her look with one of polite confusion. Celeste's eyebrows rose as she looked to Lucy for an explanation. "She doesn't know?"

"Scout's been out of touch, these last couple of decades," Lucy said, fixing Scout with another steely look. "There's a whole lot of things she doesn't know about."

"Excuse me, Marsha?" One of the waitresses interrupted. "We've got a request for a reading on table five. And everyone else is kind of backed up, so do you think—"

"I'll go." Celeste stood up quickly. She gave Marsha's hand a reassuring pat. "You three go on with your reunion." They sat for a moment watching as Celeste crossed the terrace. Marsha felt a little of the chill in the atmosphere recede as well.

"So, just what kind of racket are you guys running here, anyway?" Scout asked after a minute. Her voice had lost a little of its odd, detached quality. She sounded angry now. *Interesting.*

"Oh, my God." Lucy laughed angrily. "You know something? I'd almost forgotten how much I always hated that self-righteous attitude of yours. Jeez, Scout, how've we managed all these years without you?"

Marsha left off playing with her teacup. "What is it you want to know, Scout?" she asked quickly, hoping to avoid another confrontation.

"Why don't you tell me, Marsha? You're the psychic, apparently. Or did you just *hypnotize* your friend Celeste into thinking you know everything?"

"Oh, she doesn't know *everything*," Lucy taunted. "But if you've got any secrets you're still hiding, you might want to keep your distance."

"It's really not like that," Marsha sighed. "I had an NDE—a Near Death Experience—not too long after you left town, actually. I was in a car accident and, well, I died. When I woke up, it was as if everything had changed. Things looked different, or maybe it was just the way I was looking at them. I really can't describe it all that well. And sometimes I get these...intuitive flashes."

"Sometimes," Lucy muttered, rolling her eyes. "Riiight."

"Yes, sometimes." Marsha shot her friend a quelling look, before refocusing her attention on Scout. It wasn't at all hard to know what she was thinking at the moment. "It's *not* all the time. And it's not really that big of a deal, either. But yes, by the way, you're right. It has been very good for business."

"Lucky guess," Scout muttered.

Marsha shrugged. "Maybe. But those don't hurt, either. And, like I said, it doesn't happen nearly as often as people think—or as I'd like it to, for that matter. I mean, let's say I meet a guy who is going to be big trouble – like my ex-husband, for example. Do you think I get any kind of warning to stay clear of him? No such luck.

"As far as the rest of your accusations, this isn't a racket, Scout. I provide goods and services that a lot of people want. Things that *I* want. I'm sort of a Born-Again Pagan these days. And I'm every bit as serious about my spiritual beliefs as any of the nuns back at Our Lady were about the catechism. You know that the Midsummer Festival is this weekend, right? Well, we're gonna have a booth there. You should come out and see for yourself what we're all about."

Scout stared at her for a moment. Confusion, compassion, and a desperate need for distance warred in her eyes. "I don't know. I'll have to think about it," she said finally. She drained the last of her latte and stood up. The dog rose stiffly to her feet as well. "Look, I gotta go. I'll see you guys later...or sometime...I guess."

Marsha couldn't help but smile. "Oh, yeah, hon, count on it. I have a feeling we'll be seeing a lot of each other. C'mon, I'll walk you out."

Lucy sat at the table long after Scout left, staring into the depths of her coffee, as if she could find the answers there to the questions that filled her head. Scout-friggin-Patterson. She still couldn't believe it.

She probed the emotions the name dredged up, as her tongue

might probe an aching tooth. Bitterness, yes of course, that went without saying. Along with anger, and resentment, and...hate? Hmm. Yeah. There was definitely some hate, there. And more than a little bit of fear.

She wondered if Nick knew she was back, yet?

Twenty years ago, when everything was going to hell, Lucy had jumped to Scout's defense, insisting that their friend would never intentionally betray them. And then, when her brother had told her what Scout had done to Nick – how she'd tricked him and lied to him and used him to get back at Lucy for that hypnosis thing – she hadn't wanted to believe that, either.

But, in the end, she'd been forced to admit she'd been wrong about Scout. Because if Scout had really been their friend, she would have held her tongue. No matter how they'd threatened her. And if she'd cared *at all* for Nick– well, she wouldn't have been sleeping with Glenn, would she?

Lucy sighed. It had taken Nick forever to get over her. How many times had he asked, oh so casually, if Lucy had heard anything from her friend?

*"Forget it, Nick. She's bad news. You don't want to know."*

*"Christ, Luce. I'm just asking."*

Just asking. Yeah, right. As jumpy as he always got whenever the subject came up? And with that look in his eyes? Ha. One word of encouragement, and he'd have been in his car and halfway to the freeway before Lucy's mouth had stopped moving. And the next thing anyone knew, he'd probably turn up missing, too. Just like Lisa.

And Lucy would be left with something else to feel guilty about.

So, even if she had known where Scout was, she wouldn't have told him. But she hadn't known. No one had. No matter how many times she was asked, no matter who asked her, Caroline had refused to say.

And all that time, while Lucy was stuck here in Oberon, dealing with truckloads of grief and guilt and humiliation, Scout had been where? Soaking up the sun in fucking Florida! *Yeah, that must have been tough, all right.* Jesus.

"So, what's the deal, Luce?" Marsha asked dropping back down into her chair. "You gonna hang out here all day? Or what?"

"Shit, Marsha. Why'd you have to go and invite her to the festival?"

"Who? Scout?" Marsha shrugged impatiently. "It's open to the public, isn't it? And why not invite her? Maybe if she sees what this is all about, she won't be so freaked out by it."

"Oh, who cares if she's freaked?" Lucy played with her hair, distractedly. "What do you think she's up to, anyway?"

"What makes you think she's *up to* anything?"

Lucy eyed her friend skeptically. "Because this is Scout we're talking about. And you know what she's like. You don't *really* think she's here to find Lisa, do you? After all this time?"

Marsha sighed. "Well, if she is, she's gonna end up disappointed."

Maybe, Lucy thought as she eyed her friend closely. "And you're not even a little bit worried? You aren't afraid of the kind of mess she could cause? What about Celeste's reading? I gotta tell you, I got a bad feeling about this. If Scout's being here *means* anything, it can only mean trouble."

"Well, we'll just have to be extra careful then, won't we?" Marsha bit her lip, looking, Lucy couldn't help thinking, a lot more nervous than she wanted to let on. "I don't know, Luce. There was something really odd about her today. I can't put my finger on it, yet. But I think, if we can get her to lighten up a bit, we can maybe try some things. You know, to find out what it is? But try not to worry too much, okay? Everything's going to work out. I think."

Lucy shook her head. As if that wasn't the dumbest thing she'd ever heard. The biscotti she'd eaten sat like a lead weight in the pit of her stomach. "Honestly Marsha, how can *any* of it work out? Whatever she's up to, it's bound to end badly for someone. Just like last time."

---

1. I love big, orange tomcats. I've had several over the years. I think they're my favorite.

2. Another fun fact. I was very firmly (and happily) established in California when I wrote this book. I had no plans to live anywhere else. But plans change and although most of the Oberon books were written while I lived in California, I did end up following in Scout's footsteps. I was living in Florida when Scent of the Roses was first published. I was only there for a year and a half—just long enough to write parts of books five and seven, and all of book six.

# 5

*L*ucy was in her kitchen fixing dinner when her husband got home from work. She had a big pot of water simmering on the stove ready for the pasta; a fresh salad chilling in the refrigerator; and two trays of clary sage focaccia baking in the oven. The pungent odors of basil and garlic filled the sunny room.

"Hey there, babe. What's cooking?"

Just the sound of Dan's voice as he came up behind her was enough to send involuntary shivers of pleasure coursing through her. He smelled good, Lucy thought, inhaling deeply. He smelled of earth and sun and sweat and skin. His big, warm hands molded themselves to her waist and she leaned back into his embrace.

"Mmm, pesto huh?" His breath was a warm caress against her neck. "Bit early in the season for you to start hitting the basil this hard, isn't it?"

"I had my reasons," she muttered, her mood darkening. But then he was gently teasing one of the straps of her tank top off her shoulder, while his other hand twisted possessively in her hair. He tugged her head to the side and a pleasant thrill of anticipation drove every other thought away.

Lucy's eyes slid shut as Dan planted a string of soft, wet kisses all along her neck, from ear to shoulder and back again. [1]

When he'd finished, she turned to face him, slipping her arms around his waist and into the pockets of his jeans and smiling up into a pair of twinkling eyes the color of fresh denim.

Her breath caught in her throat, as it always did when he looked at her that way. "I had such a lousy day," she pouted teasingly, brightening only after he had kissed her. One, long, luxurious kiss that suggested he'd gladly do everything possible to ensure that her evening was very much better than her day had been.

"Mm. Nice," she purred, pulling away just enough to look up at him. "God, I missed you today. How'd everything go? Are we all set for tomorrow?"

"Yep." Dan pulled her back against him, his hands sliding over her back, and then down to squeeze her butt. He kissed her several more times before finally letting her go.

A pleasant feeling of possession washed through Lucy. She watched as he walked across the kitchen, appreciating once again his close-cropped dark hair and the comfortable solidity of his large, muscular frame.

"Yeah, we're set all right." He chuckled quietly as he took two beers from the refrigerator. "In fact, it's Seth's expert opinion that Cavanaugh's Nursery will have a 'killer display' this year. I gather he thinks it's a first for us. And all due to his efforts, you understand." He twisted the cap off one of the bottles and took a long swallow. "Swear to God, how that boy thinks we've managed out there without him—for *three generations*, mind you—is a fuckin' mystery. And personally? I blame you. He's got your attitude written all over him."

Lucy laughed. "Oh, no you don't. He's your son, too, you know. And what do you mean, attitude? Hell, he's fifteen years old, Dan. What were you like at that age?"

"Oh, hell, no. I'm not even goin' there," Dan leaned his elbows on the counter and stretched his long legs out in front of him. "But I tell you what; I think when Mandy turns fifteen, we should seriously consider sending her to live out of state for a while. You got any relatives on the East Coast who could take her?"

"Don't." Lucy shivered as goose bumps raced across her skin. *Relatives on the East Coast? Like Scout had?* She dragged her thoughts back to the present. "So, what about the herbs for the store? Everything go okay with that?"

"Mmph!" Dan took another drink from his beer and shook his head. "You know, woman, sometimes, the things I do for you—they should qualify me for the sainthood. I'm just thankful my father wasn't around today to catch me with those two young ladies, with their ceremonial knives and their special cloths, and their insistence that none of the plants be allowed to touch the ground once they'd had been cut.

"Shit, babe they're herbs! They *grew* in the damned ground! What's the deal with that? No." He put up a hand to stop the explanations that had risen to her lips. "Mm-mm. Don't tell me. I don't want to know. It's just, ohhh, you owe me for this one, Greco." He smiled wickedly. "You really, really do."

"Excuse me?" Lucy's eyebrows rose in mock severity, and she knew that the sudden rush of heat flooding her senses owed nothing whatsoever to either the late afternoon sunlight pouring in through the big kitchen windows, or to the oven at her back. "Did I hear you right? I *owe* you?"

"Mm-hm. Big time." Dan's eyes were dizzyingly blue as they raked slowly over her, from top to bottom before returning to hold her gaze.

Lucy felt her heart kick. "I see. And tell me, Cavanaugh, you think you can *collect* on that debt, do you?"

"Oh, I know I can." He grinned at her. "Damn, but I do love Friday nights."

*So do I.* Lucy returned his grin, and for several long moments neither said a word, they just smiled at each other across the sun-filled kitchen.

Eventually, Lucy reached for the glass of Zinfandel [2] she'd poured earlier and took a small sip as she considered which creative activities they might attempt later. She'd just made up a new batch of scented massage oils they hadn't tried yet, including a black pepper-mint-patchouli mix she thought might have some very interesting effects.

"So," she said at last, clearing her throat and attempting to catch her breath – an activity which was, all at once, surprisingly difficult. "Dare I ask what you might have done with our son? I didn't hear Seth come in with you."

"Huh! Nothing, yet. He's out on the drive shooting hoops with your cousin. Which reminds me, I better get back out there. I told Nick I'd bring him a beer."

"Nick's here?" Lucy felt a sudden qualm. "What's he want?"

Dan looked at her in surprise. "Don't tell me you don't remember? He's dropping Kate off to spend the night with Mandy."

Relieved, Lucy turned back to her food processor. "Oh, right. Tell him to stay and have dinner."

"Well, I'll *ask* him," Dan's voice was suspiciously innocent. "But, you know, he might have other plans."

Lucy snorted appreciatively. They were both aware just how *un*likely that was. Since his divorce, Nick seemed to spend more time than ever at work. Although he'd dated a few women, he'd shown no real interest in any of them. Which, given some of the women in question, was a damn good thing. As far as anyone could tell, Nick's social life was so lacking in excitement these days, even he was bored by it.

Lucy thought of the Nick she remembered from her youth – so wild and reckless and alive – and she wondered at the changes the years had wrought. Still, he was family. And nobody was ever allowed to mess with her family.

She shot a repressive look over her shoulder at Dan, still chuckling smugly to himself. "Just go tell him I'm making pesto, okay?"

"Oh, yes Ma'am," Dan teased, coming up behind her again.

Lucy giggled as she felt his hot breath in her ear.

"So, tell me. You really think your cooking can compete with one of your cousin's hot dates?"

For just an instant, a picture of Nick and Scout holding hands and smiling into each other's eyes across a candle-lit table sprang into

Lucy's head, and she shuddered. It wasn't that she didn't want her cousin to be happy, but, omigod, Scout would eat him alive!

"Believe me," she muttered between clenched teeth. "If my cousin had a hot date tonight, I'd know about it. I'd probably have to take out a contract on the bimbo."

Dan nipped at her earlobe. "Well, whatever makes you happy. I know I don't want to be the one to get you mad." Once more, his tongue caressed her neck. "Maybe later you could show me what I have to do to stay on your good side." And then off he went, beers in hand, to deliver her invitation.

Ruthlessly, Lucy stripped another handful of basil leaves off their stems and threw them into the blender. Thank God for basil, she thought, as she watched the blades do their work. It was good for curing headaches and gastric upsets, providing psychic protection, and warding off negative energies. Just what they'd all need tonight.

THE QUIETNESS in the empty house was like an immense, cold weight pressing slowly against Scout's nerves, pouring into her lungs, everywhere at once, until she felt like screaming. She remembered how comfortable and safe she'd always felt in this house. She hadn't expected a return to the happiness she'd once known. But did coming back here really have to be *this* hard?

*There were rumors at the time...about some of your friends.* Glenn's words repeated themselves in her mind. No wonder Lucy was still so bitter. If the talk was really that bad, maybe Scout had gotten more revenge than she'd realized. She felt a pang of guilt, and an unusual desire to pick up the phone and call...

*Who? Who can I call?*

Her mind ran down the list of people she could potentially call. It was not extensive, she realized with a helpless start.

*Well. Good, then.* She shook herself mentally. *Very good. No strings.* Just the way she liked to keep things. Simple and tidy and clean.

She wandered through the house, turning on lights against the encroaching darkness. Reminding herself that she felt not a single twinge of regret for having turned down Glenn's offer of dinner.

Of course, he'd tried to insist. Lord, she'd forgotten how annoyingly insistent he could be. He'd taken Robyn's suggestion that she could be in some kind of danger and run with it. Urging her to either stay locked in the house or to leave town altogether. Stopping just shy of suggesting he move in with her to keep her safe.

Or maybe it was just the way he said it, that made it sound like that's what he meant. One thing he'd apparently gained from being a lawyer, he'd learned to imply a lot, without actually *saying* anything.

But there was no argument he could use to convince her. She might not be feeling too comfortable by herself right now, but she hadn't been in the mood to play any more games with him, either.

Scout was glad Robyn had plans for the night, as well. She had entirely too many unwelcome thoughts to mull over. The last thing she needed was distraction and chatter. She turned on the stereo, but although music replaced the quietness, the emptiness only seemed to intensify.

After feeding the cats and the dog, she finished putting away the groceries she had bought earlier and wandered back out into the hallway. For several minutes, she just stood there, staring at the portrait hanging on the wall. That damn painting. It was the last one she ever sat for, and she remembered it as if it were yesterday, instead of twenty-one years ago.

*The sun, warm against her face and her arms. The itchy discomfort of grass beneath her bare thighs. The damp sweatiness of her skin where the weight of Lisa's arm fell across her shoulder...*

*"Quit slumping, Scout. You're falling asleep."*

*"I am not!"*

*"No? Well, I am. Shit, it's hot out here. How the hell do you stand this, anyway?"*

*"Stop fussing, Lisa. And don't fall asleep. Your arm is heavy enough as it is."*

*The clacking of the gardener's shears, barely audible over the buzz of the lawn mower. New mown grass. That was what she smelled. The crisp, green sweetness of the shattered blades as it mingled with the warmer, spicier scent of the roses...*

"Scout."

Chills crawled like spiders across her skin.

The mind can play such strange tricks on you when you're tired; Scout clung desperately to the thought. Surely, the scent of roses lingering in the stagnant air had just wafted in from the garden. There could be no doubt of that. No mystery, at all. And it was only in her imagination that she'd heard her name, echoing in the emptiness. Or maybe it was something on the radio.

But there was no one with her in the house. So, she couldn't have heard anyone whispering. Especially not Lisa.

"Scout!"

And she wasn't hearing her now, either.

She briefly considered removing the painting – just taking it down and putting it away somewhere, so she wouldn't have to look at it. But the damned thing was huge. And it had been bolted to the wall several feet above her head. Even in an earthquake, that sucker wasn't going anywhere. Not without a ladder and a set of tools and a couple of really strong guys.

Things she could maybe think about getting hold of tomorrow. But for now...resolutely, she started up the long, curving staircase that led to the second floor. She had to check things out up here sometime. She might as well get it over with.

She peeked briefly into the first bedroom. When she had lived here, it had been used as a guestroom. And although it didn't appear to have been redecorated very much since then, it was still reassuringly impersonal.

*Good. I'll take this room then.* Although she seriously doubted whether she'd sleep very soundly anywhere within these four walls, it was a cinch she wouldn't manage half as well in any of the other bedrooms.

The master bedroom was next. It was a lovely room: large, light and airy, with French doors opening onto a tiny balcony, and a view of the bay. After twenty years, there was very little to remind her of her father, but Caroline's presence practically overwhelmed her.

Her stepmother's desk had been moved up here at some point, too, Scout noticed—probably when she'd started renting out rooms to students like Robyn. Whatever information Caroline might have had about Lisa, that's probably where she'd kept it. Scout sighed. She knew she was going to have to tackle the chore sometime, but she felt her throat tighten at the thought of having to go through Caroline's personal things. It would just have to wait, that's all. She couldn't face *this* room yet, either.

As she turned to leave, she found the dog watching her. It wagged its tail hopefully.

*It's kind of nice having a dog around.* She patted its head absently for a moment, before she realized what she was doing. "Forget it," she snapped, snatching her hand away again. "I am *not* keeping you."

She headed down the hallway, each step taking her closer to the two doors at the far end.

She put her hand tentatively on the knob of the door on her right. Panic seized her. She paused for a moment and took a couple of good deep breaths before she could bring herself to turn the knob and push open the door.

She needn't have worried.

Years of occupation by a succession of students had exorcised any presence that might otherwise have lingered here, in what used to be Lisa's room. Gone was the pale, pearlescent pink paint that had covered the walls. The glittery gold trim, the deep, cobalt blue ceiling emblazoned with stars; they'd once given the room a faintly mystical quality. That quality was entirely absent now.

*It was as though you'd entered a fairy tale*, Scout thought, remembering the room as it had been back when she'd first seen it, all those years ago. *As though you'd been transported to an enchanted castle, in a magical realm, and had inadvertently wandered into the princess's bedchamber.*

But the princess was long gone, and the large, jewel encrusted, papier-mâché vases that she'd kept filled with peacock feathers had all disappeared.

The low bed – in reality, just a mattress on the floor –heaped with tasseled, jewel-toned pillows and draped with a sheer veil of mosquito netting, had been replaced with a utilitarian loft-bed-and-desk combination.

The colorful silk Kashmiri carpet had been taken up; the iridescent curtains had been torn down. And the scuffed hardwood floor, pressed wood dresser and beanbag chair that defined the room now, were the epitome of ordinariness.

It was hard to believe that it was this same room where Scout had fought with Lisa for the last time...

"You've done some rotten things before Scout, but this was the last straw," Lisa had fumed, angrily shoving clothes into her backpack. "If you think you can just steal Glenn away from me you better think again. 'Cause I've got one helluva surprise for the two of you. You just wait and see if I don't."

"Lisa, I *promise* you. I'm not stealing anything," Scout insisted.

"Oh, you got that right. Glenn is *never* going to be yours."

Scout squirmed uncomfortably at the thought. "Well, good, then. I didn't want him in the first place!"

"Oh, you didn't, huh?" Lisa turned from her packing to glare at her suspiciously. "So, then what's this all about? You just slept with him to fuck with me? Is that you're telling me? Or did you just turn into a slut overnight?"

*Wouldn't you like to know?* Scout grimaced. "Look, what difference does it make? You know he's sleeping with half the county, anyway. That doesn't seem to bother you."

"Not anymore, he's not," Lisa said quietly.

"Oh, really?" Scout felt a stab of pity. How could Lisa, so smart about so many other things, be so dumb when it came to Glenn?

"How do you figure that, Lees? What's changed, all of a sudden? You've never been able to stop him before."

Lisa smiled. A nasty, cold, determined smile that momentarily shook Scout's confidence. Maybe she'd underestimated her stepsister.

"Oh, trust me," Lisa said grimly. "This time, things are gonna be different. *Ve-ry* different."

"Yeah well, you're a fine one to talk about trust," Scout said, pulling nervously at the tip of one of Lisa's peacock feathers, repeatedly shredding and smoothing the interlocking fibers. "Especially after what you did to me. You and the others."

Lisa smiled again, even more coldly than before. "Oh? Is that what's worrying you? Then maybe you should have thought about that before you started messing around with Glenn. 'Cause we can do that – and worse – anytime we please. And you won't even know about it unless we want you to."

*No!* Scout felt her blood run cold. "Lisa, I'm warning you. Keep out of my head."

"And you keep away from my boyfriend," Lisa retorted, her eyes flashing blue fire. "And get your hands off my stuff!"

Scout dropped the feather as if it had burned her. "Fine. You got it. And as far as Glenn goes, I wasn't exactly planning a repeat performance anyway, you know."

Lisa snorted. "Funny. That's not what Glenn thinks."

"Really? Glenn thinks? How can you even tell?"

"Oh, ha-ha. Very cute. Yeah, Glenn thinks. Right now, for instance, he thinks he's going to break up with me so that you two can be together. That two-timing sonofabitch."

Scout groaned. Great. Just what she didn't need. "Are you shitting me? Look, how about I tell him I'm not interested?"

"How about you don't tell him *anything*? I don't want you seeing him, Scout. I mean it. And, come to think of it, *I* don't want to see you, either."

"That might be difficult, don't you think?" Scout said, hiding the hurt she felt behind a careless smile. "What with us living in the same house and all? We're bound to run into each other now and then."

"Yeah? Well, we'll see about that, too. Things change."

Scout stared in surprise. "What the hell does that mean?"

"It means there's gonna be some big changes around here, little sister. Just you wait and see."

And then, grabbing up her backpack, tossing her blonde hair behind her shoulders, Lisa stormed out of the room, and out of Scout's life.

It was just so impossible to believe she was gone. Even after all these years, Scout could not believe that Lisa would not come walking back in. Any minute, now...

*"And just what do you think* you're *doing here?"* Scout could almost hear her asking.

It was, she thought, a damn good question.

"Well, that's everything, I think." Marsha sank back into the lumpy, old couch in her office above the store. She released the clip at the back of her head and shook out her hair. "The van's loaded and I've gone over all my lists a half dozen times, but I swear Celeste, I still feel like I'm forgetting something. It's gonna drive me crazy."

"Here." Celeste pushed a bowl of chilled edamame and a cup of lemongrass tea across the coffee table towards her. "It's probably just low blood sugar. I'm sure you'll feel better after you eat something. Jasmine should be back any minute with our dinner. But, you know, sweetie, if you're really worried about your memory, I could pop downstairs and get you some ginkgo. D'you want the soda or the gum? Or maybe we should set you up with a nice intravenous drip?"

"How about a nice strait jacket?" Marsha said, re-doing her hair into a loose twist. So, you think I'm losing it, too, now, huh?"

"I think we've both been under an unusual amount of stress lately," Celeste answered quietly. "And, speaking of which, do you want to tell me a little bit about that friend of yours who was here today – like why she's got Lucy so twigged?"

Marsha shrugged. "Well, you know Lucy. She lives to hold grudges."

Picking up at her cup, she sipped for a moment, in silence. Then she sighed. "Actually, that's not fair. You know the story, right? How we got expelled from high school? But that was just the tip of the iceberg. What really set things off was that our math teacher got murdered. Strangled. They found her body on the athletic field, just a couple of hours after she'd left a message for our principal saying she wanted to meet with her to discuss some of our recent schoolwork."

Celeste shivered. "Ooh, Marsha, how awful! But wait, you don't mean to say that anybody thought you and Lucy were involved in her murder?"

"Well, no one ever came right out and *accused* us. At least, I don't think anyone did. But I had my accident only a couple of weeks later and was pretty much out of it for a good long while; so I missed out on a lot of the drama.

"I do know that there were a lot of unpleasant rumors at the time, and I know that Lucy took the brunt of them. I was in the hospital, you see. And Scout was in Florida, apparently; and Lisa, had run away, so—"

"She ran away? Why? Not because—"

"Because *she* killed Ms. Burnett?" Marsha couldn't help laughing. "No, of course not! Don't be ridiculous. It might have been because of the cheating thing, I suppose. But, oh, it could have been for a lot of different reasons. She'd just learned that Scout was sleeping with her boyfriend, for one thing. You know what teen-age girls are like. And Lisa always was a bit of a drama queen, anyway."

"Jeez." Celeste smiled appreciatively. "Fast times at Holy High, huh?"

"Something like that." Marsha grabbed a handful of the bright green soybeans from the bowl on the table. "But it wasn't nearly so funny at the time. After the murder we were all questioned by the police. Lucy's cousin, Nick, was sent to interview us. Everything was pretty straightforward until they got to Scout.

"I don't know how it happened, maybe that post-hypnotic suggestion we'd given her got triggered again, or something. But she just cracked. Told them everything. Told them stuff they hadn't even thought about asking any of the rest of us."

"Oh, Marsha, that must have been awful for all of you!"

"Well, it was, of course. Still, I'd have paid big money to see the look on Sister Benedict's face once Scout got started. But at the time... God, it was a mess."

She broke off at the sound of footsteps pounding up the staircase. A minute later her daughter Jasmine burst through the door, a large paper take-out bag from the local Chinese restaurant clutched in her arms. As always, the sight of her daughter made Marsha's heart swell with pride. Jasmine had inherited Marsha's red hair and green eyes, and her father's slim, long legged, athletic build, darker skin and classic African features. But what had passed for handsome on the young man Marsha had known so briefly, was devastatingly lovely on his daughter.

"I ran into Maya and Robyn on the way back, Mom." Jasmine plunked herself down on the couch beside Marsha and started fishing cartons out of the bag. "They said to tell you they got everything you wanted from the nursery today. Oh, and also that Uncle Dan said he'd drive it up to the fairgrounds for you tomorrow."

"Thank you, sweetheart," Marsha said, as she reached for the carton that contained her cold spinach-sesame noodles.

Jasmine stopped and glared at her. "How do you do that? The boxes all look alike. How do you *always* know which one is yours?"

"Really, Jasmine," Celeste admonished, with a smile. "I would have thought that, by now, you'd have come to terms with your mother's abilities."

"But it's just so annoying," Jasmine whined. "And it's not fair!"

"I know, darling, what can we do? Your mother is extremely gifted. But, if you keep up with those exercises like I showed you, you should be able to access more of your own inner vision."

Marsha sighed in annoyance. "Must you two always make such a big deal out of everything? It wasn't anything special. This is the only thing we ordered that's cold. The rest of the boxes all have hot food in them."

Jasmine turned to glare at her again. "Mom, you can't *see* temperature. We've talked about this. Remember?"

*Oh, right.* Marsha smiled sheepishly. "Sorry, darling. I forgot. Anyway, did Maya say if everything went okay at the nursery today?"

Jasmine's eyes sparkled suddenly. "Well," she drawled, "Apparently there was a little trouble with the knives they were going to use. They couldn't find them, or something? But luckily, Celeste was here, and she was able to lend them hers."

Marsha glanced sharply at Celeste. She'd dearly love to know what her friend had been up to. Why had she been carrying the ceremonial daggers around with her this morning? But she could sense that Celeste was not in the mood to talk about it.

"They said they'd get them back to you tomorrow, by the way, Celeste," Jasmine said, grinning widely. Marsha knew her daughter was always pleased when she was able to surprise her. She certainly had this time.

Celeste smiled serenely. "Thank you, sweetie. But it's like I told them this morning, there's no rush."

*No rush?* Marsha gazed thoughtfully at her friend. Lending out your magical tools was strange enough, being in no hurry to get them back was unheard of. She was concerned about Celeste's rather odd behavior of late, especially since she'd been unable to sense anything in her aura that would explain it. No big surprise, there. Celeste had probably forgotten more about psychic shielding than Marsha would ever know.

Which reminded her— "Celeste, I've been meaning to ask you about something. You know this morning, when Scout showed up? It was kind of weird. I could sense something strange in the atmosphere, but it was like she was invisible. Do you know anything that could cause someone's aura to practically, I don't know, disappear?"

"Hmm." Celeste frowned in thought. "I suppose it could just be an unusual type of shield. You did say that she had some rather extensive powers, didn't you?"

Marsha smiled, wryly. "Well, yes, but as far as I know, only when she's in a trance state. I'm pretty sure she was fully conscious this morning."

"Well, there is one other possibility, you know."

Marsha felt the atmosphere go cold once more. Just like it had this afternoon. She had the feeling that, whatever Celeste was about to say, she wasn't going to like it.

"Sometimes, a person's aura will contract to the point where you can hardly see it. But Marsha? That's usually a sign of approaching death."

Yep, just as she suspected, she didn't like it. She didn't like it at all. But despite the cold chills running down her spine, Marsha was aware of a steely determination. Scout was *not* going to die. Not now, and not here. Not if Marsha had anything to say about the matter.

Maybe that was why Scout had come home at this exact time? Maybe safeguarding her friend's life was what Marsha was meant to do? Maybe she was finally being given a chance to atone for her actions all those years ago?

"Hey, Celeste," Jasmine spoke up suddenly. "Why don't you come back to our house tonight? The twins aren't home, so you can stay in their room. Then you and I can go over those exercises again."

It was getting late, Marsha thought with a start, suddenly recalling the road her friend would have to travel to get to her house. Several miles out of town, winding through one of the many canyons that surrounded Oberon, it was badly lit and fairly treacherous at night. She should have thought to suggest this herself.

"That's a really good idea, Celeste," she said. "I wish you would."

"Well, all right, sweetie," Celeste answered, with suspicious ease. "I guess it would make more sense than to try and beat the traffic coming back into town tomorrow morning."

Jasmine smiled at her. "Neat. It'll be like the old days – just the three of us."

Marsha thought she could detect the slightest bit of mischief in Celeste's voice as she murmured. "Yes. Good thing I just happen to have brought some extra clothes with me."

IF SCOUT LOOKED one way out the attic window, she could see all the way to the bay. She could just make out the handful of vessels plying the gilded waters; mostly chartered ships offering sunset and dinner cruises to eager tourists. If she turned the other way, she was looking down on the shadowed darkness of the woods next door. And beyond that, on the glowing green gem that was the athletic field of her old high school.

The emotions she felt at the sight of it were more painful than nostalgic. Would things have turned out differently if she and Lisa had not gone to the same school?

There really hadn't been any reason why they had to send her there, after all. Her father wasn't Catholic, and he certainly hadn't raised her as one. Caroline had been, as had Scout's own mother, but Scout didn't see how Caroline could have received much comfort from a religion which condemned her for her marriage to Scout's father.

Probably another reason for the grudge Lisa had held against them.

Giving up her attempts to open the window, Scout resigned herself to the inevitable. The attic was sweltering. But she guessed it would just have to stay that way. Sighing, she returned her focus to the boxes she had been going through.

It appeared as if her entire adolescence was stored in this attic. *It's like a freakin' museum.* Posters, and records –now warped beyond repair. Stereos and lamps and unidentified neon-colored plastic... something-or-others; who the fuck even knew? Lisa's surfboard. The used, paisley-painted guitar Scout had insisted on buying, along with several peasant skirts and a shawl, during her mercifully brief folk music phase. [3]

And the clothes! Omigod, had they really worn anything so hideous?

There were also boxes of books and school papers, pictures and mementos. Her teenage handwriting filled page after page in a series of notebooks. Spiky pen and ink drawings covered the sheets of innumerable sketchpads.

She even found a crushed, half-empty pack of cigarettes in one of the boxes. Jeez. She hadn't realized Caroline was such a pack rat. It didn't appear that the woman had ever tossed anything out.

Other than her stepdaughter.

Scout held the pack close to her nose and took a sniff. They were stale, of course. Incredibly stale. But God! She'd forgotten just how much she loved the smell of tobacco. And the taste. She'd even loved the way cigarettes had felt between her fingers, smooth and cool. Or the way the smoke rose from their tips in long, curling plumes.

She glanced back at the box, and a wave of nausea hit her. Two chunky ceramic candleholders, a little glass incense burner, and a bulky old-fashioned tape recorder lay at the bottom of the box. They seemed only vaguely familiar, and she couldn't remember having seen them before; but the longer she looked at them the stronger the nausea became. Panic rose in a tide of bile at the back of her throat.

Scout sat back on her heels, breathing hard, shaken by an inexplicable storm of unpleasant emotions. Hardly aware of what she was doing, her hands fumbled with the matchbook that had been tucked in with the cigarettes.

The simple act of holding the match to the end of the cigarette seemed to steady her. She focused her attention on the flame; exhaling slowly, watching as the smoke spiraled up into the rafters. She wouldn't think about the past, she decided, as she put the cigarette back to her lips and inhaled again.

She'd stay focused on the present. Do what she'd come here to do. Then get the hell out.

She would not let it get to her. She would not let them win. The past was dead. It was gone. A locked door. A closed book.

For good or for ill, it would never come back to her, and she could never return to it. It was over. Buried. History.

With much effort, she shook off the depression that threatened to overwhelm her, piled everything but the cigarettes back into the box and went on with her task. She was finally rewarded when, against all odds, she found what she was looking for. A file box containing all the records relating to Caroline's search for Lisa. Surprisingly enough, it had *not* been in Caroline's desk. Maybe everyone was wrong when they said Caroline had continued to work to solve the mystery of Lisa's disappearance. Maybe she'd given up, after all.

Scout's fingers trembled as she unfolded a note written in Lisa's familiar handwriting. It was the letter Lucy had received from her several days after her disappearance. The words brought it all back. The pain. The disbelief. The sense of unreality.

*Do you believe what that bitch has done now?* Scout read, with a sinking heart. *Wasn't it enough that she slept with Glenn? Did she really have to go and screw the rest of us, too? I swear, this sucks so bad. Did you hear that Ms. B. wanted to talk to us? Jeez. How the fuck are we gonna get ourselves out of this one? Maybe we can figure out a way to blame it all on Scout. Wouldn't that be a pisser?*

*Anyway, I've decided you were right about stuff. You know what I mean. So, I'm gonna bail. I'll let you know as soon as I've got things arranged. And, yeah, you better believe I'm going to make Glenn pay for it!*

*You don't think Scout could really be in love with him, do you? She says she's not, but she's up to something, Luce. I know it. I just wish I knew what.*

*We gotta find a way to get back at her. At both of them. Give it some thought, 'kay?*

*Well, later, chica. Via con Dios, and all that crap. I'm so outta here. LL*

Scout put down the letter and struggled to breathe. The memories were too thick. The sense of being hounded by the past was stronger than ever. The creaking and rumbling of the old house, once so familiar, was foreign to her now.

Once again she found herself imagining things.

*"Scout."*

The whispers seemed to call her name. Warning her, threatening her, caressing her – she couldn't tell which. And desperately cold though she was, her eyes and throat felt parched and dry, as if she were sick with a fever.

*"Scout...Scout...SCOUT!"*

She scrambled downstairs, lit a fire in the fireplace, and curled up on the couch, wrapping herself in one of Caroline's crocheted blankets. Then she lit another cigarette and read and reread the letter until she could have recited it by heart. The amount of anger that radiated from the single sheet of paper shouldn't have surprised her – it wasn't anything new, after all. And it didn't really change anything, either. But it did prove one thing. Lisa hadn't planned on staying out of touch forever.

Which made it even more likely that she'd met with some tragedy, fairly soon after leaving town. Made it even more necessary that Scout keep searching for answers. More necessary, and more likely painful, as well.

*Why, oh, why did I ever think this would be easy?*

---

1.  Here's a great example of how characters can come to life and totally change the trajectory of a book—or an entires series. Originally, I thought I was writing a mystery—the first in what I believed was going to be a series of cozy mysteries (I thought the same thing when I wrote the first book in my Children of Night vampire stories too, by the way. I'm a slow learner). I assumed Marsha, Lucy, Scout, and the rest of the women at The Crone's Nest would be spending most of their time solving crimes. And I thought having a cop as a sort of sidekick— someone who could help out if they found themselves in trouble; who'd routinely scold them for getting involved in things that didn't concern them; and who'd make a great long-term, slow-burn love interest for one of the characters —made a lot of sense.

    So, Nick was always going to have something of a feature role. But the rest of the men—not so much. I thought Lucy's husband and Marsha's ex were going to be very minor characters. But that all changed the minute Daniel Edward Cavanaugh walked into the kitchen and kissed his wife.

    I LOVE the chemistry between Lucy and Dan—and it just kept getting better and better as the series went on.

You can read all about how they first got together in the free, prequel novella, *Such Fleeting Pleasures*. Join my Facebook group, The Crone's Nest, for access to your free download!

2. In the first draft, Lucy was drinking white zinfandel. But even twenty years ago, that had fallen out of favor with oenophiles (I even had a T-shirt that proclaimed, "Friends don't let friends drink white zinfandel"). Merlot would shortly suffer a similar fate, thanks to the Sideways Effect; and the ABC Club—Anything But Chardonnay—was also gathering strength. But personally, I don't think she would have paired pesto with a zinfandel. I think she would have gone with a rosé, or maybe a blanc de blanc.

3. I really had to root around in my memories to come up with items I could use to furnish Scout's attic. Scout's paisley-painted guitar was actually inspired by a denim-covered guitar I remember seeing. I always wondered how the denim would affect the sound.

   Also, for the record? I'd be very happy to see a return of 70's fashion. Scout and I disagree about that, apparently, but I don't find them hideous, at all.

# 6

---

"Thanks, cuz." Nick smiled, as he took the coffee mug from Lucy's hand. It was after dinner. Dan and Seth were out on the lawn, playing keep away with Mandy and Kate, while the dog ran around, barking madly, and getting in everybody's way.

Lucy went back for her own mug and then returned to the porch and sat down in the chair next to his. "You had enough pasta, right?" she asked, and then, more hesitantly. "Is everything okay with you these days?"

Nick sighed. "You know, that's the third time tonight you've asked me that. What gives?"

"Nothing." Lucy's shrug looked casual enough, but she was drumming with her fingers on the wide arm of her Adirondack chair. A sure sign she was either upset or holding something back. "Just, you know, making sure."

"Is everything okay with *you*?" he asked.

Lucy looked searchingly at him for a moment. Nick got the distinct impression she was trying to make up her mind about something.

"Yeah. Sure. Of course. Couldn't be better," she answered, turning her eyes back to the game on the lawn.

Watching the way her expression softened when she looked at Dan, Nick felt a small pang of envy. He didn't think that he and his ex-wife had *ever* looked at one another that way. *Must be nice.*

"So is Kate upset about missing the camping trip?" Lucy asked, rather abruptly, as though she were anxious to change the subject.

"Sure. But what are you going to do? Leave it to Lauren to schedule her vacation for the next two weeks." For that matter, leave it to Lauren to find a way to turn *everything* to do with Kate into a contest between the two of them.

"She had to know you guys were planning this, right? I mean, we've only been doing it for years, same time every summer."

Nick shook his head wearily. "Of course, she knew, Lucy. She pulls stuff like this all the time. You *know* that!"

"I guess so."

"Speaking of which, I'm going to have to meet up with you at the festival tomorrow afternoon to pick up Kate. I'm supposed to get her to Lauren by 6:30."

"*At the festival*? Christ, Nick."

"Hey, don't look at me. It wasn't my idea."

"You sure know how to pick 'em though, don't you?"

Nick glanced at her then, surprised by the anger in her voice. Like the rest of his family, Lucy had always seemed completely taken with Lauren – or taken *in*, as he sometimes thought – no matter what she did.

*What the heck's going on tonight anyway*? And why'd she say 'them'? What was with the plural, anyway? It wasn't like he'd been married more than once, after all. He wasn't *that* fucking stupid.

Lucy pushed herself out of her chair and stood up. "I'm getting more coffee. You want some?" Nick handed her his mug without speaking, then watched as she stalked back into the house.

Something was up, all right. Lucy had been on edge all evening and, Nick was getting the uncomfortable impression that whatever was bothering her, it had something to do with him. But what the hell could he have done now?

It always struck him as funny the way that Lucy, the youngest of their generation, had taken on the role of Family Matriarch after her parents and his mother had moved to Arizona. Nick knew she worried about him, and about her brother Joey—almost as though they were both still Seth's age. Which, if he were honest, could be pretty damned annoying at times. Still, he and Joey just naturally gravitated to her house at holidays.

Or maybe it wasn't so funny after all. Lucy had a gift for family, he thought, not for the first time. Despite having some pretty sharp edges, she was instinctively nurturing. She just couldn't help taking care of the people she cared about, and she was fiercely loyal.

Qualities that were conspicuously absent in his ex-wife. *Why did it take me so long to see that?*

Lucy returned with two steaming mugs, and a bottle of anisette, which she plunked down on the arm of his chair. Nick poured some into his coffee and took a sip, savoring the sweet licorice flavor it added. "Mmm. Thanks. You want me to pour you some, too?"

"Already got it," Lucy said, taking a long sip, her eyes once again following the action out on the lawn.

"So, how's Mandy feel about Kate missing the camping trip?" Nick probed gently.

Lucy shook her head. "Oh, well, you know how it is. She's still got Steffi, at least. And thank God for that. But it's not the same. She and Kate are best buds."

"I know. It's really nice to have a cousin you're that close to," he said, his eyes on his daughter. "Especially when you don't have any siblings."

"Yeah. Not so nice when you're worried about them screwing up, though, is it?" Lucy muttered.

*Uh-oh.* "Uh, Lucy? Did I do something to upset you?"

"What? No. Jeez, of course not!" Lucy turned to glare at him. "God, Nick, don't be so conceited. Do you always think everything's about you?"

"Uh, no?"

"Well, good. 'Cause it's not. Let's just...just...let's enjoy our coffee. Okay? And maybe not talk anymore tonight."

WHEN ROBYN RETURNED to the house late that night, Scout was huddled on the couch, lost in thought. A cigarette still burned in the ashtray beside her.

She tensed slightly as Robyn moved a step further into the room, perhaps with the intention of having a chat. But Scout couldn't be bothered playing polite. She took no notice of her, other than to sigh quietly in relief as she felt her retreat.

The day wound down. Once again, the night air stole through the house, and the dog settled down by Scout's feet. Once again, the cats arrayed themselves around her. Their eyes, as watchful as her own, glowed like embers in the night. Once again, it was just before dawn when she finally allowed sleep to claim her.

Only to dream...

Of Caroline's face, pale and drawn with worry, as she ushered Scout out of the school building and into the car without a word.

"Scout honey are you all right?" she asked as they pulled away from the curb. "How are you feeling?"

"I don't know." Scout stared out at the bleak landscape. Trees loomed on either side of the road, dark and foreboding, half hidden in the fog. Ghostly wisps of vapor drifted out across the black tar surface of the road. She shivered. *I hate this drive. I want to go home. I want to already be home. Now.* "I don't even know what happened today. No one's told me what I did, or anything. Do you think there's something wrong with me? Like maybe a brain tumor or something?"

"Oh, Scout, honey, no! I'm sure it's nothing like that." Caroline spoke soothingly, but Scout saw the worried glance she shot her way. "Sweetie, did you eat anything at school today? I mean, besides your lunch. Did anyone give you something? Or, or did you maybe take a sip from someone else's drink? The Sister said something about drugs—"

"Oh, my God!" Scout ground her teeth. "Sister Francis thinks everything's about drugs. She's totally obsessed. She thinks songs like *Peace Train* are about drug trafficking! [1] I'm not on drugs, Caroline. I swear I'm not!"

"I know that sweetheart. But it's still possible that someone might have—"

"I *told* you," Scout repeated grimly. "I don't know what happened."

*Not yet, she didn't. But she meant to find out...*

"FIRST YOU GOTTA PROMISE you won't get mad," insisted Lucy, later that afternoon.

Scout regarded her angrily. It had been about ten minutes since she'd heard her friends and stepsister arrive home from school. They hadn't even had the common decency to stop by her room to see how she was doing. No, they'd just gone straight to Lisa's room—as though Scout's well-being was of absolutely no concern to them. Or maybe they just hadn't had the guts to face her.

Arms crossed over her chest, chin thrust out aggressively, Lucy stared back at her. For a moment, Scout wondered if she could be imagining the guilt that seemed to lurk in the depths of her friend's brown eyes. But no. Whatever else was going on, she certainly hadn't imagined the events of the afternoon.

Marsha had pretty much admitted to knowing something about what happened. And now they wanted her to make promises? "No way. If you guys are hiding something from me, I'm already mad. Now, tell me!"

"Actually, we don't have to tell you anything," Lisa murmured, pausing to light a cigarette. She shook out the match, blew a thick cloud of smoke towards Scout and favored her stepsister with one of the infuriatingly calm, superior smiles that always made Scout want to brain her. "Not if we don't want to."

"No." From her perch at the foot of Lisa's bed, Marsha spoke up suddenly. "Scout's right. Things have gotten out of control. She has a right to know what's going on. It's only fair."

"Oh, all right! Jeez." Lucy flung herself into a chair, and began absently twisting one lock of her dark, wavy hair around and around on her finger. "So, Scout, do you remember last November, when we had that big sleep over at my house where we tried to hypnotize each other?"

"Yeah," Scout answered cautiously. Of course, she remembered. Marsha was studying Psychology and had been full of ideas. She remembered the uncomfortable feeling that she'd had afterwards that there was something they weren't telling her. Very similar to the way she was feeling right now, in fact.

Lucy flashed her a nervous grin. "Well, it worked! And, girl, you were amazing. You went into this super deep trance and then, well..." Her voice trailed away. She turned to look at the others.

It was Lisa who picked up the story. "It's really no big deal. Just a little experiment we've been working on. For math class."

Scout blinked in surprise. "An experiment," she repeated. "For math class. Tell me something Lisa, do I look stupid to you?"

Lisa's blue eyes glinted with amusement. "You don't really want me to answer that, do you?" She leaned back against her pillows. "Look, it's like this. You know how you've got class Monday and Wednesday and our class meets Tuesdays and Thursdays? But it's the exact same work, right? And the tests we get are all the same, too? Okay, so, we just wanted to see if we could get you to give us the answers from your work. That's all." [2]

"You mean cheating? There's no way I'd do that."

Marsha grimaced. "Which we already knew. So...we kinda planted a post-hypnotic suggestion in your mind. So now, whenever we say one of the code words, you go into a trance. Sort of automatically. And...anyway, I think that's what happened at school today. I think it was accidentally triggered when—"

"Wait a minute." Scout felt the blood roar in her ears as she tried to wrap her thoughts around the concept. "Since *November*? That was *five months ago!*"

She reached for the cigarettes on Lisa's nightstand. Her hands were shaking as she pulled one out of the pack. "Are you guys telling me that, ever since then you've been...? How often?"

"Just a couple of times a week," Marsha admitted.

Scout gasped. "A couple of times— *Every* week? I don't believe this! How could you?"

Lisa rolled her eyes. She tossed Scout a book of matches and sighed. "Don't be such a baby. It's not like we're hurting you, or anything. All we did was access a little information. It was like tutoring—only you didn't have to do any work. And can you really blame us? You know how you were always bragging about how you got better grades than the rest of us. It was annoying." She grinned then, so clearly unrepentant that Scout had to swallow hard before she spoke.

"You hafta promise you won't do it anymore," she told them, her voice hoarse with the fear that they wouldn't listen.

"I knew it was too good to last." Lucy frowned at her. "What's the big deal, anyway? It's not like we were asking you about a lot of personal stuff, or anything. It's just freakin' Algebra!"

"No!" Marsha insisted. She shook her head. "After what happened today? Of course, we have to stop. It's getting out of hand."

Scout saw Lisa glance sharply at Marsha. Then she turned back toward her and smiled. Sweetly. Far too sweetly.

"You know what, Lucy? I think they're right. Okay Scout, we won't do it anymore. "

"Thank you."

"I mean, if you're sure. Because it would be really helpful. How ow about just until the end of the school year?"

"No, I said!"

"Damn it," Lucy grumbled. "I was just getting used to good grades, too. What the hell are we supposed to do now?"

"I mean it, Lucy. No more."

"I know! I heard you. We said we'd stop, didn't we?."

*But they won't.* Scout knew that they wouldn't—that they couldn't. Something icy cold and nasty twisted deep inside her as she contemplated it.

If they'd been coasting for five months, there was no way they could catch up now. *They'll fail if they stop now.* She briefly considered telling someone – her teacher, her father, Caroline – but just as quickly dismissed it. What could she tell them that wouldn't just lead to more questions?

Alone in her bedroom that night, she considered her options. She was going to have to handle this herself. If she wanted them to stop, she would have to find a way to make it happen. She would have to harness the same power that they were using and turn it against them.

A car passed along the road in front of the house. Scout watched the patterns of light and shadow chase each other across her ceiling until the room was cloaked in darkness once again. She couldn't remember ever having felt so violated, so isolated, so trapped. Or so very angry.

She'd always thought of anger as being fiery and hot, but as the emotions that had been swirling around inside her all day began to coalesce into an icy knot, hard in her stomach, she knew better. Anger could also be deadly cold.

She forced herself to take deep breaths, fight down the panic that was making her teeth chatter. Forced herself to think. She didn't know how yet, but she would find a way to stop them.

And then? Then she'd find a way to make them pay...

TWENTY YEARS LATER, Scout thrashed around on the couch as the dream shattered and reformed in her mind. She dreamed next of being pursued through an endless forest of gnarled and twisted trees. Of water pouring in torrents through all the doors and windows of the house even as she rushed to close them. Of pale pink and yellow rose petals falling from the sky, burying her beneath their softness and their scent, until she couldn't breathe.

---

1. True story. I, too, attended an all-girls Catholic high school. And one of the nuns who taught there did, in fact, make this claim about the song. It was so absurd that I never forgot it.

2. As it happens, Like Lisa, I too have a sister who's a year younger than me. She also went to the same high school. And, just like Scout, she was so good at math that she was put into advanced classes with students in my grade level. So, we hung out with a lot of the same people. But, for the record, no one ever hypnotized anyone. I only mention this because there have been people (who should know better) who have actually asked me if this story is autobiographical. It is not.

   On the other hand, the rumor that I blew up a desk while teaching a class on witchcraft is only a slight exaggeration. The desk didn't blow up. It just got a bit singed. It was the incense burner that blew up.

# 7

*L*ucy woke up with a start. It was shortly after sunrise. The house was quiet and beside her Dan continued to sleep soundly. She thought she'd heard someone shouting her name, but no echo lingered in the morning air. Outside her window, birds chirped undisturbed. Whatever had disturbed her must have been internal.

Slipping quietly out of bed, she wrapped her robe around her and went outside to see about the weather.

A thick mist still clung to the trees and the earth felt cool beneath her bare feet, but Lucy felt the promise of sunlight in the warm breeze that blew across her face. She breathed in deeply, grateful for all the fresh, green scents that rose from her garden. She let her awareness flow out over the yard, savoring the feelings of rightness, of peace, of boundless energy, of eternal, joyful creativity. She soaked in it, allowing herself to become a part of it. Allowing it to become a part of her.

"I knew I'd find you out here." Dan surprised her a few minutes later, wrapping his arms around her waist and hugging her tight. "What are you doing up so early? I thought you'd want to sleep in a bit this morning. Aren't you tired?" He leaned over to nibble on her ear and Lucy felt a small tremor shiver through her – an echo of last night's pleasure. "I thought for sure I'd worn you out last night."

Lucy smiled. "Oh, did you now?" He had a point, after all. She *should* be tired. But, then again, so should he. She turned within the circle of his arms, and laid her head against his chest, hugging him fiercely in return. She listened to the slow, steady beating of his heart and sighed contentedly. "Not even close, Cavanaugh. I just couldn't sleep. Why're *you* up?"

"Eh, I figured I'd get an early start on the day. I'm going to take the truck down to the fairgrounds now. Get the booth set up ahead of time, for a change. Seth's up, too. He wants to come with me." A laugh rumbled in his chest. "God help us both. So, you'll just be taking the girls with you."

Lucy looked up at him, startled. "You're going *now*? But you haven't even had breakfast!"

Dan leaned down and kissed her. "Mmm. Don't worry about it. We'll get something there. See you later, babe."

He let her go, and Lucy watched him walk back towards the house. Striding off into the mist like some knight-errant, although she had serious doubts whether any suit of armor had ever looked as good as those jeans and work shirt did.

Just as he got to the house Dan stopped and pivoted, "Hey, babe, since you're up anyway, why don't you think about getting an early start yourself? Might be a good idea, you could beat some of the traffic." He lifted an eyebrow suggestively. "Get there before noon and I could maybe even be persuaded to treat you to some lunch."

Lunch. Right. "And here I thought I'd just throw together a couple of sandwiches for you," she teased.

Dan smiled. "Well, that could work, too, you know. We could have ourselves a little picnic. Just you and me. Way out in the woods somewhere. All alone."

"I don't know about you, Cavanaugh." Lucy shook her head in mock sorrow. "Food? Really? Is that *all* you can think about?"

His laughter drifted back to her through the mist. "Well, you know me, babe."

*Yeah,* Lucy thought, brimming with happiness and energy, *I certainly do.* So, he wanted a picnic, huh? Good idea. Perfect, in fact. She imagined soft, creamy Brie paired with some of last night's left-over focaccia. Maybe a roasted zucchini-mint salad. And, of course, some fresh strawberries and whipped cream.

Or maybe she'd save the strawberries for tonight and bring peaches instead. Yes, that was what they'd want today. Sweet, ripe peaches dripping with juice. She imagined the taste and the feel of peach skin against her tongue. Mmm. She could hardly wait. She'd better go in now and take her shower and get the girls up. That might not be so easy. No doubt they'd stayed up half the night talking.

And she would have to make sure Kate took all her stuff with her, since Nick was picking her up from the fairgrounds. Sheesh. Wasn't that a nice mess? Well, she thought as she turned to head back in, she'd better get a move on, if she wanted to get there before noon—which she absolutely did.

It wasn't until she was halfway back to the house that the words fell, clear as raindrops, into her mind and she knew what it was that had disturbed her sleep. *Scout's back.*

Anger sizzled in her consciousness. Her pleasant mood was broken.

Scout. Shit. Something would have to be done about that.

AFTER JOURNEYING out to Totawka Regional Park, and parking the Mustang in a lot near the campgrounds, Scout opened the door of her car and was immediately engulfed by the pungent odors of wood smoke and roasting meat, of sweetgrass and evergreens and incense. Gentle strains of music wafted along on the breeze – flute and fiddle, harp and drum. She felt her heart quicken. In the valley below, Oberon's Midsummer Festival was well underway.

Scout followed the music and the scents through the sun dappled woods, eagerly winding her way around the campground, with its hastily set up campsites that would later house the all-night revelers. She passed through stands of madrone and manzanita with their peeling red bark and gray-green leaves, and slipped easily through groves of scrub oak and cedar and fragrant bay laurels.

Like most of the solar festivals, Midsummer was a two-day celebration. A balefire would be lit as darkness approached and people would dance and party in its glow throughout this, the year's shortest night. Scout smiled as she remembered a time when one of her greatest ambitions had been to stay and party the night away with them.

Well, maybe that's what she'd do tonight. Since she had to be in Oberon anyway, she could think of worse ways to spend her time than in fulfilling a few of her teenage fantasies. Besides, she had to have *some* stories to take back to Larry.

She glanced down at the dog. The poor thing was already panting. "Not much farther now, girl. Then we'll see about getting you some water, okay? Would you like that?"

The dog rewarded her with another hopeful wag of her tail.

"You're such a good dog," she murmured, surprising them both.

They passed out of the trees and found themselves at the crest of a hill looking over a large flat bowl of a valley. The grassy plain below them was dotted with brightly colored booths arranged in a loose circle around the bare patch of ground where, just after sunset, the balefire would be set ablaze. Off to one side, several carnival-style rides and amusements had been set up. And tucked discreetly away in what the organizers hoped would be a more or less downwind direction, an army of port-a-potties stood at attention.

A shrill cry above her head interrupted Scout's thoughts. Looking up she caught a glimpse of a red-tailed hawk, sailing the wind currents to its home on Mount Totawka. She smiled at the pleasant tug of nostalgia it evoked, and started along the path that would lead her down to the festival, the dog, as ever, following close on her heels.

The fairgrounds were awash with colorful signs and banners. Scout let the seductive pull of the music draw her through the crowd.

She was at the foot of the stage before she recognized the insidious longing that had brought her there. The dream of being close to home, at long last, was flooding through her, again. She steeled herself against it.

*That's not what I'm here for*, she reminded herself, sternly. She was here to observe. To keep an eye on her dear, old friends, whose motives she had every reason to mistrust. To find out if they knew anything that would help her in her quest.

But that was all she was here to do. And although she might be willing to indulge herself with a few half-forgotten dreams during her stay, there was no way was she going to let any of those dreams seduce her. Squaring her shoulders, she turned away from the music and headed off in search of answers.

She found Lucy selling seedlings at a booth whose banner read Cavanaugh Family Nursery.

*We gotta find a way to get back at her. At both of them. Give it some thought...*

The words from Lisa's letter echoed in her mind. She wondered how much thought Lucy might have given, over the years, to the idea of *getting back at* Scout?

Forcing a politely neutral expression onto her face, she moved forward. "Hey," she said in greeting.

Lucy glanced up briefly from the sales slip she was writing out. "Hey, yourself."

"Quite a place you've got here." Scout knew there was still a hint of challenge in her voice, but she couldn't seem to shake it. "Is all this yours, too?"

"Yep. Well, kind of. My husband's family. They've had the business for years. Out in Abraxas Canyon, you know?" Lucy replied as she finished up with her customer.

When the woman had at last moved out of earshot, she turned to scowl at Scout. "What are you doing here, Scout? Are you actually buying something, or are you just here to bust my chops?"

Scout shrugged. "No downside either way, is there? But I'm thinking about it. I mean, now that I'm back in Oberon, I should

88

probably work up an interest in gardening, don't you think? Make Caroline proud? You know how she always loved her garden."

"You're not *really* planning on staying, are you?"

"Why not? Seeing as I'll be stuck with the house, anyway. I mean unless Lisa shows up and wants to fight me for it."

"Why be stuck? Sell it."

"And Lisa?"

"Who knows? But I'm sure that, wherever she is, she'd rather have the money. I'd imagine you would, too. So why don't you do everyone a favor, find yourself a realtor, and then go back to LA?"

"Gee, Luce. That doesn't sound very neighborly of you."

"No offense, Scout. But the idea of you and me being neighbors again doesn't really thrill me. Besides, you've never even wanted to *visit* before now."

Scout smiled grimly. "Oh, I wouldn't say that. I'd say it was more a matter of *other people* not wanting me to. But you know." She took a long look around and allowed her smile to broaden. "Now that I'm here...the place kinda grows on you, don't you think?"

But Lucy didn't get a chance to tell her what she thought, because at that moment another customer interrupted with a question, and she turned away again. Scout watched her with narrow eyes and cold amusement in her heart.

"Can we pet your dog?" a soft voice behind her asked. Scout turned around to find two girls, about ten- or eleven-years old staring at her with large, hopeful eyes.

She smiled at them. "Go right ahead. She seems like a very nice dog, I'm sure she won't mind."

The smaller of the two girls, the one with the light brown curls, bent over the dog, crooning softly. The other girl eyed her curiously. "Are you friends with my mom?" she asked after a moment, gesturing at Lucy, whose back was turned to them.

"You're Lucy's daughter?" Scout's eyes widened in surprise. She looked more closely at the girl. Yes, of course, she was. She should have recognized that shrewd, serious expression right away. "Your mom and I went to high school together. But we haven't seen each other in a really long time."

The girl nodded. "I thought you probably knew her, from the way you two were talking."

Well, there was no touching that. "Is this your sister?" Scout asked instead, nodding at the other girl.

"My cousin."

"We're actually second cousins," the other girl informed her. "Because my dad and her mom were cousins first."

"That's not what that means," Lucy's daughter corrected.

"Yes, it is, Mandy," her cousin protested stubbornly. "They're older than us, so, obviously, they did everything first."

Cousins? Scout's gaze sharpened. "Wait— You're not...Nick's little girl?"

Both girls turned to face her then. "You know my dad?" Nick's daughter asked. She had beautiful eyes. Familiar eyes. A warm, luminous, light brown shade that Scout remembered all too well.

Despite the sudden aching in her chest, Scout couldn't help but smile. "I used to. A long time ago. I think you have his eyes."

The girl smiled back at her. "I'm Kate. What's your name?"

"Scout."

Both girls giggled. "Like...Girl Scout?" Lucy's daughter asked.

"Only without the girl."

"Well, I think that's cool." Kate flashed her cousin an impatient look. "I wish *my* parents had given me a cool name like that."

"Oh, my parents didn't choose it," Scout told her. "I picked it out myself, when I was about your age."

"Really? Wow." At that, both girls looked impressed.

"Girls." Lucy was back, frowning even more fiercely. "I need you to run an errand for me. Right now. Go find Marsha and ask if she needs any more mint. Or chamomile. Or...just ask her if she needs anything. Okay? Go on!"

"But Mom—"

"Mandy, just do it. Now!"

"But Cousin Lucy, you can ask her yourself," Kate told her. "See? Here she comes."

"Scout." Marsha smiled at her warmly. "You made it. Good. Have you met my friends? This is Amanda and this—" but she got no further because a red cloud of fury seized hold of Scout, and without warning she hauled off and hit her. Hard as she could. Right in the face.

The girls gasped in shock and Lucy cursed furiously as Scout stood paralyzed with shock, unable to account for the adrenaline coursing through her veins. She stared in horrified confusion at Marsha, who had fallen back against the wall of the booth.

Marsha stared right back at her. Stared almost through her it seemed, with piercing intensity, her initial expression of outraged anger changing almost immediately, first to one of dawning recognition, and then to rueful amusement. Improbably, she started to laugh.

"Marsha!" Scout gasped. "I'm so sorry. I don't know what happened. I just, just—"

"Don't worry about it." Marsha rubbed her cheek. Her green eyes were alive with something close to malice. "I mean, ouch but...well, that's the problem with post-hypnotic suggestions, isn't it? Sometimes you just don't know what you've got in your head 'til it wakes up and socks you in the face."

*Oh, dear God.* Scout felt her throat close, just as it had in the attic the night before. Once again, a wave of nausea engulfed her. *I remember...*

It had taken her almost three weeks to come up with a plan to stop them. She'd had to research the procedures she would need to follow, and to buy all the necessary equipment. The candles. The incense. A tape recorder [1] and a blank tape—so she could record and play back the instructions that would allow her to hypnotize herself.

She had chosen a day when she knew Lisa would be out. Concentrating on her breathing, she had counted backwards and imagined herself on an escalator. Moving downward. Flight after flight, deeper and deeper. Into the darkest reaches of her mind.

Around and down. Around and down. Her breathing slowing and

deepening as she went. Her heart thudding in her ears. Her body growing increasingly heavy.

Around and down and down and...

She found herself in a large storeroom, cloaked in shadow, its dimensions impossible to ascertain. It was filled with crates and boxes, piled high and wide, as far as the eye could see. [2]

A storeroom was not exactly what she had been expecting, but then, neither was the sprightly old man who came bustling out from between the stacks of boxes to help her.

Comprehension gleamed in his bright gray eyes. "Ahh, yes," he told her. "I know just what you need."

Patiently, she followed his instructions, until she had constructed the perfect protection. Confident that she was prepared for any future attacks, as she had begun to think of them, she headed back to the escalators, circling upward this time, through floor after floor after floor.

She had thought she was safe after that. Thought they'd tire of the game once it ceased to serve them. Once the maze she had constructed within her own mind, the mirrors and traps she had laid there, had succeeded in providing enough misinformation to foul all their plans.

But after that last argument with Lisa a new fear had surfaced.

*What if they find out about Nick?*

They could hypnotize her again, and maybe cause her to say or do all sorts of horrible things. Perhaps they already had?

With a growing sense of paranoia, she considered her actions of late. Had she done anything unusual? Anything strange? Anything that she wouldn't normally have done?

Well, yeah; she'd slept with Glenn. Definitely not one of her better ideas. Still, she'd had her reasons, hadn't she? And, much as she might like to blame someone else for that decision, she didn't really think Lisa would have suggested it. But what about one of the others?

Maybe? Sadly, she couldn't say it was impossible. Given everything else she'd learned about them, everything else they'd done to her... Honestly, it was not all that farfetched.

*Okay, that's it. It's war now.*

She'd seen no other choice but to go back into her own subconscious and build new defenses. Her hands had been shaking so badly she could barely light the candles and the heliotrope incense. It had taken her a long, long time to calm her breathing, and even then, she found herself descending at a frightening speed – down and down and down and down – into the very center of the earth, it seemed.

Even before she got there, she could smell the fear. So strong it all but smothered her. A sour, clinging scent, like stagnant water thick with decayed vegetation. The atmosphere reeked with it. When the wizened old man approached her this time, there was a look of deep concern on his face. Speaking softly, he gradually calmed her until she was able to step away from the rank cloud that surrounded her. She felt cleaner, calmer, although she could still see the roiling, seething mass her emotions had created, as it hovered in the darkness at the edge of her perception.

She left it there. Turning her attention away from the fear, she focused her thoughts on what she'd come for.

First of all, she needed the code words they had implanted into her subconscious. There had to be a way to access that information. Once she had it, she could construct a kind of armor to protect herself—both from their wrath and from any further prying they might seek to do. And, finally, she would also need a way to deflect them. Something that would stop them if they ever tried to hypnotize her again. A way to force them to keep their distance from her.

The first was the easiest. In fact, she almost couldn't believe it when she'd searched their minds and found just a handful of names.

That was it? That was all they had needed, all they had used, to cause all this trouble? It was hard to believe that something so seemingly harmless could have such power. But, then again, all the old stories spoke of the power that existed in names. And, armed with this knowledge, Scout knew she could construct a suitable deterrent.

To serve her second need, the old man produced a long cloak.

Smoke gray, soft as the fall of night. It hung to the floor and the hood, when he had drawn it up over her head, was deep enough to cast even her face into shadow.

The garment was made of a thick, cloudy substance. Once she was wearing it, Scout felt as though she were clothed in fog. It distorted her perceptions, she noticed that right away, but just the tiniest bit, hardly enough to signify. Some things – things she'd barely noticed before – sprang suddenly into focus, while others receded. It felt warm and weightless on her shoulders as she allowed him to bind it securely around her.

The last thing she needed was some sort of reverse trigger. Like an early warning system, or an alarm. A way to retaliate if they ever again tried to get into her mind. But she was just so mad, and all she could think of was her own overwhelming desire to hit them. Hard. To hurt them the way they'd hurt her.

This time, it seemed to take forever to climb back to the surface. At almost every stop, she found herself wanting to wander off and explore her surroundings. The cloak, too, seemed to grow warmer and heavier as she went up. She wished she could take it off, but it was fastened in some manner she did not understand, and she wasn't sure how to undo it.

Eventually, she did make it back to her room, and her normal consciousness. At least, she was pretty sure she had. But everything around her still looked strange somehow, so she couldn't be sure.

She'd been nearly overcome with exhaustion and couldn't find the energy to figure out how exactly things were different. In fact, she had barely enough energy to blow out the candles. She lay down on the bed and curled herself into a ball. She was asleep almost instantly.

Over the course of the night, she seemed to pass from one strange dream into another. By morning the details of her dreams had blended with the events of the previous afternoon, and they had all but dissipated from her memory. She'd overslept and had to rush to avoid being late for school. The day had passed in a pleasant haze of anticipation. She was meeting with Nick at his apartment that afternoon. Each time she thought of it her breath caught in her throat and tiny tremors of excitement rippled through her.

Today was the day they would become lovers. She was sure of it.

She might have seen Lisa and the others somewhere around, during the course of the school day. But she had taken no notice. And later, when asked, she'd insist she had no memory of having seen them at all.

For twenty years, she'd have no memory of any of it.

---

1. This is one of many places where the series really shows its age. Granted, Scout is describing something that occurred twenty years in *her* past, but still. Tape recorders.

   Cassette Tapes. I feel old. lol!

2. Just an FYI. This storeroom will make a dramatic reappearance in book seven, **Visions Before Midnight**.

# 8

"*I* cannot believe you actually planned that!" Lucy was seething. The three women had gone back to Marsha's booth, where she had ordered tea and sandwiches for them all—along with an herbal compress for her cheek—but Scout and Lucy were both too angry to think of food.

"Well, I can't believe you used one of *those names* for your own daughter!" Scout snarled back at her. "What did you think was going to happen if I ever came back? Or were you just not thinking about that?"

"Of course, I wasn't thinking—I was seventeen! And why *wouldn't* I use it? The whole point was to pick names we really liked, so we'd *remember* them."

"Well, I hope you're happy then. 'Cause I sure as hell remembered, didn't I?"

"Oh, yeah, Scout. I'm freakin' delirious. Can't you tell? And just what were *you* thinking, huh? We were *friends* back when you came up with the idea. Supposedly."

"Oh, don't even go there. I am *so* not the one at fault."

"Enough!" Marsha threw the compress on the table and glared until she had gotten their attention. "You both need to calm down.

There's no permanent damage done. We'll just re-hypnotize Scout to—"

"*What?*" They responded in unison, glaring right back at her.

Scout nearly choked on her outrage. "No. Fuck no. Not happening."

"Exactly. Count me the fuck out of that!" Lucy sputtered.

"Ooookay. So, then I guess we'll go with Plan B. We'll just be real careful who we introduce her to while she's here."

Lucy scowled. "Hear that, Scout? There's another good reason for you to leave town. I'm thinking today's none too soon."

"Think again," Scout snarled at her.

Marsha sighed. "Okay, stop. What did I miss now?"

"Scout's got some stupid idea she might stay awhile," Lucy complained, leaning back in her chair and folding her arms across her chest. "Like...forever, or something."

Marsha looked thoughtful. "Okay. Interesting."

"Well, why shouldn't I?" Scout asked, somewhat defiantly. "I have a house here that I can't unload. I mean, I could, I guess. But what if Lisa comes back to reclaim her half?"

Marsha's face clouded. "Scout. I think you need to face the facts. Lisa's not coming back."

"You know what, Marsha? I'm starting to really wonder about you. What do you know that makes you so certain about that? And don't say psychic intuition, because you know what I think about that!"

"Hello ladies. Mind if I join you?" a woman's deep voice interrupted. Scout turned to see a rather large, imposing figure looming behind her.

Marsha beamed at the newcomer with what looked like a whole lot of relief. "Heather! Great to see you. Sit down. *Please.*"

"Oh, Marsha— Ouch!" Heather winced as she deposited her tray on the table and sat herself behind it. "What'd you do to yourself—run into a door?"

Marsha waved the question away. "Nothing so dramatic. Just a slight occupational hazard. Heather, meet Scout."

Heather's eyebrows rose. "Oh! Caroline's stepdaughter, right? Nice to meet you, I'm sure." She nodded briefly in Scout's direction and then turned to Lucy. "And how're *you* doing today?"

"Well, I'm just fantastic, Heather," Lucy answered with forced cheerfulness. "Never better." She raised her cup in a small salute before taking a tiny sip.

"Hmph! So I see."

"Don't mind her," Marsha insisted firmly. "She's fine. We all are. Anyway, what were we saying?" But before Scout could answer, she was interrupted again, this time by a young woman whose long red hair was arranged in dozens of tiny braids strung with beads.

"Mom?" She sounded concerned as she came up behind Marsha. "Hey. What happened to your face?"

"It's nothing, baby. Just an accident." Marsha smiled fondly at her daughter. She turned to Lucy and whispered urgently, "Do you remember any of the other names we used?"

Lucy grimaced. "Not really? But I think you're okay. Maybe."

"Well, if not, I guess I can always duck. Scout, this is my daughter. Jasmine." Marsha said, then paused while they all waited for a reaction that did not come. Smiling, she continued, "Okay, then. Jazz, this is an old friend of mine, Scout."

"Hi." The girl smiled, green eyes glowing in her honey-brown face.

"Nice to meet you," Scout returned the greeting with a smile of her own.

Jasmine turned back to Marsha. "Listen, Mom, I think there's a problem."

"What's wrong, honey?"

"Well, Celeste was reading for Robyn, right? And, uh, she...well, she sorta dropped the cup. Accidentally."

Marsha frowned. "So?"

"Yeah, well. *You know*. Kinda accidentally on purpose, I think?"

"Oh!" Marsha's eyes grew wide. She got quickly to her feet. "Oh, crap. Okay, where are they, now?"

"Well Robyn is still inside. She's just finishing her sandwiches. I don't think she even noticed anything was weird. I mean..." She paused long enough to heave a dramatic sigh and roll her eyes. "You know what she's like. I think Celeste would've had to hit her over the head with the cup for her to have realized anything was wrong. And maybe even then she wouldn't. But Celeste is in the back. And she won't talk about it."

Marsha nodded. "All right. I'll go take care of it."

"What do you think's going on?" Scout asked Lucy after they had gone. Lucy looked at her speculatively. For a moment, Scout didn't think she was going to answer.

Finally, Lucy sighed and said, "Sounds like bad news for your housemate, I guess. One school of thought says, if you're doing a reading and you see something you don't like in a teacup, you can sometimes stop it from happening by breaking the cup, or stirring the leaves back up, or...I don't know, anything along those lines. Not that everybody agrees with that philosophy, of course, but I think Celeste does."

Heather started slightly. "Wait. Say that again?"

"Well, you know, I guess it depends on whether or not you believe free will makes a difference or if you think the future's immutable. And you know Celeste, Heather, she's definitely not into immutable."

"You said one school of thought. Is this something that's widely known?"

"I don't think it's a universal thing, but yeah, I'd say it's pretty common knowledge."

"Oh, give me a break," Scout snapped. "Lucy, are you really gonna try and tell me you believe all this crap? You didn't used to be so gullible."

Lucy thrust her chin forward mutinously. "Yeah? And you used to be a little more open-minded. But I guess we'll just have to wait and see what happens, won't we?"

"Yeah." Scout grabbed a sandwich from the plate in front of her. "I guess we will." She took a big bite and chewed moodily.

*Devil worship*, Glenn had said, *Blood sacrifices. Ritual killings. Stuff like that.*

No. Not possible. Scout refused to consider the idea any further.

Lucy might be a lot of things, not all of them nice, but that? No fucking way.

"Dad! Dad! C'mere a minute. Quick, take off your glasses!"

Nick smiled at his daughter, as she came running toward him with Mandy in tow. Puzzled, he removed his sunglasses and slipped them into his pocket.

Kate tugged at him until he crouched down next to her. Then she placed her head next to his. "Okay, Mandy. What do you think? Do I?"

Mandy squinted at the two of them. "I guess. I mean, they're the same color and all."

"What's all this about, girls?" Dan asked.

"Oh, my gosh, Daddy!" Mandy turned to him excitedly. "Wait until I tell you what happened! It was sooo weird. There was this lady, right? She says she's a friend of Mommy's from—"

"Oh, and she knows you, too Dad," Kate interrupted. "She said I have your eyes, and—"

"No, Kate. Let me tell it," Mandy whined. "Okay. So. Dad. You'll never guess. She hit Marsha! We were just standing around talking and all of a sudden she just hauls off and hits her. Right in the face! And Marsha hadn't even said anything but hello!"

Kate giggled. "And then Cousin Lucy started *cursing* at her!"

"I'll bet." Dan chuckled. "Anyone who knows Lucy and goes around attacking her friends must be some kinda nut."

"Oh, no," Kate insisted. "She was way cool." Her face creased. "Except for the hitting part. But you know what the weird thing about that was? It's that Marsha didn't even seem to mind."

"I know, right?" Mandy agreed. "Wasn't that freaky? She was laughing, and everything. My Mom wasn't laughing, though. She was *really* mad."

"Better find out who she was, Nick," his cousin Joey said with a smile. "You'll probably be investigating her homicide by tomorrow."

"Oh, but I told you. You already know her," Kate chimed in. "She has a really funny name. What was it again, Mandy?"

Mandy rolled her eyes. "God, Kate. Don't you remember anything? It's Scout."

And just like that, Nick's world slid off its axis. He took a slow, deep breath as the ground beneath his feet began to tilt.

From another part of the galaxy, somewhere far, far away he heard Joey's startled exclamation, "Oh, fuck, no."

"Uncle Joey!" Mandy gasped. "You said that just like Mom!"

"SORRY ABOUT THAT," Joey mumbled in apology, a short while later, as the three men waited for the girls to get back with Kate's bags.

Dan shook his head at his brother-in-law. "I don't know about you, Joe. Who is this woman they were talking about, anyway? An old girlfriend of yours?"

Joey shook his head glumly. "Not mine."

Nick cleared his throat. He felt as though he'd been swallowing sawdust for the past few minutes. "Listen. Guys, I've been thinking about this camping trip. I have a lot of work right now and, the thing is, I'm not sure I should be taking the time off. I'm gonna have to cancel. You know, maybe take a rain check, or something."

"Aw, man," Dan shook his head. "That's a damn shame. You've been working too hard, Nick. And I tell you, pal, you're going to miss some great fishing."

From the safety of his mirrored glasses, Nick hazarded a furtive glance at Joey's face.

His cousin's mouth had dropped open. He stared at him, shaking his head in disgust. "Fucking hell," Joey muttered, just as Kate and Mandy got back with the bags.

"HELLO, LUCY. HOW'VE YOU BEEN?"

At the sound of the cool, familiar voice, Lucy felt an instant surge of dislike. She closed her eyes briefly, wondering what she could possibly have done to deserve the week she was having.

"Just fine, Paige," she answered through gritted teeth, as she turned to face Oberon's most tenacious news reporter. "And you?"

Paige Delaney's smile was the very picture of serene, but her inquisitive gray eyes glinted speculatively. Lucy suppressed a sigh. She wasn't really sure why she disliked Paige so much; the woman had never done anything to her. So far as she knew.

Maybe it was something about the way she always looked. So sleekly professional, every glossy hair perfectly in place. Standing next to Paige, Lucy knew she'd feel underdressed on a clothing optional beach. Just thinking about the woman brought out an atavistic desire for a really sharp knife. Or maybe a set of talons. *Shit. I so do not need this*. Especially not now, with Scout still at large, somewhere in the vicinity. And Nick due to arrive any minute to pick up Kate.

"I heard there was a little commotion over here earlier. A fight of some kind. Anything I should know about?"

Like her or not, Paige's talent for picking up on every stray rumor, or trivial event, was absolutely wasted here in Oberon. Lucy shook her head in disgust. In a perfect world, Paige would have long ago departed for some big city where she could play Brenda Starr [1] to her heart's content. Unfortunately, as Lucy was well aware, the world was just not that perfect.

For one, brief moment, she gave serious consideration to the idea of siccing Paige on Scout. But she quickly came to her senses. She wouldn't have a prayer of keeping the news of Scout's return from Nick once Paige got wind of it. She didn't think the two of them were still seeing each other, but there was no sense taking chances.

"Nothing going on here, Paige. Just the same old, same old." She turned her back on the conversation in the hope that it might die from lack of interest, but no such luck. The most evil and twisted of all Nick's old girlfriends leaned in closer, grinning her hallmark evil and twisted grin.

"Come on Lucy, you know better than to try and sell me a line like that." But whatever else she had to say was lost on Lucy, who had been struck, belatedly, by a shocking realization.

*If Paige is the most deplorable example of Nick's poor taste in women, does that mean that Scout...is not? Huh.*

However much she hated the idea of letting Scout off the hook for anything, Lucy was forced to admit that, whereas Paige had apparently been born this way, Scout had – perhaps – only become cruel and vindictive as a result of what Lucy and her friends had done to her.

*Damn.*

"Paige," Lucy interrupted the flow of questions she hadn't even heard, with her best imitation of her Aunt Lillian. "I have no time for this nonsense. Go snoop someplace else."

Paige opened her mouth to respond, but in that instant, they both heard Dan's voice booming over the noise of the crowd. With a profound sense of relief, Lucy turned to watch her husband stride purposefully towards the booth. He swooped down on her, wrapped his arms around her waist and pulled her close. There was a strange, excited gleam dancing in his eyes.

"Luce. You gotta help me out with something," he said, grinning widely. Then he turned towards Paige, all the warmth instantly evaporating from his voice, as he said, "If you'll excuse us, Paige, I need to talk to my wife."

Lucy was not particularly surprised when Paige turned and left without another word. She'd never understood the curious effect Dan seemed to have on the woman, but, as she contemplated her retreating form with grim satisfaction, she was damned glad for it, all the same.

"Luce." Dan's voice held a note of urgency. "You got any of that special herb soap of yours around? You know, the really good stuff?"

*Soap?* Lucy stared at him in surprise. "Now?" she choked out, suddenly aware of the strength in his muscular arms, how tightly they held her, how very easily he could pick her up and—

"Here?" She felt her face turn crimson. Her heart pounded as she glanced nervously at the crowds of people surrounding the booth. Heated memories set her blood to thrumming in her ears.

"Dan," she whispered fiercely. "We can't. What are you thinking?"

He chuckled knowingly as he shook his head at her. "Jesus, woman, get a grip on yourself. I need it for your brother's mouth. For some reason the guy can't seem to stop himself from cussing in front of Mandy and Kate."

Lucy frowned. That wasn't like her brother. "Joey? What's up with that?"

Dan told her.

"Oh, fuck, no!" said Lucy.

THE CLOUDS in the night sky glowed red, reflecting the light of the balefire. From the fairgrounds below, Scout could hear the noise and the music and could just make out the swirling shadows that were people dancing. A light fog crept slowly down the hills towards the valley floor. She could smell the rich scent of damp earth rising from the ground beneath her, mixing with the heady spiciness of the bay trees that towered all around. A familiar scent, one that had always reminded her most poignantly of home.

"There you are." A voice spoke quietly from out of the darkness as Marsha appeared at her side. "So. What do you think of it all?"

"I've always wanted to do this," Scout mused, her eyes straying back to the spectacle below. "You know? But back in the day...I just never got the chance."

"It's neat, isn't it?" Marsha grinned at her. "I'm glad you're here for it."

"Really?" Scout found that hard to believe. Still, she returned the smile. "Why's that? Have you turned into a masochist now, too? How's your face?"

"I'm fine. Don't worry about it." Marsha sat down beside her. "But how about *you*? How does it feel to be back?"

"I don't know. Strange, I guess. I think I forgot how weird this place can be."

"Well, but that's part of its charm. You know? The weirdness is definitely a selling factor."

"I suppose. I don't know if charm is the word I'd use."

They sat for a while in silence. Until Scout asked, "So what's the deal with Robyn? Lucy tells me I may be losing a housemate?"

"I don't know that I'd go that far." Marsha shook her head wearily. "Celeste is actually a pretty decent psychic, but lately she's been seeing death in at least half of her readings. Especially with the cards."

Marsha broke off, seeming to sink into thought for a few moments. "I can't figure out what's up with that, but I wouldn't go taking out an ad to find yourself a new roommate just yet. Anyway, listen, I'm going to go down now and catch some sleep. What about you? Do you have a place to crash?"

"No. I'm fine, though. I haven't been sleeping much lately, anyway. What's one more night?"

Marsha's brow furrowed. "I'm not sure that's a good idea, Scout. You've had a lot to deal with today. And we have plenty of space in the tea tent. I think you should—"

"*No*. Thanks but, I just— I need to be alone, right now. Okay? I don't want to sleep."

Marsha studied her in silence for a few moments, before sighing, and rising to her feet. "It's your call. But, if you change your mind, you know where to find us."

Scout watched as Marsha made her way back down the hill. She dug around in her bag until she found the fresh pack of cigarettes she'd bought on the way over this morning, and then shook one out.

She lit up and inhaled greedily. She'd never realized until now how truly addictive tobacco was. All it had taken was one good, deep drag and now she couldn't get enough. She wondered if she shouldn't be trying a little harder to resist. It had been years since she'd smoked, and she hadn't really planned on taking it up again, but oh, what the hell?

She needed something to help her cope with the stress of being back in Oberon. And she certainly couldn't go around hitting people every time she got upset. At least this way, she'd only be hurting herself.

The end of her cigarette glowed red in the dark chasm of the night. As red as the balefire on the fairgrounds far below. She took another hit. Felt the smoke curl, sharp and dry, against the back of her throat. Felt the ache of wounds that should have healed years and years ago. Wrapping her arms around herself, she hugged the old hurts close.

"You saw something, didn't you?" Heather's voice was gruff and hesitant. Her hands clutched nervously at the arms of the antique leather armchair. "In that teacup yesterday. The one you broke."

"Did I?" Ginny did not look up from the quilt she was working. It was a small quilt, a gift for a friend who had just had a new baby, and she was working it without a frame. She carefully laid down a few more stitches, while she thought about what she should say. She should have known that Heather would figure it out sooner or later. She should have planned for this.

"Yes," Heather insisted, her eyes were dark with worry. "You did. Didn't you?"

"What do you think I saw, then?" The best way to handle things like this, or so she'd been taught, was to give as little attention to the events you hoped to avert, as possible. To say nothing about them to anyone, and to dismiss them entirely from your thoughts.

"How the hell should I know!" Heather muttered in frustration. "But if something's going on, I think I ought to know about it, too."

"Something *is* going on," Ginny said calmly, as she folded the quilt and placed it neatly on top of her sewing basket. "The festival." She didn't like keeping secrets from Heather, but in this case, it was for her own good. "It's getting late. Time for bed."

"You're not going to tell me, are you?" Heather mumbled resignedly as she raised her eyes to meet Ginny's gaze.

"You know what your problem is Heather?" Ginny smiled at her and shook her head. "Sometimes your imagination just runs wild. It comes from reading too many thrillers, I think. You might want to watch that. C'mon now, we have a busy day tomorrow. Let's get some sleep."

MARSHA CURLED up on the mattress in the back of her van. From outside, she could hear the sounds of the festival continuing around her, but she put them out of her mind. She had other things to think about.

It never ceased to amaze her how events worked themselves out. The mysteries of karma and dharma, of cause and effect, the law of threefold return, they never failed to leave her feeling humbled. Whatever name you gave it, whatever form you imagined it to have, the universe was ruled by a force so vital, so perfect, it almost demanded your recognition of it. And more than recognition. It commanded allegiance. Devotion. Awe.

Marsha had no doubt that the sentient heart of creation was aware of her every step, her every word, her every thought. She was being guided now. She knew it.

She thought over the curious events of the last few days. Scout Patterson. Damn. *Some psychic I am. I really should have seen that one coming.*

Oh well, she thought as she pulled the sleeping bag up around her shoulders; that's just how it went, sometimes. She had missed signs before this, and no doubt she would again. But for right now, the universe had certainly found a way to get her attention.

---

1. Brenda Starr—now there's an obscure reference. I wonder if Lucy is thinking of the 1989 movie with Brooke Shields, or the [much] earlier comic strip? I, of course, remember reading the comics, but only until she and her Mystery Man, Basil St John had a baby named Starr Twinkle. Even as a kid, I had my limits. There was no way I could maintain an interest in the characters once they'd jumped the baby naming shark.

# 9

---

S cout wandered through the deserted fairgrounds early next morning. The fog that had seeped into the valley the night before lay thick on the ground, giving the empty pavilions a dream-like quality. People passed like ghosts through the pearl gray mist.

A solitary piper, half hidden in the shadows, played a haunting, mournful tune. Scout felt a melancholy longing steal through her. The wheel of the year was turning. The days would grow steadily shorter, now.

Last night, the Oak had fallen; the Holly King's reign was begun. [1] She shivered, her heart filling with grief at the loss of the sun. Until a passing breeze brought the welcome fragrance of fresh coffee to her nose.

She breathed it in gratefully. The scent evoked those tropical climes where the days never grew short. *That's what I need. The hell with this other nonsense.*

She changed direction abruptly, moving away from the sorrowing pipe. What the heck had she been thinking? It was the height of summer. The sun was rising, even now, and would soon warm the earth and burn off the fog. The equinox was still months away;

meaning the days would still be longer than the nights for quite some time.

Besides, this was Coastal California, where winter meant, at worst, a few weeks of rain. She could handle that, couldn't she? A little rain, a little mud, a little bit of wind, perhaps. No big deal. She'd have no problem with winter here. [2]

"C'mon, dog." She smiled at her companion. "Let's go eat."

The dining pavilion was mostly empty, only a few of last night's diehards, and a handful of early risers had gathered for coffee or tea and a light breakfast. When Scout emerged from the line with her tray, she saw Celeste sitting alone at one of the tables. She hesitated for a moment, then headed in her direction.

"Mind if I join you?" she asked.

Celeste raised weary violet eyes to her face. "Oh. Hello, Scout. Please do."

Scout sat, and the dog sat at her feet.

Celeste smiled as she bent to stroke the dog's head. "Aren't you a sweetheart?" she crooned, as she offered the dog a scrap of toast. She glanced up at Scout and asked, "Have you had her long?"

"No." Scout sipped her coffee. "I'm not really sure I have her now either, to be honest."

"Of course, you do!" Celeste looked shocked. "Anyone can tell that just by looking at her. She is *definitely* your dog. What's her name?"

"She doesn't have one yet," Scout replied, and was surprised when Celeste burst into a peal of silvery laughter.

"Oh, my. Sweetie. *Of course*, she does. They all have names. You just haven't discovered what it is yet. But don't worry. You will." Celeste smiled down at the dog again. "Oh. I have something for you. I knew I was supposed to give it to someone. Obviously, you're the very one."

She removed her satchel from the back of her chair and began rummaging through it. Finally unearthing a little brass medallion that she attached to the dog's collar.

"It's a protective amulet," Celeste explained. "In ancient times actual blessing rituals were performed at these festivals, you know.

People would bring their animals to be cleansed by being passed through the smoke from the bale fire. It's still a powerful time of year for working protective magic. Especially for animals."

"Mm," Scout murmured, neutrally. She found herself growing annoyed with all the magic mumbo-jumbo. "So how long have you been involved in this, uh, stuff? You know— amulets and tea leaves and all that kind of thing?"

"Oh, forever, really," Celeste said, with an airy wave of one graceful hand. "I learned from my grandmother how to read the tea leaves. And palms, as well. Not the cards, though." She shook her head and gave Scout a small, rueful smile. "Those are new. I'm still working on them. Would you like me to do a reading for you? No charge, of course. I could use the practice."

"Thank you, but no." Scout spread fresh strawberry jam on a scone. "I'm *not* interested."

Celeste's eyes glittered. "You're afraid. Now why is that?"

"I'm not afraid! I just don't believe in any of that stuff."

"Well, that's what's so nice about it, isn't it? It doesn't require Faith. It works whether you believe in it or not." Celeste dipped into her satchel again and removed a small red velvet bag, from which she slid a deck of cards.

"Really, I'm not—" Scout began, but Celeste laid a hand on her arm.

"Humor me." She smiled at her. "Pick one card. Where's the harm in that?"

Reluctantly, Scout turned her attention to the fanned deck. Her hand hovered irresolute, and then settled on one card. She drew it from the deck and laid it on the table.

"See? That wasn't so hard, was it?" Celeste teased. "Let's see...ahh. The Lovers. Well, that's always nice. Although, of course, in this case it's reversed, which suggests some sort of difficulty. Let's see if we can't find out what the problem is. One more?"

Suppressing a sigh, Scout picked another card at random and slapped it down.

Celeste nodded. "Uh-huh. See now? The Knight of Wands.

Someone fiery and impulsive and likely to be rather single minded in his pursuit of you." She cocked her head at Scout and smiled. "Does that sound like anyone you know?"

*Only if I have a stalker that I don't know about,* Scout thought. But before she could give voice to the idea, a shadowy figure loomed over Celeste's shoulder. "Scout? Can I talk to you?"

Scout glanced up, startled. Glenn's face looked gray and pinched —probably from partaking in last evening's debauchery, she supposed.

"Hello, Glenn," she replied, striving to keep her voice neutral.

Celeste gave a quiet cough and then, when she'd caught Scout's eye, tapped gently, but meaningfully, at the first card Scout had picked.

*No,* Scout mouthed, with an almost imperceptible shake of her head. "Celeste, this is Glenn—an old *friend* of mine. Glenn, Celeste."

As her companions shook hands and mumbled polite greetings, Scout sank back into her chair and thought about how much she hated Oberon. She hated the mystery and the magic. Hated that she could pick a card called The Lovers out of a deck of cards, and a moment later, have Glenn materialize in front of her.

*Jesus. What is up with this card shit?*

Belatedly she realized that Glenn was addressing her. "Sorry. What'd you say?"

"I said, what are you *doing* here? I *thought* you were going to stay home last night?" he repeated angrily. "I thought we'd *agreed* it would be a good idea for you to be careful while you're in town."

"I was careful," Scout snapped at him. "And anyway, *we* didn't decide any such thing. Like I already told you, Glenn, much as I'd love to believe that Caroline had only my best interests at heart, I really doubt that was the case."

"So, you're still determined to go through with this ridiculous plan of yours?"

*Ridiculous plan?* "You mean, am I still going to keep looking for Lisa? Of course, I am. Why wouldn't I? But, you know what I'm think-ing, with this being Oberon, and all, maybe I should start by getting a reading done on the subject. Maybe see what the cards have to say. What do you think?"

"Uh, yeah," he answered, his eyes sliding away from her face. "Sure. Whatever. You'll let me know beforehand though, right? Before you do anything foolish."

*Foolish? A little late to start worrying about that.*

Glenn's gaze fell on the cards, his eyes widened. "Wait. You haven't already started, have you?"

Scout felt mischief rise within her. "Nah, we're just fooling around. Pick a card Glenn. Let's see what the future has in store for you."

Celeste deftly folded the cards that had been on the table back into the deck, shuffled, and then spread them out. "Go ahead." She smiled at Glenn.

Looking unexpectedly grim, Glenn extracted a card and laid it on the table.

"Hmm," Celeste murmured thoughtfully. "The tower. Well, I'd say that means you're due for a change of some sort. How exciting. Would you like me to give you a full reading?"

"No. I- I can't. That is...I, uh, I don't have time for it right now," Glenn stammered.

"Oh, good gracious!" Celeste jumped up suddenly. "Speaking of time, I need to get back to work. Here." She fished in her bag once more and produced a business card, which she handed to Glenn. "My home number is there as well. Call me if you change your mind. And Scout, I'm sure I'll see you later. In the meantime, take care of that dog!"

Scout stared moodily at Glenn. What was going on here? If she'd made a list of everyone she knew in Oberon—everyone with whom she did not want to spend every waking minute—Glenn Gilchrist would likely have been at the very top. And yet here they were again. She picked up her cup and drained it, even though it was cold. Yuck. There was a sign, she thought bitterly; it was definitely time to cut and run.

"Hey, listen, Glenn," she said as she got to her feet. "It's been great seeing you and all, but I really gotta get myself some more coffee. You know how it is, I bet. Up all night, it takes a lot to keep you going, you know? So, I'll see you later, okay? I'll give you a call. Maybe in a few days."

"Not so fast!" Glenn's hand shot out. He grabbed her by the wrist. Scout heard the dog growl as she rose from under the table, her hackles raised.

"Uh, Glenn? I don't know this dog all that well yet, but I get the feeling she really doesn't like it when you grab me like this." *Neither do I*, she thought, as her temper rose. She half-hoped the dog would bite him.

Glenn smiled uneasily. "Don't run off just yet. I'll buy you some more coffee in a minute. We need to talk."

"About what?"

He frowned. "About your roommate, for one thing. How well do you know her?"

Scout's eyebrows rose. "D'you mean Robyn? I hardly know her at all. Why?"

"Well doesn't it strike you as strange that Caroline would confide so much personal information to a relative stranger?"

Scout sighed. A lawyer. With a brain like Pooh. Unbelievable. "No, Glenn. Just because I don't know Robyn, that doesn't mean she was a stranger to Caroline. You heard her – they shared the house for years. I don't know about all these long talks they supposedly had, but she had a lot more contact with Caroline than I did. So sure, why not?"

"I think I should look into it for you. You notice how she threw in that bit about being adopted? It might be interesting to see what I can find out about who her real parents were."

Her *real* parents? Scout couldn't help but scowl. *What bullshit.* The parents you picked, or those who picked you, often seemed more real than the ones you were born to. "Whatever." She shrugged his suggestions away. "Frankly, I don't see what any of that has to do with finding Lisa. It's also none of our business."

"You never know. It can't be any more farfetched than your idea to consult a psychic." He frowned at her. "You weren't really serious about that, were you?"

Scout took a deep breath and slowly sat back down. The dog moved closer to her side, still growling faintly. She pulled her hand from Glenn's grip and patted the dog until she had quieted. She didn't know what put the idea into her head. But all of a sudden, Glenn sounded like a man who knew something. Or was, maybe, afraid of something.

*What could he know?* "I'm looking for answers, Glenn. I'm serious about *anything* that could help me find some."

He fixed his sad, wounded eyes on her face, and shook his head, sorrowfully. "It won't work, you know. I think, wherever Lisa is, she doesn't want to be found."

The feeling that they were fencing in the dark grew stronger. "Doesn't *want* to be found or *can't* be? There's a difference, you know."

"Is there?" Glenn muttered darkly. "I'm not so sure."

*Damn. He does know something. I know he does.* "Glenn if there's something you haven't told me—"

He scowled at her. "Of course, there isn't. I'm just not sure your being here is a good idea, that's all. Like I said the other night, I think you should leave town. Let me deal with the rest of it for you. All the legalities and stuff. It's my job, Scout. I get paid to handle things like this. Anyway, I gotta go, too." He rose to his feet abruptly. "Just think about it, okay? We can talk later."

*Oh, no, you don't, buddy.* Scout forced herself to smile. "Hey, what's your rush? I thought you were buying me coffee?"

He turned back to her. Slowly. A cold smile curved his lips.

"You know, that's not a bad idea, either. Why don't you let me drive you back to town? We'll get breakfast...or something." His eyes flickered rapidly over her as he spoke, as if he were sizing up the possibilities. Scout felt her breath catch. He couldn't possibly be thinking what she hoped he wasn't thinking. Could he?

Well. There was no way she was letting him get away without telling her what he knew. But there sure as hell were limits to the ways in which she was willing to pay for that information. Clearly, going anywhere with Glenn right now was not a good idea. Certainly not anywhere alone.

"Gee, that's real nice of you Glenn. But I'd just as soon stay here if you don't mind. And coffee's fine, really. I already had breakfast. Maybe some other time."

He flushed angrily. For a moment, she thought he might try and argue her out of her position. *Good luck with that.*

Finally, he grimaced. "Right. Well, okay. Let's get you some coffee, then."

The sun was bright in Scout's face as she left the dining pavilion. She could smell the heat rising from the bare earth of the fairgrounds. More heat radiated from the large pile of ash and charcoal—all that was left of the fire that had burned so merrily through the night.

At her side, Glenn glowed, the sunlight behind him forming a weird halo around his head and shoulders as it cast his face into shadow. She noticed anew how aged he looked and felt a stab of pity for the young man she used to know. As beautiful as the morning, he had seemed back then. Bright and invulnerable.

*I feel sorry for him.* The thought surprised her. Feeling sorry for Glenn golden-child Gilchrist was not something she had ever thought would happen.

She supposed it wasn't really his fault that she had always found him less than fascinating. But, all the same, it was only after a prolonged, internal struggle that she was able to take his arm. And even lean against him just a little, as she guided him towards the one booth where she was sure to find, if not coffee, at least a cup of something that might wake her up; as well as the opportunity to give the rumor mills another spin.

"There you are." Marsha hurried out of the booth, her face anxious. "At last. What's going on? I've been having the strangest—" She broke off suddenly, her eyes widening as she recognized Glenn. "Jeez, I don't believe it. What is this, some kind of bizarre time-warp?"

"Hey, Marsha," Scout called in greeting. "Look who I picked up.

We'd like some coffee if you have it. Or tea, maybe? We've been up all night and we're just about dead on our feet."

Marsha looked them up and down, her focus seeming to waver. Finally, she smiled, and something in the glance she gave her made Scout wonder if she couldn't see right through the charade.

"Well, *you* certainly look like you could do with some sleep, girl. But I think Glenn here still has energy to spare." Marsha smiled at him cheerfully, and Glenn returned the smile, his face brightening suddenly into something resembling a boyish grin.

"Come on," Marsha said. "Never mind the coffee. I've got something even better."

"Marsha...what is this stuff anyway?" Scout sniffed suspiciously at the creamy foam that topped the drinks Marsha had ordered for them. The three of them were seated at one of the small tables that had been set up beneath an awning. The cushions that covered the bench seats were deep and soft and comfortable. The scents of herbs and incense filled the air, making Scout feel incredibly relaxed. Maybe a little too relaxed.

"Oh, but you have to have some, Scout. We make it special just for the holiday. You know—because milk has always been a traditional part of Midsummer celebrations. I suppose it has something to do with all those lactating cows and sheep they had around at that time of the year."

*Lactating cows and sheep? How incredibly appetizing.* Scout took a small sip. It was creamy and sweet with an elusive flavor that might almost have been almond. "Better than coffee, huh?" [3]

"Yep. This'll fix you right up." Marsha smiled encouragingly. "But come on, both of you. You want to drink it before it gets too cool."

Scout watched as Glenn obediently took a large gulp. Marsha sipped her own drink more demurely. Her eyes, gleaming above the rim of her glass, held a look Scout was not sure she trusted. Still, what could it hurt? Mentally crossing her fingers, she took another drink. It was delicious, but the pleasant tingles it left in its wake did not exactly seem energizing.

"So, Glenn," Marsha said, flashing a smile that, in Scout's opinion, seemed a little *too* bright. "I haven't seen you in ages. What have you been up to?"

Glenn was smiling, too—one of those boyish grins he seemed to do so well. Why had she thought him tired and aged looking a few minutes ago, Scout wondered. He certainly didn't look like that now. Maybe Marsha was on to something with these drinks, whatever they were. She took another sip. It really was good. Warm and...what was that flavor? Not cinnamon. Vanilla? No, that wasn't it, either.

While she puzzled out her drink, Scout was only half-aware that Glenn and Marsha had gone from discussing Glenn's law career to his houseboat in the marina and were now talking about the changes they had both observed in Oberon over the years. Glenn and Marsha sure seemed to have a lot to say to each other, all right. Glenn and Marsha appeared to be getting along famously, in fact.

Scout settled deeper into the cushions – bright, jewel-colored cushions, very much like the ones that used to be in Lisa's room – and regarded them sourly. Glenn and Marsha seemed to have forgotten her very existence. Which was a relief, in a way. And yet...

Things were not working out the way she wanted them to. Glenn was talking, all right, but not to her! And not about Lisa, either. Scout tried hard to think of a way to shift the conversation around to the subject, but she seemed to be having trouble organizing her thoughts in a coherent fashion.

And then, there didn't seem to be much point to trying, because Glenn was leaving.

Scout stared at him in confusion. She had missed something, obviously, because she hadn't found anything out, and Glenn was definitely leaving. She hurried into speech. "So, Glenn, about breakfast—"

He looked, very briefly, nonplused. "Great idea, Scout," he said, when he recovered. Why don't I call you? Sometime later this week, perhaps."

*Yeah, right.* Scout watched him walk away. *Sure. You'll call. And I'll wait for that to happen.* Judging from the expression on Marsha's face, she was thinking the same thing.

Scout crossed her arms over her chest and glared at her former friend. "I wasn't exactly finished with him, you know."

Marsha studied her thoughtfully. "Yeah, I gathered as much. Just what was it you weren't finished doing?"

A reluctant smile crept across Scout's face. "I don't suppose I could make you believe I was fanning the fires of an old flame?"

Marsha looked away, a pained expression on her face. "Oh, I think you could probably make me believe just about anything you wanted to. But *he* can't. Sorry. I'm not sure what Glenn had on his mind this morning, but I don't think it was romance."

Scout sighed. "I think he knows something about Lisa."

"He...what?" Marsha's gaze swung back to her face. "Knows something like what? What could he know?"

"Well, that's what I was trying to find out, before you ran him off," Scout snapped in exasperation. She picked up her glass and drained it.

"Oops." Marsha's eyes were twinkling once again. "Well, gee, Scout, no worries. You can always try again, you know. When he calls."

"Yeah, right. Like that'll happen." Scout shook her head wearily. "You got a real warped sense of humor, Marsha. Anyone ever tell you that?"

---

1. I've always been intrigued by the legend of the Oak King and the Holly King. So much so that ended up writing my own version—a holiday menage story called OAK

2. Spoiler Alert: Contrary to what she thinks right now, Scout might end up with quite a few problems on her hands this winter. But that's a story for another book.

Sound of a Voice That is Still

3. Back in the day, when I was first working on this book, I spent several weeks developing a recipe for Marsha's Summer Solstice Chai Latte. It had to be delicious; it had to contain ingredients that would honor the solstice; and it had to be loaded with soporific herbs, oils and/or tinctures—ideally ones that were native to California. I have NO idea what went into it anymore. Except for California poppies and local honey. I do remember that those were both part of it.

If I were writing the series now, I suppose I'd just have Marsha dose her with CBD, or maybe slip her an edible.

# 10

*It's not working.* Nick slammed his coffee mug down on the table. His usual Sunday morning routine of newspapers and coffee on the deck outside his apartment, was doing nothing to alleviate the angry confusion of emotions that had been building inside him since yesterday afternoon.

*She's back. After all this time, she's finally come back.*

He couldn't believe the way he felt. He couldn't even put a name to what he felt – angry, bitter, nostalgic, more than a little crazy. Plus, some other, inexpressible combination of hopeful sensations, part daydream, part memory, that he thought he'd buried long ago. Back when he'd finally made himself accept the painful truth, that she was never coming back to him.

*It's been so long since I've seen her.* Hell, it had been a long time since he'd even thought about her. Really thought about her, anyway. Thought about her in the kinds of ways that made sleep impossible and sent him speeding angrily up and down the coast for hours at a time. Thought about her in ways that made him drink too much or smoke too much. Not that he wouldn't mind a cigarette right now, he thought, in the instant before he remembered that his daughter had made him quit. Again. Six months ago. Shit.

What was she doing here, anyway? And why now? Not that it mattered, of course. Now. Next week. Next year. He didn't have the faintest clue, anymore, what he'd say to her if he saw her.

*What am I thinking? I wouldn't say* anything *to her. Why should I?*

She was the one who'd left him, after all. So what if she'd been a minor at the time, with no say in the matter? She had gone away and, apparently, forgotten all about him. And he'd be damned if he'd give her the time of day, now.

He probably wouldn't even recognize her, anyway, come to think of it. Although she seemingly hadn't changed so much that Lucy hadn't known her.

*Oh, hell. Does Lucy know about this? Is this what had her on edge the other night?*

Well, shit. Of course, it was. And wasn't it just like his cousin to try and hide something like this from him? To jump to the conclusion that he needed protection.

*Like I even care anymore. So, she's back. Big deal.*

What the hell kind of idiot did his cousin take him for?

Okay, so it had taken him a while to get over her. Years in fact. But he had done it, hadn't he? Nobody could say that he hadn't. He had moved on with his life. Hell, he'd even gotten married! Not like that had been an incredible improvement, relationship-wise.

*You sure know how to pick 'em, don't you?*

Yeah, Lucy'd got that right. That pretty much summed up his whole fucking love life, didn't it? But no more. No way. Seeing her now was the last thing on his mind. The absolute. Very last. Thing.

*She's probably not even up there anymore*, he thought, a few minutes later, as he stared out at the mountains.

Well, hell. No wonder he couldn't stop thinking about her—not while he was sitting here with a perfect view of Mt. Totawka and the foothills where the festival was going on. He needed to get off this deck. He needed to find something else to do, something else to focus on.

Which shouldn't be a problem. There were always plenty of things he could be doing on a day like this. He could always go in to work, for one thing. Just because it was his day off, that didn't mean he had to stay away. Or maybe he could go fishing. He hadn't been fishing in months. Or else...he could go for a hike, couldn't he? Or out to a movie...

Or he could just stay here and wash his car.

His car really needed a wash, come to think of it. Hell, he could wax it, too, while he was at it. Maybe change the oil, clean the spark-plugs. And when was the last time that he'd taken the time to really detail it?

But thinking of cars was not such a terrific idea, he realized a little too late, because so many of his memories of her included cars. That was how they met. She'd been hitching a ride one foggy April night and he had stopped for her...

*No. Stop that. Cut it out.*

He picked up his paper and tried once more to read it, but put it down a moment later, when he realized that his mind was working up a ridiculous fantasy about seeing her again. Of coming across her trying to hitch a ride back from the festival. Maybe, if he drove up there right now—

*What the hell am I thinking? She's not a teenager, anymore.* There was no earthly reason to suppose she'd be hitching a ride back from the fair.

*It doesn't matter. It doesn't matter. It doesn't matter.*

He ground his teeth, as his eyes strayed back to the mountain. It really *didn't* matter because he was *not* going up there again. He hardly ever went to any of the festivals, and he'd just been to this one, yesterday.

*There's no way I'm going back up there again. No way in hell.*

He was actually glad he'd found out that she was back in town, but only so that he could make damn certain he did not run into her by accident.

*Liar*, a small voice in his head admonished him. *Why'd you back out on the camping trip, then?*

But that had *nothing* to do with her—no matter what Joey thought. He *did* have a lot of work to catch up on. And it made *perfect* sense that he save a few of his vacation days for later in the summer, so that he and Kate could go somewhere.

*I wonder what she looks like now?*

The thought came out of nowhere, and for a moment he was overcome with the longing to find out. Jesus, but this was getting ridiculous. What could she look like, after all? She was thirty-six years old, for pity's sake. She was probably settled and dull. Probably nothing at all like the wild, unpredictable girl he remembered.

Thirty-six-year-old women did not look or behave like teenagers. Which, if he were honest, was not a bad thing. There was a whole range of really objectionable, immature behaviors that he associated with those years, and he, for one, was just as happy to have seen the end of them.

Thirty-six-year-old women did not hitch rides, for instance – a dangerous and illegal activity the whole world would be better off without. And they did not go around creating the kind of havoc Scout had positively excelled at when she was sixteen.

They had jobs and they had families and they had mortgages and commitments. And most of them wouldn't be caught dead dancing around a balefire in the middle of the night, not even with their clothes on. Most of them—the sensible ones—wouldn't even have bothered going to any damn pagan festival in the first place!

Except that she *had* been there.

And she had *not* forgotten all about him, damn it.

*She said I have your eyes.*

Her own eyes had been a smoky, warm, greenish gold; like the moss that grew in damp, secret hollows all along Domingo Creek.

And her hair had been a streaky mass of yellow and brown. The same color as the grass along the cliffs there, late in summer, after it had been bleached and debauched and blown about by the sun and the wind.

And when she smiled – but, no, he wouldn't even think about that. He'd spent *years* forgetting her smile. [2]

And anyway, none of it mattered. Not anymore. *I'm over her now,* he reminded himself again, more firmly. *Definitely and completely over her.* And he was not going to go there again. No possible way.

"Marsha, when you said this was 'better than coffee' you weren't actually talking about keeping someone awake, were you?" Scout nodded at the tall glass that had held her second drink. The glass was empty, and Scout was feeling anything but awake.

And Glenn had gotten away, she thought again, grimly.

Marsha flashed an unrepentant grin. "Nope. It tastes better though, doesn't it? At least, I suppose, if you really like the taste of coffee, you might not think so, but—"

"You think I care about taste? I can't keep my eyes open!" But it wasn't the heaviness of her eyelids that bothered Scout the most, or the warm, comfortable numbness that had crept over her entire body. It was the fact that she'd been ambushed, once again, by her supposed former friend. She felt tears of self-pity welling up in her eyes. "Damn it. What did you do now?"

"I didn't do anything. Not really. It's just that some herbs can have a mild soporific effect. That's all."

"You sedated me? Jesus."

"No. I— Listen to me." Marsha leaned forward to place a hand on her arm. "They're very mild. So much so that you probably wouldn't even have noticed it if you weren't already exhausted. I told you last night that I was worried about you. But you're obviously too stubborn to admit when you need help." Marsha sounded concerned, and there was a look in her eyes—

But no, Scout knew better than to trust such things. "What are you, my mother? I said I was fine, and I was!"

Marsha shook her head. "You were *not* fine. You needed sleep— still do, apparently."

"Well, maybe I *would* have slept, Marsha, if I could have gone home to do it. You ever think of that? How do you expect me to drive like this?"

"I don't. And trust me, my friend, you were in no condition to drive before, either."

"Says you."

"Yes. Exactly. And I wish you'd trust me, Scout. I actually do know what I'm talking about, occasionally. Now, come on. My van's out back, behind the tent, you can crash there for a few hours."

"TELL me I did *not* hear what I just thought I heard." Lucy fixed Marsha with a stony glare. "*Please* tell me that you didn't just say that...that person...is out there, right now, asleep in your fuckin' van!"

"Lucy, stop," Marsha said soothingly. "You're making a much bigger deal of this than you need to."

"The hell I am," Lucy fumed. "What is with you, Marsha? Why couldn't she just have gone home?"

"She was too tired to drive." Marsha busied herself straightening a collection of athames in one of the glass display cases. "She was practically passing out."

Lucy snorted. "Yeah. So I heard. Gee, I wonder how *that* could've happened?"

"She'd been up all night, I guess," Marsha answered, frowning slightly, her attention still focused on the knives.

"That's not the way Celeste tells it."

"Celeste doesn't know everything."

"Well, I still don't like it."

Marsha sighed. "Noted. And, while we're on the subject? I know there's something you're not telling me—the real reason why you're so upset about Scout being back."

"I have no idea what you're talking about."

"No. Of course, you don't. But be that as it may, you're just going to have to trust me on this, Lucy. I'm following inner guidance. I don't know why, but it feels like the right thing to do."

Lucy frowned. Inner guidance? Shit. That was the trump card, wasn't it? "You're sure about that?"

"Yes. I'm sure."

"Terrific. I don't know why I even bother trying to talk to you. But, if you have to, then I guess you have to. But I'll say it again. I do not like this. Not at all."

"I'll keep that in mind." Marsha smiled crookedly. "Now, are you sure you're okay here for a while? I just need maybe a half hour's break, is all."

Lucy shrugged. "Take as much time as you want. Dan and his brother have the nursery's booth covered all day today, so I'm cool. Just tell me one thing before you go. What am I supposed to do with our friend back there, if she wakes up?"

Marsha chuckled. "Oh, I'm sure you'll think of something."

*Think of something?* Yeah, Lucy could think of a lot of things to do with Scout. Or *to* Scout. She could think of a lot of things she wouldn't mind *telling* Scout, either. Mostly though, she just wished that Scout would go the hell away.


MARSHA'S PROBABLY RIGHT, Lucy decided, as she puttered around in the tent a short while later. *I probably am making too big a deal of this.*

She needed to relax. Let go. Learn to trust. Maybe she should get Tina or Wendy to make her one of those special lattes, like the ones Marsha had given Scout. That should chill her right out.

"Hey cuz, how's it going?"

Lucy jumped at the sound of Nick's voice and gave up on the whole idea of relaxing. There wasn't enough steamed milk in all the world to accomplish that feat.

"Nick? What are you doing here?" This should *not* be happening. He never came to these things, damn it. He *hated* these things. And on top of that, he was just here yesterday.

"Oh. Um, well, see, since I'm not going on the camping trip, I thought perhaps, the guys might want to borrow my stove?" He jiggled the green metal box he carried and shrugged. It was a good shrug. One that fell just short of looking casual.

Lucy narrowed her eyes. "So, you just decided to get in your car, battle the traffic, and bring it all the way up here now? Instead of simply dropping it off at our house?"

"Yep." He shook his head and laughed, shifting his weight from foot to foot, his hand clenched tightly on the handle of the stove. "That's what I did all right."

It was a weird, angry sounding chuckle, it made Lucy nervous. She had a pretty good idea what Nick's real reason for being here might be. She had a pretty good idea his real reason was less than thirty yards behind her, fast asleep – she sincerely hoped – in the back of Marsha's van.

Every ounce of mental energy she possessed was currently focused on sending powerful messages in the direction of that van. Messages that could basically be summed up by a single sentence: *Bitch, don't even think about waking up right now!*

"So, I never heard. Why *did* you decide not to go camping?" she asked, crossing her arms in what she hoped was a more credible attempt at looking casual than Nick had managed. She leaned against one of the posts that held up the awning, as though she had all afternoon to chat with her cousin, and no earthly reason for wishing him miles away.

Nick shrugged again. "No real reason, I guess. I've just got a lot of work right now."

Work? He was a cop, for Christ's sake. In *Oberon*. Where nothing *ever* happened. How much work could he possibly have? "Yeah? It's funny that you didn't say anything about all this work when we saw you Friday night."

"I just decided yesterday," Nick mumbled, turning to scan the crowds.

*He is such a liar. They almost deserve each other.*

The words she knew he wanted to hear were on the tip of her

tongue, but she bit them back. Nick was still her cousin, even if he was an idiot, and she felt compelled to save him from himself.

She straightened away from the post. "Well, whatever. Look Nick, I've gotta get back to work now. Dan's over at the other booth. So, why don't you run over there and ask him about the stove, okay? I'll see you later."

"Yeah. Fine," he said, but without conviction. And without moving away.

He looked like he wanted to ask her something, and she had a pretty good idea what that something might be. Hadn't they been here and done this enough in the past? He looked so damn miserable she was once again tempted to tell him.

The only thing that saved her was thinking about the hell she'd catch from his mother if she found out. Lillian Greco was not someone whose bad side Lucy ever wanted to be on if she could help it.

SCOUT HAD DREAMED—VAGUE images in brown and gold, soft voices that left her feeling safe and warm. She awoke to find herself in Marsha's van, where it was not just warm, but hot as hell, even with the front windows cracked and the skylight open. The dog lay beside her, panting. She sat up and looked around.

The most interesting thing about the van, was not that it looked to be about forty years old. But that it looked to have been decorated almost forty years ago, as well. The third row of seats had been removed and replaced with a mattress covered in Indian cotton, which is what she'd been sleeping on.

Stained glass patterned contact paper covered the rear windows, the now useless rear-view mirror was hung with strings of colorful plastic beads, and the entire interior had been carpeted in thick, rust-brown shag. Except for the remaining seats, of course, which were buried beneath sheepskin covers. She had a very vague memory of being driven home from somewhere once, about twenty-five years ago, by one of Marsha's older sisters. One of the twins. Probably Siobhan. In a vehicle that had looked very much like this. Talk about a time warp!

Much as she hated to admit it, Marsha had been right. Scout felt about a thousand times better than she had before. This was probably the most hours she'd managed to sleep in at least a week.

Maybe it was the van? She wondered if Marsha would consider selling it to her. Or maybe she could just borrow it to sleep in. She was tempted to lie down again and see if she couldn't sleep a little longer, but the dog looked at her so piteously that she knew she'd have to get up and let her out.

She opened the door of the van. The fresh air felt wonderful against her warm skin, cool and invigorating. The dog jumped around, wagging its tail enthusiastically as it followed Scout around to the front of the tent.

It looked like they were doing a brisk business. Most of the tables were full. She saw Celeste, along with a couple of the other women she recognized from yesterday, giving readings. She didn't see Marsha, but Lucy was there. Standing tensely at the front of the booth with her back to Scout, hands on her hips, staring off into the distance—just as though she were watching for someone in the crowd.

"Hey," Scout said, coming up behind her, making her jump.

"Oh, jeez. Scout. Fuck. Don't sneak up on me like that."

"Sorry. I—"

"Uh, no. No, it's okay. Really. Don't worry about it. Just c'mon, now. Let's go back inside."

Lucy tugged at Scout's arm impatiently, hustling her back inside the tent, and talking a mile a minute as she did so. "Scout....so. I uh, uh, I hear you were here all night, huh? Jeez, I haven't done that in years. Was it fun? Did you like it? What did you think?"

"Well, it was different. Kind of impressive, I guess," Scout answered, confused by Lucy's sudden interest in her opinion. She felt a little like Rip Van Winkle. How long had she been asleep, anyway —decades?

"Yeah, I must say, I always liked everything but the idiot Frat boys spitting alcohol at the flames. That always struck me as really stupid, you know?"

"Gee, I must have missed that part." Scout grinned. "Too bad. Anyway, is Marsha around?"

"No. She's on a break," Lucy said, her voice curt, once more. Her face resumed its usual sullen expression. *Well. So much for conviviality.*

"Okay. Well. I guess I'm going to head out, now. But tell her I said thanks, okay? Oh, and tell her I said she was right."

"You're leaving?" Lucy asked, her face brightening, again. "Now?"

"Try not to look so sad," Scout said sarcastically. "I didn't mean I was leaving town, or anything. Just the immediate vicinity."

"Ah, well." Lucy flashed a malicious smile. "It's a start."

---

1. Sunday papers—remember those? I used to love reading the paper on Sunday mornings. I used to dream of spending the whole day in bed (naked, of course) with the papers, and coffee—maybe some pastries—and my husband, of course. Unfortunately, I married a guy who couldn't spend the whole day in bed if he were dying. And who doesn't drink coffee. But, I guess it doesn't matter since he outlasted the papers anyway.

2. I love this description of Scout's eyes and hair. I love that, for twenty years, Nick drove around Oberon seeing Scout everywhere. For almost that long, I'd think of her, too—and this description—every summer when the grass would turn gold.

# 11

*B*y the time Scout had hiked back up to her car, the western sky was turning gold. The exodus from the park had already begun. Rather than join the crawling snake of cars trying to leave by the main gate, Scout turned onto a smaller service road, one that would allow her to exit directly onto Domingo Creek Road.

The San Domingo was one of several creeks that wove their way down through the foothills. It flowed in a generally southwesterly direction until it fetched up at the coast a couple of miles below Oberon. It was by then the merest trickle, whose cascade down the side of the cliffs went mostly unnoticed—unless the rainy season was exceptionally rainy. The road, which for the most part followed the creek's path, had been built on a narrow ledge, high on the canyon wall.

It was not a route that anyone not bent on suicide would care to travel after dark, or if there was even the slightest chance of a storm. But since neither of these factors were currently present, Scout decided to go for it.

She liked to take risks and she liked to drive fast. And the opportunity to travel, for even a mere two miles, along the rocky Pacific Coast on a golden, midsummer afternoon was well-nigh irresistible.

Besides, it had been a long time since she had been out that way. She was curious to see if anything was still as she remembered it.

What she mostly remembered was the way it had looked in springtime, when the hills were ablaze with wildflowers. The way the wind had whipped her hair in her face. The way her heart had pounded along with the music that blasted from the car's speakers. The way her head had reeled from excitement and blackberry wine.

She remembered they'd followed the road to a point where the cliff ledge widened enough for a turnout. Where you could stop to see the whole town laid out below you, and the ocean gleaming silver in the distance, under the vast, cloudless expanse of the sky.

And where you could also, if there were two of you, and you were young, and wild, and reckless enough, drive each other to a frenzy in the back seat...

"I don't want to stop this," Nick groaned as he sat up and pulled away from her. His breathing was as harsh and ragged as her own.

"Then...don't," Scout answered, swallowing hard as she said it – staring deep into his eyes, her heart beating wildly. And blushing fiercely because, with the way her hands remained clenched in the material of his shirt and the urgent, half strangled sound of her voice, she knew it was more than an invitation. It was a plea. "Don't stop." Please, don't stop.

"Jen. Jeez, hon, we have to. If I'm ever going to get you home on time, we have to stop now," he said it gently, insistently. But instead of pulling away further, he lowered his head and kissed her again, deeply and thoroughly, taking her whole mouth with his, completely swamping her ability to reason. She could feel the weight of him, the length of him, the heat of him, as he stretched himself out on top of her once more, pressing her back down into the seat's cushion. She slid her hands up behind his neck and fisted them in his hair, pulling him even more tightly against her, kissing him back every bit as hard as he kissed her, her tongue slipping deep into his mouth, one leg curling up to wrap his hip.

"Oh, God." He wrenched himself away again. "C'mon, babe. Help me out here." He laughed, weakly. "You could put up a little resistance, you know. What kind of girl are you anyway? Haven't you ever heard of playing hard to get?"

Embarrassment was more effective than a cold shower. Scout felt her cheeks flame as she pushed him away. She climbed into the front seat without saying a word and paid no attention to him as he slowly folded himself into the driver's seat. He glanced at her, a slight frown on his face as she pulled her clothes back into order. She grabbed the pack of cigarettes from the dash and punched viciously at the cigarette lighter, several times, before it stuck.

"Are you okay?" Nick asked, his voice hesitant, as he steered the car out onto the road.

Scout shrugged, but otherwise continued to ignore him, lighting her cigarette with hands that trembled.

"Hey." His voice was a caress when she couldn't bear to be touched. She shivered uncontrollably as his rough voice slid like sandpaper over her nerves. "Talk to me, Jen."

A sob escaped her lips, and then she couldn't halt the tears that were sliding down her face.

"Oh, hell," she heard him mutter. He sounded angry, but what did it matter? She couldn't be any more mortified than she already was. She sobbed steadily as the car flew over the narrow curving road. Had she been sober, had she not been beyond caring, she might have been frightened by the grim expression on his face and his fey driving.

In no time at all, they were out of the canyon. Nick brought the car to a stop in the parking lot of the diner and convenience store, where earlier they'd stopped to buy the wine. He grabbed the cigarette from her hand and threw it out the open window before pulling her into his arms.

"Now, tell me. What's wrong?" His voice vibrated in her ear.

"You think I'm cheap," she whispered, barely getting the words past the tightness in her throat. "You think I'm— That I..."

"I what? Aw, come on babe. That was supposed to be a joke." She felt him drop kisses in her hair, on her forehead, her nose, her cheek. "It was a really lousy joke—I know. And I'm sorry. But please don't cry." He pushed her away enough to look into her eyes. "Are you kidding me? You can't possibly think I meant it? Jeez. You must be even drunker than I thought. I knew it was a bad idea letting you have all that wine."

"I am *not* drunk!"

He quirked an eyebrow. "Uh-huh. Not much, you're not. Come on, you have to know I'd never think anything like that. Right?"

She stared at him in silence.

"Oh, hell," he said again, as he pulled her close. "Jen, you gotta know what a turn on it is when you get this hot for me."

Scout tried to turn away, but his hand tightened on the back of her head. His lips moved deliberately over her neck, her throat, up behind her ear.

Her eyes slid closed as shivers ran through her and she felt her hands clutching at his shirt once more. "Nick..."

"That's more like it." His voice was a low, compelling rumble of a whisper in her ear. "I love that you're not all cold and untouchable. I love how you shiver when I kiss you. The way you close your eyes when I touch you like this. Do you really think I'd ever be interested in the kind of girl who won't let anybody close to them? Believe me, the last thing I'm looking to get involved with is some uptight little virgin."

The sudden introduction of a new fear sobered her for an instant. She pulled away with another half-strangled sob and stared at him wide-eyed. And then the world began to spin again.

"Oh, shit. Not drunk, huh?" he chuckled. "Damn. We're gonna have to get some coffee in you, quick. You're going to be late, but it's still gotta be better than taking you home like this."

The lights were too bright. The sounds too overwhelmingly loud and confusing. A jukebox was playing, and the sound of silverware banging against thick, china plates echoed in her head. There were voices talking, laughing, arguing. The cash register was ringing. Irregular pinging sounds she couldn't identify were coming from somewhere close at hand—

She closed her eyes against the intensity and gulped scalding hot coffee, as though it were iced tea and her mouth was a desert. Not caring at all that her tongue screamed with pain. Welcoming the clarity it brought.

"Jesus," Nick groaned. "We are so fucked." Scout's eyes sprang open, and she gazed at him, warily.

"You feeling any better yet?" he asked her.

"I told you," she mumbled, as she felt her cheeks flame, again. "I'm fine." Except that he thought she was drunk. He thought she was a stupid, drunk schoolgirl. A virgin...or a slut...or too young? Shit— she didn't know *what* he thought, at this point. But whatever it was, it wasn't good. Because it probably wasn't true. "I have to go home."

"No kidding! But not like this, you're not."

He sounded amused. Maybe a little worried, a little chagrined. But not scornful. Not angry or cold. She clung to that idea. He didn't hate her. Not yet.

"Here. Why don't you have some more coffee?"

"Okay."

It was hot and bitter, and completely wonderful. It exploded within her stomach, magically clearing the fog from her head. She drank it down and pushed her cup away. "I really am fine now. Can we go?"

"Not yet. We need to talk."

"No! What I *need* is to go home!" She didn't want to talk. What did they have to talk about, anyway? Everything she had ever told him was a lie. *Almost everything.* And everything he believed he knew about her was based on those lies.

And she could not believe she'd been so stupid. Only now did she realize how truly disastrous that could be.

"Take it easy. We'll leave in a minute. All right?" Nick grabbed her hand and held it. His eyes glittered. She felt her breath go as his eyes locked on hers and held them. "First, I just want to say that I'm sorry about before. But you have to know how much I want you, right?"

She felt her cheeks grow hot again. She dropped her gaze and nodded.

"And you want me, too. Don't you?"

She nodded, again.

"Okay, then."

She heard him exhale. He sounded relieved. She sneaked a look at his face. He was smiling, but his eyes still glittered with that look that made her feel as if everything inside her had liquefied. She quickly glanced away again.

"Look at me," he ordered, quietly.

She swallowed hard and forced herself to look him straight in the face and ask, with exaggerated patience, "What is it?"

His eyes drilled into hers. "I love that you don't play games with me. I don't want to play games, either. You don't know this about me, but normally I'd have had you in bed long before now. Or I'd have been gone. I'm not real patient. And I'm definitely not into wasting my time with girls who can't decide if they want to be with me or not. All this stuff we've been doing – sneaking around like this, not being able to pick you up at home, or even call you, or spend any kind of real time with you – this is *not* stuff I do. Not ever, Jen."

She must have looked like she was about to say something, or maybe he read the fear in her eyes, because his grip on her hand tightened almost to the point of pain.

"Let me finish. Okay? I *know* that things are weird right now, but that's because of your parents, right? Not you?"

"I..." Well. There was no right answer to that, was there? So she shrugged and lied again, "Yes. Right. Exactly."

"And that's what I'm trying to tell you. I don't like it, but I under-stand. And I can handle it. For a while longer, anyway. Like I said, I don't have a lot of patience normally, but this is different. *You're* differ-ent. You're worth waiting for. But you have to understand that the only thing getting me through this is knowing that you're not stringing me along. Okay?"

It wasn't, but she nodded all the same. "Yes."

"All right. Good." Nick reached for the carafe. "More coffee?"

Scout nodded again. "Yes."

He filled her cup, and then set the carafe down again. "But then we really gotta get you home."

"I know." She drank greedily, relieved to have an excuse to look away.

"You're not upset anymore?"

"I'm not upset."

"Because, you kind of look like maybe you still don't believe me."

She shook her head, but she didn't trust herself to speak, or to meet his eyes.

"Aw, come on, Jen. Don't be like that. You gotta know how much I care for you. If I was just looking to get laid, don't you think we'd already've done it? We could be doing it right now. Sure, you'd get home late, and who knows if I'd be able to see you again, but what the hell, right? If that was all I was after, why would I care?

"But you know it's more than that. You know how much I want to be with you. And if that means we have to take things a lot slower than either of us wants, then I guess that's just the way it's gotta be." He studied her face in silence for a couple of moments. "So, please Jen, be honest with me. Are we really okay again?"

"Yes." She nodded yet again, blinking back the tears that still insisted on coming. "Of course, we are. We're fine."

But they weren't. Not really.

Oh, she was still determined to keep seeing him, too, of course. And it thrilled her to hear him talk about how much he cared for her, how much he wanted her. Not that she hadn't already known that. Young she might be, and inexperienced, but she wasn't an idiot.

But up until now, she hadn't realized how easily she could lose him. Now she did. And she knew something else, too, and wished she didn't. He could never be her first. She couldn't ever let him find out how young and inexperienced she really was.

There wasn't anything she could do about her age, but experience was another matter entirely. Before they got back in the car, she was already plotting ways to lose her virginity. Without him.

So lost was Scout in her memories, she hadn't noticed the vehicle that had been following her since she left the park. She still didn't notice when it pulled into the lane beside her, or as it sped up until it had come almost abreast of her. She didn't notice anything at all out of the ordinary.

Not until she heard Lisa's voice, loud and angry, clear as a bell. *"Hit the brakes, Scout! Now!"*

She did as she was told.

She heard the tortured squealing of the brakes, felt the blast of speed and color as something large and dark veered suddenly into her lane with enough force that, just clipping the edge of her front fender, it caused her car to spin out of control. For several excruciating minutes the entire world spun around her. She fought the skidding tires without thinking, turning the wheel this way and that, relying on instincts she hadn't even known she had. A part of her watched with total detachment as she finally wrestled the car away from the edge of the cliff. But not without sending it veering too far the other way. Sending it into a shuddering, bone jarring, glass breaking crash against the jagged wall of rock on the other side of the road.

By the time she thought to look for it, the other vehicle was gone. The dog whined softly and licked at her face, and she grabbed it and held it with arms that trembled violently.

If she hadn't slowed down just when she did, the impact would have been dead-on into the side of her car.

It would have sent her flying out over the cliff, and down into the canyon below.

She would have been dead. Just like her father. Or like...wait. *Lisa? Holy shit.*

A wave of nausea washed through her then, and she barely got the car door open in time. As the sickness subsided, it left an icy panic in its wake. This time she couldn't pretend it had been the wind, or the innocent creaking of an old house. She hadn't been in Oberon for one week, and already she was hearing voices. If she stayed here much longer, what were the chances she'd be able to get out with her mind in one piece?

She crawled out of the battered car, shivering violently with a chill that was only distantly related to temperature. *What to do?* There was an unnatural silence in the canyon. Not a birdcall, not a rustle, even the wind seemed shocked into stasis.

*What to do? What to do?*

The question echoed in her head but found no answer. She didn't want to stay in Oberon for another minute, but she had not accomplished anything she'd come here for. And, God help her, she'd more than heard a disembodied voice that had sounded somewhat like her sister's, she'd *recognized* it—from the depths of her soul.

It was Lisa's voice; no doubt about it. And something more. Her presence.

Scout rotated slowly, looking all around her, in the darkening canyon, searching for something that would explain what had just happened to her. Half-expecting Lisa to jump out from behind a rock, laughing at the fright she'd given her. But the canyon remained quiet and empty, and she remained alone.

*What to do?* Well, that was obvious, wasn't it? She should leave. Because if Lisa *wasn't* dead, and if she had –somehow – managed to engineer what had just happened, then she was clearly determined to drive Scout crazy.

A stray bubble of amusement burst out in a giggle. *Drive me crazy? Drive me off a cliff, more likely!*

Except...she didn't think she'd be driving anywhere for a while. Not if the way her car looked was any indication of how it would handle. But all puns aside, the idea might not be as far-fetched as all that. It sounded a little like a Hitchcock film, which would have been right up Lisa's alley. Except...that presence in the car, just now—

She just couldn't see how someone could fake a thing like that. And, while it had only been for an instant and it certainly hadn't felt malicious, it had been real enough to trigger a surprising response. The dogged, balls-to-the-wall competitive streak that Lisa had always been able to bring out in her – and that she'd thought she'd seen the last of years ago – was back, full force.

Scout was damned if she was going to be chased out of town by a, a ghost! If that was what Lisa had become, then she could just go haunt someone else, is all. Because, ghost or no ghost, Scout would leave Oberon when she was good and ready. When she'd finished what she'd come here to do. And not one friggin' moment sooner.

But she sure wouldn't mind getting the hell out of this damn canyon.

She returned to the car and dug her cell phone out of the bag. She'd call information, that's what she'd do. She'd get the number of a tow company. Or maybe she'd call 911. But she couldn't even get a signal.

She stared stupidly at the phone for several minutes. Stared at the little symbol that continued to read no signal and refused to change into something more amenable. Anger seethed along her shaky nerves as she got back out of the car to try again. Maybe away from the car, reception would be better? Or over here, as far from the canyon wall as she could get? But it was still no good.

Goddamn it! What was the point of having this stupid piece of technological crap, if it didn't work when you needed it to? In a fury, she hurled the phone over the cliff, stormed back to the car and turned the key in the ignition. [1]If it started, she'd just drive herself off the damn mountain. Hadn't she learned a good long time ago that she couldn't count on anyone else to save her?

Damn straight, she had.

She'd hauled her own bacon out of every friggin' fire she'd ever gotten it into. And, if she'd done it once—or, you know, five thousand times—before, she could do it again now.

The car started easily enough, but turning it proved a bit more difficult. Something seemed to be amiss with the front wheels. And there were strange sounds and vibrations that she was at a loss to account for, until she remembered that, *oh, yeah. I've been in an accident.* A random-sounding fact that somehow seemed to keep slipping from her mind.

The dog sat quietly, only occasionally giving vent to a soft anxious sigh, while Scout cursed and coaxed the car down from the canyon and back into town. She could have stopped when she got back to the highway, but by then her mind was focused too firmly on getting herself home, and she didn't even think of it.

By the time she got back to the house, reaction had set in for real. She felt sore in a dozen different places and was so distracted she barely remembered to let the dog out of the car, before she limped to the house.

Robyn stared, open mouthed, as she came into the kitchen. "Wow! What happened to you?"

Scout's teeth were chattering so hard, she couldn't speak. She had a vague sense that she might be in shock, and she remembered having heard, somewhere along the line, that brandy was what you gave to people who were in shock. Did she have brandy? Did she like brandy? Did it matter?

She seemed to recall that Caroline had always kept a bottle of the stuff in one of the kitchen cabinets. Apricot brandy. It was a key ingredient in a favorite, but seldom made, dessert. If she could find that—

"Were you out at the festival all this time?" Robyn pressed, while Scout searched clumsily for the bottle. "I saw you there yesterday. Did you stay up all night? Scout you look terrible. Maybe you should sit down. Are you sick or something? What are you looking for, anyway?"

Finally, she found the bottle; finally, she got the bottle open. Tilting it up, she took a long, long drink. The sweet, fiery liquid burned through her system, and cleared her head.

"Car crash." She got the words out, at last, and then took another swig.

"Car crash?" Robyn looked puzzled.

Scout nodded, gulping for air. *Yes.*

"Oh, you mean, like an accident?"

She nodded, again. *Yes.* And drank some more.

"You were in an accident? Just now?"

Another sip. Another nod. *Yes.*

"Omigod!" Robyn's eyes got even wider. She stared at Scout with an expression of dawning horror on her face. "Omigod! Omigod, Scout! Are you all right?"

The alcohol hit her stomach and the absurdity of the question her brain at one and the exact same instant. The only reaction Scout could manage, the only reaction that made any sense, was to fall helplessly into a fit of hysterical laughter. A fit from which she would not be able to recover until long after she had frightened Robyn into locking herself in her bedroom for the night.

---

1. Do you remember when cellphones were so unnecessary that you'd toss it off a cliff just because it wasn't getting a signal? Gee, what will Scout do now? it's almost like her whole life isn't on that phone. Oh, wait; it's not.

# 12

Marsha was not a morning person. And the bus station at five a.m. had never been her idea of a good time. But here she was all the same, with her daughter, her daughter's bike, and what still seemed like a truly excessive amount of gear.

She still did not understand why a three-week bike trip needed to begin at five in the morning. And she didn't know if she would ever get used to saying good-bye to any of her children. Just thinking about how she was going to feel in September when Jasmine went off to college – well, it was almost enough to make her go back to bed, pull the covers over her head, and stay there for a week.

At least a week.

But she couldn't do that, could she? She had too many people to take care of, too much to think about, too much to do. Like get to work, open the store, and go over the receipts from the weekend. Like find a way to stop obsessing over how much she was already missing Jasmine, and how long it had been since she'd heard from her boys. Like take care of Scout and placate Lucy.

And now, on top of everything else, she had this thing with Robyn and Celeste to deal with.

MONDAY DID NOT START out well for Robyn Smith, either. After spending most of the previous afternoon watching horror films, she'd found Scout's behavior and appearance yesterday evening disturbingly similar to that of the killers in several of the movies. As a result, she'd lain awake most of the night with one eye trained on her bedroom door, half-convinced that Scout might break it down and come after her with an axe, or a hook, or a very large knife, or some other implement of destruction.

It had taken several days for the idea that there might be something wrong with Scout to take hold in her mind. Now that it had, she couldn't shake it loose.

She thought about it when she got up late and rushed off without breakfast. She thought about it as she rode her bike to work. And while she was at work, she thought about it so much that she was quiet and distracted and so unlike her usual ebullient self, that Lucy, who routinely spent Mondays working with her at the nursery, couldn't help but notice.

"Okay, Robyn." Lucy put a steadying hand on the younger woman's arm. "What gives? Is everything all right? You seem kind of out of it today."

Robyn turned to her, a woeful look on her face. "It's the woman I'm sharing the house with. You know, Caroline's stepdaughter? She's acting so strange. She frightens me. I think – I really think there might be something *wrong* with her."

Robyn's morning was not improved when Lucy burst into peals of loud and sudden laughter. As loud and as sudden as Scout's, and every bit as disturbing.

THIS MORNING COULD STAND some improvement, Scout decided, as she continued her fruitless search for some kind of painkiller. Any kind of painkiller – as long as it was non-alcoholic. It was hard to believe that anything as sweet as apricot brandy could leave her feeling this bad, but there you had it. She was hung over, and hungry, and more achy than she'd previously believed it was possible for a person to be.

There was no food in the house. Which normally wouldn't matter, since she couldn't cook, anyway, but this was one day when she really didn't feel like going out to breakfast.

And there were no painkillers, either. Not unless you counted Robyn's feverfew tea, which Scout for one, did not.

She put some water on the stove to make coffee. It wasn't until she looked in the canister that she realized she was out of that, as well. Great. Just perfect. No food, no aspirins, no coffee. She sighed in resignation. There was no way around it. She'd have to go downtown. And she'd have to walk. Assuming she even could.[1]

Overnight, her right ankle had become swollen and stiff. Even if the thought of getting back into a car again right now didn't terrify her, she wasn't sure she could drive anyway. But between her ankle and her lightheadedness, and the bright sunlight that felt as if it were slicing into her head, walking there wasn't going to be a picnic, either.

She whistled for the dog, and then immediately wished she hadn't. But the dog came running to her anyway, obviously none the worse for wear, and they headed off. Scout did her best to keep her mind off the pain by trying to decide which made more sense: food first and then coffee? Or coffee first? But she still hadn't reached a decision by the time she got to town.

Glenn didn't usually have this much trouble making decisions but seeing Scout again had stirred up a hornet's nest of ideas. Unpleasant memories and emotions buzzed about in his head, resisting all his attempts to bat them away.

He couldn't decide what to do.

He knew he hadn't handled things well, so far. He'd acted rashly, said and done the wrong things. But he'd gotten one shock last week, when he learned she was coming back. And then yesterday—

Well. Being forced to make small talk with Marsha while Scout sat silent and distant – that had been intolerable! He could tell that she was thinking about finding Lisa, and the idea scared the shit out of him. Because thinking had always been Scout's problem.

She thought too much. About everything. Everyone always talked about how smart she was, but he'd never seen it. Why, just look at all the trouble she'd already gotten them into – planning things that were best left to chance, arranging things that didn't need to be arranged.

He'd have to see her again, wouldn't he? That's what he'd do. He'd see her and talk some sense into her. He should go to her house today. Or maybe tonight.

Or better yet, he could go right now.

They would talk some more about Lisa. Or, then again, maybe they wouldn't. Maybe he'd let this just be about them. He thought about that for a moment, and a faint wave of pleasure washed over him.

There was peace in its wake, and clarity.

Maybe, what he *really* needed to do was to stop thinking so much, himself. Maybe that's where the problem lay—where all the problems lay. He'd always been good at thinking on his feet when he was younger, hadn't he? He'd acted on impulse most of the time back then and, most of the time, things had worked out for him. Could be that was what was needed right now.

NOTHING WAS WORKING for him and frankly, Nick was tired of the struggle. He'd put up a good fight, but no matter how hard he tried to push Scout from his mind he just couldn't do it.

Maybe seeing her one time wouldn't hurt...too much. Just seeing her from a distance? He wouldn't even have to talk to her...

But what if that wasn't enough? And what if, on the other hand, it was more than he could handle?

For twenty years, he'd had his dreams and his memories of her to sustain him—during all the worst times. What if coming face to face with the reality caused those dreams to shatter, turned his memories to dust?

Was this really the chance he had been waiting for? The chance to finally free himself from his obsession with her. Or was it just another one of Fate's cruel tricks.

Lucy might know. Hell, Lucy probably knew the answers to *all* his questions. And if he and his cousin could just have a simple conversation about it, like two normal people, then perhaps he could avoid doing something as obviously stupid as the actions he was currently contemplating.

But fat chance of that ever happening. And for once, he knew just who to blame for the mess he was in. Damn it, this was all Lucy's fault.

"IT'S MY FAULT. I'm sorry. Really, I am. It's just—" Lucy paused and gasped for breath. She was trying hard to apologize, but tears still streamed from her eyes, and stray peals of laughter continued to slip past her lips. "This is Scout we're talking about, right? And you think there be something wrong with her? Might be? *Nah!*"

Robyn sniffed angrily as Lucy dissolved into giggles once again.

On the whole, Lucy thought, laughing until her sides ached, this morning wasn't half-bad.

"I LOVE THIS STORY." Marsha laughed, gleefully.

Scout shot her a weary, disgusted look. "I knew you would."

"Oh, c'mon. Your sister communicated with you from *beyond the grave* and saved your life. How can you not love this?"

Once again, Scout had to wonder what Marsha knew. Why was she so certain Lisa was dead? Granted it seemed likely, given the whole disembodied-voice-thing. But, on the other hand, it could just be imagination—couldn't it?

"I don't know, Marsha. I think if you felt as awful as I do right now, you wouldn't love much about it either."

Where was the coffee she'd been promised? Where was the food she'd ordered, or the painkillers that Marsha had assured her were on their way? "Anyway, I don't think it proves anything. Other than the fact that I have a really vivid imagination. And I think we already knew that. I tell you, though, if that really was Lisa? And if she went to all that trouble just to save my ass? I wish she could have done a better job of it. I feel like crap."

Marsha's grin grew wider. "Well, who says you can't judge a book by its cover? You look pretty lousy, too."

"Thanks." Scout sank her head in her hands. "Seriously, Marsha," she sighed. "What am I gonna do? I'm hearing voices! That's not normal."

"C'mon, Scout. Don't you think you might be overreacting? It was an extremely stressful situation. And...what do you mean *voices*? It was just one voice, right? Isn't that what you told me?"

Scout shrugged. "I guess."

"Okay. So. You hear one little voice which, not incidentally, prevents you from being killed. Where's the bad? There are a lot of people who would call that a miracle."

"Maybe."

"Besides, I really think it's probably a one-shot deal."

"You think?" Scout asked, perking up. "So, maybe I'm not losing my mind after all?"

"Let's put it this way," Marsha said growing serious once again. "There're a lot of things that you probably should be worried about right now, but I don't think that's one of them."

GLENN'S DAY was not improving. Scout wasn't home. He'd driven all the way out here and she wasn't even home!

Her car was, though. And, man oh man, the little red convertible was a real mess. She must have had one hell of a close call yesterday. But he supposed the fact that it was here at all must mean she hadn't been too badly injured.

He shook his head in frustration and came within inches of kicking the car's tires on his way to the house. But, given the way the car already looked, that would certainly be overkill.

He'd tried to warn her of the danger, hadn't he? He'd told her she ought to take more seriously her roommate's suggestions that someone might be out to get her. But she just wouldn't listen. So, if—or likely when—she did get hurt, it would be nobody's fault but her own.

When he got to the front door, he found it locked, which surprised him. He'd spent his entire life in Oberon, and like many people who lived there, he usually didn't bother locking his door, except maybe at night.

But it was typical of Scout to make things difficult. She could be lying in the house unconscious, for all anyone knew. Because no one could get in to check. She could be lying in there stone-cold dead, too. And what good would all her thinking and planning do her then? Not too damn much, that's what.

He went around to the back of the house, hoping to find another way in. There were three cats on the patio. He felt the weight of their stares and shivered. He hated cats. He had always hated cats. He couldn't understand what anyone would want with even one of them, never mind three.

And if it turned out that Scout was *not* lying dead inside the house, they were seriously going to have to talk about that.

The thought brought a smile to his face. Well, of course they'd talk, but he didn't think he was going to be bringing up the subject of cats. At least, he was pretty sure they would be a little too preoccupied for that.

The kitchen door was locked, and the French doors, as well. What the hell was she thinking? He eyed the cats again, and another smile crawled across his face. Well, as the old saying went, there was more than one way to skin a cat. Or, as his mother had been fond of saying, *when the Good Lord closes a door, you can be sure He'll open a window, somewhere.*

There was still the basement door to try. If there was one thing that he prided himself on, it was his ability to think on his feet. To accept what life brought him and roll with the punches. Unlike Scout, who probably hadn't, even now, accepted the fact that accidents were a part of life.

Well, they were. He shivered as he thought of it. No one knew better than he how true that was. Accidents happened all the time. Hadn't he seen that in his work? In his own life? Big accidents and small. Preventable, or seemingly unavoidable. Inconsequential, or life changing, or fatal. They could happen any day, anywhere, to anyone.

And you couldn't always plan for them, either.

NICK HADN'T EXACTLY PLANNED to drive by Scout's house on his lunch break. First off, he seldom ever even took a lunch break. And today he'd meant to drive out to the coast – fresh air, the open road, and a full tank of gas that's how he spelled relief. [2]

Instead, his car had practically steered itself through the narrow residential streets that led here. There were two cars in the drive, and though he knew nothing about the kind of life she'd led for the past twenty years, he had no doubts that the new red Mustang with the convertible top was hers.

It was exactly the type of car he could picture her driving. Although, he wouldn't have pictured it in quite this condition. It had obviously been in an accident recently. He wondered how she'd even managed to get it here, as banged up as it was.

He didn't know who the other vehicle belonged to, but she obviously had company, and the last thing he wanted right now, was for anyone from Oberon to see him hanging around her house. He'd come back later, he promised himself. He pressed the gas pedal to the floor and sped away. The coast was calling...

I'LL COME BACK LATER, Glenn thought, as he got back into his Montero. And when he did, he and Scout would have that little talk he'd been promising himself.

Maybe.

Maybe they'd talk, or maybe they wouldn't have to. Depending on how things worked out, maybe he wouldn't see her, or talk to her at all.

He still thought he could make her see things from his point of view – he just wasn't sure he'd have to. But, either way, it didn't make any sense for her to waste time looking for Lisa.

For a moment he allowed himself to think about Lisa. She'd been so beautiful, so vibrant. And she'd always understood him. A whole lot better than Scout ever had, to be honest.

He'd truly never meant to hurt Lisa – why would he? But there had been something about Scout; she'd been impossible to walk away from. And no matter how hard he tried to explain that Lisa hadn't wanted to accept it.

Ah well, there was no sense in dwelling on the past. It was all so long ago, what did any of it matter now? Lisa was gone and what they had together was over.

Whereas Scout, on the other hand, was here.

Perhaps...perhaps he had been too hasty. Perhaps she didn't have to go away again, after all. If he could just talk to her and make her see reason. If he could just make her listen! It might save them both a lot of unpleasantness.

His head began to ache again. Things were getting complicated. Perhaps it was best to leave things as they were. To let chance or fate or circumstances rule his course. One way or another, if he could just stay calm, he was sure things would work out fine.

"OKAY, OKAY." Lucy held up one hand to stop the flow of words from Robyn's mouth. "I get the picture." But the picture she was getting was enough to start the laughter gurgling in her throat again. "Look, you have to understand something. Scout and I go way back. I mean, I could tell you *stories*—"

Once again, she bit back a laugh. They'd had some good times, before all the trouble started. She'd almost forgotten that.

Robyn glared at her. "It's *not* funny,"

Lucy sighed. "No. I know it's not. The thing is, I honestly don't think you're in danger. Really. She's trouble, no question there, but not the kind you're thinking."

"I don't think you understand what I'm saying," Robyn insisted. "She doesn't sleep. I don't think she eats. I mean, *I've* never seen her do it. She just drinks. Wine and coffee and stuff like that—none of it healthy. She even had this bottle of brandy, or something stashed in the back of the cabinet! And now, all of a sudden, she's smoking? Nonstop? I mean, who even does that anymore?

"But the worst was last evening when she came home from the festival. She'd been in an accident, or something, I guess. I mean, I think that's what she said. But she looked like someone had beaten her up. Her hair was hanging in her face, and she didn't even seem to notice. Do you think she's, like, on drugs?"

Lucy considered the idea. Drugs? Not a bad idea. *Could be that's what Robyn needs.* Just a little something to help her calm down. But Scout? She shrugged. "I don't think so. I saw her yesterday afternoon and she seemed okay."

"Well, she was definitely not okay last night," Robyn insisted, again. "And when I asked her about it, all she did was laugh."

*Yeah, that sounds about right.* Lucy shook her head. "I wouldn't worry too much about that if I were you. She's always had a damn peculiar sense of humor. But, like I said, I don't think she's going to hurt you. Just don't get too close to her, and you'll be fine."

"You really think so?"

"Absolutely. Now why don't you go get some lunch, you look hungry."

"Okay, Lucy." Robyn smiled, happy for the excuse to return to her usual good mood. "Thanks."

Lucy sat thinking long after Robyn had gone. Accidents didn't happen to people like Scout – not unless they caused them. But it sure did sound like she was having problems. And that was bad. Because, as Lucy well remembered, Scout's problems had a nasty habit of blowing up in other people's faces.

She'd been through enough explosions of that sort for a couple of lifetimes.

She had to do something. She tugged at a piece of her hair, twirling it around her finger as she thought. There had to be some way to make sure that, if there *was* another explosion, this time Scout would be the only one who got caught in it.

---

1. Ahh, yes. The good old days when, if you were out of food, you were out of luck; you couldn't just pick up a phone and have whatever meal you liked delivered. Unless you happened to want pizza or Chinese food. Or chicken. I had a boyfriend, way, way back in the day, who worked at a delivery driver for Chicken Delight. I still remember the slogan, "Don't cook tonight, call Chicken Delight."
2. . Does this sentence seem odd to people who don't remember the old Alka Seltzer commercials? This is just one of many sentences that would have had to go if I'd updated the books. I'm kind of glad it stayed. This entire series is like a time capsule.

# 13

By the time Scout was halfway home, she felt almost human again. Her head still ached, and her ankle throbbed, but all in all, she just might live. She'd picked up some supplies in town – more coffee, a couple of frozen dinners, some canned soup, and a box of doughnuts – so she was all set for food, for a good long while.

She'd splurged on a carton of cigarettes and a bottle of blackberry wine, as well. Although she refused to think too much about the impulse that had led to her doing so. There was nothing to think about anyway. It meant nothing. She was *not* getting caught up in old memories. It was just...something she hadn't had in awhile and that she happened to be in the mood for it. It was no more complicated than that.

The dog trotted along at her side, stopping occasionally to sniff around the base of a tree, or under a bush. They'd left Main Street a block past the shopping district to hike through the greenbelt. [1]Besides offering extremely pretty scenery, Scout was sure that the detour would cut the distance she had to walk by half.

Part wilderness, part footpath, part labyrinth, the greenbelt was often described as Oberon's answer to urban sprawl—a claim that

Scout found laughable. Had any of the people who made those inane remarks ever actually been to a city?

The belt intersected most of the town's main roads as well as three of the creeks that made up part of the local watershed. It had always been something of a nightmare for local law enforcement. Scout remembered hearing stories of suspects eluding the police within the twisting maze of pathways. And other tales of high-speed pursuit by motorcycle cops which, while usually successful, had still earned them the wrath of the City Council.

As a teenager, she and Lisa had been forbidden to step foot within its shadowed boundaries after nightfall, or at any time of day at all if they were by themselves. Prohibitions which they had, perhaps not surprisingly, tended to ignore.

Sunlight slipped through the thin branches above her head as she limped along, stopping occasionally to shift the bags she was carrying. The sunbaked ground beneath her feet was hard, rocky and dry. As she remembered well, from countless school field trips here, the greenbelt had been landscaped using native, drought resistant plants whenever possible.

She even remembered some of the plants she saw now, like Toyon, whose red, holly-like berries had given Hollywood its name. And Mountain Lilac, whose fragrant blue flowers the Native Californians had made into a type of shampoo. Or the Arroyo Willows—their bark was used for something, either as a cure for headaches or in basket making, she wasn't sure which.

And those tall trees that lined the path just here were white alders. Scout couldn't remember if they served any useful purpose, although she did vaguely recall being told that she should look for them if she was ever lost in the woods and needed to find water.

*The eyes of the forest.*

That was what the early settlers had called them, or so she'd been taught. They had a habit of dropping their lower branches as they grew, and the resultant scars were supposed to resemble eyes. As creepy an idea as any she had ever heard of; it reminded her of the dream she'd had the other night. Something dark and dangerous lurked in the depths of the woods. Watching and waiting. There'd been danger, terror, and the relentless rushing sound of running water.

She came out of her reverie with a start. She *did* hear water running. Looking around her, she found that the path she'd been following had taken her to the foot of a small stone bridge spanning one of the creeks.

She stopped by the bridge and put down her bags. Her ankle was really sore now and there was a choppiness to her breathing that she didn't think was a result of exertion. Damn, but there really *was* an uncanny sensation of watchfulness here in the shadows cast by the tall trees.

Scout searched the bags for the cigarettes, tore open the new carton, and then one of the packs inside it. She must be more serious about this smoking thing than she'd originally thought. She was now working two packs of cigarettes at once.

Marlboros, too. Nothing fancy or flavored or, God forbid, extra light. What would be the point of that? And not the brand she'd been in the habit of smoking as a teenager, either – Virginia Slims, usually, which Lisa copped from her mom.

No, this was heavy duty, hard-core, mainline smoking. And she had no idea why she was doing it. Except that, somehow, it kept the sense of impending doom at bay. And that, as Marsha would probably agree, was all good.

The dog climbed down the narrow banks of the creek to drink from the water trickling between the rocks. Scout thought briefly about climbing down there herself and soaking her ankle in the cold water, but the idea didn't really appeal to her.

She recognized this place, now. This particular path would lead past the crumbling ruins of an old stone cottage whose real history she had never known, but which had, over the years, inspired several generations of ghost stories. From there it would skirt the grounds of her old high school, and curve around a small, isolated, forest pond.

She could leave the path at that point and, assuming she could find a way to cut across several yards of brush, reach the back of her property.

*Piece of cake. Sheesh. Some great detour this was. Not.*

She paused to reconsider her earlier conviction that this route constituted a shortcut. But if anything other than an excess of optimism had inspired her decision, she didn't want to know about it.

Her mental health depended on going with Marsha's take on the subject. There was nothing strange going on. She wasn't losing her mind. There would be no more voices, no signs, and definitely no ghosts.

There would also be no mysteries. No miracles. No inexplicable events. And maybe, if she were very, very lucky, she could even avoid any of the really creepy coincidences that seemed to be a daily occurrence in Oberon.

SCOUT MADE it back to the house rather later than she'd planned, tired and more scratched up than when she'd started, but without having suffered any recurrent bouts of spookiness. She felt an enormous sense of satisfaction at having found her way through the woods.

She crossed the lawn and climbed the steps that led to the brick patio. A cat crouched on the railing beside the kitchen door. When it saw her, it laid back its ears and hissed. The dog growled back at it, an eerie, low sound, ending in a whine.

Scout frowned. "Stop that," she admonished, as she unlocked the door and let herself inside.

The cat stalked into the house at her heels, yowling and complaining, as it followed her into the kitchen, the dog trailing reluctantly behind.

The kitchen used to be one of her favorite rooms in the house. It was bright and cheerful with high ceilings and a large center island topped with a marble slab. Perfect, or so Caroline had always insisted, for making pie crusts and fudge.

Scout remembered hanging out here with her friends, sneaking down late at night to raid the 'fridge for snacks when the munchies hit. Now it was just a place to make coffee.

She deposited the bags on the island with a tired sigh and stopped to get herself a glass of water from the sink before putting the food away. When she turned back from the sink, she was startled to see eight cats watching her steadily.

Seven of them crouched motionless on the floor near the door that led in from the hallway. Only her friend from the patio was still in motion, pacing back and forth, lashing his tail and uttering angry noises. When she went to retrieve the rest of the groceries from the island, he jumped on top of the counter. When she reached for the cigarettes, he jumped on her hand and bit her.

"Ow!" Scout pulled back in pain and surprise and shoved the cat to the floor. "What is wrong with you?" she yelled at the furious feline.

He responded with another long, warbling string of sounds. Ears laid back. Gold eyes glittering. The dog stood by the back door and whined unhappily. The other cats moved cautiously into the kitchen.

Their behavior sent chills down Scout's spine. She watched the cats sniff at the air, and found herself doing the same. The air was cool, and dry. It smelled faintly of the onions in the pantry. Of the coffee grounds in the garbage. Even more faintly of the food in the dog's bowl, and the small scraps the cats had left.

And underneath it all, it smelled of gas.

Scout whirled around to look at the stove. The gas had been left on. A cold chill washed over her, the sudden tightness in her chest made it difficult to breathe. She'd made coffee this morning, had she forgotten to turn the gas off? But, no, she hadn't made coffee. She'd started to and—

That was it. She must have put the gas on and forgotten about it. And then somehow, the flame had blown out.

She snapped it off, pushed the button for the fan, opened the door, and then the windows. All the time refusing to think too closely about the cats' behavior.

Cats can smell; there was nothing strange about that. Cats could smell gas and, probably, recognize that something was different in the air. Something unpleasant. Maybe even something *wrong* in a very primitive sense.

But that was it.

Cats could not make the connection she was making. Cats didn't know what cigarettes were. Or matches. And they absolutely could not make the leap from cigarette to match to gas explosion.

At least this time, there had been no disembodied voices. And while the cats may have saved her life, that was no more than luck. They didn't know what they were doing. *Yeah, right. So where are they now?*

Eight cats had disappeared in a blink of an eye. Not a single one remained in sight.

The phone rang as she was debating what to do next. She certainly wasn't going to be eating dinner here tonight, she thought, as she lifted the receiver to her ear. "Hello?"

Glenn's voice crackled over the phone. "Scout? Is that you?"

She nearly dropped the phone in surprise. "Well, hi, Glenn. I wasn't expecting to hear from you again."

He laughed. A strange noise, too loud in her ear. She pulled the phone away a little distance, but it was still too loud.

"What's that Glenn? I didn't hear you."

"I said, that's funny. What're you doing right now?"

Scout sighed. "Oh, you know, nothing much. Just trying to keep from blowing up the house."

"Oh, yeah?" Glenn's voice held a guarded note. "And how's that going?"

"Fine, I guess. I think I left the stove on this morning. And then the wind must have blown out the flame, or..."

*Or what, Scout? Where would the wind have come from? From the window which you just now opened?*

"Anyway, my cat saved me."

"They *what?*" Glenn's voice cracked in surprise. "Okay, that's it. I'm coming over. We need to talk."

"Okay, I—" Thoughts of the last time she and Glenn had been here alone rose up her throat, and she nearly choked. "No! That's – Look, I have to get out of the house anyway. I'll meet you at The Temple Garden, over on Fourth Street. We'll get some dinner."

"I'm not sure I want—"

*Well, I am.* "My treat, okay? How's half an hour sound?"

"Fine," he said at last, sounding as if it were anything but. "If that's the way you want it."

---

1. Oberon's greenbelt was inspired by Berkeley's Ohlone Greenway and Newport Beach's Environmental Nature Center. The Greenway is a park-slash-walking trail that meanders through the city. The Environmental Nature Center (where I volunteered as a docent) is a former gully that's been planted with native trees, shrubs, etc. And landscaped in such a way that it presents a variety of California eco-systems. Most of what I know about California native plants, I learned working there.

# 14

$S$cout sipped her second glass of plum wine and glanced once again at her watch. Glenn was late. Which was fine. Better than fine actually. Because she wasn't in any kind of hurry to see him, anyway. When she remembered the look in his eyes yesterday, she felt slightly sick.

He was crazy if he thought she wanted anything from him but information. And she didn't want it so badly she was going to sleep with him to get it, either.

It was ironic, considering the way she used to argue with Lisa about him. *"Can't you see what a user he is? Why do you let him get away with it?"* If she'd said it once, she'd said it a hundred times. What a hypocrite she'd been—back then, and possibly now, as well. Because, when the opportunity had arisen, she hadn't been above using him, had she? And here she was trying to do it again.

At least last time things had been a little more equitable. She was pretty sure that, last time, they'd each gotten exactly what they'd wanted...

It was a rainy Wednesday afternoon, shortly after school let out for the day, and Glenn had come to the house looking for Lisa. But Scout was the only one home, still dressed in her school uniform, eating her way through a pint of rocky road, as she brooded over life's unfairness, and the treachery of friends. Feeling generally sorry for herself.

It had been several weeks since she'd learned about the 'hypnosis experiments' her so-called *friends* had been running on her, and only a few days after she and Nick had talked at the diner. She had problems. Big problems. And the last person she wanted to have to deal with that day was Glenn.

"I can still come in, can't I, and wait for her?" he asked with that pleading, puppy dog look in his eyes.

Of course, she'd recognized the look for what it was. Hadn't she seen him use it a thousand times before? And hadn't she always been amazed whenever someone fell for it?

*"So, he's got nice eyes. Big deal. Can't you see it's just an act?"* she wanted to yell at them – Lisa and the others, falling all over themselves to please him. She was just about to send him on his way, back out into the rain where he could drown, for all she cared, when several thoughts collided in her brain.

Her first thought – and much as she hated to admit it, both then and later, it *had* been the first – was how great it would feel to pay Lisa back, even a little, for what she'd done.

Her second thought was also about Lisa, although here she could at least pretend to a measure of altruism. Lisa needed a wakeup call. She needed to see Glenn for the low life he was. And you couldn't get much lower than making it with your girlfriend's sister.

Only the third thought was for herself. She needed to lose her virginity with someone other than Nick. And she had to do it soon. The way she felt about Nick...it scared her. She loved him so much, and that gave him the power to hurt her. Badly. She couldn't bear the thought of losing him. Especially over something so trivial.

She'd do anything to keep from losing him. Even this.

What she needed was someone who would do it, and not think twice. Someone who wouldn't expect a relationship with her. Someone who couldn't possibly hurt her because she didn't care enough about him to be hurt. Someone exactly like Glenn.

So, she'd let him in. And ten minutes later he'd had her on the couch.

It was just that easy.

But first, she had a little business to take care of. "Gee, Glory, we've got this whole house to ourselves for the next hour or so. You'd think we could come up with some way to entertain ourselves, wouldn't you?"

That was all it had taken. She had seen his eyes light up with greedy anticipation, and she knew she had him. She moved quickly to seal the rest of the bargain she wanted to make.

"You know, Glenn," she told him, edging closer—close enough to brush an imaginary piece of lint from the front of his shirt, and then slide her hands up his chest, and around his neck. "I've been thinking. I've got a little bit of a situation here. Something you could maybe give me a hand with if you wanted to."

"Uh-huh. Sure. Whatever you want." He ducked his head to kiss her, but she held him off.

"Okay, good. Because you see, there are times when...I don't always want people to know where I've been. Or what I've been doing. You know the kind of thing I'm talking about, Glory, don't you?"

"Uh...yeah...maybe," he answered, his breath coming faster than before, his hands tightening on her waist as he tried to pull her closer.

Scout shifted away from him, frowning slightly. "What do you mean, maybe? Weren't you listening to what I just said?"

His throat bobbed, and he looked as if he were trying hard to think. "Yeah, sure. You, uh...you said you don't want people knowing..."

"Where I've been," Scout prompted. Shifting closer once more, until her breasts were pressing against his chest.

Glenn nodded slowly, his expression relaxing once again. "And, what you've been...been doing. Right?"

"That's right." Scout smiled approvingly as Glenn's hands slid up over her ribs. She did her best doing to ignore the quick, uncomfortable beating of her heart. The flush of heat in her face. The faint queasiness that was making speech so difficult. "And also who I've been with. So, d'you think you can help me out with that? I can tell them I was with you, and you'll back me up?"

"Sure, I can do that. I can—" His eyes widened in alarm. "Wait. With me? No, that's—"

"Only if they ask." She smiled up at him in her most entreating manner, swaying, ever so slightly from side to side. "They probably won't."

"But...what about Lisa?"

*Good question, butthead.* She pushed away from him then. Backed up a step. "What about her, Glenn?"

"What?" He stared blankly back at her.

"Lisa," she prompted, ready to call a halt. *Shit. Maybe I'm wrong about him. Maybe he really does care. How can I do this if—* "Are you afraid she'll be hurt?"

"No." Glenn frowned; his tongue darted out to moisten his lips. He shook his head. "It's not that. It's—"

*Of course, it's not. Whatever was I thinking?* Scout gritted her teeth to keep from scowling. She let her hands move to the button fastening her skirt. "Well, then what is it?

"It's just—"

She paused again, waiting. "Just?"

"Well, she'll get real mad if..."

*If? Ha!* Scout shook her head sorrowfully.

"...if she ever finds out about this."

*Never mind, if. Try when.*

Eyes wide, she smiled her most guileless smile as she popped the button and slowly, slowly, slowly lowered her zipper. "Lisa trusts me, Glenn. She'd never believe I'd go behind her back like this." Although, of course, that was precisely what she was counting on.

"Yeah, but I still don't think we should tell people we—"

"It's kinda important to me, Glenn." She pushed her skirt down over her hips. It fell to the floor, and she kicked it away. "I need to know I can count on you."

"You can! I just...I just don't see why I—"

"It's simple." She started in on the buttons of her blouse. Opening them slowly. One by one. Watching him watch her. Gauging his reaction to her every move.

*One.* "I need an alibi." She pretended not to notice the way his fists clenched and unclenched at his sides. "And, you know, Glen, someday..."

*Two.* Her blouse gapped open as she raised her hands to her head and made a big production out of undoing her braid, running her fingers through her hair. "Someday, you might need an alibi, too."

"Huh?" He stared at her blankly. "Alibi? For what?"

Her hands returned to unfasten button number *three.* She shrugged. The blouse gapped wider. Resting her hands on her hips, she took a deep, deep breath and pretended to think. "Oh, I don't know. Something we don't want anyone finding out about, maybe? Something secret?" *Something like this, you moron?*

"Oh, yeah. Yeah, maybe. I guess so."

Uh-huh. I guess so, too. *Four.* "And maybe." Her fingers toyed with the last button. "If you did need an alibi. I could be it. Right?" She cocked her head to the side.

"Uh, yeah. Sure. That's a, a good idea."

*Five.* "Uh, yeah, it is." Holding the edges of her now unbuttoned blouse together, she smiled encouragement. "So, what do you think? Are you in?"

"I...I...sure," He nodded slowly, shook his head, nodded again. "I guess. Why not?"

*Bingo.* "Good. It's a deal, then."

God, what fools they'd been. Sex had been this huge mystery, and virginity an unimaginable hurdle. Once she'd cleared it, she was so sure it would be smooth sailing for her and Nick. And her experience, which she was certain would be immediately obvious to him, would assuage any lingering doubts he might have about her age.

Plus, if they ever got caught...

Well, no one could blame Nick for corrupting the morals of a minor, could they? Not if her morals were already corrupted by someone else.

Just one more area where she considered Glenn to be expendable.

But sex with Glenn had been almost a non-event. Quick, clumsy, relatively painless – unless you counted the embarrassment she'd suffered. And virginity, she decided belatedly, was as meaningful a concept as an imaginary line drawn in non-existent sand.

She'd almost laughed out loud when they were finished. Where was the trauma and the pain she'd heard so much about? Where were the tears she was supposed to shed over her lost innocence? She had felt herself transformed far more deeply just staring into Nick's hot eyes. The passion in his gaze made her feel as though her very bones were melting. And the sound of his voice...well, nothing Glenn did made her feel anything like that!

Even now, just the thought of Nick, his eyes, his voice, his kisses, had the power to move her. Whereas Glenn—

But why was she thinking about that now? She emptied her wine-glass and signaled for another. It probably shouldn't have surprised her, how unmoved she'd been by the idea of letting Glenn have her body. Not when she'd already lost her mind to Lisa and her heart to Nick.

She'd made so many bad decisions back then. But had that really been her fault? She hadn't been herself for weeks. Or maybe even months.

She reached into the bowl of Chinese noodles, just for the pleasure of feeling them snap between her fingers. She'd given up too much back then, that was the problem. Too much control. Too much self-respect. Too much of herself. Too much of everything.

And she was doing it again, too, wasn't she? She'd been doing it all week, ever since she'd been back in Oberon. Allowing myths and memories to frighten or seduce her. Allowing herself to dream about things she'd spent years forgetting. Like the home she'd lost; the family she only thought she'd had; or the love she could never recapture.

Only this time, there was no excuse for it. She wasn't a kid anymore. It was time she grew up. Time she found the courage to walk away from her past – not run from it. To confront her ghosts, take them on, and send them packing.

All of them. The specters of Caroline, and Lisa. Robyn's elusive stranger: whoever he was. Marsha. Lucy. Glenn. Even Nick – he of the velvet voice and the brandy-colored eyes.

She had seen eyes like that just recently, her wine-dulled mind seemed to recall, but where? Oh yes. Nick's daughter. A sudden chill spread sadness through her soul. Of course, Nick had a daughter. Why wouldn't he? Obviously, Nick had a life.

And what did she have? Why was she still pining after him, anyway? Even now when it was clear he had moved on and forgotten all about her.

*Well, no more.* It was time for her to be over him, too. Time for her to get on with her own life. She searched her bag for her cell phone. Maybe she'd give Larry a call, see if he'd been able to put together that gallery showing they'd talked about. Maybe she'd take Glenn up on his offer to handle things here. How much could she really hope to accomplish, after all? But where the hell was her phone?

And then she remembered. *Oh, God. Last night. The canyon.* She'd thrown her phone over the cliff, hadn't she? The memory washed through her and left her dizzy. What the hell had possessed her last night?

She was saved from answering her own question by Glenn's belated arrival. He looked good, she thought sadly, as she watched him walk across the crowded restaurant towards her table. Too bad he moved her not at all. His somber clothing and expression were eerily reminiscent of a priest. Black turtleneck, black jacket and slacks. All that was missing was the white collar.

Not that a priest should ever be caught dead with that particular look in his eyes. She bit back a giggle. *Uh-oh.* Could be she'd have a little trouble with old Glenn tonight.

Or maybe not. It was possible she had been looking at this all wrong. It was possible Glenn was *exactly* what she needed right now.

Something to take her mind off her troubles and the sorry mess she called her life.

So what if he wasn't the man of her dreams? She was lonely, he was willing – who would it harm? What they'd had together hadn't been too awful, really. And, maybe, sometimes, not-too-awful beat nothing-at-all.

"So. Glenn." Scout greeted him with a friendly smile, as he sat down across from her. "This is kind of an interesting look for you. Dark, a little edgy, but still kinda sexy."

"Oh, yeah?" He leaned forward, smiling. His eyes for once not watchful, but wide and hopeful. In his eagerness she could still see the faint traces of the boy she'd seduced all those years ago. "Do you really think so?"

"Yeah," she answered, her mood dropping as reality hit. *Get involved with Glenn? Again? Not in this lifetime.* She felt suddenly sorry for the both of them, without quite knowing why. "Uh, yeah, Glory, sure. You got a real *Angel of Death* look goin' on."

NICK HAD SWORN he wouldn't do this. All day long, and repeatedly on the way here tonight, he'd promised himself that he'd behave like an adult. A mature, rational, mostly functional adult. Not the skewed, randy psychopath he seemed to have morphed into over the last forty-eight hours.

*I have a kid,* he told himself, again. *I shouldn't be acting like one.* But thinking of Kate really didn't help matters.

*She said I have your eyes.*

So, here he sat. Parked on the street across from Scout's house, without a clue in the world as to what he would say or do if he saw her. But wanting to see her, all the same.

Just before dark, a woman had ridden up on a bicycle, and his heart had leapt into his throat. But it couldn't be her. This woman was far too young. Her daughter, perhaps? For an agonizing minute, he considered the idea—it wasn't impossible. Finally, however, he'd recognized the girl. He had seen her before, with Lucy. Robyn some-body. One of the interns at Dan's nursery.

He didn't know why the idea that Scout might have a daughter should bother him. But apparently it did. It bothered him a lot. He didn't like to think of himself as being prone to such primitive emotions as jealousy or possessiveness, and not even his ex-wife had thought to lay those particular sins at his door. But— Oh, God. Blood flooded his face as he remembered the blind rages that had seized him during the days and weeks after Scout had first left town.

*There is no fucking way I can go through that again.*

The idea scared him half to death. Memories churned in his gut. And, shit, *nothing* was worth going through that again. He should go home. She probably wasn't even in the damn house. And the last thing he needed was for Robyn what's-her-name to mention to Lucy that she'd seen him here. His life was complicated enough as it was.

He should leave. Now. Before he got in any deeper. He could always come back and make a fool of himself again tomorrow, unless he had the great good luck of regaining his senses before morning.

But he didn't turn the car on. He couldn't bring himself to leave.

For just awhile longer, he sat there. Staring once more through the growing darkness, as he'd done so many times in the past, at the house where she used to live.

Scout sighed wearily. "Look, Glenn, it's like I told you, it was a joke, all right? I didn't mean anything by it." It was already the third time she'd said it. And what was she apologizing for, anyway? He was the one who'd knocked over the table. Spilling the water and what was left of her wine. Noodles and plum sauce flying all over the place.

Why was he such a wreck, anyway? Just because she'd used his old nickname? Could that possibly have upset him that much? Hell, he wasn't the one who'd nearly blown himself up today. If anyone had a right to be jumpy tonight, it was her.

And you didn't see her accidentally upending tables over a stupid joke.

But now, the table had been reset, their food had arrived, and still he was fretting. Fussing for no reason, phrasing every remark in such a way that it meant absolutely nothing. It was almost enough to make her long for the old, brash, obnoxiously insistent Glenn. This wishy-washy, careful crap was starting to annoy the shit out of her.

All she wanted was to concentrate on her Kung Pao chicken, find out what he knew about Lisa, maybe order some lychees and another glass of wine. And then go home. Alone. Most definitely alone.

"Why don't we cut to the chase, Glenn. Tell me what you know about Lisa, and then we can both call it quits."

He set down his Kirin with a frown. "What makes you think I know anything other than what I've already told you?"

Scout sighed. "Oh, please. It sticks out a mile. And, anyway, you called me, remember? You said we had to talk."

"How do you know I wasn't just making excuses to see you again?" The ghost of his old smile flickered on his face, and Scout couldn't help but smile back.

She shook her head. "Why—for old time's sake? C'mon, Glenn, we did this already the other night. Besides, we weren't ever exactly an item, you know? And even if we were once, we're two completely different people now."

"We could have been an item. We almost were. Who knows what might have happened, if things had been different? If it weren't for Lisa. I always thought we would have made a good couple. Maybe we still could."

Scout felt a pang of remorse. *Did he really think that? Had he always?* "Glenn—"

"We had something Scout," Glenn insisted, his blue eyes boring into hers. "You know that as well as I do."

Well, she'd asked for this, hadn't she? She'd brought it on herself.

Scout suppressed a sigh. "Yeah, we had something, all right. I'm just not sure what."

"We could still find out, couldn't we? What's stopping us? It's not too late, you know." Glenn reached across the table toward her hand, but she slipped it out of his way and picked up her glass. He sighed and stared at her sadly.

The puppy dog look was in his eyes again. Some things never change, they just become more of the same. And she still wasn't falling for it. "Actually, Glenn, I think it's very late. So maybe you should just tell me what you know."

"You know, I really would hate to see you get hurt, Scout," he said rather ponderously, with maybe just an edge of temper.

"Same here. Although I don't see any reason why knowing what happened to Lisa would hurt more than not knowing. I lost her a long time ago."

He stared at her for a moment. "No, I mean physically hurt," he said at last. "I think you should give serious consideration to the idea that somebody might be, as Robyn said, *out to get you*. These accidents—"

Scout ground her teeth. *Oh, here we go again.* "Come on Glenn; out to get me? You can't really believe that. And anyway, I think what she said was that the guy was *after me*. Which could be interpreted any number of different ways, don't you think? He could have been a secret admirer, or a bill collector. Or maybe I'd won a raffle. It could happen."

"You're being very casual about this."

"So, what, then? You're saying you think this thing with the stove was some kind of warning?"

"I didn't say that did I? But I do think you were lucky. And maybe you should worry a little about your luck changing."

No, she guessed he hadn't said that, had he? At least, not exactly. Scout speared a little piece of chicken with her fork. In fact, he hadn't said *anything* worth listening to. This entire conversation was getting her nowhere.

"Look, Glenn, why don't you just tell me what you know about

Lisa. And why you're so sure I won't be able to find her."

Glenn's expression darkened. "Lisa again. You never give up, do you? You think Caroline didn't try to find her? Of course, she did! She did almost nothing else for twenty years. Believe me, I know all about it, because she did a lot of it through the firm. Through guys we hired for her. Some of the best investigators in the state. It was a total waste of time. *And* money. What makes you think you can do better?"

"Because, for one thing, none of them knew Lisa. Don't you think that gives me an edge?"

"Are you suggesting that her own mother didn't know her? I'm pretty sure the information Caroline gave them was as good as anything you might have to offer."

Scout shook her head. "Come on, Glenn. You know better than that. There was a whole lot of stuff that Caroline hadn't known about Lisa. In some ways, yeah, I think I *did* know her better than her mother did. Hell, in some ways *you* probably did too."

"Yeah. Well. I don't think any of the things I knew about her would be of much use to a PI." He smirked as he said it, and Scout felt her eyes narrow.

"Don't make jokes about this," she snapped. "It's *not* funny."

"Okay, fine." Glenn sighed. "But you *do* know, don't you, that none of the investigators Caroline hired were able to find out a single thing, right?"

"That's not true. Lloyd Donahue said Caroline had been in touch with someone about ten years ago who claimed to have information about Lisa."

"Oh, for Christ's sake!" Glenn slammed down his fork and glared at her. "Are you kidding me? That was just some sort of scam. Caroline was contacted anonymously, and after paying a lot of money in advance, she never received the promised information, or even heard from the person again. As anyone could have told her would happen. As I did tell her."

"That doesn't matter," Scout insisted. "Maybe the reason the investigators you hired didn't find any clues, was because they weren't looking in the right place."

"Okay. So where do *you* think they should have looked?"

"Right here in Oberon, of course."

"Here?" Glenn's eyes looked like they were going to pop out of his head. Scout wondered if anyone would know what to do if he went ahead and had the heart attack he seemed to be working himself up to? "Wh— You think you're going to find Lisa *here*? After all this time?"

"Not Lisa, herself, but– Well, think about it. That letter she sent Lucy was mailed locally, remember? That means she had to be hiding out somewhere close by—at least for those first few days. Right? So, where was she? I mean, even if she'd rented a motel room for a couple of nights, someone would have had to have known about it."

"Not necessarily. There are a lot of no-tell motels out on the highway, you know. She—"

"—Didn't have any money with her," Scout reminded him. "So how would she have paid for it? I figure either she left town *with* someone—which seems unlikely. Or someone here must have helped her get away."

Glenn's face had gone ashen. Maybe she was finally getting through to him.

"You're serious about this, aren't you?" he asked, his voice subdued.

"Somebody knows something, Glenn. They have to! And whatever that something is, I'm going to find it out."

For a moment, Glenn said nothing, just picked at his Szechuan Beef. Finally, he put his fork down and fixed her with a steady gaze. "Okay," he said, sounding like he'd come to a decision. "I didn't want to tell you, because I didn't see how it could help, but, when Lisa...left town...she was pregnant with my child."

Whatever Scout had been expecting, it hadn't been this.

"No. That can't be true." Her head swam. "Glenn, Lisa would *never* have left town if she was going to have a baby. Why would she leave if—"

"Because I wouldn't marry her, that's why," he said quietly. "We

175

argued about it. She wanted to but I told her I wouldn't. I told her I was in love with you."

"Oh, my God." She stared at him in horror as he leaned forward to capture her hand. Holding it tight. Too tight. Painfully tight.

"You see what I'm saying, don't you Scout? She was angry. And she wanted to hurt me. I think she even hated me, a little. But she hated you more. I knew it would hurt you to hear that. But you just wouldn't listen. You just wouldn't stop."

Glenn paused for a moment, and then went on again. "Now do you see why you have to quit looking for her? You could get hurt, Scout. Badly hurt."

*Hurt?* Scout stared at him; her mind blank. *Worse than this?* "How—"

"Think about it." he insisted. "I think she's dead; I think she has to be. But what if she isn't? You remember what Lisa was like, don't you, Scout? You remember how she got when she was angry, or if you crossed her? She's spent a lot of time pretending to be dead. If you track her down now...how happy do you think she's gonna be to see you?"

GLENN WATCHED as Scout disappeared into the night. Going home to walk her dog, or so she said. He'd thought, perhaps, if he drove her home – but no, it was probably better this way.

He'd tried. He'd given it his best shot. But he could tell that nothing he'd said had changed her mind. She'd been shocked, all right. For all of about a minute. But not enough to give up. She'd keep prying and digging and who knew what she might find.

It was such a shame. He'd hoped they could start over, begin again – but he knew now that wasn't going to happen. He had wanted, so much, for things to turn out differently. But tonight hadn't been a new beginning, after all. If anything, it was just the beginning of the end.

Robyn jumped when she heard the door open, she ran to take a look. After sneaking a peek around the kitchen door, she had to concede that maybe Lucy had been right. Scout looked tired and she was still limping a little, but all in all, she looked so much less like an axe murderer than she had the night before.

"Hi," Robyn called out, tentatively.

Scout looked up. "Oh, hi Robyn." Her voice sounded weary, but reasonably devoid of hysteria.

"You okay, tonight?"

"What? Oh, sure." Scout yawned. "Just tired, is all. How about you?"

"I'm good. Uh, listen, I have to go out again tonight. Is it okay if I take the dog?"

"Sure. She needs a walk anyway. You'd be doing me a favor."

"Well, great. I might be out pretty late though."

"That's okay." Scout yawned again and started up the stairs. "With any luck, maybe I'll be asleep when you get back."

Robyn watched Scout walk slowly up the stairs. *Well, it looks like I was wrong about her. Maybe things will go back to normal, now. I guess I don't have to worry about being killed tonight, after all.*

She got her things together, called for the dog, and headed out the door.

# 15

Out in the garden, the morning mist had not yet lifted. Dew furred the leaves and blossoms of the trumpet vine that grew around the porch and glistened on the huge spider web that stretched between the redwood posts that supported the grape arbor.

Lucy watched as her little flock of chickens stalked across the lawn. They clucked and cackled excitedly, scratching for snails in the wet grass. The sun danced in the rooster's iridescent green neck feathers as he flapped his wings and let loose with a loud, long, undulating crow. "Show-off," she muttered fondly. Truth was, she was a big fan of testosterone-fueled displays.

In spite of the glorious morning unfolding all around her, Lucy was feeling considerably less than glorious today. Dan and the kids were getting ready for their camping trip—with Mandy still unsure about whether to go, and Lucy suddenly uncertain about being left behind.

"Are you kidding me?" Dan had protested when she'd suggested joining them. "After you've been bitching for months about how you deserve a break once in a while? You know that if you come you'll only end up complaining about how you should have stayed home."

He was right—she knew that. It's just that things seemed so unsettled right now, and it was so comforting to be with him...

"Mom!" Seth called from the porch. "Dad says do you know where the extra air mattress is? Oh, and to tell you Uncle Joey's here."

"I'll be right there," Lucy called back. A small thrill of pleasure ran through her as she contemplated her tall and handsome son. He looked more like his father every day.

Out on the driveway, Dan had stopped loading the car and was going over the maps with Joey. Her nephews, Jason and Zach, were checking out the fishing gear, and Stephanie, her niece, was showing Mandy her CDs. Lucy sighed as nostalgia tugged on her heartstrings. She'd always loved these trips the families took together. Especially when the kids were younger.

Back then, of course, Nick and Lauren were still a couple, and they and Kate had always gone, too. As had Joey's wife Janice – back before she decided that her quality of life would be radically improved if she never saw the inside of another tent.

Things just weren't the same anymore. The last few years, Lucy had ended up playing Mommy – to everyone from the big boys right on down the line. And Dan was right, she'd come to resent the hell out of it.

The truth was, they really didn't need her along. So she *should* stay home and enjoy having some time to herself. But being selfish like that really went against the grain. Besides which, she missed Dan already.

"Hey, Joey," Lucy greeted her brother as she came up behind her husband and slipped her arms around his waist.

"Morning, Lucy." Joey looked up from the maps in front of him, and then quickly rolled his eyes away again when Dan hauled her around for a kiss.

His lips tasted of coffee, spicy and just a little sweet. It was all she could do to resist the urge to explore the flavor further. But Joey and the kids were there, so when Dan pulled away from her, she contented herself with licking her own lips clean of every trace of the taste he'd left there.

"Hey babe. I had a question," Dan started, but then seemed to lose his train of thought. He frowned slightly, staring fixedly at her mouth. "Uhh...?"

"The air mattress?" Joey prompted, with a heavy sigh.

"Oh, right. Luce, do you know where our other air mattress is? I can't find it anywhere."

"Don't you remember?" Lucy said, smiling fondly even as she shook her head. "You got rid of it last year, after the kids got it snagged on those thorn bushes."

Jeez. Maybe staying home was a mistake. How would they get along without her if they couldn't remember simple things like that?

Dan flashed her a grin, as though he knew just what she was thinking. "Oh, yeah. I forgot about that. Good thing one of us can still think straight."

"Hmm."

"Five days, huh?" He reached out and pulled her back against him for another kiss. "I guess we'll just have to manage without it...somehow."

Lucy bit back a smile. She'd recognized that gleam in his eyes. She didn't think he was talking about air mattresses anymore.

"That's okay," Dan whispered, hugging her very, very tightly. "I'll let you owe me for it later."

This time she was *sure* he wasn't talking about the air mattress. She snorted quietly. "Get real, Cavanaugh."

A short time later, she watched the cars pull out of her drive. The quiet luxury of five free days, five days all to herself, settled around her. Five days to do whatever she wanted, whenever she wanted to. Maybe she'd start with a long, hot shower. Or better yet a bath. But she was just getting ready to turn on the water when the phone rang.

She should have known it was too good to be true.

Lucy was seething when she hung up the phone three minutes later. She should have known something like this would come up. The call had been from her brother-in-law, Kenny, at the nursery. Robyn hadn't shown up for work and they were shorthanded dealing with a big landscaping order. Would she come in and give them a hand? Well, of course she would.

So much for selfishness.

But, jeez. Robyn? Lucy pushed away a vague uneasiness. Of course, there was no reason to worry! People didn't show up for work all the time, and for all sorts of reasons. She shouldn't be worried. What she should be was mad! Wasn't it just her bad luck to get stuck filling in for the girl, during what was supposed to be her vacation?

Dan was going to owe her big for this, she thought, already considering a variety of ways in which he might be induced to pay her back.

Still, she remembered the fear in Robyn's eyes yesterday. And a cold dread rose inside her when she remembered having warned Marsha to expect a disaster. As far as potential disasters went, this one had Scout's fingerprints all over it.

But there was no sense jumping to conclusions, she decided, as she went to get ready for work. In all likelihood, it would turn out there was nothing to worry about. Nothing at all.

NOTHING. That's what Scout heard when she woke. Absolutely nothing.

No doors slamming, no water running in the shower or the sink, no can opener whirring, no coffeemaker gurgling, no dishes hitting the floor, or being banged together in the sink. It was like a miracle, she thought for one grateful moment.

But the moment passed quickly, and she felt herself grow tense.

It was too quiet. Why was that?

The entire house was wrapped in stillness. Six of the cats paced silently through the halls. They followed her downstairs and into the deserted kitchen and waited while she put food in their bowls.

Where the heck was Robyn, Scout wondered uneasily; and what had she done with the dog?

For once, Scout thought, she would have welcomed the noise and confusion she had almost come to expect of mornings here. Shreds of last night's dreams still clung to her thoughts, and they hadn't been pleasant.

She'd dreamt of the woods again. Of the woods and the pond that she'd passed by just yesterday. Only in her dream, she had to cut through the pond, instead of around it, to get to the house. She'd become trapped in the weeds, snagged on submerged branches, mired in the soft mud of the bottom.

What good did it do her to sleep through the night, if her sleep was so disturbed that it left her feeling more exhausted than staying awake would have? She really should talk to Marsha about borrowing her van if this kept up much longer.

By the time she'd finished her second cup of coffee, Scout had almost convinced herself that Robyn must have spent the night out somewhere. She'd probably gone straight from there to work. Which meant she wouldn't be bringing the dog back until much later today.

The thought was surprisingly unsettling. Why was that? Scout had told Robyn often enough that she could take the dog wherever and whenever she wanted, hadn't she? But that was before she had gotten used to having it around.

Scout briefly contemplated driving out to the nursery. Lucy had said it was in Abraxas Canyon. How hard could it be to find? But her car was such a mess, she wasn't sure she should even have driven it home the other day.

Also, she had neglected to report the accident to her insurance company; she really needed to get on that. And then she'd need to see about getting it repaired.

So, good. She had a plan now. Something to occupy her time and keep her from thinking too much about other things. But that sense of satisfaction didn't last beyond the time it took her to phone her insurance agent and locate a mechanic.

Glenn's news had really thrown her last night, so much so, she'd forgotten to ask him any of the obvious questions. Like whether the existence of grandchildren would make a difference to Caroline's will. Or whether anyone had thought to check birth records from nineteen years ago. She'd bet anything he hadn't thought of something so obvious. The idiot. It was only *his child* they were talking about, after all!

But had there ever *really* been a baby? A secondhand report of a possible pregnancy was not the same as an actual child, after all. Maybe Lisa had been lying. Or maybe she'd miscarried or died in childbirth. Or maybe she hadn't even lived long enough to do *that*.

Tears stung Scout's eyes, almost blinding her. The questions she'd been struggling with for a week seemed twice as urgent now, and she was more determined than ever to find the answers. She finished her coffee, double-checked to make sure that this time the gas was definitely off and then, very carefully, drove her damaged car downtown.

GLENN WAS DRIVING BLIND, so wrapped in thoughts and memories that the scenery around him barely registered at all. Last night had been a mistake. How could he have gotten things so wrong? He was sure now that Scout's claim about having to walk the dog had been a lie—a bluff to get away from him.

Enough was enough. He'd go back to her house – right now – and they would finish this, once and for all.

His vision cleared just before he came to the turn for the wide curved driveway. Nostalgia hit him fast and hard. How many times had he pulled in here? Always coming to see Lisa, and once – just once – finding Scout instead. All warm and friendly, where she was usually so cool, so indifferent.

Her eyes had glittered with need that afternoon. Her need for *him!* What a surprise that had been. Just that one time, which he still didn't understand. Why hadn't there been more days like that one?

Lisa, probably. Wasn't all of it Lisa's fault? But Lisa was gone, and now...

There was no reason why he and Scout shouldn't have gotten together again. It couldn't have been because she didn't want to.

She had been almost giddy with her delight, laughing – a deep, sexy, groan of a laugh – as he whispered in her ear. Telling her all the things he was going to do to her, how he was going to make her feel.

He had felt the way she shivered as his hands slid up her thighs, and she had opened for him so willingly. When he entered her, her body had pulsed with passion and heat. Even her voice had vibrated with it, as she urged him to hurry, not to wait, to do it now—

Why couldn't he have that again? His hands tightened on the wheel. And why couldn't he make her understand that she had to let Lisa go? Just as he had.

Her car wasn't in the drive, but someone else's was. Someone was standing on the porch, peering into the hall windows. A stranger. No, wait— *Not a stranger!* A thrill of fear shot through him, and instead of turning into the drive, he put his foot down hard and sped away.

With the distance, the fear he felt was quickly replaced by anger.

That cop. Lucy's cousin. What was he doing there? Always sticking his nose in other people's business. Always coming after people. Threatening them. Frightening them.

*Well, not this time,* Glenn thought angrily; *not now. I've waited too long for this. It's my turn now.* This time, Glenn was way ahead of the bastard.

NICK PEERED through the window and rang the doorbell again. But no one appeared in answer to the bell, except for a phalanx of cats, who sat in the hallway and stared back at him through the window, their gold eyes inscrutable and cold. The irrational fear that had propelled him out of his car and onto her porch – the fear that had come when he'd seen her car was missing, the fear that she was gone again, that he had waited too long – was mildly assuaged by the sight of all those cats.

Surely, she wouldn't have left town without them. Unless they belonged to the roommate? Or unless she'd made arrangements for someone else to come in and care for them? But he refused to let himself dwell on those ideas.

Better to focus on the car. He was pretty sure she couldn't drive it any great distance, not the way it looked yesterday. Which meant she would have to get it fixed before she tried to run away again.

So, he was probably still okay.

*Okay? Well, that's one way of looking at it!*

He sighed as he headed back down the stairs. Might as well get used to it. He was obviously bound and determined to make a jackass of himself. Nothing new there. He supposed he could live with that.

He'd have to live with it, wouldn't he?

Not certain which emotion predominated, relief or frustration, he got back into his car.

Later. He would come back later and...well, he wasn't sure what he would do, but chances were good that it would be something stupid.

*Stupid, stupid, stupid*. Scout walked away from the lawyer's office in a state of angry frustration. *God, I'm so tired of stupid people*. Glenn hadn't been in—not that she was sure she was ready to talk to him again yet anyway. And Donahue had been at his irritating best. She was just so tired of people warning her off Lisa's trail.

They all had good reasons for it. But she didn't *care* about any of their damn reasons. *Why can't anyone understand that?*

And why did everyone assume she cared all that much about Caroline's estate? None of that stuff belonged to her, much as she would have loved to claim some of it for herself. The house perhaps. Maybe a few pieces of furniture. Her father's paintings, for sure. But the reality was that she'd lost whatever rights she'd had to any of it when she'd chased Lisa away from home.

*Pregnant, homeless, teenaged Lisa, whose heart I trampled.*

How could Glenn possibly imagine she'd stop searching for answers *now*? All he'd done was compound the guilt she'd already been feeling!

*I can't believe what a bitch I was back then. How could I have been so stupid, so cruel. So...young.*

Scout was so lost in her thoughts, she didn't hear the voice that hailed her, and didn't stop until she felt the hand on her arm and looked up into a pair of shrewd blue eyes.

"Oh. Uh, h-hello," she stammered. She felt her face coloring. "It's Heather, isn't it? I'm sorry I didn't see you."

"You got that right." Heather chuckled; her short blond hair gleamed in the sunlight. "You were in a daze, girl. Nearly walked right into us."

Us? Scout noticed the other woman for the first time. Registering her height—barely five feet—a short mop of curly brown hair, and a bright pair of chocolate brown eyes, before anything else.

"It's so good to finally meet you," the woman positively gushed, grasping her hand warmly. "I've heard so much about you from Marsha and Lucy. You weren't thinking of coming in for a book, by any chance, were you?"

"A...book?" Scout asked stupidly.

"Yes, of course. See?" The woman waved one hand gracefully, and Scout realized they were standing right in front of a bookstore. "Our store. Digressions. New and used books. Hartman and Finch, proprietors. I'm Hartman, by the way. But please, call me Ginny. And really, you must stop in sometime. But not right now, I'm afraid." Ginny sparkled at her. "Because we're just going out to lunch. But perhaps you'd like to join us?"

"So, WHERE'S YOUR DOG TODAY?" Heather asked, after they had been seated at one of the small outdoor tables provided by the Red Rooster Grill – a sidewalk cafe in what Scout considered to be the true Oberon style, vegetarian with French pretensions. [1]

*Good question.* Scout laughed, ruefully. "I'm afraid your guess is as good as mine. My housemate went off with her last night and they haven't come back yet. I guess she just went straight to work, although—"

Scout's mouth went suddenly dry as an unwelcome new thought occurred to her. "I can't quite see her going to work at the nursery without stopping home to change out of last night's clothes first. I guess she could have taken a change with her, though..."

"Housemate—that's Robyn, yes? The girl's a dear, but a little impulse driven. I doubt she'd plan anything that far ahead." Ginny smiled sunnily as she dug into her soy cheese and spinach crepes. "That's partly why we were so glad when we heard that you were coming to live here, you know. It was much too lonely for the poor child, rattling around in that big house all by herself. But you do realize that she works out at the nursery with Lucy, don't you?"

"Yes. I know."

"Well, why don't you drive out and see if she's there? If you're worried about the dog, I mean."

"I'm not *worried*. Exactly." Scout picked moodily at her startlingly verdant *pate faux gras*. She wondered if the final 's' had inadvertently been dropped on the menu?

Not that it mattered. She didn't know why she'd even bothered to order anything at all – she had no appetite today. "Besides, as it happens, I just had to drop my car off to be repaired. I won't have it back for a few days."

Heather's eyes sparkled. "Well, there's always the phone, you know."

"Oh, no. That's okay." Scout sighed again. "I'd just as soon not call Lucy, either."

Over lunch, she told the women a little about her trip to the lawyer's office, omitting any mention of Lisa's theoretical pregnancy. It would be interesting to find out if anyone else had known about that.

"Well," Ginny said. "I see your point, of course. But what makes you think she's even alive?" She put a hand solicitously on Scout's arm. "Forgive me, if this pains you, but she hadn't had a falling out with her mother, had she? Surely in all this time she would have gotten in touch with her. If she could have done so."

"I know that," Scout answered, sadly. "And I do realize it's a long shot. But I still feel like I owe it to Caroline to try and find out. Besides," she added. "Caroline must have thought of the same things, and she hadn't given up."

"Well, but she was her *mother*, after all."

"Plus, there's the small matter of, I don't know, I guess it's just pride. Caroline and I hadn't seen one another, or even spoken, more than a few times in twenty years. I have to know why she did this. What she wanted from me. It's not like she just flat out left everything to me, either. I'm pretty sure she would have wanted me to continue searching."

"Maybe there's a way you could ask her. You know, through a psychic," Heather suggested. "Always plenty of those around here."

Scout shook her head. "Wishful thinking."

"Now, why do you say that?" Heather demanded. "I heard about the story you told Marsha yesterday. About the accident you had the other day? After something like that, I should think you would at least admit the possibility."

"Do *you* believe it's possible?"

Heather smiled wryly. "Oh, yes. Not that I've had much personal experience, but Ginny has had entirely too many visits from relatives who have passed over. Of course, it's not always easy to contact them, from what I understand. Excessive emotions can be a problem when you're trying to communicate. Apparently, if you're missing the person too much, that can be a barrier."

Scout picked at her *pate* for a minute with her fork. "I think I got over missing both Caroline and Lisa a long, long time ago. And anyway, if you don't think they're really gone, why would you miss them?"

She looked up again, to find Ginny staring at her pityingly. "If you loved someone, but knew you would never be able to see or speak to that person again for the rest of your life, would you be content with just knowing that she, or he, was alive?" Ginny asked softly. "Would that little bit of information be enough to keep you from missing them, or from feeling any sadness over their continued absence?"

*Never to see someone you loved, ever again? Like me and Nick, perhaps?* Scout swallowed hard, hoping to dislodge the lump that had risen in her throat. "I don't know. But I think, even if you never actually did it, just knowing the possibility for contact existed, and that the other person was also thinking of you? I think that would be wonderful."

Ginny smiled again, an even sadder smile than before. "Well, if that's true, then I envy you. But, just the same, I really do think you should consider giving it a try. I'm sure, from everything Marsha has told us, you wouldn't have any problems making contact. But I am still confused about one thing. Why do you think it was *your* fault your sister left home?"

Scout laughed. "Oh, everyone agreed on that point! She even wrote to Lucy after she left, telling her so."

"She contacted Lucy, but not her mother. Didn't that seem strange to you?" Ginny mused, breaking off to pick up the check the waitress had placed on the table. "Oh, no, dear." She smiled at Scout when she saw her reaching for her bag. "It's our treat. After all, we invited you."

"Oh. Thank you," Scout answered. "But really, I can't—"

"Nonsense," Heather assured her. "We'll spend a few minutes now, talking about how much reading you do, and what books you'd like to see us stock, and then we'll write the whole thing off as a business lunch. You're doing us a favor." Her blue eyes twinkled mischievously. "But if you really feel indebted, you can repay us by satisfying our curiosity. What did your sister say in this mysterious letter?"

Scout shrugged. "Oh, it was just typical Lisa: 'Dear Lucy, Scout's a bitch. I'm leaving now. Gotta make them pay for what they did. Talk to you later. Yadda, yadda, yadda.' Just like a thousand other notes she'd written to Lucy or Marsha – or to me, even – during class, or whatever. That's why I'm sure something must have happened to her. She was just too matter of fact about it. You know, pissed off and all, but not jumping-off-a-cliff crazy."

Heather looked at her thoughtfully. "Well, you know, one thing you should keep in mind, you were both just kids, at the time. Maybe you should cut yourself a little slack?"

"Yeah well, I guess that's a whole lot easier said than done," Scout sighed. "Because I came back to town with the idea that I was going to do just that. But so far, it hasn't exactly worked out that way."

---

1.  There's a Red Rooster restaurant in Santa Cruz, CA. I'm not sure if I named the Oberon restaurant after it, or if I noticed the real life location afterward. I don't think I ever ate there, so I'm guessing it was the latter.

    We made the drive between Berkeley (where we lived) and Orange County (where my parents lived) somewhat regularly during a few of the years that I was writing this series. I picked up bits and pieces of many things along the way and added them to Oberon.

    Then we moved to Paso Robles, CA—which, visually, is so exactly how I pictured Oberon that I started laughing the first time we pulled up to the town square.

    I was four books into the series, at that point, and really felt like I'd come home.

    There's also a Red Hen restaurant in Napa, by the way. I HAVE been there, but it's NOTHING like the one in Oberon. lol!

    Oh, and another thing. I'm pretty sure I modeled the Red Rooster's menu after some of the dishes I tried at Gratitude Cafe in Berkeley. Sadly, it's no longer there. But, then again, neither am I.

# 16

This time, Nick made himself wait until nightfall before he drove back to Scout's house. But, unlike the night before, when the lower floor had blazed with light, tonight the house was dark, and looked deserted.

Still, he wasn't overly worried. He'd checked around at the local auto body shops and learned that Scout's car had been brought in that morning for repairs. At best guess, it would be several days before it was fixed. The mechanic had even agreed to notify him before he released the car.

It wasn't much, but at least this time she wouldn't be able to slip away without his knowing.

She hadn't left town. So, then where the hell was she? He guessed he'd just have to wait and see, wouldn't he? Nothing new about that. Over the years he'd had plenty of time to practice waiting for her. By now, he guessed he'd gotten pretty good at it. And in any case, sitting around in his car wasn't so different from sitting around a campfire, or inside a tent. And that's precisely what he would have been doing right now, if she hadn't come back to town, or— Shit.

He was hit with a sudden, suffocating sense of anxiety. That's what he'd be doing if he hadn't *happened* to learn that she was in town.

Which meant— Jesus Christ. She might have come to town and gone away again, any number of times, without his ever knowing about it.

The idea filled him with dread. To have come that close, and never to have known it? How many times in the last twenty years might that have happened? How many times might he have already missed seeing her?

He and Lucy really needed to sit down and have a little talk about this. He was not a child, no matter that he was acting like one. He couldn't have his relatives making decisions like this for him. Disaster or no, he was walking into this with his eyes wide open. He had every right to mess his life up any way he wanted.

MARSHA SAT in front of her altar trying to clear her mind, but the clarity she sought continued to elude her. Tonight, she had no sense of being guided. She was unable to connect with Spirit.

It was an uncomfortable, empty feeling, and not one she felt often. She had learned not to ignore it when it happened, though, because time and again it had proven to be a reliable indicator that something in her life was severely out of balance.

Unfortunately, it also usually prevented her from seeing clearly where the problem was.

That was not the case this time, however. This time, she had a pretty good idea where the problem lay.

She tried again and again to clear her mind, to establish a connection, but it was no use. With a sense of profound frustration, she extinguished the candles and put away her tools. She had not accomplished any of the things she'd set out to do. She would have to find another way to deal with her problem.

LUCY LISTENED to the phone as it rang and rang and rang some more.[1] Where the hell was Robyn? She had half a mind to drive over there and see for herself, but the idea of appealing to Scout for information was not one she relished. Besides...what if she really had gone round the bend, after all?

What were you supposed to do, anyway, if you suspected that someone was missing? Or had maybe been hurt? Without stopping to think, she hit the button that would automatically dial her cousin's number. Again, the phone rang and rang with no answer.

When his machine picked up, she thought about leaving a message; but at the last moment, she changed her mind. What the hell was she thinking? The last thing she wanted was to get Nick involved in *anything* to do with Scout. Not unless she was absolutely forced to.

Oh, hell. She was overreacting again. She had to be. This couldn't be happening! If only Dan were here. He was always so calm and rational. Always teasing her for being such a drama queen. Always ready to distract her from whatever nonsense was worrying her. But tonight she couldn't even call him! Sure, he'd taken his cell phone with him, but she knew from experience that reception was impossible in the canyon where they were camped. She couldn't reach him or her brother unless she drove all the way out there. And now, she couldn't reach Nick, either.

Men. You just couldn't count on them either to be there when you needed them, or to keep themselves out of trouble while they were gone.

Where could Nick be at this hour? *Miles away from Scout, I hope.* But he was such an idiot, he probably thought he could handle getting involved with her again.

For one more, brief moment she reconsidered calling Scout, but what would she say? Instead, she settled for dialing Robyn's number yet again. Once again, there was no answer. Solitude was all very well and good, she thought angrily, but this was getting ridiculous!

ABSOLUTELY RIDICULOUS! Glenn fumed. Didn't that cop have a home to go to? Every time he'd tried to see Scout today, he'd found the cop was there before him – either skulking around the house itself or staked out in his car.

*And just what's up with that, anyway?*

Oh, the hell with it. He'd come back tomorrow. His business with Scout had waited this long; it could wait a little longer. Sometimes the waiting only made things better. That cop couldn't stay there forever. Sooner or later, he'd have to go home. And then it would be Glenn's turn. Again.

THE HELL WITH IT, Scout thought, sleepily. She'd been up in the attic long enough, she was stiff from sitting on the hard, dusty floor, and although she had gone through every scrap of paper in Caroline's files a dozen times, she was still no closer to finding any answers.

Caroline had newspaper clippings that spanned several months. Everything, from Ms. Burnett's murder to Marsha's car accident had been painstakingly documented. And, just as Glenn had suggested, there had been no shortage of rumor and innuendo floating around. But wherever Lisa had gone, whatever had happened to her, she – or someone else – had done a damn good job of covering their tracks.

*Or maybe the answers are right here, right in front of me, and I'm too tired to see them?* She'd always heard that clarity came with sleep.

Maybe she should try to close her eyes and forget about everything. Maybe in the morning it would all be clear.

*Yeah, right. Like that's ever worked for me before.*

She pushed her hair back from her face, rubbed her tired eyes. What if she never found an answer? What if she only found more questions? How long could Caroline expect her to keep looking?

And, speaking of questions, here was a good one. What the hell had happened to Robyn? And to her dog? *I can't believe how much I miss the damned mutt.* The cats were all well and good, and attending to her every move in a highly flattering way. But still, it wasn't the same.

Exhausted, Scout crept down from the attic and into her bedroom. She heard the phone ringing again in Robyn's room, and she continued to ignore it. What would she have to say to anyone calling for Robyn?

She got into bed feeling lonely and miserable. She hadn't had the stupid dog for even one week, and already she couldn't remember what her life was like without it. *You're being ridiculous*, she told herself, as she reached up and turned off the lamp on her bedside table. *You do not need a dog. You do not need a housemate. You do not need anything.*

Except, maybe, to get the hell out of Oberon.

NICK STIRRED IN HIS SEAT. One of the lights in the house had gone on. An upstairs light, probably in one of the bedrooms. He checked his watch. Damn, he'd had no idea it was so late. Either he'd missed her going in, which he didn't think was possible, or else she'd been in the house the whole time – sitting in near total darkness, apparently – and he hadn't even known it.

*Ridiculous.* That was the only word to describe this evening's performance. So, what the hell should he do now? Maybe he should go and ring the bell again, he thought, feeling giddy with exhaustion and disgust. *Yeah, that's good. That'll work.* He'd just tell her that he'd seen the light go on and realized she was probably about to go to bed. But he hadn't seen her in twenty years so couldn't he please come in?

Yeah, that would be brilliant, all right. Maybe he should just go right ahead and ask if he could climb into bed with her, while he was at it. That was what he really wanted, wasn't it?

To take up where they'd left off, all those years ago. To finally settle the craving that had tormented him for close to forever, that had kept him awake more nights than he cared to count.

He watched the bedroom light go off again and was appalled when he actually found himself reaching for the door handle.

*Oh, Jesus fucking Christ!* This was no way for a grown man to behave. He started the engine. It was time he took a good, long, hard look at just what the hell he was doing. He needed a plan. He was not coming back here until he had one. Something rational. Something logical. Something faintly mature, with maybe a tiny scrap of dignity attached to it. He snapped on his lights and roared off into the night.

SCOUT HEARD the sound of a car engine start up on the street outside, and a moment later, heard it peel away from the curb. Fast. Way faster than usual. *Someone's in a hurry*, she thought drowsily.

The sounds stirred up memories of other times. Times she'd rather not think about right now. But oh, she wished it could be her out there, racing away through the dark, deserted streets of Oberon. Leaving this house and all its memories far behind her.

*Take me with you*, she wanted to whisper to the unknown driver. *Take me away from here.*

Instead, she did the next best thing. She focused on the dwindling sound of the engine and allowed her attention to travel as far as it could with it. Out into the darkness, into the night. The sounds carried her far, far away. Away from her lonely room and into a deep and dreamless sleep. The dreams would come later, she knew, but for right now there was only the glow of streetlights advancing and retreating around her mind. The rush of the engine was loud in her thoughts, and the remembered feel of wind in her hair and of slick leather seats beneath her, so vivid. She could practically smell the scent of the leather, as it mingled with tobacco, and wildflowers and blackberry wine.

All the sights and sounds of an imaginary road were there for her, miles and miles of it, reeling endlessly out of her memory. Carrying her into tomorrow.

---

1. This is the first (I think) of several places where the relative lack of cellphones is strikingly obvious.

# 17

Marsha and Celeste were in the teashop unpacking a shipment of whimsical mugs when Lucy called, at about eleven o'clock the next morning.

"I won't be stopping by today after all," she began, without preamble as soon as Marsha picked up the phone. "We're short handed out at the nursery. So much for my couple of days off, huh?"

"Oh, Luce, that's too bad," Marsha murmured, smiling at the purple and turquoise spotted gargoyle that scowled at her from the bottom of a pea green mug. "What happened?"

Lucy sighed gustily. "Oh, you know, nothing *terribly* worrisome. Just Robyn's gone AWOL. And all I know is, I spent most of Monday trying to convince her that Scout was most likely not gonna try and kill her while she slept. D'you think maybe I was wrong about that?"

"You want to pass that one by me again?" The next mug was even better. Sunshine yellow with orange and black striped newts.

"No, never mind." Lucy sighed again. "She was just really spooked, is all. She kept trying to tell me Scout was acting weird, and I of course thought: well, what else is new? But then Robyn didn't show up for work yesterday, or again today. And she's not answering her phone. So, what do you think, Marsh? You got any feelings about this? Think it's worth scrying over?"

*What do I think? I think this conversation is giving me a headache, that's what.* "You're saying she was spooked about Scout?" Marsha carried the phone, and two of the new mugs, over to the serving counter. "That seems kind of strange."

"Ya think? I was figuring she'd seen one too many horror flicks lately with the way she kept going on and on about axe murderers, and knives and stuff. And of course, I didn't take her seriously. But, honestly Marsha, I'm beginning to ask myself why not. I should know better, by now, than to put *anything* past that woman. Didn't I tell you this would end badly?"

"Don't you think you might be overreacting just a tiny, little bit, Lucy? And, no, I do not need to drag out my scrying bowl to determine that Scout's not a killer. However, if you really think Robyn is missing, you should call the cops."

"Oh, that's a great idea," Lucy muttered. "Let's give Nick a *legitimate* reason to see Scout. Hard pass."

"You've lost me again," Marsha said, as she filled two tea infusers: one with jasmine tea, the other with a feverfew-willow bark blend. "What does your cousin have to do with Scout?"

"Nothing! Forget I mentioned it. If Robyn's really missing, then yes, of course, you're right, I'll have to call the police. But until I know that for sure..."

"Well, you do what you think is best. I really don't think Scout's a danger to anyone. But I do have to get back to work, now. We'll talk later, okay?"

"Yep. Just, if you see Scout, ask her if she knows what's up with Robyn. Oh, and Marsha? If you *do* see her? Better watch your back. You never know. Ciao."

"Yeah. Ciao, yourself," Marsha muttered as she hung up the phone. *What the heck was that all about?* She put the infusers into the gargoyle mugs, filled both mugs with boiling water and carried them back over to the shelves, where Celeste had taken over arranging the new merchandise.

"How's Lucy?" Celeste asked as Marsha handed her the mug of jasmine tea. "Is she enjoying her vacation?"

"Nope. One of the nursery staff has gone missing so she had to take over for her. You know the one I mean. Robyn Smith." Marsha's voice was casual, but her eyes were watching Celeste carefully. She saw the shudder of surprise as it ran through her friend. *Thought so.* "Still don't want to talk about it?"

Celeste hesitated for a moment, before shaking her head. "N-no. I don't think so. But...did Lucy happen to say anything about Scout? Or maybe her dog?"

"What about the dog?" Marsha asked, nearly choking on her tea.

"Heather and Ginny ran into Scout yesterday. Apparently, she was complaining that Robyn had gone off with her dog the night before."

Marsha inhaled sharply. A slow chill was filling her chest, stealing her breath. "You're saying Scout doesn't know where Robyn is, either?"

"I don't think so." Celeste did not look up, but Marsha thought she saw her hands tremble, ever so slightly as she clutched at the mug. "I gather she was mostly upset about the dog. Heather thought she might have been a little surprised at how much she missed it."

"I see. And how did she seem, other than that? Did they say anything else?"

"I don't know," Celeste mused. "I think they talked about how she had gotten some resistance to her attempts to find out about her sister. Or something."

"Okay," Marsha said quietly. "That's it. I'm going to need you to cover for me this afternoon. As soon as everyone's back from lunch I'm going over to Scout's."

"Okay, that's it." Lucy stripped off her gloves and pushed the hair back from her forehead. "We're done, and I'm outta here."

Her brother-in-law smiled at her. "Thanks, Lucy. I owe you one."

"Yeah, that's right, Kenny." Lucy returned his smile. "You do. Try and keep that in mind tomorrow morning when you think about calling me to come in to work again. And then don't! I'll see you guys next week."

"You heading home to enjoy the solitude?" Kenny asked as he walked her out to her dark green Explorer, the twin of the one Dan drove.

"Not quite yet," she answered, pausing, with one hand on the vehicle's door handle. "I have one little stop to make first."

SCOUT HAD SPENT the better part of the day ignoring the fear, but it was getting harder to do. Last night, she'd dreamed of hitchhiking along deserted highways. Of Caroline and babies. And she'd woken up grief stricken and crying, only to discover there was still no sign of Robyn. Or her dog.

Despite the dozens of chores she'd invented to keep herself from thinking about it, by midafternoon she knew she had to do something. The first thing that came to mind was to check Robyn's room for any clues about where she might have gone. Scout had long since grown accustomed to the presence of the cats, in the last two days they'd been particularly persistent, barely leaving her alone for an instant. Now, she scarcely noticed as four of them paced along with her.

The wallpaper was new, she noticed that right off, and smiled as she did, for it was yet another flower print. The more things change, the more they stay the same, all right.

The furniture was different, too, of course, but it didn't stop the flood of memories, mostly happy ones, that rushed to fill her mind. This was the room where she and Lisa had held parties and hung out with their friends. She had gotten her first kiss on the couch that had once stood in the very place now occupied by Robyn's bed. The same couch where she and Glenn—

No. She didn't want to think about Glenn right now. Thinking about Glenn only made her think of Lisa. But, boy, it must have come as quite a shock to him, when, after months of *no*, she'd so suddenly said *yes*. She could not resist giggling, just a little, at the memory…

She hadn't been able to stop herself from giggling then, either. When it was all over, when she'd done what she'd set out to do, and Glenn, sweaty and panting, was lying beside her.

"Oh, wow," he'd breathed in tones of amazement which she had no doubt he practiced for effect. "Jesus. That—That was incredible."

Scout was sure someone else would find it flattering. Probably, a great many someone else's already had. But, even as inexperienced as she was, she'd been certain that it had to get way better than *that*.

The giggles died in her throat as she thought about it. Maybe, with someone else, with the right someone else, it would be wonderful.

But she was sincerely grateful to Glenn for the service he'd provided. And, aware that she still needed him for future subterfuge, "Mm. Yeah. I'll say," she murmured in the sincerest tones possible.

He really wasn't such a bad guy, she supposed, in retrospect. Clueless, of course, and clumsy, but so very obliging. It could have been so much worse.

One of the cats reached up and began sharpening her claws against Scout's pants leg. Scout shook her off, and then looked around the room. But she could find nothing that would explain Robyn's absence. It didn't appear as though any clothes were missing, not that she would necessarily know if they were. And there were two rental videos stacked beside the TV that were most likely overdue.

She was just pondering what her next move should be when she heard the doorbell ring.

Glenn pushed his way past her as soon as she opened the door. "Let me in, Scout," he said, although, by the time he said it, he was already inside. His manner annoyed her, and she would have told him no, except she was caught off guard, and he was in the house before she could think of a reason to refuse. "We need to talk."

*Again?* "Why? What's up?" She crossed her arms and glared angrily at him, but then quickly realized that she had already lost his attention.

She turned her head to follow his gaze, only mildly surprised to find seven of the cats, including the large beige tomcat who had bitten her two days before, ranged along the staircase, watching Glenn intently.

"Jeez. How many of them do you have?" he said, almost choking on the words. There was no mistaking the discomfort in his voice.

"Oh, lots," she answered vaguely, sensing a possible advantage. "I haven't really counted. But there's more around here somewhere. Would you like me to call them?"

He shook his head. "No, that's all right," he answered quickly. "I don't really like cats. My mother always said they were evil."

"Evil, huh? Well, then, I guess, whatever you want to talk to me about, we'll just have to do it over the phone. I wouldn't want you to stay if you're uncomfortable. And since I can't get rid of them..."

"No," Glenn repeated, pulling his attention away from the cats with obvious difficulty, and focusing on Scout. The look on his face wavered between reluctance and determination. "It's too late for the phone. It's too late for a lot of things. I tried to tell you the other night, but you wouldn't listen." He paused and looked at her sorrowfully. "I don't want to hurt you, Scout," he said, and she didn't doubt his sincerity, but still her mind supplied the missing *but.*

Was Glenn threatening her? And with what, exactly? The icy tremors cascading down her spine had nothing at all to do with the ugly, menacing growl coming from the tomcat's throat. Before she could frame a response, the door behind her was pushed open once more.

"Oh, good. You're home," Marsha said as she let herself into the hallway. "We need to talk."

Scout noted her unexpectedly grim expression with surprise. "Do we? Okay, and how do *you* feel about cats?"

"Cats? Love 'em, why? Oh!" Marsha's eyebrows rose practically into her hairline as she took in the implacable stares of seven crouching felines. "Oh, my goodness," she breathed in tones of uncertainty, that were only slightly less uncomfortable than Glenn's.

Scout breathed her first deep breath since answering the door, she felt giddy with relief. One thing she knew for sure. Whatever else happened, she was keeping these cats. Every last, blessed one of them.

"I'm going to the kitchen to get a drink, now," she addressed her guests. "You guys can stay out here with the cats, if you want. Or," she added, wickedly, as she noticed that the cats appeared ready to follow her, "I guess we can all go."

Once in the kitchen, Scout looked around uncertainly. What did she want to drink anyway? She pulled open the refrigerator, but that didn't spark any thoughts. "Anybody want something?" she asked over her shoulder, hoping one of the others might give her an idea. Marsha walked over and looked into the refrigerator as well.

"Like what, exactly? There's nothing here," she pointed out.

Rather unnecessarily, Scout thought, frowning. "Well, there's no need to be rude about it."

"Do you have any tea?"

Scout shrugged. "Yeah. Sure. I mean, I think we do. Somewhere. Help yourself. Just make sure the fire's lit, okay? I nearly blew myself up the other day."

She leaned back against the island counter, watching as Marsha went about making tea. *That's what this kitchen's been missing. Someone with a domestic flair. Someone who enjoys cooking and is good at it. Someone who can make tea, or coffee, without blowing themselves to pieces.*

"Oh, and that reminds me. Forget about your prediction that I wasn't likely to have any more accidents, or that nothing else weird was gonna happen to me. I've had nothing *but* weird all damn week. I cut my foot this morning stepping on glass from a broken window in the basement. Oh, and on the way to doing that, I nearly fell down the basement stairs, because apparently there's a step missing. You'd think Robyn might have thought to mention that little detail, wouldn't you? And then, like I said, there was the gas."

Marsha's eyebrows rose in surprise. Scout smiled at her friend's startled reaction. "That time, like I already told Glenn, it was the cats who saved me. A little less weird than voices, I'll grant you, but still too damn strange for me."

"Yeah. For me, too," Marsha looked again at the cats, who had reestablished themselves in the kitchen. "And I have to say, they do seem unusually protective."

Glenn snorted. "That's nonsense," he said, angrily.

Scout sighed. Glenn, clueless and amiable, was hard enough to take. Pissy and moaning, he went way beyond anything she felt like handling. Especially today. "Okay, Glenn. If you don't want anything to drink, why don't you tell me what you want to talk to me about?" *And then, you can leave.*

Marsha chuckled. Scout glanced at her sharply, and then turned her attention back to Glenn. "Well?" she prompted.

He was frowning, seemingly irresolute, still bothered by the cats, as far as she could tell. "It's private."

"Oh, give me a break," she said wearily. "What could we have to talk about that's secret? And, apparently, Marsha knows everything, anyway." But she saw the strained expression on his face and relented. "All right. Fine. We'll talk later. Marsha, you're up next. What can I do for *you*?"

"I just want to know what's going on with Robyn," Marsha answered promptly. "She's missed two days of work, and on Monday she told Lucy some nonsense about being afraid of you."

It was Scout's turn to be surprised. "Robyn's afraid of *me*? Why? What did I do now?"

"Well, that's the question, isn't it?" Marsha said gently. "All I know is what Lucy told me. She said she spent most of Monday telling her that you weren't going to come after her with a knife, or an axe or something. Which, if you knew Robyn very well, you'd know is not the kind of thing you normally hear from her. So...what *did* you do to her?"

Surprise turned to shock. *A knife or an axe? How is this possible?* "Damned if I know. Are you sure you don't have it backwards? Maybe it was Lucy who talked her into the idea in the first place?"

Marsha's shoulders sagged. "So, you really don't know where she is?"

"No. I was just in her room, trying to find anything that would tell me where she might have gone Monday night. That was the last time I saw her."

"Find anything?" Marsha asked hopefully.

"No." An angry restlessness nagged at Scout. "You know, I think I'd like to find out where Lucy is, too. I think *we* need to talk."

"What a coincidence. That's just what I was thinking, myself," said a voice from the doorway. Turning around, Scout was not surprised to see Lucy standing there, with a sardonic grin on her face.

A grin Scout did *not* feel like returning. "Gee, Lucy, good to see you. Why don't you let yourself in?"


MARSHA SIGHED. *They're going to be difficult.* She could tell that they were in for another nasty scene. Unfortunately, both Lucy and Scout seemed more interested in facing off with each other than in dealing with the disturbing fact of Robyn's disappearance.

*There's no way around it.* Much as Lucy didn't seem to like the idea, it was time to call the police. So, Marsha slipped back into the hall, unnoticed by the others, and put in the call.

# 18

*L*ucy and Scout were still glaring at each other when Marsha returned to the kitchen a few minutes later. The tension between them was so thick that even Glenn seemed affected by it; he skulked in the corner as though he were trying to blend into the woodwork.

"Oh, for Christ's sake, you guys! Give it a rest, can't you?" Marsha muttered angrily. "Lucy, why don't you go and see if you can find anything useful in Robyn's room."

"Good idea." Lucy looked challengingly at Scout, as if daring her to refuse. "Why don't I?"

Scout merely shrugged. "Why ask me? Mi casa es su casa, apparently. I couldn't find anything there. But then, I don't know her as well as you obviously do." She watched as Lucy disappeared down the hallway, then shook her head. "Fuck this. I need a smoke."

"Listen, Scout," Marsha said, as she followed her into the living room. "I think you should know that I called the police."

"You did what?" Scout and Glenn both spoke at once.

"Well, someone had to," Marsha replied, a little defensively. "Because that's what you do when someone goes missing."

Scout sank into one of the armchairs, her desire for a cigarette apparently extinguished. "I was kind of hoping she had just gone off with a boyfriend or something for a few days. But I guess you don't think that's what happened, huh?"

"No," Marsha said sadly. "I don't think any of us really think that. Do you?[1]" She walked over to the big front window, pushed the curtains aside, and looked out at the street. Her eyes widened. "Oh, wow. That was fast. It looks like Nick's here already."


"WHAT?" Scout was on her feet in an instant, heart pounding. *Surely, she hadn't said—* Successive waves of hope and panic rippled through her. She took a few steps forward, and then froze as she heard a knock on the open front door, followed, an instant later, by a voice. A voice she remembered entirely too well.

*Oh, no. Oh, hell no. Oh, no, no, no, no, no! I should have known. I should have guessed!*

This was Oberon, after all. Capital of Coincidences. It would just have to be Nick, wouldn't it? They couldn't possibly have sent someone else? Anyone else? Just this once? She should have seen it coming the minute Marsha mentioned the police.

And then she should have gotten herself the hell out of town. Again.

"We're in here," Scout heard Marsha call as the room began a slow, painful spin around her. She felt herself blushing with a fierceness she thought she'd left behind in puberty. All at once it seemed that blushing was just about the only action her body was capable of. She couldn't breathe right. Couldn't speak, couldn't turn, couldn't raise her eyes to his face. She could barely even hear his footsteps, over the loud, frightened beating of her heart.

She was only dimly aware of Marsha's eyes widening in surprise once more, as she swayed away from her. Was only dimly aware of reaching out a visibly shaking hand to grasp the back of a chair for support. But the chair swam abruptly out of sight.

"Watch out, she's fainting!" she heard Marsha say. And then she did.

. . .

NICK WASN'T the one standing the closest to her, but he moved the fastest. He caught her just as her eyes rolled back and her knees gave way. And it wasn't her weight that made him stagger and his breath to go, or that caused the uneven coloring he knew the others could probably see in his face. It was having her back in his arms again, after all this time.

Her head lay against his chest. He stared at her, still not quite believing it was true, as he tried to still his breathing. He didn't even realize how tightly he was holding her until the red-haired woman smiled at him, surprise and quiet amusement glimmering in her eyes.

"You know, I think maybe you'd both breathe a little easier if you just put her down on the couch," she suggested, one eyebrow lifted wryly.

And Nick wasn't at all surprised, when he'd pivoted to do just that, to see his cousin Lucy standing in the doorway, fury writ on every feature of her face.

"Oh, hell no." Lucy stamped her foot in frustration. "Nick! What are *you* doing here?"

Nick smiled, a little self-consciously. "Well hey, cuz. Good to see you, too." He put Jen down carefully on the couch. *No. Not Jen. Gotta call her Scout, now.* Straightening up, he flashed another sardonic grin at Lucy.

"I'm here because someone called for the police. Something about a missing person? I'm guessing you're all a little old to be playing pranks. Although," He looked around at the various familiar faces, and shrugged. "I don't suppose I should put anything past this particular group."

The red-haired woman chuckled appreciatively. He recognized her now. Lucy's friend Marsha. Of course.

"A fair assessment," Marsha agreed. "But I'm afraid it's no prank."

"Damn it, Marsha. I told you we did *not* need to call the police," Lucy grumbled angrily.

Nick wondered if her friend understood what Lucy might be

annoyed about. Or whether Lucy had already guessed that when the call had come in, and he recognized the address, he had insisted on answering it himself.

"Of course, we did," Marsha retorted. "What are the police for, if not to find missing persons?"

"Well, we do have a few other areas of interest," Nick felt obliged to point out, his eyes involuntarily straying back to the couch.

"I know what you're thinking Nick," snapped Lucy. "And you can just forget it."

"Who's missing?" he asked, directing the question toward Marsha. Sometimes the best way to handle Lucy was to simply ignore her.

"One of the students who's been living here." Marsha's voice was calm and matter of fact. "Her name is Robyn Smith. She's nineteen years old. Oh, and she works out at Cavanaugh's with Lucy. They haven't seen her there since Monday."

"Here." Lucy thrust some photos and an address book into his hand. "Maybe someone in her book knows where she is. That's her." She pointed to one of the pictures. "And that's the dog."

"Uh, thanks. Yeah, I recognize her. But what do I need a picture of her dog for?"

"Oh, it's not *her* dog." Marsha chuckled. "It sort of belongs to Scout, here. But we think Robyn might have been walking the dog when she disappeared. It's missing too. Or is that too much like a cat stuck in a tree, do you think? Should we have called the Fire Department, also?"

Scout groaned. One look told Nick that she was regaining consciousness. Once again, he was quicker than the others.

Ignoring Lucy's glare, and the amused smirk on Marsha's face he bent over the couch and called the name he must now get used to using. "Scout? You back with us?"

NICK'S VOICE came from someplace in the darkness above her. Scout shivered in response. She was lying on the couch, she realized, and

Nick was leaning over her. *So close. Too close. Not close enough.* She didn't even have to open her eyes to know exactly where he was. It was as if he were taking up all the space, all the oxygen, all the energy in the room.

She groaned again and covered her face with her hands in an attempt to hide the intense irritation she felt within herself. She was frantic to get away from him, to back up, back away, get off of the couch – or even out of the room, altogether.

*I should have never come back here. What was I thinking?*

She wanted to scream. She wanted to push him away. And at the same time, despite her sudden inability to breathe, she wanted nothing more than to grab hold of him and pull him down on top of her, to feel his body against her own, his weight crushing her beneath him. *Nick.*

"I'm fine," Scout muttered thickly, as another shudder ran through her.

*God damn it*, she screamed silently at herself. *Get a grip!* What the hell was she doing, acting like some Victorian heroine? Fainting? Having trouble breathing? Feeling nauseous? Jeez, could this possibly get any *more* embarrassing?

*But, oh, God, who would have guessed he would still be wearing the same cologne?*

She took a deep, greedy breath and then another, thinking somewhat sheepishly of the bottle of scent that she had bought once, many years ago, in a moment of great weakness. All by itself it had the power to bring back hazy, bittersweet memories, and fuel even sweeter fantasies of what might have been, what should have been. *Oh, if only things could have been different!*

But the scent coming to her now, mixed with the all-but-forgotten fragrances of his hair and his skin and his breath, was infinitely more devastating. It brought everything to life at once. All her memories, alive and vivid. All the fantasies she had cherished over twenty, long, lonely years, more alluring, more compelling than imagination alone had ever made them.

"Scout? You in there?"

"Mm?" Reining in her emotions, she pushed herself upright. "No. I mean, yes. Yes, I'm fine."

And maybe she would be. It had been a long time, after all. He could have changed...enough. She opened her eyes and cautiously looked up into his face. *Damn. Not enough. Not even close.*

He was as handsome as he'd ever been. The same full lips. That strong, straight nose. If anything, the years had only added to the rugged masculine beauty that still haunted her dreams. And they'd done nothing whatever to dim the luster of those beautiful eyes. Delicious, caramel-colored eyes that had always been able to melt her with a glance. Except that...well here was a difference. Twenty years ago they hadn't ever looked at her with so coldly disinterested a gaze.

It did the trick though. She felt her own eyes narrow as she returned Nick's icy stare. She was fully conscious, now.

"I'm fine, damn it. Just give me some space, huh?"

"All right, all right. Take it easy," Nick answered, not moving an inch.

"I said—" she began, but his jaw was clenched, and he was looking so suddenly fierce that she couldn't help but look away. *Another mistake.* His body was a little heavier, a little more powerful than she had remembered it. Solid and strong. *And, if he were to lean just a little closer...*

Her tongue slipped nervously over her lips. Damn, but her mouth was dry. She'd just fainted, hadn't she? You'd think someone would have thought to offer her a drink. Water. Or...anything really, just as long as it was wet.

Pulling her mind away from thoughts of Nick's mouth on hers, she forced herself to meet his eyes again. This time, it was his gaze that faltered. She felt him take a long, deep breath and let it out again, very slowly, before speaking.

"Think you could tell me what this is all about?" His voice was dangerously soft; she felt her heart speed up again. He nodded toward the others. "I'm not sure I'm getting a clear picture from your friends here."

"Robyn. My, my housemate. I'm not... I don't know where she is," she heard herself stammer. "I th-think something's m-maybe happened to her."

"Something, huh? Okay. Like what for example?" He backed off a little then, just far enough to sit on the edge of the coffee table, his knees only inches from her elbow.

Scout shrugged and tried again for control. "Well, that's the thing, I don't know. An accident, maybe?"

"An accident? You mean like…a car accident? They just said she was missing. What kind of accident do you think she might have had?"

"I don't…know." Scout was momentarily diverted. *Another accident? That would be a little hard to swallow, wouldn't it?* "Okay, maybe not an accident. But something had to have happened to her."

"Because?"

"Because she's missing, of course!" She shot him an exasperated glance. *How hard is this to comprehend?* "Two nights ago, she took my dog out for a walk. Or maybe it wasn't a walk. She might have said something about going out somewhere. I don't remember, exactly. It was pretty late, and I was… preoccupied. All I know was they were still here when I went to bed. But then when I got up next morning they were still gone. I haven't seen either of them since."

"And she hasn't shown up for work at the nursery either yesterday or today, like we already told you." Lucy cut in.

"How did she seem – When did you say you last saw her? Monday night?"

"Yeah, Monday. I don't know. Fine, I guess. I wasn't really paying attention. I uh, had some other things on my mind."

"Well, she definitely was *not* fine Monday morning," Lucy interrupted again. "Although, what I'm thinking now is, maybe she just decided to find another place to live, and she's just been too busy to call in. She was pretty upset. And she'd probably figure I'd understand if she missed work because of it. That is," she paused to glare at Scout. "If you're *sure* nothing else happened Monday night."

Scout glared back. "I said I was, didn't I?"

"Scout was with me on Monday," Glenn cut in, much to Scout's irritation.

Nick glanced at him briefly, his eyes narrowing. "What exactly is your role in all of this?"

"I'm acting as Ms. Patterson's attorney. And, as such, I don't think she should be answering any more questions right now."

Scout shuddered at the fury that blazed in Nick's eyes when he turned back to look at her. "Is that so?"

Had he recognized Glenn? No, that wasn't possible. As far as she knew, they'd never met. And even if he did recognize him, what could it possibly matter, after all this time? What did any of it matter?

She took a deep breath. "Glenn is helping me sort some things out with my stepmother's will. And I don't have any problem answering your questions."

*Boy, isn't that the understatement of the century!* She knew she was blushing, and she didn't dare meet Lucy's gaze. *How ironic is this?* She and Nick had picked things up right where they'd been forced to leave off the very last time they saw each other—with him asking questions, and her giving answers, and both of them pretending to be strangers. *Doesn't life just suck?*

What would happen right now, she wondered, if she dropped the pretense? If she said hello, and asked him how he'd been; how would he react?

Given the look in his eyes, probably not the way she hoped he would.

She sighed. "Glenn and I had dinner Monday night—that's all. Then, when I got home, Robyn was getting ready to go out. She asked if she could take the dog with her and I said yes, and that's all I can tell you." She gazed at Nick defiantly. "Why are you so interested, anyway? You *can't* think my dinner has any bearing on Robyn's being gone?"

"Just trying to get the facts straight." He shrugged, nonchalantly. "If it doesn't have anything to do with what happened to your friend, it makes no difference to me what you did Monday—or any other day, for that matter."

"No, I can't imagine any reason why it would," Scout answered, stung once again by his indifference.

"Of course, it doesn't!" Lucy snapped. "I don't know why you're wasting your time like this Nick. Can't you just go back to the station now and put out a bulletin, or file a missing person report or something?"

In the sudden silence that followed Lucy's outburst a phone rang.

"Oops. That's me." Marsha grabbed her bag. "Sorry. I'll uh, I'll just take it in the other room."


NICK SCOWLED AT HIS COUSIN. "I don't need you to tell me how to do my job, Lucy. Don't you have someplace else you need to be?"

"No. Don't you?"

"Yes, as a matter of fact." He got to his feet. His next words were addressed to Scout, although he didn't meet her eyes. "I'm going to leave now. But I'll be in touch if I find out anything—or if I need to ask you more questions." He gave Lucy another wry grin as he left. "Bye cuz. Try to stay out of trouble."

"Oh, and you're a fine one to give advice, aren't you?" Lucy grumbled, shooting him a troubled look.

Nick chuckled in response, and swaggered from the room, pointedly taking no notice of Glenn, who had shrunk back against the wall.

Marsha was speaking into her cell phone as he passed through the front hall. "Calm down Celeste. What are you talking about? *Murder? Here?* No, honey. Everybody here is fine." She looked up and met Nick's eyes. He raised his brows in a quizzical expression but didn't pause.

"Somebody whose name begins with a G?" he heard her say, just before the door closed behind him. "Is that a first name or a last name? No, damn it Celeste, I know a lot of people whose names begin with G. What? Well, you for example. Yeah, well..."

.  .  .

MARSHA'S EYES slid over the painting that hung next to the doorway. Lisa and Scout, as painted by Scout's father, smiled back at her in dreamy serenity. Jeez, she'd forgotten how much alike in looks the two girls had been, almost as if they actually had been related. Lisa had been the more classically beautiful, but Scout had always had a sort of untamed, exotic quality that the artist had captured perfectly. In the corner of the painting, she could just make out the signature. *Gil Patterson.* Great. Just fabulous. "I'm telling you Celeste; we've got G's coming out of the woodwork around here."

But enough was enough. Celeste's agitation poured through the phone until Marsha thought her head might explode from the pressure. She took a deep breath. "Okay, Celeste, I got it. And as soon as I make sure that Scout is okay, I'll leave. I promise. And then tomorrow we can— What?" she broke off when Celeste abruptly segued into a new topic. *Paige Delaney.* What was the reporter up to, nosing around her shop? Nothing good, that much was certain.

"Look, there's no sense in worrying about it now, all right? So, just close up and go on home. We can talk about it tomorrow."

Celeste's frustrated sigh vibrated in her ear. "You're forgetting. I have tomorrow off."

Oops. Marsha sighed as well and rubbed her temple. Right. She should have remembered that. "Well, Friday morning then. Now, don't worry. I'll take care of everything."

Marsha hung up the phone and stared at it distractedly. It wasn't like Celeste to get this worked up. It especially wasn't like Celeste to let down her guard in front of Marsha like that. She knew how hard it was for her to screen out other people's emotions. Damnit. She needed a drink and some mindless entertainment. She needed to calm herself down. They were on the brink of disaster; she could feel it. And she was useless to anyone like this.

A sudden motion made her turn. Glenn was staring at her curiously. A shudder ran through her. She hadn't even felt him come up. She forced a smile and rolled her eyes. "Everyone's a psychic." she joked.

"I think we should leave." Glenn said quietly. "All of us. Scout doesn't seem to need anything else now. Except maybe to rest. I think we should—"

*You should go now,* Marsha thought, trying to focus on his aura. It looked awful. She wondered if he was sick. *Go. Now,* she thought again, with more force than before.

She tried the smile again, too. This time, putting a little more reassurance into it. "I'm sure she's fine. Really. Nothing to worry about."

She could feel his thoughts, like a dark, encroaching cloud, attempting to wend their way into her mind, but she closed herself off to them. She had enough to think about at the moment, she couldn't take on his pain, too.

"That...person on the phone with you just now. Were they with the police? I thought you said something about a murder?"

Had he been listening to the whole conversation? Marsha shook her head. "Oh, no. It was just my partner." She shrugged. "Celeste tends to get a little carried away, sometimes. She did a reading at the festival this weekend that still has her a little upset, is all."

Glenn frowned uncertainly. "At the festival? But that cop, the one who was just here—"

"Nick?" Marsha smiled, again. "He's Lucy's cousin, you know. He's maybe a little overprotective at times, but—"

"He's dangerous," Glenn whispered, still oozing darkness, like a black, bitter mist. "He threatens people."

*Not now!* Marsha pushed the thoughts away once more. "Well, I'm sure he can appear pretty intimidating when he wants to be, but I'd guess that, most of the time, his bark is worse than his bite." *Go home. Leave. Now.*

"He's dangerous." Glenn repeated, more firmly, as he turned to go. "I have to go now. I need to think."

Marsha shook her head as she watched him leave. Was he always this weird? What the hell had they all seen in him, back in high school?

Back in the living room Scout was still lying on the couch with her eyes closed, and Lucy was still sitting across the room glaring at her. Marsha took a look at the two of them and quickly reached a decision.

"Okay," she announced briskly. "It's getting late and there's nothing else we can do about Robyn today, and Scout, you have nothing in the house to eat. So, what I think is...the three of us should go out to dinner. Make a night of it."

"Well, count me out of that," Lucy said, folding her arms across her chest, and glaring at her now, too.

But Marsha could handle Lucy. "No, I won't either. I was thinking of going to that Brewery place, out on the coast. You know the one I mean. And you're the only one I know who remembers exactly where the turn off is. Besides, you know my night vision is terrible, and even if Scout had her car, she's too banged up to drive that distance. So, you have to come. You two are both adults, and I'm sure you can manage to be civil to each other for one night. Maybe a couple of beers will help. Now, let's go." She smiled at them both. "It'll be fun."

---

1. An address book. How cute is that?

# 19

*N*ick slammed his car into gear and sped off down the street. For as far back as he could remember, the only thing that seemed to help him let off steam, or deal with any of the bad things life threw at him, was speed. Before it was cars, it had been dirt bikes, bicycles, skateboards – the pattern went all the way back to one of the most vivid of his early memories:

*Tears had blurred his vision as he raced down the driveway on his tricycle. His hands clutched the handles as if they were the only things solid in the whole world. His feet pushed the pedals harder, faster. Down the driveway and around and around the block he sped for hours that day.*

*The day they told him his father was dead...*

There wasn't really any place he needed to get to right now. He'd go back to his office later and see what he could learn about the missing woman. But he hadn't been lying when he said that he had to leave. He couldn't have stayed in that room any longer. He couldn't have stayed and not said or done something he would regret.

He turned away from town, headed for the narrow, winding highway that stretched along the coast. With its unexpected dips and rises, its relentless, irregular curves, and its unobstructed view – straight out and down – of the endless, blue Pacific, it was the kind of road that made tourists quail. But Nick had lived all his life in Oberon and these roads held no terror for him. The real terror in his life was in that house he had just run away from.

He'd put his lights on, and now, all along the road in front of him, slowly moving cars pulled over to the side to let him pass. He felt a small flare of amusement. This had to be one of his favorite job perks. Everybody falling all over themselves to get out of the cop's way. He stomped down harder on the gas as he fished around in the side pocket for the pack of cigarettes he'd remembered leaving there after the last time he'd quit.

*Kate missed this one*. He felt a tiny stab of guilt as he punched the cigarette lighter in. His daughter hated his smoking and had already convinced him to quit three times. But Kate was vacationing with her mother. And Scout was back in town. And this was no time to be worried about something as innocuous as tobacco. His other addiction had always been far more hazardous to his health.

Nick knew trouble when it stared him in the face. Growing up, he'd been nothing *but* trouble. He'd been an almost constant source of worry for his mother, his aunt, his uncle, the sisters at St. Dominic elementary school, and later for the brothers at Navarre County Catholic High School. He had barely avoided expulsion countless times solely—and he had this on the best authority—due to the grace of God. Not that he'd ever done anything that was *too* illegal, but he liked trouble and he liked to fight, and he never could resist the chance to pull a prank or take a dare.

By the time he was fourteen, he was on a first name basis with most of the cops in town. By the time he was seventeen, he had decided that, seeing as he didn't seem able to beat them, he might as well try and join them, instead.

Power, control, the opportunity to get a little action now and then, and the chance to drive real fast whenever he wanted – who could ask for anything more from a job?

He hadn't really changed all that much from when he was a kid. Although he knew he had somehow managed to convince most of the people who were close to him that he had. It was better that way.

Simpler. Less worrying for the people he cared about. But the truth was, he had always liked trouble, and he still did. Which is why his obsession with Scout made perfect sense. She was trouble personified...

He'd been just twenty-two, that misty April evening, when she materialized at the side of the road. A tall, leggy hitchhiker, wreathed in fog, with a guitar and a backpack thrown over her shoulders. When he stopped, she threw open the door, tossed her bags in the back without a word, and slid into the seat next to him. All with a fluid, graceful motion, that was mind-blowing in its sexiness.

"Whew! Thanks!" she said, exhaling a deep, gusty breath as she turned to face him.

And then she smiled.

It was no ordinary smile. It was a grin that started at her mouth in a spark of mischief and traveled over her face until it hit her eyes and ignited twin flares of such merry devilment that he knew, beyond any shadow of a doubt, that he'd just met his match. Her gaze swept the car's interior, and then back to his face. *"Oh, hey,"* she breathed in tones of awe. *"Nice car!"*

Nick felt as though choirs of angels had just launched into the Hallelujah Chorus. He could think of no better response than to return her grin with one of his own, put the car in gear and spin out – *fast*. She let out a whoop of delight and bummed a cigarette from his pack on the dash without even asking. They tore off into the growing dark in companionable silence until his brain dredged up something coherent to say to her.

"So, uh, where are you going?" he asked with much originality.

Mischief twinkled in her eyes. "Well, I was on my way home from school, but I'm not actually in a hurry to get there, or anything. So...I don't know?"

"You're local?" Nick sent a brief prayer of thanks to whatever divine agency had sent her to him. "That's good."

He thought fast. Oberon Community College was only a mile or so beyond where he had picked her up. She had to be a student there. And the guitar— "Are you a music major?"

"No, not really. I'll probably major in art."

"Oh, a sophomore, huh?"

"Yeah. How'd you know?" She seemed mildly disappointed.

"Well, you'd have already picked your major if you were a junior, and the Community College is only two years anyway, so…"

"Oh! Right." She flashed him another blinding smile. "Exactly. Next year I'll probably transfer to State. That is, if I'm still around."

"Oh? You're thinking of leaving town?"

"No. I don't know. Maybe. I get restless sometimes."

"I know what you mean. Hey, maybe you know my cousin. He's at Community, too."

"I don't think so," she answered, a little too quickly. And then she hesitated. "I mean, I don't really know that many people there. What's your cousin's name?"

"Joey Greco."

She inhaled on some smoke and began to cough. It was several seconds before she could answer. "But that— Wait. Joey Greco is your *cousin?*" she gasped at last, and then started coughing again.

"Yeah. Are you okay? D'you know him?"

"I, uh…yeah? I mean, maybe? I think I might've heard of him." She giggled suddenly. "I think maybe he and I have some friends in common."

What could she possibly have heard about Joey, to make her giggle with such wicked, breathless delight, Nick wondered. His cousin's reputation was almost the polar opposite of his own – good tempered, well behaved, popular with the right kind of people, not given to erratic behavior, steady and hardworking.

Nick shot her a quick, sideways glance. She was staring straight ahead, seemingly lost in thought, a small, blissful smile glimmering across her face. He felt his heart sink.

Despite the two-year age difference and a lifetime of having the younger man held up as a role model, Nick had always counted Joey as one of his best friends, the closest thing he would ever have to a brother. He wondered how jealousy would change that?

"He's got a…a sister, doesn't he?" the girl asked next with wide-eyed candor. "Your cousin, I mean. Over at that girl's high school, Our Lady of the Angels, isn't it?"

"Yeah, that's right. My cousin Lucy."

"I have a...an ex-step-cousin, sort of, who goes there. I think she might know her."

"Oh yeah? So, your cousin knows my cousin, huh? Small world."

"Yes, isn't it? Absolutely unbelievable," she said, as she giggled again.

She told him her name was Jen. It was a popular name. A generic, nonspecific name. His cousin, when asked, could think of at least half a dozen girls called Jennifer, Jeni, Jenna or Jen from school. Although none, Nick was relieved to note, in whom he seemed to have more than a casual interest. The fact that she hadn't mentioned a last name didn't even occur to him until much later. Even then, it didn't strike him as unusual. He hadn't told her his last name, either.
1

Afterwards, he had actually resisted asking her for it. He kind of liked the aura of mystery that clung to her, especially since he half sensed that she cultivated it to intrigue him.

Looking back, Nick could see that he had been a damned idiot not to have guessed the truth that very first night. He had been completely taken in by the ridiculous stories she told him. The nameless friends and relations who just happened to have mentioned his cousins to her. Her vague plans for the future. The pathologically over-protective parents who wouldn't let her date, or even receive phone calls. The theft of her car, which had necessitated her hitching a ride home in the first place.

On some level, he knew he simply hadn't wanted to see the truth. His instincts must have been screaming warnings, but he'd suppressed every one.

He was so busy thanking his lucky stars that he'd found her, that he didn't even spare a thought to wonder why, when he'd never seen her before, he was suddenly running into her everywhere he went. After the third time he'd run across her hitching a ride somewhere, he'd stopped to lecture her about the dangers. He was in his squad car at the time. His partner at the time, Dave, listened to the exchange in disbelief…

"Do you have any idea how much trouble you could get yourself into doing this?" Nick asked, as she smiled at him from the curb, totally unrepentant, her arms crossed casually just below her breasts. He tried not to pay too much attention to the subtle sway of her hips as she rocked slowly from foot to foot.

"Yeah. But, uh, you know, how else am I supposed to meet guys?" Her eyes, half hidden beneath long lashes, gleamed wickedly.

*Cute look.* But he was being serious. And he didn't much like the idea of her trying to meet guys, anyway; especially not like that. He frowned. "That's exactly what I'm talking about, Jen. Trust me, the kind of guy you're likely to run into that way could be very bad news."

"I guess you're right." She bit her lip, looking suddenly troubled. "I met *you* that way, didn't I?"

"Well, but," he broke off, somewhat startled, himself. "That was different. You just got lucky."

"Hmm." The corner of her mouth kicked up. She narrowed her eyes. "I'm pretty sure that's supposed to be *my* line."

"Is it?"

"Could be," she answered softly, as her smile grew slowly wider. Her voice sent warm tremors running all through him. "Are you feeling lucky, Nick?"

"Oh, yeah. I'm feeling very lucky. C'mon, hop in. I'll give you a ride."

"Uhh…I don't know if that's such a good idea." She glanced again at Dave and frowned. "Maybe some other time."

"Jesus. Are you out of your fuckin' mind?" Dave hissed. "Look at her, Nick. That girl is *jailbait*."

"The hell I am." Jen's head reared back, and she planted her fists on her hips, and all Nick could think about for a few moments was the way her crop top hugged her midriff as she stood on the sidewalk, taking deep, angry breaths.

"Oh yeah?" Dave leaned across him to challenge her. "So, tell me kid, just how old—"

"Okay! Enough," Nick interrupted, feeling suddenly irritated. Feeling suddenly, a whole lot less lucky, as well. "C'mon, Jen, get in the car. Where're you going, anyway?"

She hesitated for almost a minute, and then she smiled again, slow, and sensuous, looking deep into his eyes, as if they were the only two people in the whole world. "I wasn't *actually* going anywhere," she answered, cocking her head to one side. "I was just kind of, you know, hoping I'd run into you again."

He returned the smile. "Well, we could *actually* arrange to meet each other somewhere, you know. I'm thinking it might a whole lot be safer for you." What he was really thinking was that it might be a whole lot more private, as well.

She lifted one shoulder in a small shrug. "'kay."

"So. What are you doing tonight?"

"Nothing I can't get out of," she smiled in answer.

"How's the bowling alley sound? About seven, seven thirty?"

"You want to go bowling?" she asked, sounding about equal parts surprised and doubtful.

"No." It was his turn to smile, and then smile wider, as he watched awareness flood her face with color.

"Oh. Okay, uh, sure."

"Good. I'll see you then. Sure you don't want a ride now?"

She sneaked another look at Dave and rolled her eyes. "Oh, yeah, I'm sure. I'll see you later, Nick."


THE SUN WAS low in the sky when Nick pulled into the parking lot of the Buena Vista Bar and Grill. The current owners had only had it for about five years, but the restaurant itself had been there for decades. Its location made it a favorite with generations of surfers and beach goers. He'd been coming here since he was a kid, although back then the place was known as the Shake Shack, [2] and had sold mostly health food – date shakes, wheat grass, homemade yogurt and granola, and fresh juices.

Now, the place was a glorified diner. He got himself a sandwich and coffee and a fresh pack of cigarettes –marveling, as he did every time he started smoking again, at how much the prices had gone up since he'd quit. He took his purchases and sat outside on the bluff. He loved the wild beauty of the coast and the sagey, resinous fragrance of the chaparral. He'd come out here to find solace during all the most painful times of his life.

After he'd found out about Scout, and again when his marriage was breaking up, he had practically lived here. Most of what little sleep he got during those periods was in the front seat of his car.

God, she was something else though. Even now, even half-unconscious with bruises on her face, she had damn near taken his breath away. It had always been the little things that had gotten to him, anyway. The purr in her voice. The flash of fire in her eyes.

Or that smile. Beginning at one corner of her mouth and sliding, ever so slowly across her face.

Even the way she moved, like some sort of wildcat, nothing tame or domesticated about her. A part of him had been hoping she'd lost that. That she'd somehow outgrown the ability to drive him out of his mind with just one glance. But she was still as beautiful as ever. And even though she hadn't smiled at him once, and the flashes he'd seen, deep within her hazel eyes, had reminded him more of ice, this time, than fire, she'd still made his head spin.

Of course, there were differences. She'd filled out a little since he'd seen her last. She most definitely was not a kid anymore. But the new fullness of her breasts and hips didn't exactly do anything to diminish her appeal.

She looked better than ever, damn it. And the effort he'd had to make this afternoon to keep himself from finding out exactly how much she'd changed, had been almost enough to slay him. Sitting across from her, as she'd lain there on that couch, he had barely been able to contain the urge to jump her.

But whether he wanted to kiss her or kill her, he just didn't know.

Things sure had been simpler twenty years ago. Back then, he'd known *exactly* what he'd wanted to do with her.

Given her age and apparent willingness, he supposed it was a damn good thing she'd left town when she had. But try telling that to his body, which still remembered every detail of that last afternoon they'd had together...

He was supposed to have been working, instead he'd talked Dave into dropping him off at his apartment. She was waiting for him when he got there, wearing jeans, and a loose, flannel shirt so soft and thin that he could feel the heat of her skin right through it.

His need for her had pulsed in him, like a drug through his veins, until even the tips of his fingers were on fire with it. Until just the buttery smoothness of the buttons as they slipped, one by one, from their holes for him, was excruciatingly erotic.

By the time Dave had come back to tell him to drop whatever it was he was doing and get his ass in the car, she hadn't been wearing anything at all.

Nick groaned and dropped his head into his hands. It was ridiculous be feeling this way after all this time. But, oh God, he'd wanted her. And he'd come so close to having her. He could see her still in his mind's eye – the same image that had tormented him for twenty years – lovely and vulnerable and naked. Looking up at him with such heat in her eyes that it had taken every bit of will power he possessed to pull himself away from her.

He hadn't expected her to still be there when he got back, shaken, and deathly cold, fresh from his very first homicide case; and of course, she wasn't. But he hadn't been worried. He could be patient, for a while longer. She was worth waiting for. Hadn't he been telling himself that for weeks?

He'd never dreamed, then, that twenty years later he'd still be waiting, still be wanting her. And nothing had prepared him for the shock, and the anger he'd experienced the next time he saw her.

When he'd learned her real name. And her age.

And then, while he was still reeling from the first blow, she'd callously dropped the other shoe on his head. Telling him, with utter, cool detachment how, while he'd been waiting – and waiting – for her, she'd been out getting it on with her sister's boyfriend.

Did he say anger?

Oh, no. No. Anger didn't come close to describing the murderous rage that had filled him then.

*Glenn.*

Not too likely he'd forget about him in a hurry. That same sonofabitch who was there today. Her *attorney*, for Christ's sake. The guy who'd had dinner with her Monday night. And whose battered, black Montero – he realized it now, having seen it there again today – had been parked outside her house on Monday morning, as well. The implications of that hit him with the force of a fist in his gut, and he groaned aloud.

*Just dinner, Jen? At ten in the morning? I don't think so.*

He'd be damned if she wasn't already up to her same old tricks. And damned if she still didn't lie better, and way more easily, than anyone he'd ever known. He felt an unwilling rush of admiration. The woman was amazing, all right. Trouble with a capital T.

Probably, she hadn't figured on his recognizing Glenn, after all this time. Most likely she didn't even know they'd met. But, oh yeah, they'd met. He'd made it a point, twenty years ago, to find out just who the fuck this *Glenn* person was.

And then later, after Scout left town, when the same sonofabitch had come sniffing around after Lucy, it had been Nick's enormous pleasure to scare the crap out of the kid. Picking him up late one night – just him and Dave and Joey. Taking him for a drive and a friendly little chat out in one of the more isolated of the nearby canyons. Not that they'd threatened him – oh, no sir. Nothing like that – they'd just explained, in real explicit detail, about some of the more unpleasant things that could be made to happen to anyone who came within spitting distance of Lucy – or any of her friends either, for that matter – ever again.

Glenn had gotten the message, all right. But just to be sure, Nick kept his eye on him anyway, over the next couple of years.

It had helped some. Not enough, but some. Hell, what else did he have to do, anyway, while he was waiting?

Those first few years, he'd never had any doubt she'd be back. They could keep her away while she was a minor, sure. But after that, he knew she'd come back to him. When she turned eighteen, maybe. Or, if not then, then after college.

He had tried to talk to Lucy about her, but his cousin would launch into a string of invectives whenever he mentioned her name.

*Do you know where she is*, he would ask; *or have you heard anything about how she's doing? Or when she's coming back? Or how I can reach her?*

"What I know about Scout Patterson," Lucy had snarled, "Is that she's a bitch and a liar. The kind of liar who wouldn't know the truth if it jumped up and bit her on the ass. That girl would lie to the Pope. To Jesus Christ himself. She can lie under hypnosis – did you know that? And do you have *any* idea how completely impossible that is for a *normal* person to do?"

"Lucy. I don't give a shit about any of that. I just want to know if you've heard anything? Or, you know, if you maybe knew how somebody could get in touch with her?"

"Why? You plannin' on arresting her for something?"

"What? No. Of course not."

"Oh. That's too bad."

"Luce..."

"Trust me on this, Nick, you don't want to get anywhere near that girl. I don't know where she is. I don't know how to reach her. And if I did, I wouldn't tell you, anyway. Not in a million years. Not for a million dollars. Not for nothin', cuz!"

She'd been gone for several years before Nick began to wonder if maybe – just maybe – she might not be coming back, after all. And by then, when he finally tried to track her down, he found the trail had grown too cold for even a cop to trace. [3]

In desperation, he'd even tried asking her stepmother about her. He remembered the pain and the deep wariness that had filled the older woman's eyes. "Where's Scout? Someplace far away," was all she'd tell him. "Someplace safe."

"Forget her," she'd snapped at him the last time he'd asked. "You'll *never* find her. She's *gone.*"

"But...isn't she ever coming back?" he'd asked, despairingly.

"Not if I have anything to say about it," Caroline Larson told him with a harsh, humorless laugh, as she closed the door in his face. "Not for a very, *very* long time."

Well, she'd got that right, Nick thought bitterly. It had been a fucking lifetime.

Twenty years. Shit. Anyone would think he'd be over her by now. Hell, even *he* had thought he was over her. Mostly. Until today. Until he'd come face to face with her again, and finally realized what he should have figured out a long time ago. He'd never be over her.

Not ever in this life.

He climbed into his car and headed for home. He had the road all to himself for most of the way, which was just how he liked it. Watching the needle push past ninety. Watching the scenery blur by the windows. Feeling the blast of noise from his stereo vibrate through him, as adrenaline mixed with the caffeine and nicotine already in his bloodstream.

The closest thing to perfect that he knew.

With the shattering clarity that came at times like these, Nick was conscious of a hot flood of determination smoldering within him. *Has it always been there? Or is this just the product of the last few days?* Only one thing was certain. Now that he had seen her again, he wanted her as much as he ever had.

If she'd stayed in Oberon twenty years ago, he'd have had a hell of a time keeping away from her – even at the risk of losing his job or going to jail. He didn't care now if the risk this time was of going to hell itself. He had to have her.

By the time he got back to town, his mind was consumed with dark, bitter rage and furious need. He drove past the station and on through town without even slowing, until he was back on her block. The house looked dark and empty as he passed by, but there was an old van parked in the driveway, and when he saw a flutter of movement near the front porch, he swung back around for a second look. He could have sworn it was that sonofabitch, skulking around again. Glenn.

"*Oh, please, oh please, oh please, oh please,*" he muttered between clenched teeth; his tires squealing as he forced the car back through the turn in the road without braking. *"Let it be him. Let it please be that sorry ass bastard!"*

He so very much wanted to smash his fist into something, and at this moment there was nothing he would have enjoyed smashing it into more than Glenn's fat face. But he must have been mistaken. He saw nothing out of the ordinary on either the second, or the third, or the fourth pass he made. On the fifth pass, he saw a curtain drawn briefly aside in the next house over, and reluctantly gave up for the night.

No sense in calling any more attention to himself than necessary. He was quite capable of making a fool of himself all on his own. He didn't need some concerned citizen calling in a complaint about a suspicious vehicle in the area.

He drove slowly back through town. His windows rolled down, sucking deeply on a cigarette, as he thought about what to do next.

He'd have to think of something. And damn fast, too. Because he couldn't go on like this. This was no good. This was gonna make him nuts in no time at all.

---

1. Sometimes when you write something, you don't actually recognize the significance of it at the time. For instance, I love that Scout doesn't make up an entirely fictitious name for herself when she's with Nick. Despite how much everyone always beats up on her for lying, she's actually her authentic self with Nick. And yes, I'm just figuring that out now. lol!
2. The original "Shake Shack" is a tiny little place in Southern California. Located on PCH, its situated on the bluffs above Newport Beach. We used to stop there for date shakes whenever we were passing through...which, given that we lived in Newport Beach and my sister lived in Laguna Beach was more often than you might think.
3. Again, what a difference forty years makes. I'm reasonably sure a modern day Nick would've had no problem discovering Scout's whereabouts—even if he weren't a cop!

# 20

The Totawka Brewery was a dark, noisy barn of a place, with sawdust covering the old wooden floorboards and the rich smells of hops, mesquite and whiskey mingling in the air. A vaguely country-western band was playing at a volume that made conversation nearly impossible.

A hopeful, anticipatory mood engulfed Scout as she looked around. This was the kind of place they used to try to sneak into with their fake IDs when they were teenagers. In fact, she had the strangest feeling she might actually have gotten in here once or twice, back then. Only then of course, it wouldn't have been a microbrewery.

"Well?" Marsha shouted in her ear. "What do you think?"

Scout beamed back at her approvingly and sneaked a glance at Lucy. She too was looking around with an expression of grudging enjoyment on her face. When their gazes met, Lucy shrugged and rolled her eyes, but for once she wasn't scowling.

"That's better," Marsha shouted, approvingly. "C'mon, you two. Let's get a table. I'm starving."

"Marsha, I still don't understand why you wanted to drag us all the way out here," Lucy said, when they were seated at a booth in the slightly quieter back room and the waitress had taken their drink order. "This is a hell of a funny place for a vegetarian to pick, that's all I can say."

"Are you both vegetarians, now?" Scout asked, a little nervously. She'd been thinking of ordering a steak, but she was already feeling wrung out from her unexpected meeting with Nick. If it came with a side of even more grief from Lucy, she'd be happy to take a pass on the beef.

"No," Lucy said shortly. "Just her."

"Order whatever you want, Scout," Marsha said reassuringly. "It's just a personal choice. I don't claim any sort of moral superiority."

"She's been like this since her accident," Lucy said, sighing a little as she twirled her fork between her fingers. "I think she musta had some kinda hallucination about a cow or something while she was in her coma. Or maybe it was a chicken."

"Lucy, we've talked about this," Marsha replied with some asperity. "It wasn't a cow *or* a chicken. And it wasn't an hallucination, either. It was a vision. A profound spiritual experience which brought me face to face with my personal guardian. My Power Animal. And as I've told you many times before, I have no intention of revealing exactly what form she took. So quit fishing."

"Ahh. A fish, huh? Was that it?"

Marsha smiled. "You'll never know. Anyway, I like this place. It's got great energy. And for your information they happen to make killer nachos."

"Well, I'm going to have my usual," Lucy announced closing her menu emphatically. "Whiskey-mesquite ribs and a side of fried green tomatoes." She hesitated a moment and then, rather reluctantly it seemed, she turned to Scout and inquired politely. "What are you having, Scout?"

"Well, I thought...maybe a steak?"

"Uh, huh. That sounds good. Sirloin or porterhouse?"

"The ten-ounce sirloin with the burgundy onions," Scout told her. "And maybe some garlic fries."

Lucy nodded. "Oh, yeah, I love those. The fried baby artichokes are very nice, too."

"Mm. I haven't had those in years. How are the salads here, by the way?"

Lucy appeared to consider the matter for several minutes. "Well, the Caesar is nice, but the Cobb salad is boring; I haven't tried the spinach salad yet. Maybe Marsha could tell you."

"Christ," Marsha muttered. Their drinks had arrived, and she took a long sip from her margarita. "Look, I know I said you guys should be civil to each other, but you're both being so damn sweet that it's kinda making my teeth hurt. You're also boring me to tears. Can't you just relax? We're here to have fun, remember?"

"I don't know Marsha," Scout said. "Having fun was *your* idea. I'm not sure Lucy and I are really up to having fun together yet."

"Yeah, if ever," Lucy chimed in. "This might be as good as it gets, you know. Besides, this business with Robyn has me way too upset to even think about having fun. You really think something bad's happened to her, don't you?"

Marsha nodded unhappily. "It doesn't feel good, Luce. That's why I called the cops. Oh, and by the way, I oughta tell you that when I talked to Celeste tonight she happened to mention that Paige Delaney was in the shop this afternoon. Asking questions."

"About Robyn? Already?" Lucy frowned in surprise. "Shit. What is it with that woman? She's like a fucking shark. You'd think she could scent blood in the water from clear across the globe, or something," she broke off, on a shudder. "I don't know why she gets to me like she does, but...damn."

Marsha grinned, suddenly. "She really pushes your buttons, doesn't she? Maybe it's some horrible, unresolved past-life trauma, or something. 'Cause, whatever it is, it's mutual. She's not real fond of you, either."

"Yeah?" Lucy looked briefly interested. "Well good. I was never sure, you know? I always feel like I amuse her. Like maybe she can sense how pissed off I get whenever she's around, and she thinks it funny."

"Oh, no," Marsha assured her, looking serious again. "She's definitely not amused. And Celeste wasn't amused this evening, either. In fact, I don't think I've ever heard her sound so rattled. I know she's still totally unpredictable with the cards, but those were *tea leaves* she was reading on Saturday. And today, I think she'd been reading her own."

"This whole thing has a real bad feel to it," Lucy agreed, drumming her fingers on the table pensively for a moment. "I suppose you're sticking to your story, too?" she asked, shooting a mutinous glance at Scout. "Nothing happened Monday night? You and Robyn didn't fight? She didn't say anything before she left?"

"What do you want me to say Lucy? 'Oh, gee. You're right. I've been lying?'"

"Dunno. Maybe. Are you?"

"No." Scout regarded her former friend, angrily. "But I promise you, if I'd really come back to Oberon just to commit murder, I would *not* have picked a total stranger for my first victim. Not when I've got you guys."

"Good," Marsha said, encouragingly, pausing to gulp down some more margarita. "That's much better. You two have lots of issues. You need to get them off your chests. Might as well be now. I think you'll both feel better after you've talked this stuff out."

Lucy sighed. "I don't know Marsha. It's a nice thought, but I don't really want to talk to her all that much. No offense, Scout, but I mostly just want to kill you, too."

"Yeah, yeah, welcome to the club."

"You know, another thing I like about this place," Marsha mused. "It's so loud. I'm sure no one will mind, or even particularly notice, if the two of you were to start screaming at each other."

*Uh-oh.* Scout eyed them both warily. Was that what this was about? Was Marsha trying to set her up for a fight? Just when she'd been lulled into thinking they could be friends again?

"Good thinking, Marsha." Lucy sounded as unhappy about the suggestion as Scout. "Because I'm sure the last thing either of us wants is for someone to get upset with all the noise we're making and call the cops on us." She turned on Scout and asked challengingly. "Or, on second thought...would we?"

Scout smiled at her coldly. "Are you just making conversation, Lucy? Or do is there actually something you'd like to say to me about your cousin?"

Lucy's face assumed a look of mock surprise. "Who, Nick? Oh, that's right! You two knew each other, didn't you? I keep forgetting how you *told me all about it*!"

"You know damn well why I'd've kept something like that to myself, back then," Scout grumbled.

"Because you were such a bitch?" Lucy suggested, sweetly.

"No. Because you'd have opened your big mouth and fucked everything up for me."

"Yeah?" Fury sparked in Lucy's eyes. "You want to talk about big mouths?"

Scout ripped a long strip of label from her beer bottle. "Oh, please, let's."

"Because, as I recall, *I'm* not the one who spilled the beans to Sister Ben, or to my cousin either, about our little math project."

"Ooh. Having problems with the famous memory, are you?" Scout snapped. "Because I don't recall hearing anything about *our* little math project either. Not until after I'd blacked out in the middle of class because of it. And, while we're on the subject, don't you *ever* dare call it '*our project*' to me again. I was never in on any damn project. I was nothing more than your goddamn guinea pig!"

Marsha gurgled as she drained the last of her margarita, and Scout couldn't tell if she was laughing or choking. She glanced at Lucy, who appeared momentarily speechless. "Ooh. A hit, a palpable hit. I think we'll have to give that round to Scout, Luce. She's got us there." And though the words were spoken lightly, Scout could not detect much humor in her tone.

The waitress returned with their food just then, and Marsha took the opportunity to order another round of drinks.

"Look, Lucy," Scout said at last, breaking the silence. "The truth is, I don't know why I told them everything, like I did. I really hadn't planned to. It was just...your cousin was there and I, I lost it. It was a crappy thing to do. I'm not saying it wasn't. But they kept asking me questions and...I couldn't seem to help myself. I just kept right on answering them.

"I don't know, maybe I was in shock or something? I just could *not* make myself shut up. I had been trying so hard to keep everyone from finding out about Nick and me, and...all of a sudden, there he was. And I knew it was all over between us. The rest is just a big blur."

Marsha nodded understandingly. "Repressed memory. Happens all the time with trauma victims."

"What repressed memory?" Lucy demanded, nearly choking on her beer. "It sounds to me like she remembers everything just fine."

Marsha shrugged. "Not really. It's like the other day with, uh, you know, Mandy? She hadn't remembered anything about that, either. Did you, Scout? Until afterwards, I mean?"

"No," Scout answered, shuddering as she thought about it. "No, you're right. I didn't remember anything about it."

Marsha's gaze was compassionate, her voice quiet. "I have a feeling there's a whole lot of stuff that you don't remember yet. It's really not that uncommon, Luce. Take my accident, for example. I don't remember why I went over that cliff. Was there another car? Maybe I swerved to avoid an animal in the road."

"Yeah, maybe it was your power animal," Lucy suggested. "Maybe what you thought was a vision is really just a repressed memory of having run it over. That would explain the whole vegetarian thing, too, if you ask me."

Marsha grinned. "Oh, I don't think so Luce. I think that would be extremely unlikely. On either count, actually. But forget that." She turned her glittering green eyes toward Scout. "I'm dying of curiosity here. And I can't believe that you *both* have been holding out on me like this. What's the deal with you and Nick?"

"Remember back in high school," Lucy asked, answering before Scout had a chance to open her mouth. "How we all knew she was seeing someone, but we didn't know who it was? Turns out it was Nick."

"You're kidding?" Marsha looked impressed. "I mean, wow! He's cute and all, but he must have been, what? Twenty-two? Twenty-three?"

"He was twenty-two," Scout answered quietly.

"Well, what the hell was he thinking, running around with a fifteen-year old?"

"Obviously he didn't know she was only fifteen," Lucy snapped. She gave Scout a withering glance. "She lied to him. Big surprise."

Scout nodded. "He thought I was nineteen or twenty. He got the idea I was going to the community college, and I didn't tell him other-wise. And anyway, I was sixteen."

"Just barely," Lucy argued. "And it wasn't *only* your age you were lying about either, was it?"

Scout sighed in exasperation. "No, of course not. I also had to lie about where I was going to school. And about my family, 'cause, you know, he wanted to know why we couldn't go out like normal people. And about why I didn't drive. And my name."

"So, basically, it was all a scam."

"That's not how it felt at the time, but, yeah, I guess it was. I had to lie about pretty much everything."

"Well, you have a real talent in that direction." Marsha beamed admiringly. "I've always said so."

"You make it sound like it's an achievement or something." Lucy scowled. "Believe me, she's got *nothing* to be proud of here."

Marsha shrugged. "Still. You gotta admit, it's pretty damn useful, at times. So, uh, where did Glenn fit into all of this?"

"She was screwing both of them," Lucy said, answering for her, again—something Scout was beginning to feel more than a little annoyed about.

"Not exactly," Scout corrected. "I was never really interested in Glenn. I just— I needed a way to divert everyone's attention away from me and Nick. Glenn agreed to give me a hand."

Lucy snorted. "Oh, I'll bet he did. Both hands, would be my guess. As well as a few other assorted body parts."

Scout ignored her. "Honestly," she said as she turned to Marsha.

"I couldn't *believe* how easily you all fell for it. You all knew how I felt about Glenn. You knew I could never understand what everyone else saw in him."

"What we saw in him? That's funny. I was wondering the same thing myself, just this afternoon." Marsha smiled at her. "But he was sooo cute, back then. You have to admit that. He and his whole family were like...local celebrities. *Everybody* knew the Gilchrists. Plus, he was captain of the high school swim team. And that was back when they actually won occasionally." She turned to Lucy. "Remember all the fuss senior year when he dropped swimming altogether and decided to train for the biathlon? I mean, skiing? Here? What was up with that?"

"Yeah," Lucy agreed. "The shooting part didn't go over too well with anyone, either, as I recall. But, you know, in a way it was just typical. I mean, the reason everybody knew about his family was because they were all so weird."

"That's true." Marsha chuckled. "Remember his mother? Anyway, he's still kind of cute. Don't you think? In a weird, wounded sort of way."

"I suppose." Scout shrugged. "But he's still not my type. I mean, did you all really not remember how I kept telling Lisa to dump him?"

"Well, sure." Lucy nodded. "That was why. We figured you were just saying that because you wanted him for yourself."

"Wait, a minute," Marsha interrupted. "I don't understand. If you weren't involved with Glenn, why was Lisa so sure you were sleeping with him?"

Scout hesitated. She'd been wondering how to bring the conversation around to Lisa. It had been easier than she hoped it would be. Easier, and about a thousand times more awkward. The ensuing conversation was likely to destroy the fragile bond Marsha had been trying to build between the three of them.

She was surprised to feel a pang of disappointment, but she suppressed the emotion, ruthlessly. She could not afford the luxury of friendship right now. Or pride either, for that matter. She needed answers.

"Okay, I'm not saying I *didn't* sleep with him." She shrugged. "But it was only the one time. And I told Lisa I didn't want him. She just didn't believe me."

"Gee, imagine that," Lucy drawled. "Because nothing says, 'I don't want to bone your boyfriend anymore' quite like doing the nasty with him in the first place."

"Besides," Scout continued. "She didn't leave just on account of me and Glenn."

Lucy looked disgusted. "Oh, right. Of course, she didn't."

"No, really. You read her letter, didn't you? She had other issues."

"Maybe. Other issues to do with *you*," Lucy said, eyes narrowing. "Like the whole math thing."

"Oh, don't even go there. You guys *promised* you'd stop. But you didn't, did you? You think *Lisa* was upset about that? Well, so was I! And, I'll tell you something else; if there were repercussions, she had it coming. You all did."

"Repercussions? Scout, we got expelled!" Lucy glared at her. "My parents decided they couldn't trust me about anything after that. It took me *years* to live that down. Not to mention that just about everyone in Oberon thought we were freakin' Satanists, or something."

Scout nodded. "So I've been hearing. And, for what it's worth, I'm sorry things turned out the way they did. But I'm not the one who started it." She took a quick sip of her drink and then continued, "Anyway, Lisa had other problems too, you know. Problems that had nothing at all to do with me. Like the little matter of her being pregnant."

Lucy's face went white. "You— You couldn't have known about that."

"Oh? Well, you did, obviously." Scout eyed her coldly. "I wonder what else you've been keeping to yourself?"

"She'd only just found out about it. She wasn't going to tell *anyone* yet."

"Well, she did."

"Not you." Lucy shook her head solemnly. "She might have told someone, eventually, but it wouldn't have been you."

"It doesn't matter," Marsha said gently. "It wouldn't have made any difference."

"How can you say that?" Lucy demanded, turning on her. "How can you be so sure? Maybe, if Scout hadn't made things so hard for her just then, she wouldn't have left!"

"The Lisa I remember would never have left anyway," Scout said quietly, surprised at the tears that glittered in Lucy's eyes. "Not like that. Somebody has to know something about what happened to her. Something they're not telling."

Someone like who?" Lucy looked perplexed. "And what could they have known? And why would anyone have kept quiet, if they knew something that would have helped find her?"

Marsha sighed. "I don't think the *who, what, why* are all that important. Sometimes things just happen." She looked at Scout sorrowfully. "I'm sorry. I know this isn't what you want to hear, but you're *not* going to find her on this plane. You need to move on with your own life, now, Scout. Just let it go."

"You may be right, Marsha. But I can't. Not yet, at any rate."

"So, you're still planning on sticking around?" Lucy asked, the muscles around her jaw clenching tensely.

"Yeah. I am. Sorry to disappoint you."

"Well, I still think that's wonderful," Marsha insisted, adding—in what Scout could only imagine was an attempt to restore their previous good humor. "So, what are you gonna do for a social life while you're here? Any plans?"

"Social life?" Scout looked startled. "I don't know what you mean. What kind of plans?"

"Well, I know you said you were out with Glenn the other night, but it doesn't sound like you're interested in pursuing that. So how about you and Nick? Are you going to start seeing him again now, too?"

Lucy's beer glass hit the table with a loud thunk. "No. Bad idea, okay? Nick's already got a life. He does not need Scout coming back here and fucking with it."

"Well, I don't know, Lucy. Maybe he'd like it." Marsha twinkled. "What do you think Scout? You want to fuck with his life? Or, you know, maybe just with him?"

"I'm not here to socialize," Scout said, carefully avoiding Lucy's glare. She shrugged. "Besides, for all I know, Nick is happily married by now with half a dozen kids."

Then she busied herself with cutting and chewing a piece of her steak while she waited to see if either of them would answer the question she hadn't exactly asked.

"That's not the point," Lucy replied, after a moment, her voice edged with frost. "I'm sure you're both over each other by now. And I can't imagine why either of you would want to do anything so purely stupid, anyway. You can't pretend you were *good* for each other, back then, can you?"

"Maybe not," Scout admitted softly. But her heart pattered excitedly. He wasn't married. He couldn't even be seeing anyone seriously, or Lucy would surely have mentioned it. Maybe there was a chance she could bring a few of her fantasies to life, after all?

"But maybe you could be good now. Right?" Marsha asked with a small, knowing smile. "Now that you're both older and unattached?"

"Don't be ridiculous," Lucy snapped. "Whatever they had – or thought they had – that was twenty years ago. I'm sure they're both over it by now."

"Over?" Marsha stared at Lucy in disbelief. "What're you talking about? You saw the two of them today—I know you did. They were almost as bad as you and Dan."

"I have *no* idea what you're talking about," Lucy replied coldly. "Dan and I are — Wait. What do you mean, *bad?*"

"Lucy, please." Marsha's smile widened. "You and Dan aren't nearly as subtle as you think you are. When you two get into one of your moods everyone knows about it. And, this afternoon, you could have set off a bomb in that living room and neither one of them would have noticed it. Whatever else it is, it ain't over. Am I right, Scout?"

Scout merely shrugged. She was aware of Lucy fuming beside her. There didn't seem to be any way to answer that question without making her angrier.

"Well. Don't worry about it," Marsha said, at last, breaking the long awkward silence. "Things happen if they're meant to. Otherwise, they don't. Eventually, everything works out for the best."

Lucy snorted. "If that's not the most nauseating, Pollyanna-esque piece of crap I've ever heard, I don't know what is. A lot of things that happen in the world are just shit from start to finish. What are you supposed to do then?"

Marsha smiled. "Well, Luce, in cases like that you just have to look for the lesson in it, you know? And just keep believing that things will work out the way they're supposed to. Like I said. Eventually."

"*Eventually?*"

"Mm-hm."

"And what are you supposed to do in the meantime?"

"Well, that's what dessert's for." Marsha's eyes twinkled. "Which reminds me, did I mention that they also do a really incredible Kahlua Cheesecake here?"

# 21

"*O*h, yeah," Marsha moaned, eyes closed in ecstasy. "Oh, that's good. That's *really* good." Along with the cheesecake, the source of her present bliss, she had also ordered coffee laced with more Kahlua, and topped with whipped cream.

"So, I'm guessing you like Kahlua, huh?" Scout asked, as she dug into her chocolate parfait.

Lucy paused, with her coffee cup halfway to her mouth, and rolled her eyes at Scout. "You wanna know *how much* she likes the stuff? She named her daughter after it."

"What? No way." Scout stared at her. "Marsha, is this true? You have a daughter named after a liqueur?"

"Oh, like that's a big deal?" Marsha put her fork down on her plate and stared at Scout, challengingly. "I suppose no one has ever been named Brandy? Or Sherry? Or...oh, I don't know, I'm sure there are more names like that. Anyway, it's just her middle name. And it made perfect sense to call her that. After all, she probably wouldn't have been conceived without it.

"Of course," she said as she picked up her fork again. "My mother has never forgiven me for it. I mean, she's gotten over the fact that I didn't marry Jasmine's father; that he was just some guy I met on vacation in Jamaica; that I didn't even really know what his last name was, or how to reach him. But I'll never live down Kahlua. She didn't take on half so much when I had the twins. Although, my in-laws were absolutely devastated over their names. Which still surprises me, I hafta say. They're English...or British, I guess? Whatever. They live in England. And I didn't even think they'd make the connection."

"What are the twins' names?" Scout asked curiously.

"Frank and Jesse," Marsha said around a mouthful of cheesecake.

"Oh." Scout blinked in surprise. "Well, okay. The outlaw motif is a bit much, I suppose. But I do see your point. It is an American thing, after all. And they're both really nice names. I like them."

"Mmph," Lucy quickly choked down a bite of her dessert. "Just wait. You haven't heard the half of it yet. Go ahead, Marsha. Tell her what Alex's last name is."

"My ex-husband's name," Marsha announced grandly. "Is Alexander Harrington James the third."

"Which would make the boys..." Lucy prompted, a crooked smile lifting one corner of her mouth. Scout felt her eyes widen as it hit her.

"Oh, no," she whispered, trying hard not to laugh. "Not Frank and Jesse *James*?"

"Got it in one." Lucy chuckled.

"Oh." She took a deep breath and fought hard for an even tone. "Well. What can I say? They're still nice names."

Marsha sniffed. "Well, that's what I've always said. Although Jasmine's name is still my favorite. It has such a nice ring to it, no matter what my mother says. Jasmine Kahlua Quinn. There ain't nothing wrong with that."

"I've always liked it," Lucy agreed, as she savored the last of her key lime pie. "'Course, if I'd gone with that philosophy, I'd have named my kids Weed and Hot Tub." [1]

She paused and considered the idea. "Now that I think about it, Weed wouldn't be so bad a name. I mean, it kind of makes sense, you know? What with the nursery, and all. And he's always grown like one. But can you imagine Hot Tub Cavanaugh? Jeez. It sounds like...well, actually I don't know what it sounds like. But it doesn't sound good. What about you Scout? You ever think about having kids?"

Scout grimaced. "That's a joke, right? I obviously can't even keep a dog for more than a couple of days without losing her. Besides, I don't know anyone I'd want to have a baby with."

"Really? Well, what if you and—" Marsha began. But stopped when she saw the others' faces. "All right. Never mind. Shutting up, now. Anyway, speaking about your dog. I've been thinking we should put up some flyers. You know those missing pet flyers you always see? We could put one up at the shop, about your dog, Scout. Maybe someone has seen her."

"But what about Robyn?" Lucy asked. "I mean, sure, let's find Scout's dog, by all means. But Robyn is a little more important, don't you think? Maybe some posters would help us find her, too."

A look of pain crossed Marsha's face. "No," she said quietly. "I don't think we'll find Robyn that way. In fact, don't think we're going to find her at all."

"Just like Lisa," Scout mused. She finished up the last of her parfait, took a sip of coffee and pretended not to notice the startled look the other women exchanged. It seemed to Scout that they both knew more than they were telling her. Maybe about a lot of things.

"So, help me out here, Scout," Marsha said, in what once again seemed to Scout to be a deliberate attempt to change the subject. "I'm still trying to understand this. If you and Nick were so hot for each other, why did you sleep with Glenn? That was pushing the diversion thing a little far, don't you think?"

Scout groaned. "Please, it's too embarrassing. I don't want to talk about it."

"Well, what's up with that? We can tell you *our* embarrassing secrets, but you won't tell us yours?"

Scout stared at her in surprise. "What embarrassing secrets did you tell me?"

"My kids' names! Shit, just ask my mother. She assures me every time we speak that they're an endless source of embarrassment to her. Which is probably why we don't talk very much, come to think of it. So...?"

"Yeah, Scout." Lucy leaned forward; her eyes glittered maliciously. "Tell us. What was it like with Glenn? Must have been pretty special, given that he was ready to dump Lisa for you."

"Like I said, we only did it once. But, no, if you must know, it wasn't all that special. At least not for me."

"So, what're you saying? That when you made love with Glenn the earth didn't move?"

"Glenn and I did not *make love*, Lucy." Scout was stung into answering. "It was just sex."

Lucy shrugged. "Oh, well, if you're gonna split hairs. Having sex, making love – what's the difference?"

"You don't think there's a difference?"

"Not at sixteen, I don't," Lucy retorted. "Or eighteen, or however old he was." She waved her hand dismissively. "At that age, I think it's mostly too many hormones and too little practice. Although, I guess that wouldn't have applied in this case, would it – the lack of practice, I mean. Not on his part."

"Oh, I don't know," Scout mused. "Maybe that's true most of the time. But, even at that age, even without a whole lot of practice, it could still be great, I think." She sensed the unasked question hanging in the air and left it to hang there. If Lucy wanted to know anything else about her and Nick, and their non-existent sexual relationship, she could damn well ask him herself.

"Oh, I'm with you, Scout. One hundred per cent." Marsha nodded in agreement. "And Lucy, I can't even *believe* I'm hearing shit like this from you, of all people. I was nineteen when I met Jerry – you know, Jasmine's dad? But man, it was cosmic." She sighed, a little wistfully. "I guess that's why I was kind of thrilled when I learned I was pregnant. I was scared as hell, of course, but part of me was so happy that I was going to get to keep a little piece of that magic."

"What do you mean, *me of all people*?" Lucy demanded, coloring angrily. "I don't know what's gotten into you this evening, Marsha, but I don't think I like it."

"Oh, cool your jets, Lucy. We're just having fun. Anyway, maybe it just seemed so special with Jerry because it was my first time, you know? Maybe I just made it into something more special than it really was."

"No." Scout shook her head emphatically. "I don't think so. Glenn was my first, and I knew even then that what we did was no big deal. I just—" she broke off, aware that the others were looking at her with identical expressions of surprised confusion on their faces. "What?"

"But you said he wasn't even your type," Marsha reminded her, gently. "Your first time? Why him? I mean, why wouldn't you wait and do it with someone you at least cared about?"

"Because I couldn't, okay? The person I cared about had made it real clear that he didn't even *date* virgins." Scout glanced challengingly at Lucy, braced for another sarcastic comment, but for once, Lucy didn't appear to have one. "Of course, I *wanted* my first time to be with him, but...well, not if it meant losing him. So, I had to, you know, get it out of the way. Before we could— Not that we did anything like that," she added quickly. "So, don't get bent out of shape, Lucy. Okay? And as for 'why Glenn' I guess maybe it was because I knew I wouldn't be risking rejection."

"Well, that's for damn sure," Lucy agreed, having at last found her tongue. "You wouldn't have had any worries on that count."

THE PHONE by her bedside rang later that night. Scout snaked one arm out from beneath the covers, feeling around in the dark for the receiver. Too sleepy to turn on the light, or to sit up, or even to open her eyes. "Hello?" she yawned into the phone.

"Scout? It's Nick."

At the sound of his voice, she felt a warm thrill run through her. He had never called her before, she realized. The fact registered with a sad little shock. They had been cheated out of so many things. They had never even spoken on the phone. Maybe that was why the sound of his voice in her ear now seemed so incredibly, almost unbearably, intimate. As if he were right here in the room with her. In the dark. In her bed.

Desire swept over her like a tidal wave, without any warning at all. She felt her breath catch in her throat. Several seconds passed before she was able to speak. Even then, she could barely manage a whisper.

"Oh...hi," she breathed the words softly. And then waited while another, even longer pause stretched itself out into the darkness before she heard him clear his throat.

His voice sounded painfully impersonal when he spoke. "I, uh, I've been thinking about your dog."

"My...*dog*?" she repeated, stupidly. He'd been thinking about the dog? He was calling her in the middle of the night to talk about...a dog? *Our very first telephone conversation* ever *and he wants to talk about—*

"You didn't say whether you had checked the shelters in the area. Or whether anyone has been in contact with you about it," Nick continued, relentlessly. "But I'm assuming it was wearing tags. Would that be correct?"

"Tags? Jesus, Nick, *I* don't know. She wasn't even really my dog. Well, I mean she is *now*, sort of. She belonged to Caroline. You know, my stepmother? But I think she'd just gotten her, so I don't know."

"So, you don't know if the dog was licensed?"

"As far as I know, Caroline hadn't even gotten around to naming the damned thing. So, I'm guessing not."

"Okay. Fine. So, about the shelters. Have you checked with any of them? There are several in the area, you know. And dogs can range pretty far, especially if they've been gone a few days. Animal Control hasn't contacted you?"

"No. Actually, I haven't really been thinking about this too clearly. I've had a bunch of other things on my mind. But I guess I'd better get out there tomorrow and check, huh? Oh, no, wait. I can't." Scout sighed. "I forgot. My car is being fixed. I guess I could still call around, though."

"Might be hard to get a firm ID on the phone," Nick said. And then paused. "I tell you what. As it happens, I'm not working tomorrow. And I'm probably more familiar with the shelter locations than you are, anyway. If you don't have a car, I could...I don't know...maybe drive you around to a few of them?"

"You mean...you'd want to go there together?" Scout struggled to keep her voice level. She felt the blood rushing to her face, pounding in her ears.

"I have a few hours I could spare. It would have to be first thing in the morning, though." Nick's voice held all the softness of wrought iron. "But if you think it would be helpful...?"

"Yeah. Okay," Scout said weakly. "Sure."

"Fine. I'll see you about nine, then." The cool, crispness of his voice was almost instantly replaced with a dial tone, but it was several moments before Scout dropped the receiver back in its cradle.

*He called.* She stared up into the darkness. A small smile slowly lifted the corners of her mouth. *I'm going to see him again. Tomorrow.*

The coldness in his eyes today, the indifference in his voice just now, what did they matter? They did nothing to disguise the flimsiness of the excuse he'd used. Help her check the shelters for her dog? Oh, please. What the hell was that all about?

*He wants to see me.* An incredulous thrill of delight tingled through her. After all this time, despite everything Lucy had insisted upon, and everything logic would suggest, he still—

*It has to mean he wants to see me, doesn't it?*

Lucy was going to have her hide for this, but Scout didn't care. She'd deal with Lucy when the time came. Rolling over onto her stomach, she groaned her impatience into the pillow. Tomorrow. She couldn't *wait* until tomorrow. She stretched out against the cool sheets and wished that she knew his phone number or had the nerve to call him back with some equally pointless excuse, just to hear his voice again.

*He called. I'm gonna see him again. Tomorrow.*

If she could only fall asleep right now, so that it would be morning before she knew it. But she knew it would never happen that way. She knew she would lie awake for hours imagining what other surprises tomorrow might bring.

NICK STARED at the phone long after he had hung up, berating himself for being a fool.

*This is a mistake*. He'd known it the instant he heard her voice, all soft and breathless. Just the way he remembered it; the way it had always sounded in his dreams.

If she sounded like that when he picked her up tomorrow, he couldn't even imagine what he might do.

He should have listened to his cousin. *"Stay away from her, Nick,"* Lucy had warned. *"She's nothing but trouble. And I do know what I'm talking about. If you get involved with her, mark my words, cuz, sooner or later, you're gonna regret it."*

Well, he already regretted it, but what could he do? He *couldn't* leave it alone. He had to see her again. He had to at least try to find a way to break the hold she had on him. He closed his eyes and saw her again, the way she'd looked that last afternoon they'd had together, staring up at him with lust and longing in her eyes.

*I have to have her.*

He knew there was no point in thinking like that. It wasn't going to happen—not tonight, and probably not tomorrow either. But a tiny voice kept insisting, anyway. *It wasn't all a lie. She wanted me back then, just like I wanted her.* He would go to his grave believing that.

Still, twenty years...that was a hell of a long time to carry a torch for someone. And what were the odds they were *both* that obsessed? Perhaps the best thing he could do tomorrow would be to wipe the slate clean and pretend that they'd only just met. Because, really, it wasn't that far from the truth.

They could start over as strangers, and it would still be okay. Because even twenty years later, he was certain he could make her

want him again. Or, at least, he was pretty sure he could. He remembered, oh, so many things about her. Things that, even after all this
time, couldn't completely have changed.

If only he could know for certain how much of what he remembered had actually been true.

Given enough time, a fantasy can take on a life of its own. But
he'd had enough of this particular fantasy. It was time he got a taste
of reality.

---

1. Just want to take a moment to reflect on how authors make their lives more...
   interesting. I had no idea when I gave Lucy this line of dialogue that it would
   have any repercussions down the road. But then in the next book, we learned
   more about the circumstances surrounding Seth's conception, and then in book
   four—Lucy and Dan's story—I needed to tell the whole story of that night.
   Which was great until I remembered that weed needed to be involved!

   It worked out great though, IMO. And it remains one of my favorite scenes.
   Disclaimer: I have a lot of favorite scenes.

# 22

From the deck of his houseboat, Glenn looked out across San Bartolo Bay. The early morning sunlight gleamed across the surface of the water and the silence was broken only by the calls of gulls wheeling in the sky above him, and the faint bell-like tones of the wind as it vibrated in the lines of the nearby sailboats.

In the distance, to either side, the long, green arms of the shore reached out to embrace the bay. Everything looked bright and safe and warm. Everything but the dark, murky depths where the secrets were hidden. Thinking about that now, he was conscious of a deep thrill of mingled fear and satisfaction. He liked the irony of his choice to live on the water. Once, he'd practically lived in it. He swam every day, and when he wasn't swimming, he was running – training his muscles so that they'd propel him even faster through the water. But it was in the water that he felt most comfortable. It was the one place where he could forget about the troubles at home and let go of every-thing that disturbed him.

It had been years since he'd felt that way. Too many long years, during which the very sight of a large body of water was enough to make him break out in a sweat. No one knew, of course. He'd hidden his discomfort too well. His move here had been a stroke of genius, forcing him to confront his demons head on. And while he still could not bring himself to actually enter the water, he had progressed to the point where he could, as he was doing now, gaze at the surface without panic taking him. Without the thought of everything that lay drowned within the depths making him sick.

What did make him sick, however, was the thought of Scout and that cop. He'd seen the way they'd glared at each other the day before. It had made him not only sick, but nervous, as well. That man was dangerous – crazy – and now he was after Scout. He should have seen it coming days ago, but he'd been so preoccupied with other things, he hadn't made the connection. Now, he had. And he knew that it was up to him to find a way to take care of this, too.

There were always demons to be faced. No matter how many you put away, there always seemed to be another coming at you.

JUST AFTER NINE O'CLOCK, Scout slid into the passenger seat of Nick's car. Her heart pounded with excitement. After all those years, years when she'd given up even dreaming about it, she couldn't believe this was happening. A rush of excitement speared through her. This was how they'd spent so much of their time together.

It didn't matter that this was a different car than he'd driven twenty years ago. *He* was still the same. And the excitement she felt at being close to him was exactly as she remembered it.

Nick's eyes, hidden as usual behind dark glasses, were unreadable, but Scout thought he had looked just a little uncomfortable when she first got in. She hadn't had time to wonder about it though, in fact she'd barely gotten her seat belt fastened before he peeled out of her driveway.

*God, he looks great*, she thought, glancing at him from the corner of her eye. She was mesmerized by the way his hands slid lightly over the wheel as he spun around a curve, the way the muscles in his arm tightened as he changed gears. She remembered the way those hands had felt on her skin, so many years ago, how those arms had held her. And suddenly, she found it hard to breathe.

"This was really nice of you," she said, stumbling into speech to cover her confusion, annoyed when her voice came out sounding breathless and weak. "Thanks."

"Sure," Nick ground the single syllable out.

She couldn't help but notice that his jaw was clenching again. Was he angry about something?

"Here," he said suddenly, as he twisted around to reach into the back seat. He retrieved a couple of small, brown paper bags, and thrust them at her. "I didn't know if you'd already eaten, so I picked up some stuff for breakfast."

He was driving fast, which was just as she remembered. But he kept his eyes fixed on the road for the most part, which was not. He nodded towards the cup holders on the front console. "I also got you some coffee. I wasn't sure what you'd want to drink. We can stop again if you want something else."

"No, this is great." Scout busied herself with extracting a raspberry filled pastry from the bag. "Just like old times, huh?" [1]

"No." Nick shook his head emphatically. "It sure isn't."

"I only meant that—"

"I know what you meant." The steel in his voice surprised her. Scout found herself suddenly wishing for her dog. She missed her warm, comforting presence.

"Well, it was nice of you to do this – help me find my dog."

"Yeah." he replied, curtly. "You said that already. Why don't you give me one of those pastries, 'kay?"

"Sure. What kind do you want?" she asked, her own voice subdued.

"Doesn't matter. Any of 'em. What'd you say your dog's name was, again?"

He sounded irritated and preoccupied. He sounded so much as if he would rather be doing something –almost anything else. She had a sudden, horrible and totally irrational thought. Could Lucy have put him up to this? Was he only doing this as a favor to his cousin? Could Lucy have called him last night, after dinner and—No. Impossible. Lucy would walk barefoot over flaming coals before she'd do anything to help Scout. Or, for that matter, before she'd throw her together with her cousin. She'd made that crystal clear.

"It's like I told you on the phone, I haven't had her for very long. I haven't actually even named her yet," she admitted.

He shook his head, looking disgusted. Looking so, so bored.

"Well, I hadn't exactly planned on getting a dog, you know," she was stung into explaining. "I mean, I'm only back a week and boom! Suddenly I'm dealing with a house, a dog, a dozen cats, a missing roommate..."

"Sounds like you got your hands full, all right. So, what was it that finally brought you back to town?"

"What, Lucy didn't tell you?"

Nick smirked, and she thought she saw his hands tighten on the wheel. "Oddly enough, your name didn't come up in conversation all that much these last twenty years."

Scout sucked hard on her coffee. "I just thought she might have mentioned that my stepmother had died. That's why I'm back. For some reason Caroline decided to leave everything she had to me and my stepsister. Her daughter, Lisa."

"Yeah? So, where's she at?"

"Who, Lisa? Well, that's the question, isn't it? That's what I'm here to find out."

"Wait, you're not talking about the same stepsister who ran away all those years ago, are you? She's still missing?"

"Apparently. As I'm just about the last to find out."

"And you think *you're* going to find her? Now? After all this time?"

"Seems like a long shot, right?"

"Little bit."

Scout sighed again. "I know. And that's pretty much what everyone else says, too. But I've got to try, you know?"

"No, not really. I mean, do you have any investigative training, or experience that makes you think you can do this? Or are you just gonna wing it?"

"Look, given the fact that Caroline and I hardly spoke to each other over the last twenty years, I really wasn't expecting her to put me in her will at all. Never mind to leave me everything! There's no other way to explain it; she must have known that I'd feel honor bound at least *try* to find out what happened to Lisa. That I'd feel I owed them both that much, since it was mostly my fault that she left in the first place."

Nick frowned slightly. "How d'you figure that?"

"C'mon, Nick, it's what *everyone* thought, right? Lisa and I had a fight, after which she left the house and never came back. A few days later, she sent Lucy a letter blaming me for everything, and then nothing. That was the last anyone ever heard from her."

"Yeah." Nick shook a cigarette out of his pack and jabbed at the lighter with his thumb. "So," he said between puffs as he lit it. "Refresh my memory. What was it you two were fighting about?"

*Here we go again.* Scout sighed. "Mostly her boyfriend."

"Oh, right. The *boyfriend*. That'd be Glenn, right? Your lawyer?"

"You recognized him?"

"I recognized his name. You were quite the social butterfly back then, weren't you? Or maybe you still are?" A cold smile flickered briefly on his lips. Scout felt herself bristle with sudden anger.

"Are you *sure* that you and Lucy haven't been comparing notes? 'Cause she and I took this same stroll down memory lane just last night."

"Nope. It never came up."

"Well, maybe we can let it drop again. All right? I just want to find my dog and go home. And then, as soon as I find out what happened to Lisa – and to Robyn now, too, I suppose – I can get the hell out of town again."

"Hmph." Nick puffed quietly for several seconds. "Well. I gotta say, you sure do have a knack for losing things, don't you?"

The frost in his voice was palpable, but Scout more than matched it, folding her arms and turning away from him as she muttered,

"Yeah. I guess I do. It's just too bad a few more of them don't stay lost." Digging in her bag, she pulled out her own pack of cigarettes, and was soon puffing away as furiously as he.

IT WAS ANOTHER PERFECT MORNING. Still June. And once again the sun was shining, and a gentle breeze caused the nasturtiums to shiver and sway on their stems. On the terrace, three women talked quietly, their lattes and herbal tea all but forgotten in the seriousness of their conversation.

"You really think she's dead, don't you?" Ginny asked quietly.

Marsha shrugged. "Well...let's put it this way; it doesn't look good."

"So, we're just taking Celeste's word on this?" Heather demanded. "Marsha, much as I love the woman, we don't even know what she's basing her ideas on. No offense, but it seems a little premature. What do the police have to say? Are they buying into this idea, too?"

"I guess they're not ruling anything out, at the moment." Marsha shook her head. "But it's not exactly a matter of belief, you know. I mean, Robyn *is* missing."

"Is she though? I mean, it's summer, right? And she's what—nineteen? It's not like she owes your friend an accounting of her whereabouts. Maybe she just took off for a few days?"

"What about what she owes Lucy?" Ginny asked. "What about her job? She didn't tell anyone at work she was leaving, either. That doesn't sound like Robyn, does it? Oh! And, what about the dog? How do you explain that?"

"Well, what about the dog?" Heather asked, perking up suddenly. "Who the hell would try and abduct Robyn *and* her dog? That doesn't make any sense, either.

"I still think it's much more likely that Robyn just wanted to take off for a few days, you know? Or maybe she got real attached to the dog and decided that her only course of action was to steal it. Maybe she took off with the dog and went back home to...Where is she from, again?"

"I don't know. But I don't think that's what happened," Marsha told her. She was suddenly very, very weary. She thought of her own daughter, just a year younger than Robyn, out there right now, all alone, riding a bike along a deserted highway. Not that she was *really* alone, of course. There were other riders out there with her. It was supposed to be safe—but then, so was walking a moderately large dog in a residential neighborhood in a little town like Oberon. But still, things happened. No matter what kind of precautions you took. Things – sometimes very bad things – happened anyway.

*We're such small, fragile creatures,* she thought. *And we're all just out there, all the time alone, out in the great unknown. And ultimately there's nothing – not friendship, not family, not caution or common sense, not even precognition – that can save us.*

She thought again of the painting she had admired yesterday in the hall at Scout's house. Such happy, happy faces. And yet, just look what happened there.

"It's a mystery," Marsha said at last. "You can never really know what someone else is thinking. Or what they're gonna do. You might think you know. But you never do. Not really."

"You gotta do what you can, though," Ginny said softly. "Don't you? To help people? To try and make sense of things?"

Marsha shrugged. "Yeah, I guess. You do what you can. For all the good it ever seems to do. You do what you have to do, and you hope for the best." *And still, bad things happen. Bad things happen all the time.*

THIS WAS SUCH A BAD IDEA, Nick reflected moodily as they pulled away from the third shelter on his list. Definitely a bad idea. He should have gone by himself. That way, if he'd found the dog he could have brought it back to her. Not that he'd have a clue what to look for – a nondescript mutt, he'd seen only one blurry photo of, with no name and no tags? *Good luck with that.*

But, if he'd pulled it off, he'd have been a hero. And she would have been grateful—he could have worked with that. Instead, they had immediately gotten off on the wrong foot, and stayed there.

It was his own fault, he supposed. He hadn't exactly overwhelmed her with his charm. But all it had taken was her getting into his car this morning, and he was a goner. Memories surged to the forefront of his mind. Desire slammed into him with the force of a gunshot, setting all his nerves on edge.

Twenty years older and she still moved like a kid, damn it. *It just isn't fair.*

Hell, this was *worse* than yesterday. At least then, when she'd fainted, he'd gotten the chance to put his arms around her. That wasn't likely to happen again anytime soon. And having her this close, without being able to touch her? Sheer torture.

*Just like old times,* she'd said. Oh, God, what was that—some kind of twisted joke? In the old days there had never this tension between them. Things had been simple. Easy. Clear. Being with her had been like breathing, normal and right and effortless. And if he'd felt like kissing her—which he usually did, like he did right now—he would have gone ahead and kissed her.

In the old days he knew where he stood with her. Or at least, he'd always thought he did. But now..? What would she do if he tried to kiss her now? He sneaked a glance in her direction. She sat staring out the window, arms crossed tightly, a grim, angry expression on her face.

Shit. He didn't have a prayer.

"Hey, listen," he said as he stumbled into speech. "There are a few other places I want to try, but it's getting kind of late. So how about we grab some lunch?" He had to do something to get her out of this car, at least for a little while. Maybe a little space would help him get things under control.

"Lunch?" She looked at him doubtfully, and Nick found himself growing even more annoyed.

Why was she looking so damn surprised? Didn't people eat lunch in...where the hell *has* she been living all this time? "Yeah. You remember. It's that meal that comes between breakfast and dinner?"

"But don't you have to get back soon? I thought you could only do this for a few hours?"

*Uh-oh.* He had said that hadn't he? *Well, who knew it was going to take so long to find the dumb mutt?* "I thought you wanted to find your dog?"

"Of course, I want to find her! It's just—"

"Well, I got the time, and I don't mind the driving. But if you've got something else that you'd rather be doing..."

"No. I just thought— Oh, never mind. Just...thanks. Again. For doing this, I mean."

They lapsed into an uneasy silence, and Nick still didn't know if she wanted to eat. "Look, I think maybe we got off on the wrong foot this morning," he told her, after a moment, trying a different tactic.

"Oh?"

"Yeah. What happened between us— you know, before? That was a long time ago. It's in the past. It's over."

"I see," she said, very quietly.

"We aren't the same people we were back then. Agreed? Far as I'm concerned, I don't know you, and you don't know me."

She said nothing for a minute. And then, "So then why are you helping me find my dog?"

Her voice held a hint of challenge, and he found himself replying more sharply than he'd planned. "Well, it sure wouldn't be because of the way you used to jerk me around, now, would it?" he said, and was instantly sorry as all the softness and uncertainty fled from her face.

"Oh, I get it." She glared at him through narrowed eyes. "So, the only part of the past we're *not* forgetting about is the part where I screwed up?"

"Okay. Good point," he answered, trying to think fast. "From now on…we'll just forget the whole thing. None of it happened. Or, if it did, it was to two other people, two strangers. How's that?"

"If that's the way you want it."

"Absolutely. We don't have to talk about it, or even think about it. Not ever again." *Yeah, right.*

"Perfect." Her voice was distant and cold. "And what did you say your name was again?"

*Shit.* He ground his teeth together, but finally he had to ask. "So, what do you think? D'you wanna get lunch, or not?"

"Well, gee, Nick, that'd kind of be like taking candy from a stranger, wouldn't it? Seeing as how I don't even know you." She shrugged. "But, sure. I can live dangerously. Why not?"

*Strangers? Oh, good thinking. Just when the fuck did I lose my mind?* "Okay. Good."

"Good."


*WELL, this is just perfect*, Scout thought as they raced down the coast: Destination Unknown. Well, unknown to her, anyway. She assumed Nick knew where they were going, even if he wasn't in the mood to share that information. She wasn't sure *what* he was in the mood for, to be honest. Not *this*, to judge from his glum expression. Even though it had been his idea.

"You know this was your idea." The words were out before she realized she was going to say them.

He scowled. "Yeah, I know."

"So, I guess…what I'm wondering is…why are you doing it?"

He hesitated, seeming confused. "Why? Because I'm hungry. Why else would I want to eat lunch?"

"No, not lunch. This. Spending the day together."

He choked back something that sounded suspiciously like a laugh. "Oh, is that what you think we're doing?"

The hint of amusement in his voice was more than she could take. "I don't know what we're doing," she snapped. "And please don't say we're looking for my dog because that's not what I meant either. I just can't help thinking that you might have some...other reason for doing this."

"I see." She saw the muscles of his jaw bunch. "Okay, and what about you? Do you have another reason for being here?"

Scout found her mouth had abruptly gone dry. There was no way she was going to mention any of the foolish ideas she'd had the night before. "No. No, I just want my dog back."

"Ahh."

She fumbled to light another cigarette. "You know, come to think of it, I don't think I want to stop for lunch, after all."

"Too bad," he answered, swerving suddenly off the road and into an unpaved parking lot. "Because we're already here."

Scout looked around her, and gasped. "Oh! I've been here." The words were out of her mouth before she could stop them. They'd stopped here on the way back from Domingo Canyon. What was he trying to do to her, anyway?

"Sure, you have." Nick shrugged. "It's been here forever. Everybody's been here."

She was about to say more, was about to say that she had been here with *him*, and more than once, but the indifference in his voice hurt too much. If he didn't remember, she wasn't going to be the one to remind him.

*"We aren't the same people we were back then."*

*"We're two completely different people now."*

The words he had spoken a few minutes before, the words she'd said to Glenn Monday night, came back to haunt her.

*We had something.* Glenn had insisted. *You know that as well as I do. Who knows what might have happened, if things had been different? I always thought we would have made a good couple. Maybe we still could.*

Oh, God. She could imagine herself saying the exact same things to Nick. Was it possible? *Oh, no. Surely not?* That the way she felt about Glenn, was the same way Nick felt about her?

*We had something...you know that as well as I do.*

And if she said that to Nick now, would he answer, as she had answered Glenn the other night?

*Yeah, we had something. I'm just not sure what.*

She swallowed hard, blinking back her tears and looked with unseeing eyes at the scenery.

"It's changed some," she said finally.

"Yeah. You're in luck," Nick drawled. "The food's better now."

THEY ATE OUTSIDE, perched on one of the picnic tables, both of them facing out toward the ocean, their feet on the bench, and about half the length of the table stretching between them. This was nothing like what he'd had in mind when he'd called her last night. Back when he still believed that they could spend some time together, maybe get used to being with one another again, without it driving him crazy.

Back before it even occurred to him how maddening it might be to sit across from her in the intimate confines of a booth. Even more frustrating than sitting beside her in the car had been.

"You want to eat inside or out?" he'd asked her, hoping she would choose one of the picnic tables at the bluff's edge. Not that she had given him any reason to suppose she even noticed the tension he was under. Whatever reaction he might be having, she clearly didn't share it.

"Does it make a difference?" she responded; her voice as unenthusiastic as he'd ever heard it.

"Well, if we eat out here, you can still smoke." He nodded towards her hand, where her cigarette was burning away.

"Oh. Right. That's fine, then." Scout shrugged, and then, once they had gotten their food, she proceeded to lose herself in the view. Apparently, she was more hungry for the scenery than for her sandwich, which sat untouched on the table beside her.

What was she thinking about, anyway? He sneaked a look at her from the corner of his eye, but her face told him nothing.

"You know," he said, finally breaking a long silence. "I think we just might be the last two cigarette smokers left in the entire state."

She shook her head. "Not really. I haven't smoked in years. It's this place. I just started up when I got here. I'm sure it's only temporary. I'll probably stop again as soon as I leave Oberon."

"Yeah. Me, too," Nick replied absently—adding, when he saw the confused expression look on her face— "I just started again recently, I mean."

"Oh, yeah? Why'd *you* start?"

"Oh, you know." He waved his hand in a vague, casual gesture as he improvised. "Reasons. My ex-wife was being a pain in the butt. She messed up my vacation plans with my daughter."

He took a deep breath before continuing, in a voice he had to struggle to keep casual. "So, I guess maybe my problem's not as temporary as yours. I take it you haven't moved back here for good?"

"Oh, hell no," she answered, with a fierceness that surprised him. "Are you kidding me? I hate this place. All the magic and the mysticism and stuff? Shit, if I even hear the word *synchronicity* again any time soon...I really think I might scream."

*Wow. That much, huh? Terrific.* "The view's nice, though," he said, hoping he might get a smile, or even a laugh. "You know? The buena vista of bar and grill fame?"

But she just snorted, without mirth. "Yeah." She sighed. "Yeah, the view's nice, all right." After a moment she continued. "You know, I had a car accident out here the other day,"

"Yeah, I know. I saw your car," he answered, again without thinking.

"What? You did? When?"

"No, I mean...I saw that your car was gone. Yesterday. You mentioned last night that you were having it fixed."

"Oh. Right."

"So, uh, what's that got to do with mysticism? Or are you saying you only get into accidents here in Oberon?"

"Sometimes it does seem that way. Hunh..." She paused for a moment, as if struck by a sudden thought. And then, shook herself and began again. "Anyway, I was up at the festival, right? And when I was leaving I, uh…well, I thought I could beat the crowd, by sneaking out the back way. You know, by going through Domingo Canyon?"

She wasn't looking at him, when she said it, and he didn't think she saw the look he shot her way. "It's a tricky road," he said quietly, between gritted teeth. "What happened?"

"Oh, the usual. Some car tried to pass me. Yeah, on *that* road, if you can imagine. But, you know, I'm sure it happens all the time after the festivals. I'm sure there are a lot of folks who get too drunk, or stoned, or sleep deprived and lose their judgment. Anyway, he just clipped my fender, but it was enough to make me lose control and smash into the hillside.

"And, the thing is, he came really close to hitting me broadside, which would have probably run me off the road." She laughed again – the same short, humorless sound as before. "Well. There's no probably about it, I guess. And you know, when I say *off the road* up there, I mean really *off the road*. The only reason I'm still here is that just before it would have hit me, I heard a voice in my head that told me to slam on the brakes."

"Jesus!" Nick felt his throat tighten in panic. He had to clench his fists to keep from grabbing her. *She was nearly killed? I came that close to losing her forever?*

"That's what I mean about this place," she continued, unaware. "After a couple of days I'm not only smoking like a chimney, I'm hearing voices. What's next? Visions? Transmogrification? Full scale possession?"

She slid off the table, and stood facing him, her arms wrapped around herself as though she were suddenly cold. "I don't know, Nick. You think the *nice view* is enough to make up for losing my mind? 'Cause I'm thinking I'm gonna maybe need a little more incentive than that, to stick around."

He didn't answer right away. He couldn't. "What kind of car?" he got out at last, his voice cold and flat.

"What? Mine?"

"The one that hit you."

Scout shrugged impatiently. "No idea. It happened too fast. I just got one look as this big, dark *thing* flashed passed me, you know? It was big. An SUV or something, I guess. But what's the difference? Who cares what kind of car it was?"

"Well, there are laws," he reminded her. "Did you report it?"

She stared at him in amazement. "You see? This is why I can't ever live here! I tell you I'm hearing voices and you don't even blink. All you want to know is did I report the accident."

She sighed and shook her head. "Are you finished? I'd like to get going."

Nick took out a cigarette and concentrated – very hard – on lighting it. He needed something to occupy his hands. Something to occupy his thoughts. Something to occupy his mouth.

*I can't live ever here.*

Well, she'd certainly said that loud and clear. And that, he thought somewhat bitterly, certainly answered one of his questions.

---

1. My husband and I met when we were both sixteen. We went on a lot of breakfast dates like this. He'd pick me up, early in the morning, and we'd stop at the bakery then take our coffee (well, *my* coffee, anyway—I forget what he drank back then) and pastries down to the river. We'd park and have breakfast. Or, you know, watch the submarine races. IYKYK

# 23

$\mathcal{I}$t was late afternoon when Nick pulled back up in front of Scout's house. They hadn't found her dog. They hadn't spoken much after their disastrous exchange at lunch, either. But they had each managed to maintain a cold civility, and he guessed he'd count that as a win.

He couldn't help but be aware of her growing disappointment as shelter after shelter had yielded no success. And now...man, she looked unhappy. Which was not at all what he'd wanted or hoped for. Not at all a part of his plan.

His plan had been, first of all, to make sure she understood he had not spent the last twenty years obsessing about her. He had tried this morning to make it crystal clear that he was totally indifferent to the events of twenty years ago. That he didn't still hold all the lies she'd told against her.

But, in retrospect, he had to admit that he might have gone a little overboard there. If only being with her wasn't making him so fucking nuts.

The second part of his plan had been to find the damn dog. If he had, it would have made the rest so much simpler. She would have been happy. Perhaps even grateful.

Grateful could have been very, very good.

Instead, she was silent and sad, and now – he watched as she eased the car door open – now she was leaving.

"Well, thanks for trying," she said, turning back to him for a moment, a small smile tugged at one corner of her mouth. "I guess I'd better go."

"I'll walk you to the door," he replied grimly, wondering if there was any possible way that he could still salvage this disaster.

At the door, Scout paused with her hand on the knob. "Do you want to come in?" Her voice was toneless, she didn't even bother to look at him, and her entire body had gone rigid—just as though her desire to get rid of him was at war with some notion she had of good manners. She took a deep breath. "I mean, the least I can do is get you a drink. Or something, I suppose?"

It was quite probably the least enthusiastic invitation he had ever received from a woman in his life. And if she had been anyone else—anyone at all—he would have turned her down flat. But this was Scout, and he'd take whatever opening she gave him.

"I guess I could go for a drink," he said, carelessly. *Drinks? Sure, why not. Plenty of possibilities there.* "I'll call the station, while I'm here. Maybe there's some news about your friend."

Scout was searching the kitchen for something to offer him when Nick joined her. She glanced at him hopefully, but he shook his head. She felt discouragement settle more heavily in her chest. "Damn," she said softly.

"So, what've you got?" Nick came up behind her, peering over her shoulder into the refrigerator, just as Marsha had done the day before. Scout had to resist the urge to shut the door before he could see inside. The shelves were nearly empty, and suddenly that seemed too pathetic for words. "Jeez. Don't you have any food? What do you do? Eat all your meals out, or something?"

She sighed. "I guess it looks that way, doesn't it? Anyway, there's beer, some wine, a couple of spring waters. Sorry. I wasn't exactly planning on entertaining.

"It doesn't look like you were planning on eating dinner tonight either."

"I'm not really hungry."

"No? Well, I am. How about I order us a pizza?" he suggested in a disinterested voice, still staring absently into the open refrigerator.

She glanced up, startled by his suggestion. He met her eyes briefly.

"I was gonna pick one up on my way home, anyway," he said with a small shrug, as he returned to his pointless perusal of the empty white box. "And I figure you gotta eat, too, right?"

*What's going on here?* Scout wondered. She really couldn't stand to see any more of her fantasies crash and burn tonight, but every once in a while, like now, he said or did something that left her thinking there was still a chance.

Oh, hell, she was probably about to make another huge mistake, but she supposed things really couldn't get any worse. And she could use the company. Anything was better than the loneliness she was sure to feel when he left. Or almost anything. And if there was even the slightest possibility—

"Okay," she said making up her mind, at last. "But this is my treat. You didn't have to spend your whole day looking for my dog the way you did. I really am grateful."

"It's a deal," Nick said, and she could actually feel some of the tension leave his frame. But before she had even a moment to wonder about that, his face was suddenly illuminated by a dazzling smile, and she lost the ability to reason at all.

He reached around her for one of the beers, and as his arm brushed against hers, she shivered. He was so close, now. She could feel his breath, warm against the side of her neck. She slipped quickly under his arm, and away.

"Help yourself to anything you find in there," she called as she headed towards the phone. "I'm just going to make that call now. Be right back."

*Oh, God, that was close.* She leaned her head against the wall in the hallway for several long minutes, waiting for her heart to stop hammering. Way too close. How could she have forgotten what it did to her when he smiled like that, or when he touched her?

How could she possibly have imagined she could keep up the pretense of indifference once they were here? In this house, of all places! And alone. With all these rooms, and all these possibilities and without the comfortable, familiar barriers of seat belts and stick shifts between them?

She should just turn around, go right back in there and tell him she'd changed her mind. She could say she wasn't hungry, or she had a headache, or she'd forgotten an appointment. It didn't matter what she said. Any excuse would do.

*But then he'll leave.*

And even though his leaving was the best, most sensible, safest thing that could happen, it was also the last thing she wanted him to do.

*I can do this*, she told herself, as she forced herself to breathe; *there's no need to panic.* She'd managed all day, hadn't she? She was sure he didn't have a clue how she was *really* feeling.

She would be all right as long as he didn't touch her.

She could handle anything else, but not that. And no more smiling either. As long as she kept her distance, she was sure she'd be fine. But distance was critical. Because if he touched her...who knows what she might do?

THEY TOOK their drinks out to the patio while they waited for the pizza. And if Scout thought that being out of the house would be an improvement, she quickly realized her mistake. Her younger self had imagined scenes like this one far too many times...

*There would be music playing, and the two of them would be right here on the sun-warmed bricks of the patio, with the hot tub, and the Mexican ceramic fireplace, and the large, old, Royal Palm tree strung with tiny white lights...*

She'd turned on the lights tonight almost without thinking—the stereo as well. And now she felt almost as though she'd entered one of her own fantasies.

Except that the hot tub had always figured a little more prominently in most of those fantasies.

Nick was standing a slight distance away from her, leaning on the railing, taking in the view. She found her own gaze returning, again and again, to his profile. She swallowed hard, as she wrenched her eyes away, forcing herself to focus on the larger view, instead.

She had filled the bird feeders early that morning in a fit of enthusiasm; now, what seemed like dozens of house finches darted and swooped across the yard. Two of the cats sat motionless on the deck, watching them through slitted eyes. The gardens, always lush with flowers anyway, positively shimmered as the slanting rays of the sun glinted off the wings of the butterflies and hummingbirds that fluttered around the blossoms. The mingled scents of honeysuckle, jasmine and rose was almost overpowering.

To the left of the yard rose the dark, graceful woods, through which she used to travel back and forth to school. And in the distance, partially obscured, a sliver of ocean view could be glimpsed – sparkling, pure shot silver –between the large, old bay laurel trees that bordered the property line at the back. [1]

It was impossibly romantic, Scout thought, with a flash of irritation. It was completely, totally and unfairly romantic with the golden sun gilding everything it touched. With the soft sounds of bird calls filling the perfumed air. And with Nick—actually here, and looking so impossibly good.

*Oh, fuck my life.* She was staring at him again. But she just couldn't help herself. There were those soft curls at the nape of his neck that just brushed against his collar. And his arms, looking so strong and tanned—

How could you look at arms like that, and not wonder how it

would feel to have them wrapped around you? The problem was, she remembered all too well what it felt like. And she wanted to feel it again.

*Forget it,* a harsh voice in her head kept saying. *That was years ago. He doesn't care now. Hasn't he made that perfectly clear? He's moved on with his life Why can't you?*

Scout took another sip of her Shiraz. The smooth, peppery coolness slid down her throat to turn warm in her stomach. And all the while a smaller, softer voice was insisting, *but he did care, once. And I bet I could make him care again.*

"Nice," Nick said appreciatively, turning back to face her. Forcing her back to reality.

"Yes. It is." Scout sighed wistfully. And, struggling to recapture her former coolness, she made herself add a casual, "It's just about the only thing in Oberon I really missed." *Almost the only thing.*

"Huh. Well, you couldn't have missed it that much, I guess. Seeing as you somehow managed to stay away from it all this time."

She retreated to the table and busied herself with lighting a citronella candle. "It wasn't really that simple. Or that easy."

"So, tell me," he suggested softly. He was leaning against the railing with his arms crossed, and a look in his eyes she found disturbingly similar to those of the cats'.

Watchful. Predatory. Dangerous.

She felt a small, familiar thrill of excitement. Nick had always seemed just the slightest bit dangerous. It was a big part of what had attracted her in the first place, the idea that she was playing with something wild. Something that might turn unpredictable and scary without warning. *Like now.* But she was older now, and hopefully wiser. *I can handle this.*

Still, she shook her head. "It's a long story."

He shrugged. "Well, we've got the time. The pizza won't be here for another ten minutes you said."

*Right. Shit.* "Okay, well...to start with, my father was dead. I think things might have turned out very differently if he'd lived, but..."

"How'd he die again?"

"Car accident and...well, I think my stepmother wished I had died instead. Actually, no, I know she did; she told me so."

"Jesus."

"Well, it was my car, so..."

"So...were you the one driving it?"

"No, I wasn't in the car at all. I was still grounded for life, at that point."

"Well then...?"

"I don't know what else to tell you. It never made any sense to me, either. I guess she thought I *should* have been the one driving it, or something?"

"Well, that doesn't seem very fair."

"What's fair got to do with anything? Nothing was fair. Her husband was dead, her daughter was missing and, as far as she was concerned, the person who was to blame for all of it was me. Safe to say I was *not* her favorite person at that point.

"So, I had no family left to speak of, and my friends were more than happy to see the last of me. So, you know," She shrugged. "What did I have to come back for?" *You, maybe?* She held her breath while she waited to see what he'd say.

But Nick just stared at her for a long, tense moment with an odd, slightly confounded expression on his face. As if she'd told a joke but blown the punch line.

"Did I miss something?" he said at last, picking up his beer again, and taking a slow, casual swallow. "I thought you said this was a *long* story."

"Right," Scout said with a tired sigh. "I lied. It's not long. Just really depressing. Can we please talk about something else?"

"Sure." He shifted position, slightly. "How about...what have you been doing with yourself for the past twenty years?"

"Oh, enough about me! How about we talk about what *you've* been up to, instead?"

Nick assumed an expression of innocent surprise. "You mean Lucy didn't already fill you in on everything you never wanted to know about my life?"

"I thought we weren't going to do this again?" she begged him. "Please. I can't take any more."

"Okay, fine. Seriously, though. What is it you do, when you're not here searching for lost relatives, lost roommates or lost pets? Do you realize I don't even know where you live now?"

"Well, it's hardly a secret." She shrugged. "I live in Venice Beach. I — God, I hate to call myself an artist, it sounds so pretentious, doesn't it? But I guess you could say I'm a sculptor. At the moment, anyway. I work with ceramics mostly, and some bronzes. I have pieces in a couple of galleries. I also do some other stuff – vases and tea sets, stuff like that – for some of the local art fairs. That's it, really. I was an actress for a while. But I kinda quit that."

He looked amused. "Really? Why's that? I'd have thought it'd be right up your alley."

"Yeah, well....it was fun, I guess, but acting is such a collaborative thing. There were always so many people around. I found I was more suited to working alone."

"Ever been married?"

She snorted. "After the great example my father set for me? No. No way. Never. How about you?"

"Yeah, well, marriage didn't really work for me, either. I have a daughter, though. Kate."

"I know." She felt herself blushing again. "I, um, I met her at the festival last week."

"Oh, yeah." Laughter glinted in Nick's eyes. "I heard about that. You and Marsha got into some kind of brawl, didn't you? Was that the first time you'd seen each other, or something?"

And she *so* wanted to discuss that subject. "Not exactly. So, what happened with you and your wife?"

He frowned. "It's kind of like your story, short and depressing. Let's not talk about that, either."

"A fine pair of conversationalists we are," she muttered grimly. "Were we always this chatty?"

A smile lifted one corner of his mouth. "Well, I have to admit, it's not really our conversations that I remember most when I think about the time we spent together back then."

She couldn't read the expression in his eyes as he pushed himself off the railing and crossed the deck to sit down opposite her, but she felt her skin pebble up in anticipation, all the same.

*Close. Way too close.*

Maybe it had something to do with the way the light was reflecting in his eyes, she thought irrationally. He didn't look like a cat after all now, but something even more fearsome. Something that relied less on cunning and more on deadly strength. She found herself staring into his eyes and couldn't look away. Her breath caught in her throat. Above the sudden pounding in her ears she heard a faint chime. *Thank God.*

"Doorbell," she said as she jumped to her feet. "That must the pizza. I'll go get it."


NICK WATCHED her run off to answer the door. Shit. She'd looked like a scared rabbit just then, which was a hell of a thing. Man, he sure hadn't seen that one coming. He'd better just eat his pizza, assuming he could even swallow past the disappointment in his throat and leave. Because it was becoming pretty damn obvious that she didn't want him around.

Maybe it had been a mistake, stretching the day out this long. Maybe he should have cut it off this morning, like he'd originally planned. Maybe she felt he was rushing her? He sure hoped that's all it was, because at least he could do something about that. Except... well, no, maybe he couldn't, either.

No matter how much he tried to tell himself they were strangers – that he needed to take things slowly, get to know her, give her a chance to know him – his body wasn't buying it. Not for a minute. As far as it was concerned, she was his, and always had been.

All the years of waiting had only sharpened a need that had been there forever. The need was so sharp now, he was having real trouble thinking of anything else.

It didn't help that attempting to talk to her was like walking through a minefield, either. So many subjects to avoid: the past, the future, his marriage, anything at all to do with Oberon apparently, and worst of all, how much he wanted things between them to go back to the way they used to be.

Probably best to stick to safe topics. Like work. Work had been good for oh, a whole five or six sentences already. A record, of some sort.

So, she was an artist now. Yeah, well, that was no surprise. It's what she'd always said she'd wanted. And LA; yeah, he could see that, too. He could imagine her there, hosting glittering parties on the terrace of some beach house. Always dressing in white to highlight her tan, accenting her outfits with colorful silk scarves, nothing at all like the clothes she'd wear here in Oberon. He could see her attending gallery openings and private shows. Always the center of everybody's attention, surrounded constantly by throngs of admirers.

It was nice to hear that her life had stayed on track. Too bad he'd wasted so much of his own life, waiting for her to come back to him. But that wasn't actually true, was it? What would he have done differently? He'd gotten married. He'd fathered a child. Maybe he wasn't very good at either of those things, but that was hardly her fault.

And his work...no, there really wasn't anything he would have changed there. Oberon might not have a huge crime problem, but it did attract some strange people, from time to time. Unpleasant people. The kind of people who liked to cause trouble. It was his job to find them and stop them before they caused too much. Over the years, he'd gotten real good at it. He loved his job. It was the only part of his life that actually worked. And, no matter what Lauren had always claimed, it was never boring. At least *he'd* never found it boring.

On the other hand, he'd already outlasted two partners who had, so maybe his was not a universal opinion. He worked alone most of the time now, ran his own investigations and, like she said, he found it suited him better.

*So, there you go.* He knew a fleeting moment of hopefulness. There was something they had in common, after all. A promising topic for conversation. When she came back, maybe they could discuss how much they both liked being alone.

*Oh, that would be smooth, all right. Shit.*

Maybe she was right. Maybe they *did* have nothing to talk about; maybe they never really had. After all, most of what they'd said to each other twenty years ago had been based on lies. But he had not exactly told the truth when he said he didn't remember their conversations. They had driven around for hours at a time back then, and they had talked plenty.

It couldn't all have been lies—could it?

Even if it was, who cared? What difference did it make? The truth was, he just liked the way it felt to be around her. He still did. That had to count for something, didn't it?

But not like this. He couldn't take much more of this shit. The distance thing was becoming a real problem for him. The more he felt her pushing him away, the more it made him want to push right back.

*What did I have to come back for...*

He still could not believe he'd heard that right. That she'd actually had the nerve to say that –to him! Or that he hadn't grabbed her right then and there and given her a good example of just what she'd had or could have had.

He tossed back the rest of his beer and went off in search of another. Maybe he should do the smart thing and go home. Cut his losses and walk. Now. Before he embarrassed himself. Or, before the anger flaring up inside him could reach the flashpoint. Give it up as a hopeless cause. A dream that had died. A fantasy he should have buried years ago.

*Walk,* the voice of reason insisted. *Do it, now.* Except...he didn't want to end it yet. He wanted more time with her. He *needed* more time. After all these years, was that really too much to ask for? Just to spend a little time with her before she disappeared again—as he knew she would?

*Walk away from her!* The voice was screaming now. But it didn't matter how loud it spoke, or how often. Walk away from her? He knew he never could.

———————————————

1. The summer before we moved to Berkeley, we spent a lot of our time camping outside San Rafael in a grove of bay laurel trees. It still remains one of my favorite scents. But, other than that, I modeled Scout's backyard mostly on the house I was living in at the time I wrote the book. All except for the brick patio: that was taken from the house I grew up in. AND the royal palm, strung with lights—THAT was taken from a house that we considered buying. And THAT house makes an appearance in books seven and eight; I gave it to Chenoa

# 24

$\mathcal{N}$ick pushed his way into the house, almost colliding with Scout in the dimly lit kitchen. She gasped, and all but dropped the pizza box she was holding. They regarded each other in silence.

There it is again, he thought irritably, that same wary, frightened look he'd seen in her eyes earlier. Twenty years he'd been waiting for her. Was one lousy smile too much to expect? Couldn't she even give him that much?

"Is- is something wrong?" She stammered breathlessly.

"Yeah. Why are you so damn jumpy?" Nick snapped at her, in reply.

Scout blinked. "I'm not...jumpy." But he could see her hands clench more tightly on the box.

He grabbed it away from her and dropped it on the counter. She closed her eyes, briefly, involuntarily it seemed, almost as if she expected him to strike her. And that thought caused his temper to flame even higher. Dangerously so. Christ, what the hell did she take him for, anyway?

"You look like you're scared to death of me right now," he insisted, taking a step closer. "And you're shivering." His hands closed on her arms. "What's going on here, Scout? Do you want me to leave?" His voice was low, hoarse, and he didn't know what he would do if she said yes, since leaving now was out of the question.

"No," she whispered.

That whisper was going to drive him mad. He let her go abruptly, backing away from her, his hands tensing into fists at his sides. His next words were out of his mouth almost before he thought them. "Have you seriously gotten involved with that jerk, again?"

Her head snapped up at that. "Have I...? What jerk? Who're we—?"

"Glenn. Your lawyer?"

"What? No! Jesus. Why on earth would you ask *that*?"

"You saw him on Monday, remember? You had *dinner* with him? At least that's what you said yesterday."

She looked away. "Oh, that. Look, the situation...it's a little awkward, okay? When he first showed up I...well I couldn't exactly tell him to get lost, now could I?"

"Why not? Was it because you're hoping he'll help you find out what happened to your stepsister? Or is it awkward because you slept with him?"

"All of the above, I guess," she answered, reaching for the wine bottle on the counter to pour herself another glass. "You know something, Nick, this is starting to get a little old. I feel like all I've done for the past week is apologize for mistakes I made back when I was a kid. Ever since I got here, I've had to deal with all these people who think I screwed them."

"Only, in Glenn's case, it's literally."

She made a face. "Gee. Thanks for bringing that up."

"Unlike me."

"What?"

"You didn't—literally—screw me."

"Oh." She colored slightly and took a long drink. A hint of something—mischief, anger, interest, he couldn't decide what—gleamed in her eyes as she studied him appraisingly over the rim of her glass.

"Yeah, but you know," she said she lowered the glass. "I really don't think I can take credit for that. You just got lucky, is all."

*Lucky?* "Interesting choice of words. How do you figure that?"

But, at that, her eyes turned cold. She turned on him. "Look, I get it, okay? For all your fine words about starting over, you're still upset about everything that went down twenty years ago. Right? Well, fantastic. Join the club.

"But you know what? Sure, I made mistakes—it happens. People *do* that. Only, for some reason, it seems like I'm never gonna be allowed to forget about mine. Which is yet another reason why I never came back here before now. *And* the reason why I don't plan on staying an instant longer than I absolutely have to. But as far as you're concerned, I think it's time for a reality check. You got off easy."

"You think so?"

"Yeah, I do. If we'd kept going the way we were going, then yes. You would have been screwed. Literally *and* legally. And maybe then you'd have had a reason to hate me. But it didn't happen, so..." She shrugged and took another sip of wine. "You're off the hook. Sure wish I was."

"Oh, I see." Fury raged inside him. He took a deep breath and reminded himself to stay calm. "So, you came to your senses just in time, and dumped me for Glenn in order to save me from myself? I'm touched, really. But I gotta tell you if *that's* your definition of *getting lucky?* Then I could think of a much better one."

Scout's frown turned puzzled. "I dumped you? When did that happen? Is that what you thought?"

"No, Scout. What I thought is that you were just a kid who liked to play games. And I'm sure you got a real big kick out of pretending you were attracted to me just so you could piss Lucy off."

"That's not—"

"Forget it." Nick shook his head. *Jesus Christ, some great seduction this is turning out to be.* How in hell had they gotten off on this tangent, anyway? "It's like we agreed earlier; it was a long time ago. So, what difference does it make now—right? Water under the bridge." He reached over and flipped up the cover of the pizza box.

He picked up a slice and took a bite. "Come on, we better eat this. It's not gonna get any warmer."

She didn't move. And for a moment, she didn't speak. And then, "You're wrong, you know," she said, staring at the island in front of her, her voice low and husky. He looked at her. Two bright spots of pink burned on her cheeks.

*Now what?* He eyed her wearily, chewing pizza with dogged determination, although he might as well have been eating the box for all the flavor it had for him. "Wrong about what?"

"I'm not sure, exactly, where Lucy comes into all this, but I certainly didn't dump you, Nick. And I wasn't pretending to be attracted to you, either."

*Yeah, right.* "Whatever." Nick shrugged and busied himself with opening another beer. He was curious to see if she would continue, but she just fiddled with the stem of her glass and refused to look at him. *So, what else is new?*

He leaned back against the counter and started on another slice of pizza. He could wait her out, if that's what it was going to take. It was what he did best, after all. If he said nothing, sooner or later, she was bound to start talking. Bound to say something – anything – to fill the silence. He gave her a cool, considering look. How long before she cracked? Already he could see that her lower lip was trembling, ever so slightly. And...ahh, hell.

"Okay," he said, dropping the slice back into the box and folding his arms across his chest. "I'll bite. You lied to me, not because you were trying to get me in trouble or tick off your friends, but because... you were madly in love with me? Was that it? And then, let's see, you slept with your sister's boyfriend, instead of with me, because...? Help me out here, Scout. What was it? You were trying to protect me? You couldn't resist him? The opportunity to piss your sister off was just too good? What?"

"It was a mistake!" she yelled, and then she shook her head. "I just — No. Forget it."

"Uh-huh." He took a long, steadying drink before he asked her, "So, just for the record, when were you planning to tell me the truth?"

"About my age and...and my name and everything? Well, not before I turned eighteen, anyway."

"*Two years?*" Nick set the bottle down on the counter hard and stared at her in shocked amazement. "Holy shit, babe. I realize you didn't exactly have a high opinion of my intelligence—with cause, I'll grant you that—but you actually thought you could get away with lying to me about something like that *for two whole years?*"

"Well, I was hoping I could." A small smile flicked at the edge of her mouth. "It'd worked so far. And anyway, it wouldn't have been two *whole* years, really. I just...I wanted you."

She looked straight at him then, and Nick felt as if her eyes were twin lasers, piercing their way through all the years of doubt.

"I wanted you and I couldn't stand the thought of losing you. And I would; I knew I would. I knew that when you found out, if you found out, you wouldn't...you wouldn't want me anymore."

"Oh, I still wanted you." Nick grimaced, remembering just how much. He pushed himself away from the counter then, moving slowly across the narrow space that separated them, his eyes never leaving her face. "Learning the truth didn't change *that*. I still wanted you as much as I ever did. But you're right. I would not have kept seeing you. And I *definitely* wouldn't have slept with you. At least, I'd like to think I wouldn't've."

He stopped, then. He was breathing hard with the effort it was taking to keep himself from grabbing her. He wanted to believe her. Oh, how he wanted to believe that she was telling the truth now, that this wasn't just another lie. But there were still a couple of feet between them, and although she hadn't moved away from him, neither had she made any effort to close the gap.

He needed her to make a move. Some move. Any move. Anything to show that she meant what she said, that it wasn't just empty words.

He forced himself to stay where he was, and smile as he said, in an attempt at easing the tension, "I had *some* standards, you know— even back then." *Oh, like hell I did.* Whatever standards he'd had left at that point wouldn't have held for more than another week – at the absolute outside.

.  .  .

284

SCOUT TRIED hard to return his smile, but she was just too tired for the effort. And too unbearably depressed. "Yeah. I know." She swallowed hard and lifted her chin at him, defiantly. "Unlike me, you mean?"

"You want the truth, babe?" he asked, sounding angry again. "I didn't give a rat's ass about your standards. I wasn't expecting you to be a virgin. Hell, you *knew* that! But what I never suspected that I was just priming your pump! That you were taking all the passion we had, all that heat, everything I was building between us and just... just giving it away to some asshole!"

His face had grown dark again. Dangerous. An icy rage was burning in his eyes. Scout's breath caught in her throat as terror flooded suddenly through her veins.

*Oh, shit. No. Not again. Not again!*

She'd seen that look before. Just once before had he looked at her with that same mix of anger and passion and pain burning in his eyes.

"It wasn't like that," she croaked, trying to fend off the rising panic. She felt as if she'd been sucked off her feet by an undertow; dragged, with no warning, out beyond her depths. [1]

Twenty years ago she'd seen that look in his eyes and knew she'd lost him.

For twenty years, she had buried the memory, and the pain that went with it. She had stayed away from home for all that time because having nothing, feeling nothing, was better than having to endure this pain ever again. She felt the room whirl around her. And suddenly...

She was sixteen, again. Frozen where she sat. Hands clenched on the arms of the hard wooden chair, feeling the wood give slightly beneath the pressure of her nails.

Sister Benedict's office. Her father sitting beside her because a parent had to be present when a minor was questioned by the police. Sister Benedict sitting across from her because it was her office, her school, and that was the way she wanted it.

*Do they sense it, too?* she wondered. Could anyone else feel what was happening? Was the sudden drop in temperature perceptible to anyone but her? She felt their eyes on her. Their hard gazes seemed to hold her in her place – like two arms of a vise – when she would otherwise have bolted. But she saw only Nick.

Her eyes were locked with his, and the look on his face lanced through her. Like a stake through her heart.

It was several seconds before Scout understood she hadn't died from the pain. That she would not die. That something far, far worse was occurring. Several endless seconds before she understood that the booming silence in her head, and the slicing, tearing, cold sensation she had taken to be the blood draining from her heart, was merely the way it feels to watch your world come crashing to a halt.

*The undead,* she thought in the absurdity of the instant. *That's what I've become.*

Stupidly, she thought of Juliet waking in her tomb and finding Romeo dead beside her. Her mind flashed on the image of the dagger-shaped letter opener she remembered having noticed on the desk in front of her. But she couldn't tear her eyes away from his to search for it.

She couldn't tear her eyes away from his until they had finished the job they had begun. Until they had burned through to the very center of her soul and turned to ash every last bit of life and joy and love and happiness that had been contained there.

Until she had been left as empty and cold and unfeeling as a dry husk.

Abruptly, the pressure in her chest receded and she found she could breathe again. She sighed and blinked and, realizing that Sister Benedict was speaking to her, she turned to her tranquilly, and answered her questions, and then all of Nick's queries as well, with unassailable calm and total indifference.

As if he were no one she had ever met before. As if the information she gave them was of no consequence, whatsoever.

*Oh, there's that letter opener,* a part of her thought incuriously. Not that it mattered. She had no need for it, now.

She did realize, in a detached, abstracted, disinterested sort of way, that this calmness was something different, something of a surprise, something that might have worried that part of her that had cared about things. If that part still functioned. But since it no longer did...

With a complete lack of concern, she answered truthfully all the questions that were posed to her, except for one. When she was asked for her whereabouts on the afternoon of Mrs. Burnett's murder, she turned cool, blank, passionless eyes to Nick's face and, in a voice devoid of all emotion, she lied.

The excuses she'd prepared ahead of time, the story she'd always planned on using in just such an event, sprang from her lips without any hesitation at all.

"I was with Glenn," she heard herself tell them. "At his house. All afternoon. We were making out." And she saw that look again, full of pain and hate. Only, this time it had no power to touch her at all...

Now, twenty years later, Nick stood before her, in the kitchen grown dark and cold. And once again, his eyes were dissecting her soul. Suddenly, the memories flooded back. Her heart awoke in such an agony of feeling, it was all she could do to keep from crying out.

This time, there was no one to stop her from moving. A distance of only two feet separated them, and Scout launched herself across it without a single thought. Blinded by her need, she threw herself against him, clutching desperately at his shoulders. Her lips sought and found his mouth, and she kissed him with every ounce of strength that she possessed.

HER ASSAULT TOOK him by surprise. He staggered backward a step at the impact. But then his arms wrapped around her, and he hugged her to him, as if it were possible to pull her any closer.

The taste of her mouth, something he hadn't even thought it possible to remember, almost made him cry. *Oh, God, it's been so long!* His hands slid under her shirt and over her back. And then down to her waist, and up again, over her ribs this time. Until at last he felt the weight of her breasts pressing against his thumbs, and her soft, soft, skin under his palms. His brain reeled at how unbelievably good she felt, how soft and warm in his hands.

The blood was thundering in his ears, and through the haze he heard her give a soft, shrill cry, like that of a wounded bird. Startled, he pulled his head back to look at her. Her eyes met his and the unremitting need that blazed there took his breath away. He bent his lips to hers again and felt her respond as if her very survival depended on what only he could give her.

And now, it was her hands that were moving—first grasping, and then tearing at the front of his shirt. With trembling hands that did not want to loosen their hold on her, he let go only long enough to help her pull it off. And then he took her shirt off, as well, pushing it over her head in one quick motion, stroking the straps of her bra off her shoulders and down her arms.

He groaned as she slid her hands over his shoulders to lock around his neck. She pressed herself back against him and her greedy mouth was on his again, and he was lost once more, in a lengthy exploration of her mouth. For a long, long moment he could think of nothing else. Then his hands were reaching behind her to undo the clasp of her bra, and he was dragging his lips away from her mouth, and across her neck, and then down, down to her breasts. To her nipples, already hard and taut. She raised up on her toes and arched herself closer to him with a soft, feral growling sound that drove him to the edge of madness. Her nails were digging into the back of his head now, holding him just where she wanted him to be, and his hands were cupped around her butt, pulling her closer, tight against him, while he suckled and licked at her.

A desperate voice in his head was whispering urgently of the need for a bed, a couch, the kitchen counter, the goddamn floor. *Just pick a place, damn it. Any place. Now!*

He pulled himself away and fought to get the words past the ragged rasping of his breath, as he held her close against his chest, where his heart was pounding far too fiercely.

·  ·  ·

"Your bedroom. Where—" she heard him say.

But she stopped him, her fingers trembling against the softness of his lips. "Don't talk," she told him, shaking her head slightly. She began to kiss him again, soft, hungry kisses. "Don't say a word."

*The undead don't crave words,* she wanted to tell him, *or even blood.* What she needed was a soul.

---

1.  . It's funny how some scenes just stick with you. Even all these years later, I still remember exactly where I was when I wrote this scene. I was in Ghirardelli Square in San Francisco, seated at a table on the terrace, overlooking San Francisco Bay. My sister-in-law was visiting from Virginia and she and my husband were sightseeing while I drank coffee and worked on my book. And, because I'm a little bit of a hoarder, it's entirely possible I still have the notebook I was writing in at the time. Although, on the other hand, that was nine moves ago, so maybe not.

## 25

Somehow, they made it up the stairs and into her bedroom, stumbling to a halt so many times Nick thought they'd never get there. He'd never known such greedy desperation. And then, finally, down, down, down, they were tumbling onto the softness of her bed.

They'd already lost most of their clothes along the way, and the sensation of naked skin on skin ignited every nerve he had. Her mouth had found his chest now, her tongue was tickling, licking, tasting, teasing. He groaned and levered himself up on top of her, and then over, rolling her with him, refusing to let her go for even an instant, as he worked at removing whatever last bits of clothing they still retained.

Thoughts began percolating up from the bottom of his brain, again. Thoughts he *really* didn't want to listen to and had, so far, managed to ignore.

*I didn't think this would happen tonight. I didn't come prepared.*

But his body didn't care. His body screamed for his mind to shut the fuck up! Just go away. Just please, please let me have this.

*Please, God, let me have her now.*

But he knew it was no good. And finally, with a shattered groan, he pulled himself away from her. "Scout," his voice raked against his throat, and his body trembled with the effort he was making. "Stop a minute. Honey, we can't...no, wait. Wait! Listen to me."

She stopped. In the cold moonlight coming in through the windows he could see her eyes glowing black, hard as obsidian.

"I'm sorry," he gasped, not believing what he was forced to say. "I wasn't thinking. You— you kind of took me by surprise, you know." He tried to smile. "We can't do this. We need...we have to wait...we have to have some, you know, protection. Unless...do you have something? A condom? Anything?" *Oh, God, please let her be on the pill.*

"No." Her voice was low. Quiet. Final. *Shit.*

"Honey, I..."

"No," she repeated, with a shake of her head. "And I don't care, not about any of that. I want you." The glittering black spheres of her eyes were fixed upon his face. "Now. I want to do this now."

Yeah, so did he, but, "Listen to me. We can't—"

"No!" *Oh, surely, surely he's not gonna do this to me again?* Scout thought in disbelief. *Not again? Not now?*

Desperation flared inside her. What was he waiting for? What more did he want from her? Dear God, hadn't they always stopped, before? Hadn't *she* always stopped? Whenever he'd asked her to? Every damn time?

And look where it had gotten them. Where it had gotten *her*. For twenty years her soul had been dead within her, and she hadn't even known it. How long would he make her pay, and go on paying, for the sin of loving him too much? Her eyes held his and would not let go, would not relent, would not back away. *He is* not *going to do this to me, she thought fiercely. Not now. Not again.*

But still he hesitated.

*Oh, God. This can't be happening.* Scout's pulse pounded frantically. Already, she could sense icy fingers reaching out to seal her heart back up in the soulless darkness.

"No, please," she whimpered, "Please." *Not that!* She could not go back to that. Could not bear to feel her newly re-awakened heart turn to ice again. With a desperate cry she pulled him down to her. "What more?" she whispered, her voice a broken sob against his neck. "Nick, please. What do you want from me?"

"EVERYTHING!" he gasped, as his resolve broke and he took what he had wanted for so, so long. His mouth found hers again, and all reason fled. He thrust both hands up through her hair, holding her head captive as he nibbled and sucked and licked his way slowly down her throat. And then he was taking her breast with his mouth again, while his hands stroked and caressed every part of her that they could reach – as if he would commit the feel of her entire body to his memory.

He was conscious of every gasp and whimper that she made, the sweetest sounds he'd ever heard. Of the taste and the smell of her. The wondrous, soft sleekness of her skin.

And when he could no longer stand not being inside her, he rolled on top of her, groaning at the eagerness with which she received him—her arms reaching up to clasp him to her; her legs parting to cradle him between her thighs. He slid his hands up under her arms, sliding his fingers along the length of them, until he'd grasped her hands.

Until their fingers had locked together on the bed above their heads. Their bodies stretching out together, in one long, fluid line, perfectly matched. Their mouths devouring each other with insatiable hunger.

Scout wrapped her legs around his back and clung to him and he thrust into her, felt himself enter and join with her, merge with her. Felt himself pulse hot and mindless into the melted core of her.

And then they were rocking together, lost to everything except the rhythm that was building between them. The room, the night, the world, all contracting around them. Shrinking into a dark, hard, tight point of power and light and life. Shrinking down and down and down until it could no longer contract and could only explode. Hot, sweet, ecstatic. Catching them both up and flinging them, gasping, against each other.

Slowly, Nick felt awareness returning. His breathing slowed, and then his heartbeat. He could feel Scout beneath him, and where their bodies were still joined, he could feel her shuddering softly. He bent his head to look at her, curious to discover her mood. She raised damp eyes to his.

"You won't leave?" she asked, softly hopeful.

He shook his head.

"Not ever?"

*Ever? What are we even talking about?* He hesitated for the smallest fraction of a second, and then shook it once again.

"Never," he promised as he gently, reluctantly, pulled out of her, and then reached down to pull the blankets up around them both.

"Never," he murmured as he kissed the curve of her shoulder and felt himself drifting toward sleep.

Her head nestled against his shoulder, and he was aware of her soft, contented sigh, of her eyes falling shut.

"Never," he whispered it softly, once again, with his lips against her hair, though he didn't think she still could hear him. And then his own eyes closed, and he knew nothing more.

WHEN NICK AWOKE, several hours later, he was lying on his back with one arm still clasped around her shoulders. She was on her side, the entire length of her body pressed tight against his own. One arm lay draped across his chest. Her head rested in the curve of his arm. He sighed happily into the darkness. He wasn't sure how he'd ended up here tonight, but sweet Jesus, it felt good.

Dazedly, he reviewed the events of the evening. One thing was certain, he'd probably never be able to figure out where he stood with this woman. One moment she'd been cold and distant, glaring as if she hated him, as if she'd just watched him murder a puppy, or something equally heinous. And then the next— Nope, he'd never be able to figure that one out, not if he had the rest of his life to try.

*Jesus. Is that what this is? The rest of my life?*

He smiled at the thought. It sounded good. He could take this for the rest of his life. No problem.

But then the palest, shadow of a doubt crossed his mind. Okay, problem. Possible problem, anyway. Possible *big* problem.

*You won't leave?* she had asked. But what had she meant by that? What *could* she have meant, when she'd just spent the whole day telling him how much she couldn't wait to leave town?

*And since when have I ever been the one to leave?*

Had she changed her mind then? Did she mean to stay? Again, he heard the words she had said at lunch, as they echoed in his memory. *I can't ever live here.* She'd sounded pretty sure of that.

Presumably she had a life in...LA, wasn't it? Would she really give that up? For him? When he hadn't even been a reason for her to come back in all that time, not even once? *What did I have to come back here for?* she'd asked.

*Not me, apparently.* But all the same; *she can't leave. She has to stay!*

Despair swamped him. He couldn't stand to lose her a second time. It was one thing to have gone without her for all these years— hell, it might even have been for the best. If she'd unleashed all that passion on him twenty years ago it would most likely have killed him. But now? Aww, hell. Now, it would kill him to let her go.

*She has to stay.*

He turned to her then, pushed himself up on one elbow, pulled back the covers so he could look at her. So that he could make certain that this time, at long last, it had not been a dream. He nuzzled her neck, her ear, kissed her softly, reverently. Kissed her ever so gently awake.

Her eyes fluttered open. She looked startled at first. Uncertain, but so lovely. She reached one hand up and softly touched his cheek, her mouth curving in a small, hesitant smile. "It's really you, isn't it?" she whispered. "We're really here? Together?"

He chuckled. "Yeah. I think so." *Oh, God, I hope so. Please don't let this be just another dream.*

"I was so afraid. I thought we wouldn't ever..."

"It took us long enough, huh?"

"It was all my fault." Tears shone suddenly in her eyes.

He shook his head. "No. Stop that. It wasn't *anybody's* fault. It's just the way it was, is all."

"But if only I—" she broke off on a sob, the tears sliding down her cheeks, and when he bent to kiss her, he could taste their salt on her lips.

"Shh," he whispered as he continued to kiss her tears away, kissing her cheeks, her eyelids, her mouth. "Don't cry, sweetheart. It doesn't matter, now, okay? None of it matters. Let's forget the past and just...enjoy the present." He didn't want to dwell on the past. And he couldn't bear to contemplate his future, either. But the present. Ah, now, that he could handle. The present was just about perfect.

She nodded, and kissed him back for several minutes, her sobs growing quieter and quieter and then, just when he thought his heart could not contain any more happiness, she looked up at him again. And smiled.

It started at one corner of her mouth, and spread, slow and sexy and certain until it had covered her face and flamed in her eyes. A rapturous smile that held love and wonder and desire.

A smile that held the promise of forever.

A smile he recognized from the depths of his soul.

"Oh, God," he groaned, as he wrapped his arms around her. "Jen. Oh, I've missed you. I've missed you so much!"

Scout's fingers raked through his hair as she pulled his face down to hers, and a deep throaty chuckle erupted from her throat. "Good." she said, just before she kissed him again. "Me, too."

Nick felt desire stir to life again, along with a nagging sense of guilt. They were acting like kids, which was certainly understandable given the circumstances, but even when he had been a kid he'd known better than to act as irresponsibly as this. Never in his entire life had he allowed himself to get this swept away, to lose control like he'd done tonight.

"I can't believe we're doing this," he groaned against her lips.

"I know," she giggled slightly as she returned his kiss, and then gently bit his lip.

"It's crazy," he muttered, grasping her head in his hands. Kissing her harder. Not wanting to think about anything else. But thinking about it anyway. "Crazy."

"Mm-hm." She kissed him again. And then, again. "Absolutely."

"It's so irresponsible. Really, I've never—"

"*Shhh!*" Scout laid fingers against his lips. She felt a sudden chill as his meaning finally got through to her, as she finally understood what he was saying. *He wants to stop.* They lay still for several moments, neither one speaking.

He sighed. "Look, it's not like— I mean, I've always been careful. So, you know you don't have to worry or, or anything, but..." his voice trailed off into silence.

Her cheeks burned. "I know. Me too," she whispered hoarsely, and then cleared her throat, and tried again. "I don't usually...that is, I've always...but tonight, well, it was *you!* And everything was so weird, and—"

"Right. But, there are other issues, too, you know."

Scout nodded. He was right, she knew that. But for once, oh God, she didn't care. No. If she were honest, there was more to it than that. She remembered her conversation with Marsha and Lucy. Remembered how their faces changed when they talked about their children. She knew exactly what Marsha meant when she spoke about Jasmine. She wanted to have that, too.

A tiny part of him that would always belong to her. An unbreakable bond between them.

*A piece of the magic.*

It wasn't fair. She knew that. And it probably wasn't right. It was, in fact, incredibly selfish. Not to mention absolutely insane, given their situation, and their history, their lifestyles, and all the craziness going on right now. But all the same...

She sighed and stroked her fingers lightly over his arm. "Would it really be so terrible?" she asked at last, in a quiet, sad, little voice.


*TERRIBLE?* Nick felt a thrill of surprise run through him. *To have a child with her? To see that smile of hers reproduced in miniature? And to know that there's a part of me there, too?* Unbidden, an image of himself holding a newborn appeared in his mind. Their baby.

Could that possibly be what she was thinking? It seemed extremely unlikely. Even more unlikely than the idea that this one night could prove that fateful. But if it *were* the case? "Nothing that comes of this could ever be terrible."

He gathered her back into his arms and took her mouth with such fierce possessiveness that Scout felt her breath go. She shuddered as an answering thrill surged through her as well.


*MINE. Mine. Mine.* The thought chanted in her brain, accompanied by an intoxicating feeling unlike anything she'd ever known. He was hers, if only for this one night, or this one moment. She knew beyond all doubt they belonged to one another, as surely as if their images had been seared into each other's souls. She didn't know if he felt it, too, but, oh, how could he not?

Tiny ripples of excitement ran through her as she thought of the days and weeks and years of wanting him and all the glittery danger that she had sensed in him. And now, finally, finally, at long last, they were together. And he was kissing her again, with those sweet, leisurely kisses that always made her lose her mind. He lay beside her, his arm cradling her neck. His free hand stroking through her hair, then tracing the line from her cheek to her throat, down over her breast to her waist, to her hip, the top of her thigh, and then back up again. His thumb grazed her nipple, and she gasped as she felt it harden again, in response to his touch.

He moaned softly and slid his mouth down to her breast, while her hand clenched in his hair, and she shuddered at the warmth of his mouth against her skin. She felt his lips tugging gently at her nipple, and then his tongue, sliding across the tip. And she was arching against him, again. Mindless with pleasure. Again.

She slid her own hand down between their bodies, her knuckles and the back of her hand trailing against his belly – over hair and skin and muscle, all of it shuddering under her touch –until she found the hard shaft of his penis, where it lay pressed tight against her thigh. She curled her hand around it, grasping and stroking the length of it. Thrilling to the smooth slide of his skin through her fingers, his deep rumbling groan of pleasure, and the heat of his breath against her wet nipple as he panted "Oh. God. *Yes.*"

She wanted to feel him deep inside her again, filling her and stretching her, but before she could tell him so, he had moved up to kiss her mouth again, his tongue licking deep into her, his breath coming harder and louder than before. The very sound of it excited her. Once again, she felt his hand slip down and down the length of her body. She let her legs fall open and his hand slipped between them to cup her gently, his touch stroking fire into her flesh, one finger sliding deep inside her, and out and then two fingers, again and again and again.

His lips were warm and wet against her neck, and then behind her ear, kissing and licking. His warm breath sent shivers skittering across her skin. She heard herself moan beneath the pressure of his hands and his lips and his tongue on her and in her. She clutched at him more tightly, her hands moving more rapidly over his body, delighting in the feel of him. His skin was damp with heat now, his muscles sliding and bunching underneath. She dug her nails into his shoulder, pressing herself against him, desperate to feel all of him, all over her, everything everywhere, all of it at once.

And then his hand was cupping her face. "Look at me," he begged with quiet urgency. She opened her eyes and found him staring down at her.

Her breath caught in her throat. He looked deeply, searchingly into her eyes, while she stared back into his. As though they could read each other's souls, in their depths. And everything she read there was open and trusting and true – as if there had never been a single lie between them.

He bent his head and kissed her mouth again—softly, with such sweet passion. And she knew, in the instant before her mind spun away, what it was that made her fall in love with him all those years ago. It hadn't been the lure of the danger after all, although that had certainly fueled the fire. It was this underlying sweetness, this purity, that had gotten to her, made her mindless with desire. Made her want to give him nothing less than everything. Anything he could think to ask for. Anything at all. Just for the chance to belong to him like this.

She pulled him close and lifted her body against him. She felt him pushing against her and again she opened for him; felt him stroking into her – deep, deeper, more deeply—and was once more overwhelmed with the sense of how right it was. How good he felt.

She had known it would be like this between them. She had *always* known. Today, yesterday, twenty years ago, a hundred years ago, a thousand years, forever.

She moaned, low in her throat, as she wrapped herself around him; longing to take him even deeper into her, to take all of him, to claim him for her own. To make him hers. Her breath came faster, hard, sharp, gasping breaths. She writhed to feel him, so hard against her. Her toes curled as everything inside her spiraled out of control, faster and sharper. She heard herself cry out as her body clenched and clenched and clenched around him. Heard him echo her cry as he drove himself into her one last time. Felt him convulse in her arms as she shuddered for breath.

In that moment she had no doubt but that they had been created for each other in the same fires, and by the same Power, that had brought the universe into being.

They belonged together; they had always belonged together. She felt the entire universe coalesce around them, a golden, glistening benediction.

And knew herself to be healed, whole, complete.

AFTERWARDS, they lay together amid the tangled sheets. She sprawled across his chest, while his hand traced idle circles against the small of her back. Scout sighed happily as she ran her fingers through the hair on his chest, brushing it first one way and then another.

"What are you thinking about?" Nick asked. His voice dreamy and quiet.

She ducked her head, shyly, and tugged at the hair beneath her hand. "This. It's different than I remembered. I think there's more of it. Isn't there?"

He chuckled sleepily. "I guess. Maybe."

Giddy, curious, she had to ask. "Am I different?"

"Mm-hm."

"How?"

He yawned. "You're even more beautiful now."

"Liar."

"Nope." He rolled over on his side then and smiled into her eyes as they lay face to face. The look in his golden-brown eyes made her so dizzy, it was all she could do to make sense of the words he was saying.

"You were beautiful then, too, of course. But it wasn't real. It was all just...some kind of lovely fantasy. I mean, if it was so obvious to everyone else how young you were, how could I have missed it? If I didn't see it, it could only be because I didn't want to see it. I wanted so much to believe you were who you said you were."

He shook his head. "I think a part of me must have known or at least sensed the truth. I was not exactly famous for my patience back then. I think I even told you that once. But there I was, taking it slow as hell...well, as slow as I *could,* anyway. And for no reason I would admit to. But this, now..." His hand stroked down her back, and he was smiling as he pulled her tight against him, belly to belly. "*This* is real. You. Me. This. And I don't need that fantasy, anymore."

He kissed the tip of her nose. "And you are *so* beautiful now. And every bit as sexy as I remembered."

"Mmm. So you're saying it was worth the wait?" she asked teasingly.

He didn't answer for a moment, but she felt his warm breath feather the hair at her temple. And then he rolled over onto his back again, taking her with him, closing his eyes and wrapping both arms around her. Holding her very, very tightly, as though he feared she'd slip away if he gave her even half an inch of space. His voice when he answered was quiet and ragged. "Oh, hon. I guess... Well, I guess you'd be worth waiting a hundred years for. But, to tell you the truth, I really could have done without most of the last twenty. Why'd it have to take you *so long* to come back to me?"

"I don't know." Scout sighed. "Life is strange, isn't it? Marsha says things always work out for the best, eventually. You think this is what she meant?"

"Maybe. I guess. Could be it's just as well we didn't get to do it all back then. If I'd known what I was *really* missing all these years, I don't know that I'd have been able to stand it. Just the fantasy of you was hard enough to live without."

They lapsed back into a thoughtful silence and Scout found herself thinking about what he'd said. Maybe he'd wanted the fantasy all those years ago, but she never had. It had come at too high a price. Sure, she'd been able to lie to him and to everyone else, and steal a few precious hours of bliss, but her happiness had been tempered by the knowledge of how easily it could all be taken away. And how much she'd have to give up to get it.

But things were different now. Now, anything was possible. Wasn't it? Anything at all?

# 26

*H*ours later, Scout awoke to sunlight streaming through the windows and the bed beside her empty. She sat up in a state of near panic, searching the room with frantic eyes. *Had it all been a dream?* "Nick?"

He stepped out of the bathroom, adjusting his clothes. Her heart slipped back down her throat and into her chest. He smiled at her bemusedly and shook his head. "I have to go to work." He sounded almost astonished. "I completely forgot about it. I wish I didn't, but I called in to see if anything was happening, and...I'm sorry, Scout, but I really do have to go." He sat back down on the bed, his eyes hungry and hot on her. "Dear God, you're beautiful."

She blushed and reached out wordlessly for him. He took her in his arms and held her close. His hands stroked her hair and her back and then, slowly, he eased himself away from her. "I have to go."

"But you'll come back, right?" she asked. "Later?"

He smiled. "Count on it. But never mind me, what about *you*? You're not going to disappear while I'm gone, are you?"

"N-no?"

"You sure about that? I'm not going to come back and find you missing again? I won't have to spend another twenty years, waiting and wondering?"

She shook her head, her lip trembling, tears starting in her eyes.

"All right then." He kissed her lightly on the top of her head, and then got up quickly and walked across the room. When he got to the door, however, he stopped to look back.

NICK PAUSED IN THE DOORWAY. *God, I hate leaving her like this.* She looked so lonely, so forlorn, and so damn lovely. Perhaps he could stay for just a little while longer...? But Jesus, who was he kidding? If he didn't go now, he wouldn't leave for...oh, hours at least. He could spend hours just looking at her, and looking was the least of what he wanted to do. Still, he hesitated.

"Are you going to be okay?" he asked her gently, almost hoping she'd say *no*, and give him a reason to stay. But she nodded, only a little uncertain.

"I love you; you know." The words were out of his mouth before he knew it. And with a shock he realized that it was true. It had always been true.

She stared at him, a tiny smile just barely warming away the sadness in her eyes.

He waited a moment longer, hopeful, but she didn't say anything. "Okay, well. I guess I'll see you later, then," he said and left her, without looking back.

*I love you, too,* Nick thought bleakly as he started up the car. Why couldn't she have said it? Even if it wasn't true. It wasn't as though she'd never lied to him before. It had been on the tip of his tongue to ask her, but somehow, he couldn't do it.

You couldn't ask a woman who'd made love to you all night with so much warmth and passion—and then begged you not to leave her —if she loved you. But did that mean you could take it for granted? He sighed and pulled the car away from the curb. He'd probably never understand that woman. And it was probably way past time that he got used to it.

. . .

Scout sat in the empty room, hugging the pillow to her chest, listening to Nick's footsteps descending the stairs, and then crossing the hallway. She heard the sound of the front door closing. Then the car door. Heard the car start up, slowly pull away, and slowly, slowly disappear down the block. His words still rang in her unbelieving ears.

*He loves me? How could he? What does that even mean?*

If *she* didn't know who she was anymore, how could he? But, oh, how she wanted to believe him. And oh, how she had wanted to tell him that she loved him, too. That she always had. But how fair would that have been—to say it now, while everything was in such a mess?

Well. She just wouldn't think about it, that's all. She wasn't sure she could think about anything right now, anyway. Not the way her head was already spinning with all the conflicting thoughts and emotions that swirled around within her. It was going to take some getting used to—having all these strange, yet achingly familiar feelings back.

Not that she wanted to go back to feeling dead inside, of course. But a little bit of balance would have been nice.

Everything looked and felt and sounded so much fresher and sharper. So much more painful and more fragile, too. Like a soap bubble that would burst if you breathed too hard upon it. A tide of happiness was rising within her like a flood of warm water, carrying the promise of stability.

*But it's not deep enough, yet.* She needed time to heal, to get her strength back. And she couldn't do that here. She couldn't stay in this empty house, where she suddenly felt as though the walls were closing in around her. *But where else am I to go?*

The phone rang, causing fear to whipsaw through her. *Just don't be bad news*, she prayed as she reached to pick it up. *I can't take bad news right now.*

"Hi, Scout." Marsha's cheerful voice rang in her ear. "I think I might have some news about your dog. Can you come down to the shop today?"

"Yes," she answered hesitantly, and then, more warmly. "I can do that, yes. I've gotta get out of here anyway. I think I'll end up losing what's left of my mind if I stay here much longer."

"Well, come on down, then," Marsha chuckled. "'Cause we don't want that. Come now and I'll treat you to breakfast."

Scout tried not to think too much as she hurried to get ready. *Enjoy the present,* Nick had told her. That was good advice. Fear gnawed around the edges of both the future and the past. But the present! Oh, the present was bright shiny bubble!

She would go see Marsha. And she wouldn't think at all about tomorrow, or tonight or about anything that might make the bubble break. She wouldn't think at all if she could help it. Not until she could be sure that thinking wouldn't ruin everything. She'd hold her breath and pray. And maybe, just maybe, things would be okay.

# 27

Marsha looked up from the counter as Scout walked through the door. "Oh, hey, Scout. You made it. Good. You want some coffee? Or..." *Holy shit.* Her voice died away as she took another, closer look at her friend. *What's up with this now?* She scanned Scout's aura a little while longer. "You know what," she said slowly. "Forget the coffee. I've got this great tea I'd like you to try. All right? We still don't have to read the leaves or anything, if you don't want to, but..."

"Actually, what the heck, right?" Scout smiled faintly, a cautious, hesitant smile. "Read my tea leaves, if you want. I don't mind. At least — Okay, I do have one condition."

"Yeah?" Marsha could barely suppress the giggle that rose in her throat. "And what would that be?"

"If you see anything bad? Lie to me, all right? I just don't want to know right now."

"You got it. No bad news. Now, why don't you go grab us a table I'll bring some things out."

Scout wandered out on to the terrace. The sunlight felt good. No, *she* felt good. No again; she felt *great*. And the sunlight felt wonderful. And the jewel-colored hummingbirds flitting and darting around the honeysuckle and the hibiscus were gorgeous. Breathtaking. The morning was bright and full of promise and maybe, maybe, maybe, if she could only hold it together a little while longer...

Marsha bustled out, a few minutes later with a tray. She set cups and plates and a steaming pot down on the table. "Okay. I think you're going to like this. It's very special. It's made with rose leaves and a couple of other things. But it's still gotta steep for a few minutes, so we can't drink it just yet."

"Thanks, Marsha." Scout took a deep breath. "It smells wonderful, very...flowery."

Marsha sat down and leaned forward conspiratorially. "Okay, so tell me. What is up with you today? Something's different. You look... oh, jeez, how do I put this? *Well rested*? Like maybe you've just gotten a really, *really* good night's sleep. Although, what I'm wondering is, would you have really slept that well if you'd been alone?"

Laughter erupted from Scout's throat.

"Hey. What's going on?" Lucy asked as she pulled up a chair and sat down.

Marsha saw the way Scout jumped at the sound of her friend's voice. She took note of the flush spread over Scout's cheeks.

Lucy, on the other hand, appeared not to notice anything was amiss until after she'd lifted the cover of the teapot and examined the contents. "Rose leaves?" she demanded, scowling at Marsha accusingly.

"Excuse me a minute, Scout," Marsha said, rising quickly to her feet. "I'm just going to find out what's keeping the rest of our stuff. Lucy, why don't you come and give me a hand, okay?"

"Rose leaf tea?" Lucy whispered again, as soon as they were out of earshot. "For real? Jesus, Marsha. What the hell are you up to now?"

"Lucy." Marsha clutched at her arm and whispered urgently. "Did you look at her? I don't know what's going on but... Well. It's gotta be your cousin, don't you think? But could they really have gotten together that fast? Like, yesterday maybe?"

"Oh, my God." Lucy stared at her horrified. "Are you shitting me?"

"Well, something's happened. And that's the only thing I can think of to account for it. I mean, if I didn't know any better, I'd think someone had gone in and done a soul retrieval. Or something fairly major."

"Oh, yeah. Right." Lucy snorted. "A *soul retrieval*, she says. And who do we know who could have done something like that Marsha? It sure as hell wasn't *Nick*."

"Well, it wasn't me, either. All I know is, all week long she's had this weird, defensive thing going. I've tried everything I could think of to soften it up—even a little—and nothing even made a dent in it. But now? The minute she walked in this morning I could tell it was weakening. Weakening? What the fuck am I saying? It's more like it's melting—like an ice cube in a blast furnace."

"Awesome," Lucy responded glumly.

"Well, I think it is. And, I tell you what, I can't wait 'til Celeste gets a load of this." She chuckled at the thought. "Approaching death, my ass. Besides, she looks happy, you know? I mean *really* happy. And I don't think she's had that for a very long time. So, don't you *dare* go spoiling this for her."

Lucy threw her hands up. "Oh, God forbid. Sure, Marsha. Whatever! As long as Scout's *happy*. That's all that matters, right?"

"Would you listen to me?" Marsha insisted. "She's actually agreed to let me read her tea leaves."

"Oh fuck, is *that* what this is about?" Lucy muttered, resignedly, and shook her head. "You don't know Marsha. You have no idea what Nick went through because of her. And now...ah, hell, I don't know why I even bother. Maybe they deserve each other."

"I think they do, actually." Marsha craned her neck for another look out at the terrace. "And I don't think that's a bad thing. If you could just see her aura, maybe you'd understand. Because, damn, I have never seen anything like this."

"Auras, huh? Yeah, too bad you can't show her aura to my Aunt Lillian. 'Cause mark my words, if you're right about this, there's gonna be hell to pay." Lucy shook her head wearily. "I can't believe this is happening. Thank God it's Friday, that's all I can say. 'Cause this would be way too depressing to deal with on any other day."

Marsha patted her friend's arm in a soothing manner. "Don't worry, Lucy It'll work out—you'll see. But, right now, I want you to go back out there and keep her company while I get us some food, okay? I don't think she should be left alone. I mean, if I'd known about this, I wouldn't even have let her walk all the way over here by herself. But hopefully there's no harm done. Oh, I know. Why don't you tell her about the dog. That should be safe enough."

"So, Scout," Lucy said, as she sat back down at the table, "Did Marsha tell you about the woman who thinks she's found your dog?"

Scout looked at her blankly for a moment, and then smiled, a tentative, wavering smile. "I'm sorry, what? Oh, the dog! Yes! I mean, no. Not really. I think she started to, but—" She broke off and looked around, vaguely. "I'm sorry. I'm not thinking too clearly, just now. How are you today, Lucy?"

"Uh, fine. Thanks," Lucy replied, startled by the unexpected change in subject. "How 'bout you?"

"Good, I think. In fact... Yeah, I'm really good. Aren't those nasturtiums incredible? The colors are just so... so *vibrant*."

Vibrant, huh? Lucy felt herself frowning. "Uh, yeah. So. Let me tell you about the dog, all right? You see, there was this woman who came in yesterday afternoon, looking for some homeopathic teething pills for her baby, not that it matters why she was here. And I was here because— Oh, never mind, that doesn't matter either."

A BABY, Scout thought, suddenly. *I think I'd like to have a baby. Maybe I will. Maybe last night— Is it possible?*

A warm rush of memory shot through her and she shivered with pleasure. *What would I call a baby conceived after last night? Cold Pizza? Second Chances? Redux?*

.  .  .

Color flooded Scout's cheeks as she was overcome with a sudden fit of coughing. "I'm sorry," she gasped at last, with a suspicious gurgle in her voice. "Go on. You were saying?"

But Lucy just stared at her, bemused. *Rose leaves?* Marsha was way off base with that. The last thing this woman needed was anything that might promote or, *God forbid,* strengthen what all the classic Herbals euphemistically called *romantic feelings.*

Or any feelings, for that matter. Hell, she appeared ready for a straitjacket as it was. What on earth had happened to her yesterday? *Forget tea leaves. I better check and see how Nick is doing.*

"Lucy? The dog?"

The dog. Right. "Well. Marsha put up a notice, like she said she'd do. We had one made up about Robyn, too, of course. Not that anyone— Well, never mind. Anyway. So, this woman came in—"

"The woman with the baby." Scout said helpfully.

"Uh-huh. And she saw the poster, and then she said that she and her husband had found a dog, which they'd taken to their vet, and she thought, from the description you know, that it might be your dog. Who, by the way, really needs a name, if you get her back. 'Cause that's the first thing everyone asks."

Names? Scout's mind drifted off track again. *I'll really have to think about that, won't I? Names are so important...*

In the past, Nick had always called her Jen. Would he want to call her that again now? Did she want him to?

"I love you." he had told her. But who was he thinking of when he said that? Who was she now, anyway?

"Uh, Scout? Can you even hear me?"

"Huh? Oh, yeah, you were talking about names. What do your children think of their names, by the way? Do they like them?"

"I don't know, Scout. But we weren't really discussing names as such. What I was trying to explain is that your dog might be at this vet's office. Are you with me so far?"

"A vet? *Omigod.* Lucy! We never even thought of that! We checked all the shelters yesterday, but she wasn't at *any* of them. And I was so depressed."

"Depressed?" Lucy eyed her skeptically. "Sure. Of course, you are." She signaled to a passing waitress. "Tina. Could you please get me a double, no make that a triple, espresso? Pronto?" And then she turned back to Scout.

"I gotta be honest, Scout. You don't look all that depressed to me. Like...at all."

She wasn't surprised when Scout dissolved into laughter, but she sure did have to wonder, with a sinking sense of inevitability, exactly to whom Scout was referring when she said *we.*

"Sorry that this took so long," Marsha said balancing what seemed to be a very heavy tray on the edge of the small Table. "We're a little shorthanded at the moment," she added, unloading plates of scones and muffins, bowls of granola and fresh fruit, and dishes of preserves, honey, butter and Devonshire cream.

"I don't know where Celeste is. She hasn't shown up yet this morning. Scout, that tea should be just about ready now, so why don't you pour yourself a cup? And you really should eat a good, big breakfast. I think you need a little bit of grounding this morning."

"Marsha, I'm totally with you on the grounding thing, but what I *don't* think she needs is this tea," Lucy insisted. "Maybe you got some chamomile or lemon verbena or valerian maybe, or I don't know... something a little more soothing?" *Like triple strength kava-kava. Or knock out drops, perhaps?*

"This is soothing," Marsha said, lips curving in a mischievous grin. "Sort of. I added some lavender to it."

"Oh, Christ," Lucy groaned.

Marsha made a face. "And also, jasmine, cloves, and cinnamon. And just the tiniest bit of clary sage. So there."

Lucy rolled her eyes as Marsha ticked off the list of aphrodisiacs.

*Oh, good thinking. Sure, why the hell not?* "That's it? Why, what happened? You run out of yohimbe and mandrake root?"

"Oh, be quiet," Marsha scolded her. "And besides, I think Scout looks very soothed already." She chuckled, wickedly. "I should only be so lucky. Go on, Scout, try it. It's very good."

"Mmm." Scout took a sip and closed her eyes in ecstasy. "Oh, you're right. It's wonderful. Delicious."

"Where the hell is my coffee?" Lucy muttered, rolling her eyes, again. "So, what's this about Celeste? Did you call her?"

"Of course. But there was no answer. So, I figure after we check about the dog, I'll drive out to the cabin. Maybe she's sick or something. I've been getting the strangest feelings all night." She turned her bright eyes back on Scout who was staring off into space again and smiled gleefully. "C'mon, Scout. Drink up. This ought to be good."

NICK POURED himself another cup of coffee, looked at the telephone on his desk and told himself for maybe the two thousandth time, that he was not going to call again. Just because he longed to hear her voice, didn't mean she would pick up the phone this time, either.

He'd already called too many times. Either she'd already gone out, or she just didn't want to talk to him. Which he refused to believe could possibly be the case, but he couldn't help worrying about, all the same.

After all the years of waiting for her, it was hard to believe his luck had finally changed.

It was probably just as well that she wasn't picking up the phone. He still wasn't ready to share the news he'd gotten when he'd called in this morning. News that a body had been found, washed up on a beach several miles up the coast. A body that may or may not turn out to be that of her missing roommate.

He didn't want to tell her anything about that until he knew for sure, and if he talked to her before then, he might end up saying more than he planned.

There were so many things they needed to talk about; so many details that needed to be hashed out between them; so many questions he still desperately needed to have answered.

He would see her tonight, and that...would be soon enough. And the sooner he got his mind back on his work, the sooner he could finish up and go home. Not that he was going to do anything like a decent amount of work today, of course. He really couldn't expect to. After all, he'd been through this before, hadn't he?

But at that he smiled. No, actually he had not been through this before. Not this or anything even close to it. All the other times he'd been unable to work because of Scout it had been a bad thing. This was very, very different. Wonderfully different. But all the same, every bit as distracting.

He picked up the files he'd been looking at earlier. What were the odds he wondered idly, of two young women walking out of the same house – twenty years apart – and just disappearing? It was strange. And he didn't like strange.

Even before the body turned up this morning, he'd thought the chances were pretty good that Scout's roommate had been killed. And given the fact that she'd been missing for twenty years, the chances were even better that her stepsister had met with a similar fate. But what evidence had there ever really been to support the theory that Lisa had run away in the first place?

As far as he could tell from the reports he'd been reading, she hadn't taken much of anything with her. Okay, there was the letter. Apparently, no one had thought to question the handwriting. The paper was hers...but did that make any sense? She ran out in a huff, too rushed to pack any clothes, but she grabbed a piece of stationery on her way out the door?

But if Lisa had *not* run away, he was left with two women who had simply disappeared, under mysterious, but oddly similar circumstances, from the same house. Twenty years apart. If he assumed foul play, what would account for the gap?

His blood ran cold, but he had to consider the most obvious connection. Scout's absence coincided a little too neatly with the pattern he was positing. And, another unsettling similarity, both women had reportedly been very upset with her shortly before they disappeared.

*Okay, that's enough*, he pushed the though away. *Let's just get a grip here.* He pulled out a note pad and began to make a list of any extraneous events that could be connected to these two disappearances. What events had surrounded Lisa Larson's disappearance? She'd had a fight with her sister, her math teacher was found strangled, several of the woman's students – including Lisa herself and two of her friends – had been accused of cheating and were subsequently expelled for it, her stepfather was killed in a car accident, and her stepsister — Scout — also left town.

Twenty years later, Caroline Larson dies, apparently of natural causes, Scout comes back to town, for the very first time, and another young woman disappears.

*I can't see it*, Nick thought. He was conscious of an intense feeling of frustration. *I just can't see it.* He was onto something; he was sure of it. The pieces were there, waiting to be put into place. But he just... couldn't...see the pattern yet.

Gil Patterson and Caroline Larson. Could their deaths be connected? A stroke and a car accident? Nothing there. Except, of course, that one death precipitated Scout's departure and the other her return.

He remembered the last time he'd seen Caroline, standing at the door of her house, facing him down, wary and defiant.

But why?

*You'll never find her,* she had insisted, which was the same thing she'd always told him; the same thing she'd been telling him for years.

But why had that been so important? Why had she felt she'd needed to send Scout *someplace safe?*

Just whose safety had she been thinking about, anyway?

SCOUT SAT on the terrace and soaked up the sun. It felt good just to sit. The water tinkled pleasantly in the fountain. The gentle murmur of conversation blended nicely with the music wafting from speakers hidden throughout the garden. And she was pretty sure she had gotten a nice little buzz from the herbs in the tea Marsha had served her.

"How are you feeling?" Marsha asked, sitting down across from her. "Things settling down a bit yet?"

"How am I feeling?" Scout shook her head. "Right now, I've got so many feelings I don't know how to answer that. But it's good, you know? At least, I think it's good. It's different but... No, it is good. It's just a lot, all at once."

"Do you mind telling me what happened?" Marsha peered at her curiously. "I'm not just being nosy, you know. I can tell there's something different about you this morning."

"Can you?" Scout smiled. "Gee Marsha, maybe you really *are* psychic, after all. I don't know what to tell you, though. I was with Nick yesterday and we finally — Oh, but it was more than that really."

"More than what?"

"I don't know if I can even explain it. We made love and, it was everything I always [1] knew it would be. But there was more to it than just sex. I know this probably sounds stupid, but I feel kind of like, like I just got my soul back. Or something."

"Yes! Yes. I knew it!" Marsha crowed.

Without warning, Scout's emotions shifted from elation to fear, from surprise to horror. Her pleasant buzz morphed into panic. "Marsha, what did you do?"

"Here," Marsha thrust a cup of tea in her hands. "Drink. Take deep breaths. Better now?"

"I'll be better when you tell me what's going on," Scout said tightly.

"Well, as to that, this is only a theory, you understand. But there are times when we disassociate from parts of our self, from our memories. Usually it's the result of trauma, events that are too painful to face. It's like our soul shatters, almost. And it doesn't have to be an instantaneous thing, either. It could be something that happens slowly, over time. But, fast or slow, the results are the same. We become crippled emotionally." Marsha shrugged. "Of course, there are various ways of dealing with it. There's a very specific Shamanic method, for example, involving trance journeys and special soul-catching crystals, known as Soul Retrieval."

*Oh, God.* "Marsha, I trusted you! *Please* tell me you didn't mess around with my head again."

"No! No, I didn't do anything—I swear. I don't think anyone is responsible. I think it was spontaneous. Not that I've ever heard of that sort of thing happening before but— Well. Here you are. But whatever it was, it was nothing to do with me. Promise!"

Scout slumped back in her chair. "Okay. Fine. So, what do I do now?"

Marsha smiled. "How should I know? It seems to me you already did everything you needed to do. Don't be scared, Scout. This is a good thing. I think you just need some time to get used to it. A couple of weeks, maybe a month at the most, and you'll be fine. Why don't you relax here a little while longer, and let me I finish up inside? Then we'll go see about your dog. But before we do that – let's take a look at those tea leaves."

---

1. Paige plays an even more crucial part in the next book in the series. But that's not what's most interesting to me. You know how people always talk about writers putting people that they know into books, and maybe killing them off? Well, Paige is that person for me. The inspiration for the character was a model I knew when I lived in NYC and my husband was working as a fashion photogra-pher. I'll go into this more in books two and book four, but no, I'm not going to tell you who she is However, I might provide hints...

# 28

*I'm too close to this*, Nick told himself; *that's the problem.* Either he was imagining a connection where none existed or there was some variable that he was still missing.

And there had to be something missing, because otherwise—

Once more, he fought down the urge to pick up the phone. He was not going to call her.

*Because you know she wasn't involved,* a voice inside his head insisted.

To which another voice—jaded and cynical—replied: *because you know you'll believe whatever lie she tells you.*

He was still staring moodily at the phone when he heard the knock on his office door.

"Hey there, Nick. Long time no see." Paige Delaney lounged in the doorway, a winning smile on her face. "Aren't you going to invite me in?"

"I've never known you to wait around for an invitation before, Paige," he answered, aware of the undercurrent of tension that moved into the room along with her. She was after something. But, when it came to Paige, that was a given.

He and Paige had dated for several months. It hadn't taken him long to figure out that she never did anything without there being a good reason for it. It had been obvious, right from the start, she was only involved with him because she wanted an inside track when it came to police information, but that was fine by him. His own involvement had been equally predatory and shallow, and he had no objection to a little quid pro quo. Besides, after what he'd just gone through with Lauren, it had been a relief to be with someone he didn't have to pretend to care about.

"Are you busy? I had some questions I wanted to ask you." Paige had taken the chair on the other side of his desk, and as she sat forward eagerly, he had to fight the absurd impulse to cover the notes he'd been making.

He smiled at her wryly. "I'm always busy, Paige. Remember?" His preoccupation with his job had been a popular refrain with all the women in his life. And, in the end, even Paige – every bit as hopeless a workaholic as he – had not been able to resist the urge to sing it. "What is it you want to know?"

"Missing person. Name of Robyn Smith. What d'you know about her?"

Direct and to the point. Classic Paige. "Well, I know she's missing." Nick leaned back in his chair and watched her through narrowed eyes. Must be a slow news day, if she couldn't dig up anything more interesting than this to grill him about.

"Yeah, thanks. That's real helpful. C'mon, Nick, level with me. I hear you've been spending a lot of time out there all week, investigating the scene. Rumor has it you even canceled your vacation. We both know you don't handle routine disappearances. I figure you must be onto something a whole lot bigger. So, what is it?"

Alarms began ringing all up and down Nick's mind, as he realized how his actions could have been misinterpreted. Shit. He'd pretty much been staking out Scout's house since Monday. As luck would have it, the same day Robyn decided to disappear. He must have been crazy thinking that would go unnoticed. The question was – who had done the noticing?

"You figured wrong, this time, Paige. I haven't been investigating anything there. Just visiting an old friend."

"Oh, really?" Paige's gray eyes lit up with an even more proprietary interest. "Who would that be, I wonder?" She paused, expectantly, and when he didn't respond, she continued, thoughtfully. "I don't know Nick; this isn't like you. There's something you're not telling me. It certainly is an interesting set-up over there though, huh? A missing person, an unexpected death, lots of money changing hands. There's gotta be some story in it. The old lady who was living there—"

"Was an old lady, Paige. She died. It happens. Natural causes."

"Maybe. She wasn't *that* old, however, and she left an awful lot of money behind. It'd sure be interesting to know if that has anything to do with the missing girl?"

"To tell you the truth, I don't know what any of it is about right now, Paige." He sighed as he reached for his cigarettes. "But somehow, I kinda doubt that it's got anything to do with the money." He searched in his desk drawer for a lighter, and then took his time lighting up.

"I got nothing for you on this, Paige. It's early days, yet. I tell you what, though—you got any friends over on the Bartolo force? I hear they just pulled a body off the beach last night. It may turn out to be our missing person, or it may not. Either way, it's more of a story than anything I can give you."

"Oh, yeah? Well, thanks Nick. I'll check it out." Paige leaned across his desk so that he could light her cigarette, as well. Then she sat back again, and studied him carefully for a moment, in silence. "So, uh, what gives? I thought you'd quit smoking?"

"Yeah, I did." He closed his eyes, using the hand that held his cigarette to massage the bridge of his nose. Smoke drifted lazily across his face. "Several times now. But you know what they say, old habits die hard."

"Yeah, yeah," Paige said as she stood up to leave. "And old sins cast long shadows, and old dogs can't learn new tricks. And much as

I'd like to sit here 'til we're both old and gray, trading clichés with you, I've got a story to track down. I'll see you around, Nick."

"See ya, Paige."

As he watched her go, Nick couldn't help but wonder how long it would take her to make some of the same connections he had made. Knowing Paige as well as he did? Not too long at all.

"WHAT'S WRONG WITH HER?" Scout stared through the mirrored glass window of the kennel where her dog lay in a miserable crumpled heap. She could tell she was hurt, just by the way she lay there. She tried to picture how she should be lying, how healthy dogs – normal dogs – looked, but she couldn't. She looked at her and saw the *wrongness*, but she didn't know what it was.

"Well, as far as I can tell, she was hit by a car, and then dragged for some distance." The veterinarian told them. "That's what did most of the damage. Other than the head injury. Apparently, she was also shot."

The room spun. For a moment, Scout was certain she was going to be sick. "Oh, my God. What kind of person would do that? Who'd want to shoot my dog?"

"I mean, it's possible the person who hit her was just trying to put her out of her misery. Luckily, he botched that, too."

"Is she—?"

"Her pelvis was broken, and one of her legs, there's been some tissue damage. Plus, she lost a lot of blood. But I'm confident that she'll recover. However, I would like to keep her here for another few days, or so. Maybe a week."

"Can I see her? I mean, can I go in there with her?" *Can I hold her? Can I tell her I'm sorry?*

"It would be better if you didn't," she said gently. "If she saw you, she'd probably try to get up and it's much better if she stays quiet, now. I'm sorry."

"Come on, Scout," Marsha said, sounding miserable. "There's nothing else we can do for her, right now. Let's go. We'll check on Celeste and then maybe get some lunch. It'll be okay."

Scout nodded. *Someone shot my dog. Someone hit her with a car!*

*My dog.* She'd never wanted a dog, but it seemed she had one after all. And she had been hurt. Someone had hurt her dog.

And what about Robyn? How did she fit in with this? "Did he... did the people who brought her in, say anything about... I mean, was there any sign of—" She stopped unsure how to go on.

"A friend of ours had taken the dog for a walk several days ago," Marsha explained. "We haven't seen either of them since. I guess we're wondering if there was any sign that maybe she, our friend I mean, had been hurt, as well?"

"Oh, my goodness." The doctor stared, looking alarmed. "I had no idea. I mean, I can give you Mr. Rachett's phone number, if you want to contact him, but you should probably be calling hospitals, or— I presume the police have been notified?"

"They know," Scout said quietly.

"Oh. Well, then. I guess that's all you can do. I hope you find her."

Scout nodded. "Me, too."

"All right, well, give me a call in a couple of days and I'll give you an update." As they passed back into the waiting room, the doctor asked, "Oh, by the way, you never mentioned. What's your dog's name?"

"Sara," Scout replied, without stopping to think. "Her name is Sara."

"SARA, HUH?" Marsha echoed curiously, as they crossed the parking lot towards her van. "Interesting. Where did that come from? When did you decide to name her?"

"I didn't decide anything." Scout answered, not knowing how it could be so, but knowing it to be true. "I just knew. That's her name."

"Well, good then. Cool." Marsha smiled as she pulled the car door open. "I'm glad you finally got that settled. Now, let's go see about Celeste."

As they headed out towards Celeste's cabin in Hidden Canyon, Marsha cast a quick glance at Scout's face. She seemed to be handling the news about the dog—Sara, apparently—pretty well. But shit. Who could have guessed the dog had been shot? This was one of those times when Marsha's wonderful intuition had really let her down. It would've been nice to have had a little advance warning. At least Sara was still alive.

She considered the dog for a few more minutes, wondering again whether there was any connection between it and the dog she'd seen in Scout's teacup that morning.

Depending on where it was located in the cup, a dog meant either a faithful friend, or a secret enemy. But the problem with interpreting symbols was that, other times, a dog was just a dog. Which might very well be the case, this time around.

And, of course, the same could be said for the bear she had seen lurking in there as well. That could indicate either healing, or a journey. Or it could have a more personal meaning.

*If only Celeste had been there.* She was the best tea leaf reader Marsha had ever known, but what sense would even Celeste have been able to make of the figure that could have been either a knife or a dagger?

Marsha was almost certain, herself, that it was a dagger, which would indicate a friend would shortly do Scout a favor. A knife, on the other hand, suggested that disaster could result from a quarrel.

However, given Scout's weird mood and peculiar talents, as well as their shared history, there was a pretty good chance that Scout's subconscious, which was responsible for the symbols in the cup, had been picking up cues from Marsha's mind. She certainly had been worried enough, these past few days, about those knives of Celeste's. *Nobody* just happened to have spare athames and bollines on hand for no good reason.

Scout was still staring moodily out the window. "How're you doing?" Marsha asked her softly.

"Okay." Scout flashed a brief smile and continued. "Really Marsha, I'm fine. I think I've even gotten over my insomnia. Looks like I might not be needing to borrow your van again, after all."

"Borrow my van?" Marsha asked, perplexed.

"To sleep in. Didn't Lucy tell you? I told her to. You really did me a favor Sunday, making me get some sleep. I owe you one."

"A favor, huh? Good to know. But listen, are you hungry, yet? We could stop for lunch on the way, if you wanted."

"No, let's just go see about Celeste, okay? I know you must be worried about her."

Worried? Yes, she was worried about Celeste, very worried, indeed. But at this particular moment she was more worried about Scout.

True to the condition Scout had set, she had given her only the good news she'd seen in her teacup. She'd told her about the chair and the apple tree and the castle – symbolizing an addition to the family, a change for the better and a legacy.

And she'd made no mention at all of clouds or unicorns. Or coffins.[1]

NICK GROANED when he heard the second knock on his office door. He steeled himself for another confrontation.[2]

"What are you doing here, Luce?" he asked, feeling at once relieved and just a little perplexed by the fact that his cousin was smiling.

"I wanted to talk to you, cuz," Lucy said as she advanced into the room. She dangled a large paper bag temptingly in front of him. "And, seeing as I know you've got a bad habit of skipping lunch when you get busy, I thought I'd play Good Samaritan and bring you something to eat."

There was an odd, speculative gleam in her eyes, which added to Nick's uneasiness. She was up to something –just as Paige had been – but she was looking a little too pleasant for it to have anything to do with more rumors about him and Scout.

"Thanks, Luce. That's real nice of you, but I've got a lot of work to do this afternoon, so—"

"Mm-hm. So I've heard." His cousin sat down and began taking sandwiches and drinks out of the bag. "You know Nick, there are those of us ...here take these...who think you may have been working a little *too* hard this week. Or maybe just a little too *fast*. What do you think?"

"I think I don't have the faintest idea what you're getting at. Is this about the camping trip, again? I'm sorry I had to bail, but like I told Dan and Joey—"

"No!" An exasperated frown appeared on Lucy's face. "Cut the crap, okay? You know what I'm here about. And I'm not leaving 'til you tell me what's happening. So quit stalling."

"Lucy, I swear. I'm clueless. Why don't you just tell me what it is you want?" *And get it over with.*

Her eyes widened. "Isn't it obvious? I want to know what you're doing."

*Obvious. Right.* "Well, what I'm doing right now, is working. Or attempting to."

"So I see." Lucy arched one brow at him and bit into her sandwich. She looked at him thoughtfully as she chewed. "I gotta admit, I'm surprised. You look like shit today."

"Gee, thanks. It's always nice to see you, too."

"Seriously. You're not even eating your sandwich. What's the matter with you?"

"You know something, Luce? You're starting to sound more and more like my mother all the time," he muttered, but he unwrapped the sandwich and took a bite. "Other than the fact that she doesn't say shit nearly as much as you do. This is very good, by the way. Thanks."

Lucy regarded him curiously. "I just... I guess I kind of expected to find you in a better mood."

"Really? Why's that?"

"Well, I mean, after—" She stopped mid-sentence, as if another thought had struck her, and not a particularly pleasant one, at that, to judge by her expression. "Oh. Shit."

"What now?"

"Nothing. I just... Huh. I was so sure. But if it's not you, then who is *we*?"

*Clear as mud.* He sighed. "Lucy? Am I ever going to find out what you're talking about?

Lucy shook her head. "No. I mean, it's nothing. Forget it. I was just worried about you, but I can see you're fine. A little grouchy, but otherwise intact."

To his surprise, she got up and started gathering her things. "But, you know what? I should just go. And let you get back to work. I'm sorry I bothered you."

Huh? "Well. great. I'm glad we got that cleared up." He chewed on his sandwich in obstinate silence, watching as Lucy packed things back into her bag, biting back the curiosity that almost had him asking her to sit back down. He had no time for that today.

"I just cannot believe this," Lucy muttered. "What the fuck is that bitch up to now?"

*Oh, Christ.* If he were smart, he'd keep his mouth shut. But he just had to ask, didn't he? "Who're you talking about now?"

"Who d'you think?"

"Scout, I assume." Nick let his head fall back against his chair. He pressed hard on his temples, where he could feel a headache forming. *Shit. Here it comes.* "What'd she do now?"

"Oh, nothing. I was just thinking out loud. I mean, she couldn't have gotten back together with Glenn, right? That wouldn't make *any* sense at all."

"What?" Nick sat up, startled, all thoughts of a headache vanishing.

*She couldn't be.* His mind reeled in shock. *She wouldn't.* Surely, she wouldn't—not after last night? *Damn it, is that why she's not answering her phone?* Images formed in his mind, and his insides turned to ice. Lucy regarded him with wary surprise.

"Lucy," he said with ominous quiet. "What do you know? Start talking. *Now!*"

"Jeez, Nick, chill out. I don't know anything for certain. It's just that I was talking to her at the teashop this morning, and she was, you know, in a really good mood. Totally spacey and weird, of course, but... Well, okay. I guess, because of some things she said the other night, Marsha and I got the idea that—"

"What time?"

"Huh?"

"*Time,* Lucy! What *time* did you see her there?"

"I don't know. Jeez. Stop yelling, already! It was early. We'd just opened."

"You're sure?"

"About it being early? Yeah, I'm sure. She got there before I did. Why?"

Nick breathed a deep sigh of relief as his world settled back into place.

*Good. Okay.* So, that was why she wasn't answering the phone at her house. She would have had to have been home to answer the phone there, now wouldn't she? [3]

And she would've had to leave shortly after he had, to get downtown as early as that. She wouldn't have had time to see...*anyone else*...beforehand.

He began to laugh, quietly. He felt giddy with relief. Jeez, what the hell was the matter with him? Of course, she wasn't seeing anyone else. He knew how she felt about him. Maybe she hadn't said the words yet, but—

"Nick?" Lucy was still gazing warily at him.

"Never mind, Lucy. It's nothing." But he couldn't resist asking. "So, she, um ...she seemed like she was in a pretty good mood, you said?"

"Pretty good? Jeez, did I say anything about *pretty good*? No, Nick. I'm talking mega-blissed out, here. I don't know what the hell happened, but I'm telling you the woman could've made it to the moon and back without any spacecraft at all."

Her eyes narrowed – suspicious once again. "And...why do I get the feeling that this is not coming as a surprise to you?"

Nick tried to hide the sheepish grin that spread across his face, but it was no use.

"Oh. My. God," Lucy uttered in tones of disgust. "Nick, are you out of your fucking mind?"

"No. But it's no thanks to you," he retorted, trying to invest some sternness into his voice, but failing.

Lucy shook her head. "I sure hope you know what you're doing."

"Yeah. Me, too. Listen, sit back down a minute. I want to ask you something. Did you ever have any reason to suspect that Lisa Larson didn't run away?"

"No. Why?"

"Well, what about this boyfriend of hers. Would she have really been that upset about his behavior?"

Lucy plopped back down into the chair and fixed him with an incredulous look. "Aw, gee Nick, I don't know." He winced at the sardonic sweetness of her tone. "Do I think Lisa would have gotten upset over a little thing like Glenn and Scout sleeping together? Hm, let's explore that, shall we? 'Cause it seems to me you were getting pretty worked up yourself not more than a minute ago, when I mentioned the exact same possibility to you."

"Never mind that." He shook his head. "What I'm saying is, it sounds like it wasn't exactly the first time this had happened."

Lucy's smile turned even more incredulous. "And, you know what? That's real funny, too. Because I thought that was *exactly* the point I was making. But, yeah, Glenn was never what you'd call amazingly faithful. Still, this time was maybe a little different. It being her sister, and all."

"But would she have been upset enough to leave home because of it? Some people might see that as an overreaction."

Lucy sighed. "I don't know, Nick. You might have a point. But she was young, all right? We don't always make good choices at that age. Plus, there were a lot of other factors, too, you know. And, however you want to look at it, it was all still mostly Scout's fault. No matter what she wants to think." Her eyes narrowed. "Why? Is that how she got around you this time? The old 'more sinned against than sinning' routine? I thought you had more sense than that."

*Thanks for the vote of confidence.* "The two things have nothing to do with each other."

"Really? So, what's it all about, then? 'Cause I swear I just went over this exact same shit with Scout the other night. Where's the mystery, Nick? Like I said, teenagers get worked up over nothing, or next to nothing, and run away every damn day, don't they? It sucks, but what are you going to do about it?"

"I'm just trying to figure out if she maybe didn't run away. Because I'm starting to see a pattern here. Between her and Robyn Smith."

"What kind of pattern?" Lucy frowned. "Do you know any more about Robyn? Did you get some news? Have you found anything out?"

"No, not yet. But I do think there's a pretty good chance she's dead. That she was either kidnapped or killed."

"Oh, God; no. Tocca ferro! Don't say that, Nick! What do you know that you're not telling me? And—wait a minute, are you saying that maybe the same person killed *both* of them?"

"It's possible, isn't it?"

"No, of course, it isn't! I mean, why would you even think that? Lisa disappeared twenty years ago. Where's the connection? Omigod." Lucy's face grew pale, and he knew she had made the same connection he had. When she spoke again, her voice was barely a whisper. "Nick—no. You can't possibly be thinking— You're not serious, are you?"

"Lucy, I am not saying or thinking anything right now. I'm just brainstorming."

"Look, I know I haven't exactly been Scout's biggest fan, but if you're thinking she's some kind of half-crazed serial killer— Omigod. Oh, shit." She began to laugh. "I can't believe this."

"Lucy, I didn't say—"

"And you're *sleeping* with her? Nick! You are so fucked up!"

"Lucy. Listen to me. I don't—"

"No, Nick, you listen to *me*. Scout might be a lot of things, but I honestly don't believe she's a cold-blooded killer. Although, I gotta tell you, it's a little scary that I've had to have this same conversation twice in one week. Talk about déjà vu. But you, of all people—how can you sit there and even think about anything so heinous?"

She shook her head, as if to clear it. "I'll tell you one thing, cuz. They may have had their problems, but Scout would no more have killed Lisa than I would."

"Not even if it was some kind of accident?"

"What kind of accident? And what—did Robyn have an accident, too? Or no, let me guess. Maybe Scout buried Lisa's body in the backyard, but then the dog dug it up. And Robyn found it. So then of course, she had to kill Robyn. And then maybe she killed the dog! That's brilliant. Why didn't anybody ever think of this before? All you have to do now is dig up Caroline's rose garden. That has to be where the bodies are buried!"

Nick sighed. "All right, look, I don't really believe Scout killed anyone. Got that? I'm just trying to make sense of things."

"Well, good. Because it's just about the crappiest idea I've ever heard. I mean, after listening to her the other night, and seeing the way she looked this morning, and then to come in here, and listen to you talk about her like she's a suspect..."

"It's okay, Lucy. You can calm down now."

"Maybe I don't want to calm down, damn it," she said, her eyes flashing angrily.

"Well, fine. But then maybe you can leave. Because I've got work to do, and you freaking out isn't helping."

"Fine. Go work, then." Lucy got to her feet. "But let me just say one more thing before I go. You think there's a pattern involving women disappearing from Scout's house and being killed? Well okay, let's say you're right. But, if that's the case, then what makes you think she won't be the next one to disappear?"

He scrubbed his hand over his face. "Believe me, I've thought about it. But she doesn't seem to be in any immediate danger at the moment, so—"

"What about that car accident she was in earlier this week? And I know she said something the other day about a gas leak, and a broken window in the basement, or maybe it was something to do with the stairs? I wasn't really listening, but—"

"What?" Nick felt his chest tighten. "Jesus, Lucy, why am I only hearing about this now? Why didn't anyone tell me any of this before?"

She glared at him, exasperated. "Maybe because none of us realized that it could be important before."

The phone on his desk rang and Nick answered it. Lucy saw the color leave his face. She watched as her cousin sank slowly back into his chair and began taking urgent notes, his face intent, grave, hopeless.

Lucy didn't think she'd ever seen anyone look so completely drained of energy.

"What is it?" she asked, as soon as he hung up the phone. "What's happened?"

"Celeste Greene was attacked in her home last night," Nick said, in a voice as devoid of emotion as his face had become. "They've taken her to the hospital, but it doesn't look good."

Lucy's heart skipped several beats. "Oh, my God, Nick... Marsha and Scout were going over to her house, to look for her."

"Yeah, well," he shook his head, his eyes bleak. "It looks like they found her."

1. Clouds = serious trouble; unicorn = scandal and difficulty; coffin = sorrow or loss.
2. This chapter sets up a pattern that continues throughout most of the books in the series. Poor Nick is in his office trying to get some work done, only to be interrupted time and again by his friends, co-workers, and relations. I don't know if everybody else is enjoying his repeated frustration, but I sure am. I've spent a lot of time, over the years, trying to determine which character is at the heart of the series. Usually it seems to be Marsha, or Lucy, or even Scout. But honestly, I think just as good a case could be made for its being Nick.
3. Good old days, part deux. People had to be at home in order to answer their phones. Unbelievable. Kids today will never believe it.

# 29

The clatter of hospital noises washed over Marsha, but she paid them no mind. Though her body sat, still and erect, on the thinly padded vinyl chair in the waiting room, her spirit was on a journey. Far removed from the reality her body occupied, it moved through a gray, mist-enshrouded landscape in search of guidance.

The answers were here—they had to be. And she would find them. With an inner eyesight far keener than the one her body possessed; she would hunt down the knowledge she needed.

*I need to fix this. I must. I will.*

Up until now, her power animal had kept pace at her side [1] as she traveled, but now it paused and gazed at her, sending thoughts of peace, compassion, wisdom, love.

Marsha turned to it, impatiently. "We don't have much time. Why have you stopped?"

"*You know why.*" The thought formed in her mind, wrapped in loving support, but all the same, implacable in its opposition. "*You need to go back. You carry too many emotions to continue with this journey.*"

"No," Marsha protested. She knew that what she was attempting was dangerous. Her spirit could sense the wisdom in not continuing. But she refused to listen. "I won't give up. I *can't*. We have to go on."

But her companion would not be moved.

"Then how?" Marsha asked, at last; almost crying in despair. "If not like this, *how*?"

*"You must accept that which you cannot change."*

"And if I can't? Or if I don't want to accept it?"

*"Then your interference will only serve to make things worse."*

"I'm not interfering; I'm *fixing* things. Isn't that what a healer is supposed to do?"

*"Not this time."*

"But there has to be a way. What's the answer?"

*"You know the answer."*

*Do I, though?* Her brow furrowed as she considered the matter. But after a moment's thought she realized that, of course, it was true.

"Yes," she sighed in grudging acceptance. "All right. Fine. I'll stop. For now."

Still, it was with great reluctance that she turned and headed back, her spirit slowly retracing the path it had taken. Spiraling back to that place where her body waited. Guided by the steady rhythm of the egg-shaped rattle she clutched in one hand; while the soul catching crystal she would not be using – not this night, possibly not ever again – rested lightly in the other.

Marsha opened her eyes just as Lucy and Nick came into view. By the time they reached her side she had composed herself. Both rattle and crystal were back in the embroidered canvas shoulder bag at her side. Her anger, and the knowledge of what she must do were carefully concealed behind a face that showed only her grief.

Lucy took the chair beside her and swept Marsha into a tight embrace. "We came as soon as we heard. How is she?"

"She's in a coma, Luce. She's still alive, but just barely." A sob escaped her as she added, "I don't think she's coming back from it."

Lucy looked stricken as she pulled away. "I just can't believe this is happening." She shook her head sadly. "How is it even possible? Was it a burglary? An accident? What—"

"It was murder." Marsha's eyes filled with tears. "Except that the killer got sloppy and didn't take the time to finish the job."

"Murder!" Lucy stared, open-mouthed. "Here? In Oberon? But that— That doesn't make any sense. Why would anyone want to murder Celeste? I mean, of all people!"

Marsha was silent for a moment. How much to say? That was always the question, wasn't it? With every reading, every consultation. Really, when you came down to it, every conversation was built word by word on what to say and what to leave unsaid. There was so much that she didn't want to say just now. But a certain amount of the right information might be helpful.

"Apparently she'd been strangled," she said, at last, hardly able to get the words past her lips.

The muscles tightened at the corners of Nick's mouth, and she could tell he'd made some kind of connection. But had she reinforced something he had already suspected, or given him something new to think about? In any case, what she really needed, right now, was to talk to Lucy. Alone.

She wanted Nick to leave, but...oh, hell. Maybe that would be another mistake. The way things were going, Marsha couldn't help but second-guess all her decisions tonight.

Whatever she decided, she knew there would be a certain amount of risk involved. But she couldn't think about that now. That was a problem for another day. Tonight, there were other things she needed to focus on. She needed to gather her materials. And she needed to talk to Lucy. And she needed for Scout to be kept safe. Safe and preoccupied. She took a deep, deep breath and smiled at them both.

"You look worried, Nick," Marsha said, very quietly. [2]

NICK STARTED as his train of thought abruptly derailed. Something in Marsha's expression, or maybe it was something in her tone, had set his adrenaline running again. He felt a new and pressing sense of urgency take hold.

"Where's Scout?" he asked, looking around the nearly deserted waiting room.

Was there a hint of worry in Marsha's voice as she answered him, or was he only imagining it? "Well, she, uh... She went home. A little while ago. I called her a cab."

"You did *what?*" He turned back to stare at her. "She was supposed to stay here. With you."

Marsha nodded. "I know. But being here wasn't doing her any good. Her emotions are a little too volatile right now." She smiled apologetically at Lucy. "You might have been right about the chamomile."

"I told you," Lucy said as she adjusted her seat, clearly settling in to wait. "She could barely focus on anything as it was. Oh, hey, what happened with the vet? Was it her dog?"

Marsha sighed. "Yes, but it's pretty badly injured. Besides being hit by a car, it was also shot."

"What?" Lucy recoiled. She stared at Marsha in alarm.

"Where was the dog found?" Nick heard himself ask, in a voice that sounded far calmer than he felt.

Marsha shrugged. "Not very far from Scout's house, apparently. Just a few blocks away, in fact."

"And Robyn?" Lucy asked. "Was there any sign of her?"

"No," Marsha answered shortly. As her eyes strayed back to Nick's face. He felt a deep sense of unease grip him.

"I need to go," he said abruptly. "Lucy if you want a ride—"

"I'll give Lucy a ride." Marsha smiled at him, reassuringly. "You just take care of Scout. She said something about expecting you. And I know you don't want to keep her waiting. She was a little shook up by everything that had happened. Probably didn't even think to lock her door."

Nick turned and hurried for the exit, his mind racing ahead of him. Well, he'd wanted a pattern, and here was another piece. He had two women missing – Lisa and Robyn. And two more women strangled – Celeste and that teacher who'd been murdered the same day Lisa disappeared. *And* two car accidents, one this week and the one

335

twenty years ago that had killed Scout's father. Both of which – why hadn't he seen this earlier – had involved cars ordinarily driven by Scout.

And now the dog. He didn't understand where the dog fit in, but he couldn't worry about that right now. He had enough other things to be worried about. By the time his car flew out of the hospital parking lot, his mind had been all but shut down by the surge of adrenaline through his veins.

"OH, LORD, WHAT A DAY." Lucy shook her head. "Marsha, can I get you anything—tea or something from one of the vending machines? I can't believe you're so calm."

A small laugh escaped from her friend's lips. "Oh, I'm not calm at all. Unfortunately," Marsha said, looking suddenly, very, very tired. But her voice was unexpectedly firm. "But I don't need anything here. In fact, we should go now."

"You want to leave? But...shouldn't we stay? Don't you want to be here if anything...happens?"

"Nothing is going to happen," Marsha said roughly. "Not yet. And there are things we need to do elsewhere. I'm going to need your help on this one Lucy."

Lucy looked at her friend then—really looked at her. She took in the grim certainty on Marsha's face, the unexpected flash of steel within her eyes. She saw the helpless fury mixed with pain. Understanding dawned inside her, she nodded gravely. A small smile lifted one corner of her mouth as she reached to clasp Marsha's hand. "All right, Cailleach. I'm with you. Lead on."

NICK MADE the trip to Scout's house in record time, afraid to even think what he might find when he got there. He noticed how badly his hands were shaking as he tried to light a cigarette, and spared a fleeting thought for how annoyed his daughter would be with him. Very seriously annoyed. Because for as long as this thing was going on he was bound to be living on cigarettes. On cigarettes and coffee. He couldn't even remember when he'd eaten last.

And he couldn't believe he was even thinking about something like food right now, but it was probably good that he was. It kept his mind off where he was going. What he might find when he got there.

His mother, for instance, he thought, determinedly steering his mind back on track, would be particularly appalled by his current diet. No self-respecting Italian American should ever pay so little attention to what he ate. She'd be saying Novenas if she knew how bad the situation had become. He'd had only a few bites of the sandwich Lucy had brought him today, and before that?

Oh, yeah. Last night. The pizza. Thinking of that, and the events that followed, brought him too close to his fears, but he was almost at her house by then, and could no longer keep his mind from sliding into terror.

The house was ominously dark as he pulled up in front of it. Adrenaline propelled him out of the car at a flat run. The front door couldn't be unlocked, could it?

Damn Marsha for putting that idea in his head. Because it wouldn't mean a thing, even if it was. There were a lot of people in Oberon who never locked their doors at all. He knew this for a fact, but still a shudder of fear went through him when he tried the knob and felt it turn in his hand. He entered the house in a state of cold dread.

The hallway was dark, still and empty. There was not a sound to be heard other than his own breathing and the panicked racing of his heart. A flicker of motion on the second story landing made him look up. And there she stood, at the top of the stairs. Her eyes were wide and watchful in her pale face, but she was here. And alive. And that was all he cared about.

337

For a moment, Nick just stared at her, almost unable to believe what he was seeing. He'd been so sure he'd lost her, again. Then he was crossing the hallway, quickly, intent on reaching her and holding her, as if she were still in imminent danger of slipping away from him.

SCOUT HAD BEEN ALONE in the house for what seemed like hours. Curled on her bed. Too lost in her own inner darkness to notice the way that night had swallowed up the house. Only the sound of Nick's car in the drive, and his footsteps in the hall had been reason enough to propel her up and out of the room.

She knew the instant he sighted her. He'd looked up, and she'd seen his body tense, and then he was crossing the hall with a predator's sure, purposeful strides. Her own body tensed in response as she watched him take the stairs two at a time with graceful, effortless speed.

As he reached the top of the stairs and wordlessly folded her into a close embrace, she was conscious of an overwhelming sense of relief. All the pain and fear and tension dissolved. They stayed that way, locked together and unmoving, for what seemed like a very long time.

Scout couldn't remember ever having felt so safe, so comforted, so cherished. *This is what it means to come home.* This – what she was feeling right now – was everything she had craved her whole life. Everything she had needed and had only ever come close to finding. She neither sobbed nor shuddered, but tears coursed, unchecked, in rivers down her cheeks.

AFTER A WHILE NICK STIRRED. He dropped kisses on her head, and gently pulled away so that he could look at her. "I was so worried," he breathed, his eyes taking in every detail of her face, anxiously reassuring himself that she really was all right.

"Were you? Why?" Scout smiled up at him. A faint, flickering smile, her eyes still bright with tears.

"What do you mean, why? When Marsha told me you'd gone home, that you were here alone, I—"

"You were worried...about *me?*" She sounded surprised, he realized with a shock. And something more. She sounded almost pleased by the idea.

"Of course, I was worried about you," he growled. "What did you think? After what happened to Celeste—"

She cringed. "No, don't! Please, don't talk about that. It was so awful; I can't even stand to think about it. But, Nick, why would that have anything to do with me?"

He considered telling her about some of the things he'd been thinking, some of the fears that had consumed him for the better part of the day but decided against it. There was no sense in frightening her, not until he knew more, until he had his facts straight.

"I don't know," he said at last. "I don't know what it is you do to me. I feel like I'm half out of my mind all the time now."

She smiled at him, then. Really smiled. That lustful, luminous look he always found so hard to resist.

"Hmm," she purred. "Only half? Seems to me we should be able to do better than that. Why don't you come back to bed with me and let's see if I can't find some way to drive you completely crazy?"

He was tempted. God, was he tempted. But he had to keep his head. He had to get her out of here, take her far away. *Get her someplace safe.* The thought seemed to originate from somewhere outside his mind, but it resonated deep within his soul. *I need to protect her. To save her. Whatever the cost.*

His cousin was forever on his case about how insensitive he was to things like atmosphere, but tonight even he could feel the hints of terror and grief that lurked in the enveloping shadows. There was little that was seductive about the darkness filling the house tonight. He only wondered how it was she failed to sense it, too.

"Listen," he said urgently. "I don't think that's a good idea, right now. I want to get out of here. Do you think you can get some clothes together?"

"Where do you want to go?" she asked, eyes widening in hurt surprise.

"My place. C'mon," he urged, ignoring the hurt, and his own incipient claustrophobia, as well. "Let's go get your stuff."

"Your place? But—" She stared at him. "I don't know if I— Why, Nick?"

He sighed; his mind grasped wildly at straws. "Honey, when's the last time you ate something?"

"I don't know. I had something earlier today with Marsha and Lucy— This morning, I guess?"

"Uh-huh. Well, I think we ought to fix that. Also, it's late and I've still got I lot of thinking to do, and I won't be able to do it on an empty stomach."

He was still smiling, and his eyes were warm and dark and reassuring. Scout could think of no reason why she should feel uneasy right now, but she did, just the same. Cold trickles of fear ran down her spine. Nothing was making sense anymore.

"Why can't we just stay here?" she protested. "I'm sure we can find *something* to eat. What is it you have to think about, anyway? It's been such a long day and I'm so tired and you...you just got here. Now you want to leave again?"

"It's like I told you," he repeated, stubbornly. I'm hungry. And whether you feel like eating or not, you probably should. I know you've had a really stressful day."

"But I don't—"

"And, this is just a guess, but you didn't happen to go food shopping today, by any chance, did you?"

"Did I...shop? No, of course I didn't! For God's sake, Nick. How'd you expect me to think about anything like that when I—"

"Right. So, like I said. I'm gonna take you home and feed you. And then... Well, then maybe we'll see what else we feel like doing, okay? Maybe I'll take you up on your offer to drive me crazy, after all."

"What's going on, Nick?" she asked feeling suddenly very, very frightened.

"Oh, hell." Sighing, he gave in to the inevitable. "Look...let's just get moving now, okay? I'll tell you all about it on the way."

---

1. Just and FYI. We do find out what Marsha's power animal is at the end of the next book, **A Sight to Dream Of.**
2. I love that Marsha remains ruthlessly manipulative to the end. No matter how often it blows up in her face. Hopefully it's not a spoiler to mention that she continues in this vein throughout most of the series.

## 30

*L*ucy breathed deep, inhaling the pungent scents of the herbs she was wrapping into bundles, and felt herself instantly refreshed. Her lips moved in a silent incantation as she carefully wound the colored yarn around wands of lavender, sage, sweetgrass and cedar. So absorbed was she in her task, she barely noticed when the door opened.

Marsha entered, carrying a large box which she put down on a bench inside the door. She sighed wearily as she joined Lucy at the table. "Well, I think we've got just about everything."

Marsha's face was drawn and pale and there was a bleakness in her eyes that made Lucy's heart ache.

"You look terrible," Lucy told her. "Here, have some tea." She nodded at the pot that sat on the table then watched as Marsha poured herself a cup. She knew a sense of relief after Marsha had taken a few sips and some of the strain left her face. "I sure hope you're right about this."

Marsha nodded. "About Scout, you mean? So do I."

Not *just* about Scout, but yeah, that, too. "And you really think you can talk her into cooperating with us?"

Marsha's lips quirked. There was an odd glimmer in her eyes, not amusement, exactly. Confidence, perhaps? Lucy couldn't be sure. "I don't just *think* it, Lucy; I *know* I can. Although I'm hoping it won't come to that. I think she'll want to do it. Don't you?"

"Ha." Lucy shook her head. *No, not even. Not if she has any sense at all.* "Have you met the woman?"

"I just wish the timing were better," Marsha fretted. "I mean... honestly, she's pretty fragile right now, emotionally. And if anything were to go wrong—"

Fragile? Was she still talking about Scout? "Well, that's where I come in, isn't it?" Lucy felt herself smile for the first time all evening. She gestured at the pile of herbs on the table. "Don't you worry about that, Marsha. I'll take care of Scout. She and I have some old debts to settle too, you know. And it looks like tomorrow, they're all coming due."

THE FIRST WAVE of fatigue hit Scout just as Nick turned into the driveway of his apartment building and pulled smoothly to a stop. He cut the engine, and they sat silent and still for a moment. Scout tried to fight back her exhaustion, as well as the overwhelming sense of isolation she'd been feeling – more strongly every minute – during the ride from her house.

The things Nick had told her on the way here, the ideas he had planted in her imagination, were too frightening to think about. She yearned desperately for the feeling of safety she'd experienced earlier when he'd held her in his arms at the top of her stairs.

Somehow it did not seem wise, or even possible to retreat to that safety now. She shot him a quick, nervous glance. He stirred then, and smiled at her, but she thought his smile seemed oddly strained.

When he bent to kiss her, she did not resist but only closed her eyes so he would not see the tears that had sprung into them. The touch of his lips was soft and sweet, but the driving need that had always marked his kisses before now was absent.

*What's happened to change that? What else has gone wrong since this morning? What is it he's not telling me?*

She could not shake off the feeling that he'd kiss her in just this same manner when he finally kissed her goodbye.

"I'm not sure it was such a good idea, coming here," she murmured when he ended the kiss.

He smiled, and kissed her again, lightly, on the forehead. "We'll feel better when we get inside," he said, but she doubted whether she would ever feel *better* again.

She'd followed him into the kitchen, where she'd slumped in one of his chairs, barely noticing when he brought her a glass of wine, before disappearing into his bedroom to shower and change.

Now, she watched as he went to work fixing them a meal. He was barefoot, wearing only a T-shirt and jeans, and he seemed relaxed and casual, completely in his element. It was a side of Nick she'd only ever glimpsed before, and she liked it a lot. Even tired as she was, she couldn't help imagining what it might be like if she could actually have this life – the life she'd always dreamed of having.

What would it be like to live here in Oberon, with Nick. To always have his warm, comforting presence filling her life. Only this morning, it had seemed like anything was possible. But this morning had been a lifetime ago. Tonight, it was hard to imagine that this happiness could be hers, that this dream had even the smallest chance of ever coming true. It was hard to believe, and it became progressively harder, as exhaustion fed her growing despair.

Her mind was a roiling mass of thoughts and emotions—all of which seemed to wriggle out of her grasp, the moment she tried to catch one. The only thing clear to her was the distant wariness in Nick's eyes. She'd asked what was wrong, and he'd claimed he was hungry. But surely there had to be more to it than that?

Desperate to distract herself, she wrenched her thoughts away from the small, cluttered kitchen and forced herself to think instead, about what he had told her on the ride from her house...

. . .

AS THEY'D SPED through the empty streets, Scout had tried hard to feel exhilarated by the speed, by the darkness, by the danger that had always before caused adrenaline to run like a thrill through her veins. Tonight, however, she wasn't thrilled by any of it. She was scared. And everything Nick told her only scared her more.

"Look," he'd said. "Twenty years ago, your sister disappeared. And a short while later a car that you were in the habit of driving was involved in an accident, right? It was *your* car your father was driving when he went over that cliff—isn't that what you told me?"

"Yes."

"Right. And then now, just this past week, another woman has disappeared from the same house. And once again, your car was involved in an accident with suspicious similarities. And about the only connection I can figure between then and now, is that you were in Oberon on both those occasions. And during all the time in between – you were gone."

He paused, and glanced over at her as if he expected a response, but she could think of nothing to say. Was he suggesting that it was all her fault—like everyone else had always done? He couldn't mean *that*, could he?

After a moment, he went on again. "Okay. So. Now, on top of that, we have Celeste being strangled only two days after I overheard part of a phone conversation between her and Marsha regarding some information that Celeste thought she had uncovered about a murderer." He paused again. "You with me so far?"

"I guess," she answered reluctantly.

"Good. Now, listen up. That teacher who was murdered, back when you were in high school—she was your math teacher too, right? The same math teacher Lucy, Marsha and your sister had?"

"Uh-huh."

"And that class you helped them cheat in – that was her class, right?"

Scout opened her mouth to speak, ready to argue that she hadn't done any such thing, but what was the use? "Yes," she said, instead. Calmly. Just as if her heart were not breaking from the unfairness of it all.

*That's what he thinks of me? That's how he thinks it went down? Doesn't anyone understand that it wasn't my fault?*

"I remember that case. She was strangled, as was Celeste. So, I guess what I'm wondering is, could Celeste have known something about that? Could she have had some information – maybe about this test thing – that someone was willing to kill for?"

"What? No! That's too fantastic. What could she have known? Celeste wasn't even in Oberon twenty years ago. Was she?"

"I have no idea. That's why I'm asking."

"Well don't ask me! I just got here, remember?" She frowned at him, feeling hurt, perplexed, overwhelmed. "So, are you saying that you think someone— No. What *are* you saying, exactly?"

"What I'm saying is that...somehow...you seem to be at the center of a lot of these events. I don't know how yet. But until I find out what's going on, I'm gonna feel a whole lot better if you're out of that house. If you're somewhere else. Someplace where I can keep an eye on you. Someplace safe."

THE SMELL OF SAUTÉED ONIONS, of garlic and basil and green peppers and other fragrances she could not identify brought Scout back to the present. On the stove, steam rose from a large pot of water. The contents of two saucepans sizzled. Nick stood at the counter next to the stove, chopping basil.

"Hey." He smiled at her over his shoulder. "We're almost there, don't fall asleep yet, okay?"

Scout nodded weakly, but then decided conversation might be the only way to focus her attention. "You really look like you know what you're doing over there. I'm impressed. I didn't know you could cook."

Nick flashed an amused grin at her. "Well, of course I can cook."

"Why *of course*? Lots of people can't, or don't cook. Like me."

"Well, that's different," he said with a shrug as he sprinkled the basil into one of the pans and then stirred, with a graceful twisting motion of his wrist. "You're not Italian."

Scout thought about that. "Are you saying it's a cultural thing?"

"Nah, I think it's more— oh, I don't know, genetic, I guess."

"Genetic? Like...anyone with Italian blood in their veins can cook?"

"Pretty much." He bent to open the oven door and removed a fragrant, crusty loaf of bread, which he quickly deposited into a cloth-covered basket. Then he slid the basket across the table towards Scout, along with a small bowl of warm olive oil to which a clove of garlic, crushed red pepper, and several sprigs of fresh rosemary had been added. "I'd say that's a pretty fair assessment. At least, we all *think* we can cook," he said with a wink, then gestured toward the food. "Why don't you get started with that, okay?"

Scout broke the bread apart and dipped a piece into the fragrant oil. The taste revived more than her energy; she felt warm all the way through to her heart. She'd had no idea she'd been so cold.

"You don't mean that you all cook well, though, do you?" she asked.

Nick had gone back to chopping – sun-dried tomatoes, this time – which he added to the mixture cooking in the other pan. Now, he nodded. "Of course, I do."

"Really?"

"Absolutely. You can't call it cooking if it's something no one wants to eat, right?"

"I don't know about that."

"Trust me. It's true. Anyway, the real secret is that each of us, in our heart of hearts, believes not just that we cook *well*, but that we cook better than just about anyone else. At least when it comes to certain, special dishes. I think that's why Italians, in general, tend to eat at home so much."

"So, is Lucy a good cook?"

"Well, of course she is—that's what I'm saying. She makes a mine-strone that even my mother can't touch. But, you know, she'd pretty much have to be especially good with herbs, and with vegetables and stuff like that, given that she spends so much of her time at the nursery. But if you really want to taste something special, get her to fix you some of her homemade gnocchi with pesto sometime." He flicked the heat off under both pans and tilted the contents of the pot into a strainer in the sink. Steam rose to envelope him.

*Ask Lucy for a favor? Yeah, that'll be the day.* Scout shook her head. "I don't know, Nick. I can't really see Lucy jumping at the opportunity to fix me dinner. Unless maybe it was for a going away party."

"Oh, I don't know," Nick said as he assembled everything onto two plates, which he then carried to the table. "Give her a chance. One of these days, she just might surprise you."

He set the food down with a flourish and slid into the chair across from her. The plate in front of her had been piled high with multicolored pasta bows in a delicate basil cream sauce, tossed with a mixture of red and green peppers, onions, broccoli, yellow zucchini, sun-dried tomatoes, and cubes of grilled chicken. All topped with more basil and paper-thin slices of Parmesan cheese. Nick watched her with amusement as she inhaled the fragrances greedily.

Scout sighed, happily. "It smells wonderful."

"Yeah, but it tastes even better – mangia!"

"So," she asked, between mouthfuls. "Is this one of those special dishes that you cook better than anyone else?"

"Nah," he answered with a grin. "This is just what you get when you throw a lot of leftovers together. It's nothing really – just a snack."

Scout eyed him curiously. "I've been wondering. What's the deal with you and Lucy, anyway? I know you're cousins and all, but she seems awfully worried about you."

"Well, we're double first cousins, that might have something to do with it. [1]

"Double first cousins? What does that mean?"

"My mother and her mother are sisters, and her father and my father were brothers. Plus, for a short while, after my father died, my mom and I moved in with her and her family."

"Sounds like you're all pretty close."

Nick nodded. "Yeah, we are."

"You're lucky."

"You keep telling me that," he observed, grinning wryly.

"And you don't think you are?"

"I guess I am." He shrugged. "Luckier than my daughter, anyway."

"Oh, come on. I know something about families, too, you know. Especially the ones that don't work. I saw your daughter with her cousins. She knows she's loved. She's got you and she's got her mother, and even if the two of you aren't still living together, it's still better than being abandoned."

He nodded. "I know you're right. And, honestly, I know it's better now than it was when Lauren and I were together—although, there are plenty of people who'd maybe tell you otherwise." Nick's voice was harsh. It pained her to hear it. "But still, it's not what I ever wanted for Kate."

"I'm sorry."

"Ah, it was just a mistake, that's all. As Lucy would probably be the first to tell you." He shook his head, thoughtfully. "She says I make a lot of them."

"You? Are you kidding?" Scout smiled, trying to make a joke of it. "Remember me? The queen of galactic mistakes? I'm pretty sure I hold the record for royally screwing things up, as far as Lucy's concerned."

Nick shot one piercing glance at her, but just when she thought he was about to say something, he seemed to change his mind, and looked away again. The moment stretched out uncomfortably. When he finally did speak, he caught her completely off guard.

"I need to ask you something," he said. And the quiet, serious tone of his voice sent a tiny warning tingle through her. "Last night, when you asked if I would stay, I didn't know if—that is, you didn't mean— Ah, hell. What *did* you mean?"

The second wave of fatigue hit her then, and her hand closed convulsively on the stem of her wineglass. She struggled to keep her voice as steady as she could make it when she answered, "Nothing, Nick. I, I didn't mean anything by it. Really. I guess I just got caught up in the moment, that's all. It's not like I was ever going to hold you to it, or anything. It wasn't a promise. Like you said, let's just enjoy the present, all right?"

He took a deep breath and let it out again slowly. "From what you told me yesterday, I kind of got the impression that you're pretty much settled in LA now. I mean, with your work and all?"

She could hear the carefully controlled tension in his voice, the wariness, the fear, and it just about broke her heart. She should have known it was too good to be true. What was it Lucy had said, again? *Nick's got a life. He doesn't need Scout.* She supposed she was lucky to have had even this much. "Yeah. So...?"

"I mean, you probably have a really nice place there, and friends, and...and everything?" he prompted.

She thought of the life she had made for herself. Her little condo near the beach was nice enough, she supposed. Nice and empty. Sterile. Impersonal. Lonely. "Sure. And, you know, like you said, I've got my work, too." She took another sip of wine, not wanting him to see the bitter smile she could not keep from her face as she thought about that. Thought of all those dry, hollow, life-less shells of clay that awaited her return, "In fact, I fit right in there." She ran her trembling fingers lightly over the top of the table. Wanting so much to be touching him instead, but not daring to.

"Oberon can be a nice place, too, you know. But...you don't really like it here. Do you?"

She laughed at that. She couldn't help but laugh. "Well, I mean, there have always been so many reasons not to!"

He nodded. "I was thinking that maybe, now that you had the house, and all, you might— But I guess there's still no reason for you to move back here. Is there?"

What was one more lie between them? "No. No reason. And anyway, you know, I still don't really feel like the house belongs to me. It was Caroline's house. It really should have gone to Lisa."

She felt him shift restlessly in his seat. "I don't think she's coming back, Scout."

"Yeah, that's what Marsha keeps saying."

His eyes narrowed. "You think Marsha knows more about Lisa's disappearance than she's let on?"

"I don't know. She seems awfully certain that she's dead—that she's been dead for a while, I mean. And it's not like she just *thinks* so. The feeling I get from her is that she has no doubt whatsoever. Like she believes it for a *reason*."

"And what do you think?" Nick asked quietly.

Scout sighed. "I don't know. After all this time? I think if she could have come back, she would have already done it. At the same time, I don't really want to believe that she's gone because – Well, don't you see? Then it's like I really did kill her."

"Of course, it's not," he insisted, a little too vehemently, she thought. "You're not a murderer, Scout. Whatever might have happened to her, I know it wasn't your fault."

Scout smiled. It warmed her heart to have him jump to her defense. But all the same, "It really was, Nick. I mean, she would have never left if it weren't for me. And if she'd stayed...then nothing would have happened to her."

"Are you so sure of that?"

"Yes! How many times do I have to say it? Lisa left because of me. Because of all the stupid things I did back then."

"Tell me about it. I never heard the whole story. What was the argument about—exactly?"

*Oh, no. Not again.* "You already know what it was about, Nick. Why do we have to go into this again? What's going on here, anyway?"

"Just tell me," he said quietly. His face so serious it scared her.

Scout sighed and leaned back in her chair, hugging herself fiercely. "We fought about Glenn, okay? Is that what you wanted to hear? She knew I'd slept with him, and she accused me of trying to steal him away from her. Then she more or less ordered me to stay away from both of them.

"And I guess I said something like, 'that'll be hard, since you and I both have to live here.' And then she said 'that's gonna change,' or something like that. I don't know. She said I was in for a surprise; I think. And then she left."

"Did you try to stop her? Did you go after her, or anything like that?"

"No. When she left – I had no idea that she was, you know, *leaving*."

"And that was the last time you saw her?"

"Pretty much, I guess."

"Pretty much?"

"Well, it was twenty years ago. It's all a little vague at the moment."

"Okay, so then what happened?"

"Nothing. That was it. After she didn't come home from school the next day Caroline asked me if I knew where she was, and I didn't. But even then, we didn't realize she was gone."

She sighed as the memories tugged at her heart. "Up until the point where Lucy got that letter from her, I don't think the idea that she might have run away had even occurred to any of us. It was just such a stupid thing for her to have done, especially when she—"

"Wait a minute. Are you telling me your sister was missing for practically a whole day and night before you and her mother even noticed she was gone?"

"What? No, of course not. She was in school all day. At least... well, I didn't see her, but I assume she was there. I never heard otherwise."

"And the night *before* was when you two had this argument? So, where'd she go after that?

"Well, she was with Lucy, obviously."

"Lucy?"

"Yeah. Sure. She'd spent the night at her house. Said they were working on a project or something. I thought they were plotting their revenge, if you must know. Trying to figure out how to get back at me."

"So...the two of you argued, then Lisa went to Lucy's house. And then when exactly did she disappear?"

"The following day, like I said. Sometime after school."

"But, if she was at school, wouldn't you have seen her?"

"Not necessarily. To tell you the truth, I was trying to stay out of her way."

"And then after school?"

"Well, after school I was with you." Scout felt her heart lurch a little at the thought. She smiled at him, sadly.

"Right," he said without returning her smile. "I remember that part. And then you were with Glenn."

"No, I wasn't," she said in surprise. "After that I went home. Why would you think I was with Glenn?"

"I guess, because you told me you were," he answered dryly.

*Huh?* "When did I do that?"

Nick sighed. "That day at your school, when I was there to question you, do you remember that?"

*Oh, yes.* She nodded, swallowing hard. "I remember."

"I asked where you'd been, and you said you'd been with Glenn. At his house. Making love."

Scout gasped. His words, and the ice in his voice were like an assault. "I *never* said any such thing!" She half stood, slamming her palms down on the table in front of her in sudden fury.

"You did, you know," Nick told her quietly, playing with his empty wineglass. "I was there. I heard you."

"No. I might have said that we were *making out*, but I never—"

"But you did, didn't you? You slept with him?"

"Well, yes, but that was earlier. Not *then*."

"What's the difference?"

*So long ago. Won't I ever live it down?* She sank back into her chair. "Look, I know I said I was with him that day. And I guess you're right —it doesn't really matter how I phrased it—but, you knew it wasn't true. Right?"

When he didn't answer, she looked at him questioningly. What she saw in his face surprised and puzzled her. "Nick, you had to have known that I wasn't with Glenn that afternoon. The afternoon of the murder," she repeated, more firmly. "The day that Lisa ran away."

"No," he said at last, even more quietly.

She stared at him in disbelief. "But you knew where I really was that afternoon. Because I was with *you*. At your apartment. Don't tell me you've forgotten?"

"And afterwards?" he prompted, very gently. "After I left?"

She shook her head. "After that I went home. How could you have thought—"

He got up and began to pace the room distractedly. "But you did see him—right? Later that day?"

"No, damn it! Will you *listen* to me? I didn't see him at all! I didn't see anybody. I went straight home. I stayed in my room. I lay in my bed and...and I thought about what had almost happened. What might happen the next time I saw you. What I *hoped* was going to happen, if you must know." She smiled weakly. "And then later that evening, I guess it was about eight or so, Caroline came in and asked me if I had any idea where Lisa could be."

"So then, when he backed you up – about your being with him, that was also a lie?"

"Oh, that." She laughed at that – a low, mocking laugh. *God, what an idiot I was back then—and probably still am now.* "Well sure, that's what made it such a great partnership, you know? If one of us lied the other would swear to it."

"Just like now, I guess."

"Now?" Once again, she was startled as much by his tone and the hard look of fury on his face, as by the words themselves. Was he reading her mind? "Wh-what do you mean?"

"I meant what I said. Now. This week. You're still lying to protect each other, aren't you?"

"No. What the hell are you talking about?" she asked coldly.

"You said you had dinner with him Monday. *Just dinner*, you said."

"Yeah, so?"

"So, you weren't with him earlier in the day? Say, at about, oh, ten a.m.?"

Scout had no idea where he was going with this, but if he was still suspicious of her relationship with Glenn, he could go to hell. She'd be damned if she was going to trot out any more of her emotions for him to stomp on. Especially not now, when he'd made it abundantly clear that he didn't want her on any kind of a permanent basis.

"We had dinner." She repeated, her voice flat. "That's all."

They exchanged a long, wordless look. Nick was the first to look away. "Forget it," he said, sounding tired and disgusted and angrier than he had any right to be. "I don't know why we're having this discussion, anyway. I really don't want to talk about this now."

"That makes two of us."

His eyes flashed for a moment, and then his expression went blank. She could actually see him closing himself off from her. Shutting her out. "Maybe you should think about trying to get some sleep," he said coldly. "I think we're both dead on our feet."

But she barely heard him, because that's when the third wave hit her and took her under.

Nick had been watching Scout sleep for over an hour, now. Right there in his bed, on the other side of the room, her hair splayed out across his pillow. His body was screaming with its need for her, but he refused to give in to it.

*She doesn't love me.*

Blind as he had always been where she was concerned, even he could see that. She didn't love him, and she wouldn't stay.

Whatever he'd thought last night had meant, whatever he imagined he'd seen when he looked into her eyes, he'd been mistaken. Last night hadn't meant a damn thing to her. It couldn't have. Not if she could still look him right in the eye, as she had tonight, and lie about having been with Glenn all day Monday.

Oh, hell. If he were smart, he wouldn't even have brought that up. He would have just forgotten about the whole damn thing. What did it matter, what went on before yesterday? It still would have come to this in the end, wouldn't it?

Hadn't he felt her pulling away from him all night? The whole time they were here, as he cooked for her, as he ate with her, as they talked?

*Can't you see how good we could be together?* he'd felt like shouting. *Can't you feel how right this is?*

But what good did it do him to feel that way, when he knew she wouldn't stay? All he had left to hold onto now was the frail hope that this time, perhaps, she wouldn't disappear as completely as she had before. And, right now, even that seemed like too much to expect.

God, but he was tired. He wanted nothing so much as to crawl into bed and take her into his arms, wipe the whole rotten day from his mind, and find again what he had found with her last night. But it wasn't real. And it wouldn't last. It was a fantasy. A dream. Another lie. And he'd had enough of those for a lifetime.

So, he'd just stay where he was, and watch as she slept...

SCOUT AWOKE WITH A START. She had no idea where she was, or what had awakened her. But then she heard it again. A soft, snoring sound, it came from the other side of the room, where Nick had fallen asleep in an old armchair.

He hadn't even wanted to get into bed with her? A cold bleakness settled around her heart. Only yesterday morning he'd said he loved her. And now— Oh, God, it hurt to realize it wasn't true.

*This is not his fault,* she told herself fiercely. They were only words. She had heard them often enough before. Heard them spoken casually, lightly, insincerely. She'd even used them that way herself, hadn't she? On more than one occasion?

She fell back on the bed and lay there, staring at the ceiling. It was funny, though, she had never thought of Nick as being the kind of man who'd say things that he didn't mean. Not that she had any right to expect honesty from him. Not after all the lies she'd told.

The empty bed seemed to stretch cold and lonely, for acres all around her. Obviously, she'd made a mistake lunging at him in the kitchen the other night. Hadn't he told her as much at the time?

*You took me by surprise,* he'd said. And still she allowed herself to read far too much into the way his body had responded. If she had given it any thought at all, perhaps she would have realized when he tried to stop – not once, but twice – what it was he was *really* trying to say. But she'd loved him for so long, and she had wanted, so much, to believe that he felt the same way about her.

To be sure, if he was just being *kind,* he had carried it a little far. Had it really been necessary for him to kiss her quite so thoroughly and with such devastating sweetness? To make love to her so passionately? To claim that he loved her? To promise that he'd stay?

But, given the way she had acted, what the hell else had she expected him to do? He probably figured he was doing her a favor – giving her what she needed or wanted. Or something like that. Just for the one night. Or perhaps, just for old time's sake? And she had no one but herself to blame for thinking it meant any more to him than that. Stifling a sob, she rolled over and pressed her face into his pillow and tried to make herself believe that none of it mattered, that things would look better in the morning...

NICK'S EYES sprang open in the darkness. He thought he'd heard her call his name. But no, she must have been talking in her sleep. Once again, he fought down the urge to cross the room and take her in his arms. What would be the point of that? It wasn't going to make her change her mind about him, and it certainly wouldn't make his feelings for her go away. Nothing had ever done that. There had to be some way to get over wanting what you couldn't ever have. And, if he were really as lucky as she kept insisting he was, maybe someday he'd stumble across the answer.

---

1. I've always loved this scene—for a couple of reasons. First of all, Nick and I have similar philosophies on Italians and cooking. And this is one hundred percent accurate, in my opinion. When it comes to food, we're opinionated as fuck and we all think we know what's best. It's actually kind of irritating.

   A few other things to note, while we're on the subject. A) Greco was my paternal grandmother's maiden name, so I've always felt a tad proprietorial about Nick and Lucy, et al. B) The idea of multiple siblings from one family marrying into another was very common among my grandparents' generation, especially among immigrants. Sidenote: ALL four my grandparents were first generation immigrants from either Ireland or Italy. C) My maternal grandmother's family thought it would be a great idea if she married her sister's brother-in-law; unfortunately for that plan, she was already secretly married to my grandfather. But that's a story for another time. And, finally, D) My paternal grandmother had *two* sisters who did marry her husband's brothers. Which resulted in my father having *two* sets of double-cousins. Talk about tightly knit families! (return)

# 31

Bright sunlight and the tantalizing fragrances of coffee and cinnamon filled the room the next time Scout awoke. For a moment, with her face still buried in the pillows where Nick's scent lingered, a pleasant warmth crept over her. But it was quickly chased away as last night's horrible isolation returned full force, along with an undefined restlessness, an inchoate anxiety that pulled her out of bed.

She dressed quickly. She couldn't stay here, and it was best not to linger over the reasons why. She had work to do. If Nick was right, then someone, possibly someone she knew, had killed both Lisa *and* her father. Someone had stolen her family, ruined her life, and left her believing it had all been her fault. She was going to find out who that someone was if it was the last thing she ever did.

No. Not the last thing. Because the *very* last thing she was going to do was to make sure that someone paid.

Nick was at the stove when she entered the kitchen a short while later. He had set two places at the table with place mats and napkins, and a little vase of blue and purple morning glories from the vine that grew up the side of the building.

All these homey little touches should have made her happy. They had to mean he cared, at least a little. Had to mean he wasn't still as angry as he'd seemed last night. But a desperate longing seared her all the same. *I can't keep this,* she forced herself to remember. *This was never really mine to begin with.*

So, she slid into the chair she had occupied the night before. She fought down the urge to run to him, wrap herself around him and never let him go. And she waited until she had her voice under control before she spoke.

"I guess you weren't kidding about the whole liking to cook thing, were you?" She even managed to smile, as she added. "Something sure smells good. What's on the menu, this morning?"

Nick turned toward her for a brief moment, a look of something very like annoyance on his face. And then he quickly turned back to the stove. "Nothing fancy, I'm afraid. Just some French toast and a red pepper frittata. And sausages. Or fruit, if you want it. I have to leave for work pretty soon." His voice was cool, indifferent, as he added, "Why don't you help yourself to some coffee, while I finish up here?"


NICK BUSIED himself at the stove, keeping his back to her as long as possible. He didn't understand why *anything* she did should surprise him, but disappointment swamped him anyway, weighing on his chest so heavily he could barely breathe. She was back to acting as though they were mere acquaintances. Was there nothing he could do to bridge this distance between them even a little? No way at all to reach her?

"You look tired," Scout said when he finally brought the food to the table. "Is everything okay?"

Nick stared at her for a long, long moment, while his mind rejected every honest or accurate response that occurred to him. How was it possible for her to rip his heart apart like this, and never even have a clue?

"I'm fine," he lied, his voice as dispassionate as he could make it. He sat down and concentrated his attention on his coffee for several minutes longer than was practical. Surely, he could only spend so much time stirring nothing into plain black coffee without looking like an idiot. But no, she didn't even notice that.

"Listen," he told her. "I don't want you out at your house all alone today. Is there someplace I can drop you off on my way to work?"

Scout looked up, startled. "Like where?"

"I don't know." He hesitated, then took a deep breath. What the hell, maybe it was worth another try. "But if you can't think of anyplace else to go, you could always stay here."

"No."

It was just one word, quietly spoken, but the flush in her cheeks and the frost in her voice left him with no doubt that she was turning down more than just his apartment.

He gritted his teeth. "Look, it's not a big deal, all right? We just need to figure out how to keep you safe." He heard the pleading note in his voice and hated it.

"I can take care of myself," Scout said, rejecting even his right to worry about her.

"Oh, I don't doubt that." Nick lashed out, as exhaustion combined with the pain in his heart to catapult him over the edge of worry and straight into rage. "Not for one, instant have I ever doubted that. Somehow, you always manage to land on your feet. It's the people around you who need to watch their backs."

"NICK DOESN'T LOOK happy this morning," Lucy said, as she chewed her lip. They were parked on the street across from her cousin's apartment building. She'd caught just one glimpse of Nick's face when his car tore out of the drive, a moment earlier. He looked like death—not even warmed over; just fresh, and raw and...

Marsha stirred. "Something's happened. If we don't want to waste the rest of the day trying to scrape Scout off the floor, I suggest we go and get her out of there. Now."

"Shit. Are you still sure you want to do this?" A nasty, cold nervousness had seized Lucy. She glanced anxiously across at Marsha.

"I'm sure." Marsha said, sounding very sure, indeed. "Let's go."

Lucy put the car back in gear and slid across the street and into the parking space her cousin had vacated so abruptly. "Whatever you say. But just so you know, I don't like this. Not one little bit."

SCOUT SAT AT THE TABLE, staring at the untouched plates of food, her hands still clenched around her coffee mug. Nick's last words reverberating in her ears.

"I give up," he had ground from between clenched teeth. "Do what you want. There's a key hanging inside the door if you want it. Just lock up when you leave and...stay safe out there."

Now someone was knocking at the door, and she wasn't sure if she was supposed to answer it, or not. Whoever it was, they were probably looking for Nick, but he was gone. And—

"Scout?" Marsha called through the door. "Are you in there? Open up."

Or maybe they weren't looking for Nick, after all.

A strange chill passed through Scout when she opened the door. Lucy and Marsha weren't dressed in long, black robes, but they might as well have been, given the fell expressions in their eyes and on their faces, their air of having come here on a mission.

Deep within her, something came awake, as if a horn had sounded, summoning her to battle. Scout eyed them warily. "Hey, guys. What's going on?"

"We need to talk to you Scout," Marsha said, asking with almost frightening formality. "May we come in?"

Scout shrugged. "I guess so." It wasn't like Nick had told her otherwise. She took a step back so they could pass through the open door and then couldn't help but notice the familiarity with which Lucy moved through the room; how she crossed immediately to one of the armchairs, casually removed a stack of newspapers from its seat and then dropped them on the floor beside it, before seating herself.

Scout could tell that this was the chair she was used to choosing whenever she visited her cousin's home, and for a moment she was consumed with envy for what she knew she would never have.

Oh, how she wanted to be the one who felt at ease here, to be the one who was comfortable enough to rearrange the furnishings without a second thought. Instead, she perched uneasily on the edge of the couch, while she waited to learn what they wanted.

Marsha sat beside her and took hold of her hands. "I need your help," she said simply, but Scout thought there was something hard and implacable in her eyes, as if her acquiescence was something Marsha was determined to gain, by whatever means necessary.

"What for?"

"Actually, a couple of things." Marsha sighed. "First of all, I need to do something about Celeste."

Scout frowned. "You mean...you want to heal her? Or, you know, bring her back, somehow?"

"No," Marsha said, her voice bleak. "Only if she—" She paused, dropping her head, swallowing hard before continuing, "Her soul, or whatever you want to call it, has to *want* to come back. And I don't think it does. But I don't think she's able to move on yet. And I feel like it's my fault, like I'm responsible for what's happened to her. So I need to do something, whatever I can, to help her. But the thing is, I can't do it alone. I tried, but I'm too close to it. Also, I can't shut off my emotions like you can."

Scout's eyes widened in surprise. "You make it sound like a faucet. Like I can just turn my feelings on and off whenever I choose to."

"That's oversimplifying things, somewhat." Marsha shrugged. "But yeah. I think that, for whatever reason, you've been doing exactly that for a while now."

Scout thought about the implications. She wasn't sure she liked them. She wasn't sure she believed it, either. Maybe once that had been true, but even if she could still do that...did she want to?

"You said a couple of things. What else?"

"I want this guy—or whoever's responsible for all these attacks. I want to know who they are and I want to stop them."

Scout nodded. "Good. Me, too."

She felt the anger coalesce inside her, and it scared her almost senseless. Her eyes closed as an involuntary spasm of nerves shook her. Only one other time had she felt this way. And she was still living with the fallout from that explosion. She opened her eyes again and cast another nervous glance at Marsha. She recognized this particular emotional brew. Guilt, anger, pain, coupled with a furious need for vengeance. She recognized it all too clearly. And a very large part of her wanted nothing at all to do with it.

Unfortunately, that part was no longer running the show. She shrugged. "All right, I'm in. Let's do it."

"*Let's do it?*" Lucy sputtered. "That's it? Don't you even want to know what you need to do? Or if there are any risks involved?"

Scout looked at her, sitting there so comfortably in that chair. Nick's chair. A chair she would have given almost anything to be able to claim as casually as Lucy had just done. It was just a chair. There was nothing special about it. She didn't even particularly like it. But all the same, jealousy flared out of control.

"What's the difference, Lucy?" she snapped impatiently. "*I* want this more than either of you could. Someone stole *my* family, wrecked *my* life, and hurt a lot of people that I cared about. They need to be stopped. I figure you guys must have *some* plan in mind, or you wouldn't be here, right? And I've got nothin'. So, who cares what your plan entails, or what I have to do? And as for risks—" She swallowed hard, as she thought about Nick. "What do I have to lose, anyway?"

"Well. Actually." Marsha cleared her throat, "To be honest, there is some risk. Do you remember what we talked about yesterday, about how some parts of your soul, or your psyche, might shut down when things get painful? I have to assume we'll be getting into some painful areas with this. If we're not careful, we could trigger another episode. You could end up shutting down all over again. And, if that were to happen, I still don't know how to fix it."

Scout felt the truth of her words. She winced at the thought of what it would mean to go back to the way things had been. But the cold fury building in her gut was going to find some outlet anyway, so it wasn't as if she *really* had a choice now, was it? And truthfully, compared to the way she was feeling right now, the way she'd been feeling all morning, what was so bad about closing herself off to pain, anyhow? It might be a relief.

"I'll take my chances," she told them. "But whatever we're doing, I don't want to do it here."

Not here, where Nick lived. Where reminders of him were everywhere. Where he'd cooked for her. And where she couldn't help but imagine what her life might have been like, if only things had been different.

"Agreed," Marsha said, standing up. "We'll go to your house. I think that's where this all started, anyway."

Lucy closed the door behind them as they left. Scout considered taking the key Nick had offered, but in the end, she didn't. *I have to remember who I am*, she thought, stubbornly. *Who I really am, when I'm not here playing pretend; and what my real life is like. Simple. Clean. No ties.*

Still, when she heard the lock snap shut behind them, she felt as though she'd let go of her last handhold to sanity. She was in a freefall, now. Whatever doom lay before her, there was nothing left to hold it back.

# 32

*L*ucy was not happy. They had serious business to conduct and Scout... Well, it was all very well for Marsha to go on and on, as she had the night before, about Scout's ability to detach from her feelings. Hell, she might even be right about it. But the tension and unhappiness that had permeated the atmosphere in Nick's apartment this morning had been unbearable. And it didn't take any particular psychic talent to guess where it originated from. However far-removed Scout might be from her emotions, it sure didn't mean she didn't have any.

While Marsha went into the kitchen to boil water for the various infusions they'd be working with, Lucy set out the materials she would use to cleanse and rebalance the energies in the area where they'd be working.

They had decided that Robyn's room was the logical place to set things up. It seemed like a bit of an intrusion, since they were all still hoping she'd be back to claim it; but it occupied an auspicious position on the ba-gua grid, it had the right energy – *or it will have*, Lucy thought, *once I've finished clearing it* – but, even Scout-the-imperturbable had been unable to repress a small shudder when they first walked in.

Now she sat huddled on the edge of the daybed, like some kind of freaking zombie, staring out through the French doors that led to the patio, her eyes glassy and cold—like chunks of serpentine.

Lucy found her mind wandering away from the work at hand. "I thought Nick looked a little stressed when he left for work this morning," she said, keeping her tone casual. "Everything still okay between you two?"

Scout turned to her, her eyes two blanks, her lips curved in a mockery of a smile. "Between me and...Nick? But, Lucy, there isn't anything between us. You, of all people, should know that."

*Excuse me?* Lucy rocked back on her heels. "That's...uh, not the impression I was getting from you yesterday."

Scout laughed. A horrible parody, totally devoid of humor, it sent chills down Lucy's spine. She finally began to understand what it was about Scout's manner that might have scared Robyn.

"D'you know what he called me the other night? A fantasy. One that he no longer needs."

Lucy gaped at her. "Oh, c'mon, Scout. That's ridiculous. There's no fucking way Nick told you that!"

"I know you think I'm a compulsive liar, Lucy," Scout said coldly, "But I assure you I'm not making this up. Why would I?"

"But, hello? Yesterday? You and...and then Nick...I mean...?"

"He's very kind."

"Nick is?"

"And I think I read too much into that. I really need to start paying more attention to what people actually say. Like the other night. You told me he wouldn't want me messing up his life, but I didn't want to hear it."

"Yeah, but Scout, that—"

"And you were right. He was very relieved when I told him I had no reason to stay here in Oberon."

"Wait— You told him *that*?" Shit. No wonder her cousin looked upset. "How could you do that? He— Jesus, Scout, I thought you were in love with him?"

Tension sizzled suddenly between them, and for a moment all of

Scout's control seemed to dissolve. The blank coldness melted from her eyes, leaving them incandescent with pain; her voice was raw with it.

"Don't," she rasped.

Lucy felt the impact slam into her solar plexus. Too shaken to speak, she could only stare at Scout in surprise. It was not the first time she'd experienced an assault to one or the other of her chakras, but it had been a long time since she'd felt anything with this kind of punch behind it. It left her shaking her head. *I sure hope Marsha knows what she's getting us all into.*

Abruptly, the tension was extinguished. Scout sighed, and even managed another brief, brittle smile. Her eyes resumed their dull, soulless glaze. "Well. I guess it doesn't matter, does it? I'll be leaving as soon as we get this mess cleared up. I hear you've become quite the cook, but I think we'll skip the good-bye dinner. Don't you agree?"

"Listen," Lucy began. "About Nick—"

But Scout cut her off. "I don't want to talk about that anymore. Tell me what all this is for." She gestured at the herbs and candles Lucy had laid out, her brass bell, the bowl of flowers, the containers of water and salt.

"Basically, these are the tools I'm going to use to clean the atmosphere," Lucy said, still trying to shake off the aftereffects of Scout's outburst. "Before we do anything else, we need to get rid of any old negative energy patterns that may exist, and then re-energize the space. It makes it easier to work in."

Scout's eyebrows rose. "You can do that?"

"Yeah." Lucy bristled defensively. "Actually, I can."

"Well, good." Scout looked around the room, and shivered, slightly. "Too bad you weren't here last week. Hey, you think maybe when you're finished in here, you can do the attic?"

"Maybe. We'll see." Lucy considered telling Scout she was wrong about Nick—that he probably loved her, that he maybe always had. But if he hadn't told her that himself...? What if he had some reason for wanting her to think he didn't care? What if Scout was only going along with their plan today because she was convinced of his indifference? Lucy had already kept his secret this long, would it really hurt to keep it a little longer?

Shit. She hated these moral dilemmas. Hated having to decide where and with whom her loyalty lay, whose side she was supposed to be on. All things considered, it was probably best not to say anything, just yet. She could always tell Scout the truth later. Once she knew for sure what the truth really was. Right now, she had work to do.

She took a moment to center herself. It took longer than usual, but she recognized when she'd achieved the proper state of mind. She took several deep, cleansing breaths, said a brief prayer, and then lit the first of the smudge sticks she had prepared the night before. Solemnly, she offered the smoke to the four directions, and then above and below, before centering it in front of her.

The smoke washed over her, bathing her in its essence. As always, the heady scent of the herbs took her to another place. A place where all the worries and conflicts she had been obsessing over could not penetrate. She felt her mind focus and clear as she passed her bell, and then the rest of the tools she and Marsha would be using, through the spiraling plumes.

Moving slowly and carefully, she made her way around the room. Feeling with her right hand for any areas where the energy felt stagnant. Ringing the bell with her other hand. Listening as the tones became clearer, brighter, as the heaviness was dispelled. This step, too, took longer than such things usually did, but she had moved into an area of focus where time didn't matter. Everything simply took as long as it took.

When she was done with the bell, she picked up the canister of salt. Moving clockwise once again she sprinkled it in a widening arc over the floor. The crystals felt as though they were charged with purity. As they left her fingers and flew through the air, she could almost see the wake of brightness they left in the atmosphere. She repeated the process with the atomizer. Taking deep, appreciative breaths as the cool mist filled the air with the scents of basil and thyme.

. . .

SCOUT SAT QUIETLY, watching Lucy's performance. She was tempted to dismiss the whole ritual as so much nonsense—especially because the small part of her that thought there might be some validity to it was quaking with fright.

*I can't believe I let myself get talked into this.*

She looked up as Marsha bustled in, bearing a tray on which she'd arranged a large steaming pot, and several mugs. She set the tray down on the coffee table and handed Scout one of the mugs.

Scout sniffed suspiciously at the yellow liquid. "Ugh. What is this stuff?"

"Nothing too lethal," Marsha replied as she took a seat beside her and took another mug for herself. "Just yarrow, clover, mugwort, with a few threads of saffron thrown in."

"And why, exactly, are we drinking it?" Scout gasped, choking down a sip.

"Well, it's supposed to increase any psychic tendencies you have, and protect us all against negative energy – stuff like that. Mugwort is traditionally used prior to scrying; I figure what we're attempting is pretty darn close, so it ought to be good for this, too."

The second sip was worse than the first. "Is this really necessary?"

"It's not exactly essential, but it can't hurt. And we haven't had a chance to prepare you as much as I'd have liked. So I figure, better safe than sorry. You know?"

"Right." Scout sighed. It was hard to argue with that, she thought as she downed the rest of the mug in one long swallow. "Okay, what's next?"

"I'd like to talk to you a little about what we're planning to do today," Marsha told her. "I think I want to attempt the soul retrieval first. I think we should ease you into this and...that should be less traumatic for you than the rest. Plus, if we're successful in reaching Celeste's spirit, we might be able to get information from her that would help us with the other matter. It might even mean that we won't have to do anything else. But that's probably a best-case scenario."

"Information? Like the name of the killer, you mean?"

"Wouldn't that be nice?" Marsha rocked her head from side to side. "I don't think we should count on getting anything as obvious as a name. But it's worth a try."

Scout nodded. "That seems reasonable. And if we're not successful?" she prompted when Marsha seemed to hesitate.

"Well...the next thing I'll want to do is to see if we can induce a light trance state in both of us at the same time. And then establish a chakra link; if that's all right with you. It would mean we'd be joined on a psychic level."

Scout had no idea what that even meant, but they were wasting time. She nodded her assent.

"And then, if *that* works, and if we don't have any problems, we could do a regression." Marsha spoke decidedly, but Scout thought there was something uncertain in her manner. "I'm not sure if we'll be able to find the answers we're looking for in the here and now, but I'm a lot more confident that we can learn everything we need to know by going back into the past. Or at least...I think *you* can."

"Why is that?" Scout asked. "I mean, why me instead of you. And also, why would the answers be more available in the past?"

Marsha looked even more uncomfortable. "Well, to answer the second part of your question first, I'm assuming that the person who attacked Celeste and injured your dog and did who-knows-what with Robyn was also responsible for Lisa's disappearance and possibly Ms Burnett's murder as well, right?"

"I guess so." It seemed farfetched to Scout, but that was what Nick had said, too. If he and Marsha had both arrived at the same conclusion, independent of each other, she guessed they probably stood a pretty good chance of being correct.

"And if that's the case..." Marsha broke off on a sigh. "Okay, look, back when we were in high school, I didn't have any idea how important it was not to abuse this kind of thing. And, to tell the truth, I don't know that I would've cared all that much, even if I had known.

But, because of what we did then, I know a lot about what you can accomplish in this kind of state. You personally, I mean."

Marsha shot a quick look at Scout's face, and then away again. Color stained her cheeks as she continued. "For example, I know that you can – well, I guess it's a form of astral projection, or remote viewing, or something along those lines – but you can move your consciousness outside of this room and see things that are occurring someplace else. You can even move your consciousness into someone else's mind and learn what *they're* thinking."

Marsha paused, as if waiting for Scout to say something. But what was there to say? She'd known their experiments had gone way beyond math. In the five months they'd had to play with her mind, Scout was sure they'd found out a whole lot about her that they'd had no business knowing. But she'd deal with that later.

After a moment Marsha went on again. "I think if we take you to a particular point in the past, you could do the same thing. Especially if the connection between you and the other person was strong enough. For example, like the connection between you and Lisa."

A cold dread settled over Scout; her heart began to pound. "You're saying I might actually see what happened to Lisa?" Shit. It was one thing to learn the truth about what happened to her stepsister, it was something else again to have to bear witness to it. "You think I could find her, and follow her and learn what she was thinking?"

"And what was happening to her. Yes." Marsha swallowed hard. She hesitated again before continuing. "Like I said. I've had a lot of experience with hypnotizing you. You seem to work better if you have a familiar essence to aim at. A target, if you will.

The problem is, if everything works out the way I hope it will, you'll most likely be very...involved...in the events you observe. Almost as though they were happening to you."

"Oh, God," Scout breathed softly. How badly did she want to know what happened to Lisa? Enough to live with the memory of how it had felt, maybe for the rest of her life?

"Look, before we begin, I'll give you instructions to keep you calm and allow you to stay detached. But it's possible the experience might still be somewhat overwhelming. That's why the chakra link is so important. It will allow me to monitor things internally, so to speak. Also, Lucy'll be on hand; and there's no one I'd rely on more. It'll be her job to pull you out if things look like they're getting too rough."

*And what if she can't?* Scout wondered, shooting a look at Lucy who was arranging crystals in each of the room's corners. *Or, more likely, what if she doesn't want to? What then?*

But it didn't matter. None of it mattered. She'd come this far, and there was no turning back. She *had* to know the truth. Whatever else it cost her. "Terrific. Wonderful. So, what do we do now?"

Marsha gave her a twisted grin and handed her a dishtowel. "Here. Drape this over your head and breathe in the vapors from this pot for about three minutes."

Scout shook her head in disbelief. "You mean I can get a facial and lose my mind at the same time? Cool."

MAYBE IT WAS THE TEA, Scout thought, a little while later. Or something in the steam, or it may have only been the power of suggestion, but despite the smoke hanging in the room, everything, including the air itself, seemed clearer than before.

Marsha approached her with a small vial of oil and rubbed some in the center of her forehead. The smell of sandalwood reached Scout's nose. She felt both her apprehension and her sense of calm detachment increase.

She studied the intricately embroidered cloth Marsha had laid on the floor in the center of the room. Several implements had been placed upon it – including a small iron cauldron, a large single-headed drum, and a surprisingly sharp-looking knife. Now, as Scout watched curiously, the other women exchanged glances. Lucy nodded once, affirmatively, and Marsha bent to pick up the dagger. Scout felt a shiver of anticipation run through her.

The solemn, removed look on Marsha's face was at odds with her normal expression. And whereas Lucy had looked dreamily abstracted as she worked – the look of someone listening intently to music that no one else could hear – Marsha's eyes gleamed with fell purpose.

Extending the dagger out in front of her, Marsha turned slowly, her hand describing a circle around the room large enough to encompass them all. Lucy's eyes swept around the room, as well, following the motion of the dagger, as if she were willing the same circle into being.

Returning the knife to its place on the altar cloth, Marsha next picked up her drum. As the very first beat reverberated in the air something within Scout snapped to attention. She knew, without needing to be told, without needing the words that followed each rapid crescendo, that the sound was a summons to powers she could neither see nor sense.

Or could she?

As the ritual continued, with Marsha moving purposefully from North to East to South and finally to the West, calling to Spirit at each stop along the way, Scout began to feel a change come over the room, as though some force, immensely powerful, ancient and protective, was gathering itself around them.

*It's probably just Marsha's voice*, the small whisper of the skeptic inside her insisted. *And the power of suggestion.* Marsha had always had the capacity to be extremely persuasive when she wanted to be. That had been true twenty years ago. No doubt her abilities had improved over the years.

Given their history, the idea that Marsha was once again attempting to exert some form of mental persuasion over her should have been frightening. Yet Scout did not feel afraid. The dread and apprehension she had experienced earlier were slipping away as the atmosphere around her became charged, more and more strongly, with a warm, comforting energy.

Beyond the warmth however, hovering on the edges of consciousness, she was aware of something else. A watchfulness. A readiness.

Another type of tension altogether, like that which preceded an electrical storm, was building within the room. Still quietly biding its time but buzzing with angry anticipation.

*Look at the cats. They feel it, too.* Their casual, relaxed movements gave nothing away, but there was no hint of relaxation in their unfathomable eyes. They settled around the room and crouched watchfully as Marsha, who had seated herself on the floor, motioned to Scout to join her.

Briefly, while Lucy lit more incense, Marsha explained the process. Soon the mingled scents of frankincense and myrrh had filled the room. Scout lay quietly on the floor, breathing in the thick, fragrant air, and listening to the steady beating of the drum. She closed her eyes, knew a brief moment of disorientation, and then the drum began to pull at her.

She found herself drifting steadily towards the entrance to a cave. Floating. Sinking. Moving inward and downward. Spiraling slowly through a cavern hewn of solid rock. Heading inexorably down, down, down into the earth.

The thing was, though...she wasn't at all certain she wanted to go there.

As soon as she thought it, she paused in her descent. She could feel herself hovering in place, becalmed in a pleasant solitude. *Now, this is more like it*, she decided with a rapturous sigh of relief. There was no stress here. Plenty of breathing space. No worries. No pain. No heartbreak.

*I want to stay here. Right here. Maybe forever.*

"Scout?" Marsha's voice broke into the peaceful isolation she had allowed to collect all around her, like a thick, dark cloud. "Scout, can you hear me?"

She could hear Marsha just fine. But, mesmerized by the flood of pleasant sensations, she couldn't answer. No, that wasn't true. She could have answered, she just didn't want to. Instead, she settled in deeper, nestling into the smoky darkness.

She was rocking now on a calm, almost waveless sea, awash in color and sound. And if Marsha and Lucy would just stop talking to her, she could sail away completely.

She was a balloon adrift in an endless, endless sky. Another moment, and she would be the sky, itself. Vast and boundless, everywhere and nowhere, all at once. She would be gone. Ended. Finis. No longer in torment. No longer a captive. She would finally be free.

A bitter, acrid smell of burning herbs assaulted her nose and she groaned inwardly. It was as though the harsh smoke had thrown an anchor around her mind.

"Can you hear us now?" Lucy asked her.

*Yes. Go away.*

"Come on, Scout. How about now?"

Her mind tugged restlessly at the invisible tether. "I could hear you just fine before," she answered, peevishly.

*Damn them. Why are they doing this? Always messing with my mind. Why can't they just leave me alone? One of these days, I'll show them. I'll make them stop. Really, they have to be stopped.*

"Scout?" Marsha's voice this time. "You've gone too far. Come back up a bit. Come on... Okay, there we go. That's better. Are you ready now?"

Scout sighed in resignation. "What's next?" But even as she said it, she was aware of the picture forming in her mind. She knew she was still lying on the floor, but she could also see and feel herself standing in an unfamiliar location looking again at the entrance to a cave.

She heard the beating of the drum start up again and once again, she felt herself begin to move, downward always downward, through a seemingly endless series of tunnels. She felt the rock beneath her feet change to gravel, and then to sand. Gradually the darkness gave way to a shadowy, pearly gray light. The soft beating of the drum faded, faded, and was lost beneath the sighing, crashing sound of the waves as they broke against the shore that was suddenly right in front of her.

She stood at the far end of the cave, looking out at a fog-shrouded beach. She had the sense she was waiting for something, but she didn't know what. The crashing of the surf echoed loudly within the cavern, and she felt herself growing increasingly agitated. A sound in the cave behind her caught her attention and she spun around. A strange, cold thrill ran through her. It was her dog. Sara whined and wagged her tail. Scout stared at her, perplexed.

*How did she get here?* she wondered. "Where did the dog come from?"

"Just relax, Scout," Lucy spoke soothingly, but Scout could sense her underlying uneasiness. "Everything's fine There's no dog."

Marsha chuckled. "Oh, sure there is. Don't worry, keep going. You're doing fine. I had a feeling about that." Scout heard Marsha say smugly, to Lucy, or maybe to herself. "That first day last week? All that was missing was the bow and arrow."

*It's the kind of beach you see in dreams*, Scout thought. Hauntingly familiar, but never a place you could actually recall having been to before. The sky above was overcast and gray. And the sounds – the lapping of waves, the cries of sea birds – were all oddly muffled.

The dog took off down the beach at a run and Scout had to work to follow her. The sand was soft and deep, which made walking difficult. Far down the beach in front of her, she could just make out an indistinct figure warming itself by a fire set in an old oilcan.

As she got closer, she could tell that the person was definitely a woman, although she was not sure how she knew this. Whoever she was, the woman was bundled in an odd assortment of mismatched garments, making identification difficult.

And the fire, Scout realized now that she was closer, was not actually in the oilcan, but underneath it. In fact…it wasn't an oilcan at all, but some type of large pot, which the woman appeared to be stirring with a pole of some sort. Or maybe…

*What the hell? Is that a broomstick?*

"*You might want to watch out for some of those stereotypes.*" a soft, amused voice spoke in her mind. "*They're awfully clichéd, you know. And, as it happens, a lot of us find them offensive.*"

"Celeste?" Scout whispered. "Is it really you? Are you okay? Where is this place?"

"*Oh my, so many excellent, difficult questions. Let's just pretend they're rhetorical, shall we?"* Celeste twinkled at her. *"What is it you really want to know, dear?"*

Scout thought for a moment. Or tried to think. Her mind was still struggling to make sense of her surroundings. "I want to know what happened," she said at last. "Who did this to you? And why? And... what's going to happen to you now?"

*"Ohh."* Celeste's sigh was a long, drawn-out windy sound. *"I don't want to think about that just yet. It was too traumatic. That's why I'm still here, you know. Even with all the signs I'd received, it still came as a shock when it happened. And I'm not quite ready to deal with that, yet.*

*"But I do know that it was time for me to move on. I'm not going back."* She smiled, somewhat sadly. *"But you tell Marsha to hang on to that crystal. It'll come in handy, later. She'll find a use for it. Just not now. Not for this. Oh, and before I forget; here's something for you."*

Scout watched as Celeste dug into a pocket in the strange shape-less coat she was wearing and brought out a small velvet bag. *"I want you to have these,"* Celeste said, pressing the bag into Scout's hand. *"Tell Marsha I said so. She'll know how to get them to you."*

"What are they? What's in here?"

*"My tarot cards. You're going to need an outlet of some kind for your energies. And, to tell you the truth, I think you'll do a lot better with them than I ever did. Although, I guess I really was getting better at it, wasn't I?"*

For a moment, Scout thought she sounded wistful. But then she smiled. *"Listen, we're almost out of time. Tell Lucy to keep a close eye on those chickens of hers. And tell Marsha to stop blaming herself. This wasn't her fault. Oh,"* she broke off with a small giggle, *"and please. Tell Marsha to stop worrying about the knives. They were never that important. I just knew they'd be needed. Ask her if she thinks she's the only one who ever had a premonition."*

Without warning, Scout found her focus wavering. Celeste's face began to fade. A buzzing, humming noise filled her head, and through the mist that suddenly enveloped her, she heard Celeste's voice again, whispering urgently. *"Wait. One more thing—don't go yet! Open your eyes again, Scout. Someone wants to talk to you."*

Scout hadn't even realized that her eyes were closed, but she opened them anyway. And there, standing right in front of her, her arms open wide was Caroline. Without a thought Scout threw herself into her stepmother's arms and was at once engulfed in a cloud of emotions.

Love and laughter burst around her, and through her. A blazing white light washed over her obliterating any other reality. A single word reverberated through the brightness.

"*Remember...*"

CAROLINE HAD GOTTEN no response when she'd tried knocking on the door to Scout's bedroom. The door remained locked. In the end, she'd had to use her key to open it.

Scout was lying in bed when she entered the room, not sleeping, just lying there. Her expression that same controlled remoteness that Caroline had already, God help her, almost begun to accept as normal.

It was only in the last few days that she'd begun to worry about drugs and cults and psychotic conditions. Clearly, there was something wrong with Scout. Something dreadfully wrong. Dear God, not even her father's death had put a crack in that hideous, cold façade!

She couldn't believe she'd almost missed the signs. But then again, there had been so many other things to worry about. Sorrow and pain washed through her once again.

*What's happened to us? How did everything go so wrong?*

Only two months ago – less than two months, really – they had all been together. Happy. Alive. They had celebrated Scout's birthday, none of them with the slightest notion of what was coming. And now? Now it was just the two of them. And whatever Caroline had to do to preserve what was left of her family, she would do it. No matter what the cost to her heart might be. No matter how much it tore her apart to send Scout away, she would do what was necessary to save her only remaining child.

*I just hope it's not too late.*

This new coldness, this wall of ice Scout had erected around herself – what could have caused her to do such a thing? There was no way to reach her through it. Each attempt at discussion only seemed to increase the blankness in Scout's expression.

Caroline could only hope that, given time, Scout would find her way back from wherever it was she had gone.

But worrisome as even *that* was, it was still not Caroline's most pressing problem. Her number one priority had to be to ensure Scout's physical safety, and that meant getting her away from here. Fast. And far. And for as long as necessary. Because, as had become terrifyingly clear, it was no longer safe for Scout to remain in Oberon.

Caroline had never fully accepted the idea that's Gil's death had been an accident. He was too good of a driver, for one thing. But it was only today, when Rose Greco had called to offer her condolences, that she realized what she should have seen immediately. With Lisa missing, anyone who knew the girls would have assumed – as Lucy apparently had done, when she first learned about the accident involving the Honda – that it had been Scout who was driving the girls' car through the canyon that night.

"Scout. Honey, listen to me a moment," Caroline said. "I'm going to need you to pack some of your things. I've made arrangements for you to go and stay with your grandfather for a while. You have a flight out the day after tomorrow."

"What? No!" For a moment, only a moment, Caroline saw a glimpse of the real Scout. But then the cold stranger immediately reappeared, to say with icy politeness, "I don't want to do that Caroline. Why can't I stay here?"

She fought hard to keep her voice calm, to keep from screaming in impotent rage, *Who are you? What have you done with my child?*

"Scout...please don't make this more difficult than it already is. I can't... I just can't have you here. Not anymore. You have to go away. That's all there is to it!"

Blank eyes regarded her coldly. "Why are you doing this? This is my home."

"But there have been so many... problems, lately. Don't you see that? Too much has already gone wrong. It— it's not safe. After your father's death I realized—"

"What does *that* have to do with me?" queried the stranger.

"Because, it could have been *you*. It was *your* car. Anyone who saw it, would have thought— It *should* have been you driving the car that night. Don't you understand that yet? *You're* the one who should have died that night—*you,* not Gil." Her voice cracked, and before she could start crying, she hurried from the room.

If she broke down now and Scout attempted to comfort her, how would she ever find the strength to send her away?

And if she broke down and Scout merely continued to stare so coldly at her? Then, Caroline knew without doubt, her heart would shatter beyond repair. She ran down the hall and slammed the door of her bedroom behind her...

SCOUT FELT as though her head were coming apart. The buzzing, whirring, stinging sensation grew louder and more and more painful. It was as if her skull contained a horde of angry bees, all desperate to escape. She could feel something sucking at the edges of her mind, pulling and tugging at her consciousness. Forcing her to respond. To return. To—

"*No!*" her voice exploded from her throat in a roar of anger. She hurled herself into a sitting position and found herself face to face again with Marsha and Lucy. "How could you do it? How? I could kill you both for what you did to me!"

# 33

"It's too dangerous," Lucy's voice was a whisper, barely audible, shaking with emotion. "You said it yourself; she goes too deep. And this chakra link is gonna double the risk. What are you trying to do here, anyway? Drive the both of you completely over the edge?"

Scout paid no attention to the argument raging quietly between Lucy and Marsha; she didn't care what they thought. She'd deal with the two of them later.

Lying on the floor, blinking back tears, she tried to deal with the sudden realization that she had thrown the last twenty years of her life away over a stupid misunderstanding.

Nothing had been what it seemed. Caroline had *not* kicked her out, as she'd always believed. She'd been trying to save her. Robyn had been right, and as for Scout—

*I've been a major fucking idiot, haven't I?*

And she had to learn that *now*. Now, when it was too late to go back and change anything.

"I disagree," she heard Marsha insist. "I think the chakra link is critical. It's not going to increase the risk. If anything, it'll provide a safeguard."

"How can you know that? How do you know that you won't get sucked right down with her to...wherever it is she goes? And just what in the hell do you expect me to do if you *both* get lost like that this time?"

"I *don't* think that's going to happen."

"Well, *I* thought the whole point of using Scout for this was because she wasn't going to get all emotional. But if that wasn't emotion, I'd sure like to know what the hell you thought it was. This whole thing is turning into a gigantic clusterfuck. And I don't want any part of it!"

"There were several reasons we needed Scout for this, Lucy. She can do things that you and I can't. You're just afraid you're gonna lose control of the situation."

"Well, hell, *yes*, I'm afraid, Marsha. I don't know why you're not. I wouldn't go under with her like you're planning to do for...well, for anything, really."

*Enough is enough.* Scout propped herself up on an elbow. "Lucy, if you want to back out now, you go right ahead." The two women swung around to face her, looking tense and unhappy. "And that goes for you too, Marsha. I don't suppose there's any reason why I can't try this on my own. But now that we've come this far, I'm not turning back."

"You think you can do this on your own?" Lucy glared at her; her arms crossed stubbornly over her chest. "Seriously?"

"If I have to."

"Then you're delusional—on top of everything else. And you have no idea what you'd be getting yourself into."

Scout felt a slow, unpleasant smile crawl across her face, she couldn't help but indulge in a little bit of malice. "Ah, but this *isn't* anything I got myself into, Lucy; is it? It was you two who got me into it, all the way back in high school."

"That's not—"

"Yes. It is. This is all a direct result of what you guys did back then." Lucy's face turned dead white as Scout continued, "Now you don't like dealing with the consequences of your actions? Well, neither do I. But I've had to. For twenty years."

"Scout..."

"No. I'm tired of talking about it. I'm all talked out. So just quit your whining about how you *don't like what's happening*, and let's finish what you started, okay? And then maybe, if you geniuses can figure out a way to undo whatever it was you did to me, I can get the hell out of here, go back to LA, and get on with what's left of my miserable fucked up life. How's that for a plan?"

"Damn," she heard Marsha mutter softly. Her face had not gone quite as white as Lucy's, but it was noticeably pale. Her expression was as grim as Scout had ever seen it, but her eyes didn't waver as they locked with hers.

"All right. I hear you." Marsha said quietly. "Let's get this over with."

"Good. Let's do that." Scout laid back down and closed her eyes again.

"Fucking hell!" she heard Lucy mutter. And that, she thought, pretty much summed things up.

Scout breathed deeply and willed herself to relax. She was aware of Marsha lying on the floor beside her. And of Lucy, sitting nearby, with Marsha's drum in her lap. Beneath the soft, steady beating of the drum, she heard Marsha's voice invoking protection for them upon their path. She soon found herself sinking into a deep drowsiness.

When Lucy began speaking, it seemed to Scout as though her voice was coming from somewhere very far away, only barely penetrating the lassitude that had claimed her. She listened while Lucy described the arcs of colored light that she claimed were flowing between Scout and Marsha, linking their chakras, red, orange, yellow, green...

Scout could almost see them. She felt strength and energy and a curious warmth pouring into her. And as the process continued, she became more and more aware of Marsha, lying beside her. Blue, purple, indigo...White.

*It's pretty*, she decided, feeling mesmerized. Bright. Sparkly. Real. But also...more than a little unnerving. And even more unnerving was the awareness that deep inside her, another, even more curious sensation was slowly uncoiling itself. As if something very dark, very powerful – something which had slumbered there for ages, waiting for this very moment to arrive – was at last waking up.

Scout could sense Marsha's relief at the ease with which the link had been achieved. She felt a tiny flicker of amusement. What kind of difficulties had Marsha envisioned?

There was a brief, answering flash of humor that seemed to come from Marsha and then, without warning, a swirling darkness was upon them. Scout fought for breath, trying desperately to steady herself against the sudden vertigo. Her heart pounded wildly. For an instant she felt as though she were caught in a whirlpool, sliding away into darkness at incredible speed. But the sensation was gone again as quickly as it had come, leaving her cold and shaken. The glittering arcs of light and the bright, comforting cocoon-like warmth that had been building around her had all disappeared in a single flash of black lightning.

"What just happened?" Lucy's voice was tight with tension. "What the hell was that?"

"I don't know," Scout answered, but with great difficulty. Her tongue felt thick and unwieldy in her mouth. Her heartbeat was returning to normal, however; and she no longer felt gripped by panic.

"Sorry." Marsha's harsh chuckle broke the silence in the room. "I think maybe we jumped the gun a little bit there. I guess Scout still has some defenses we haven't uncovered. Let's see if we can't try and work around them."

Huh? "Wait. What do you mean, *I have defenses*?" Scout asked, in disbelief. "You're saying *I* did that? That was *my* fault?"

"Let's not worry about assigning blame right now." Marsha

sighed. "We can discuss it later. Lucy, maybe try it a little more slowly this time?"

Again, they attempted to visualize the colored bands of light that glistened between them. Again, Scout felt her awareness begin to merge with Marsha's. Again, she became aware of that deep watchfulness stirring inside her, like a snake gathering itself up for another strike.

This time, however, she could tell that Marsha felt it, too. She could sense her friend's wariness, the faint fluttering of nervousness as it grew into alarm. She could feel the distance stretch between them as Marsha began, ever so cautiously, to withdraw.

*She's going to stop?* Scout knew that's what Marsha was thinking. She knew it as surely as if the thoughts were originating from within her own mind. Marsha was giving up. Maybe she'd try something else, something different, or...or maybe not. *Oh, hell no.*

*Wait a minute,* Scout thought fiercely. *Don't I get a say in this? Come back here, you coward! We can't stop now! I don't want to. It's too important!* But even though she felt certain that Marsha could hear her thoughts, could sense her objections, she could still feel Marsha's mind sliding carefully away.

With steely determination, Scout concentrated on strengthening the connection Marsha was trying to break, holding it fast with her own mind, refusing to allow it to fade or stretch or weaken. At the same time, she dug deeper, seeking out that buried awareness she'd felt earlier, willing its cooperation, bringing it into the light.

Almost immediately, she felt it swell within her. A swirling, viscous cloud, small at first, it expanded rapidly, exploding in a bright, chromium yellow blast of heat and fury.

The sensation was that of a heavy, metal door that had suddenly slammed wide open with a deafening, resounding boom.

Energy sizzled across all seven bands at once. Suddenly, they were more than just imaginary; they were a solid reality. Power poured through them. Marsha jerked, as though she'd received an electric shock. Scout heard the sharp intake of Lucy's breath. Her own senses reeled.

And when they settled back into place, she found that her awareness had increased beyond anything she had ever known.

Suddenly, Scout had the feeling that she could sense colors and sounds and other unnamable nuances she had never been aware of before. And she knew intuitively that some of what she was experiencing now, was how Marsha saw things every day.

But there was more to it than that. Scout was aware of...*everything*. She could sense Marsha's heart beating, could even feel the thrumming of blood in her veins. She knew the shaky intake of her breath was caused by her attempts to regain control. But, *oh, no. I don't think so,* Scout told her, tasting cold, bitter triumph. *At last!*

"I knew this was a bad idea," Lucy muttered, and Scout didn't need to open her eyes to sense her fear. Or to see her moving around within the circle, reaching for the tools she needed. She understood even before the herbs ignited, that Lucy was planning to burn sage and lavender again, in an effort to tame the swirling clouds of energy.

"Not this time, girlfriend," she chuckled, as a savage, unholy glee ballooned inside her. "That shit ain't gonna work." *It's a whole new ballgame, now.* And to prove her point, she kicked things up another notch. An invisible fireball spiraled through the room, sweeping over the cats with tiny little darts and flickers of light.

Like a mini tornado, energy blazed across the circle, upsetting everything in its path, all but sucking out the flames of the candles. *Holy shit,* Scout thought; *this is amazing.* And, damn, but it was funny, watching as they scurried about.

*"I'm glad somebody's able to enjoy this."* The thought appeared, unbidden, in her brain, accompanied by a tight, shrieking lance of something akin to panic.

*Hmm.* Scout was momentarily diverted from the chaos she'd been creating. *Now, isn't that interesting?*

She let her mind probe the panic, touching and circling it. Picking at the edges, until it was ready to erupt into terror... Well, she certainly knew how that felt, didn't she? Hell, she'd lived with that feeling for years.

Fear, pain, panic and a lifetime of guilt and regret...

Yup. She knew all about those puppies. And what was it they said? Oh, yeah. *Paybacks are a bitch.* Well, ain't that the truth!

*"Scout, please! Stop this."*

Scout closed her mind to Marsha's appeals, and fled back into the swirling power storm, reveling in the torquing pressure that only just reached her from the others' minds. But she could not suppress the slightest twinge of...was it conscience?

*"Damn right, I'm enjoying it! I deserve to. I've waited a long time for this. You didn't care what it was doing to me. You wouldn't stop—not even when I begged.*

*Give me one good reason why I shouldn't enjoy it, now that the shoe's on the other foot?"*

But she knew why. She knew better than anyone what it felt like, when you couldn't call your thoughts your own; it was a feeling she wouldn't wish on her worst enemies. She wavered for an instant, clinging tightly to her desire for revenge; then reluctantly let it go.

Scout took a deep, slow breath and allowed the scent of lavender to ease its way into her mind. Gradually willing the fierce hot anger that held her to relax its grasp.

As the storms around them settled slowly down, she felt Marsha's breathing slow as well. Slow and deepen and ease.

A wave of remorse washed through her, but she couldn't tell if it originated with her, or with Marsha. *"I'm sorry,"* someone thought, and *"I know. Me too,"* came the response.

The lavender fragrance was stronger now, stronger and heavier. Scout let herself focus on it and found herself drifting with the rising smoke, letting go of the anger and the sadness, releasing years of bitterness and hurt. Not completely, of course. Not yet. But enough. Enough for now.

Marsha took a deep, shuddering breath. "It's okay Lucy. We're all right now," she said, her voice still shaky. "And...I think we're ready to continue."

"Jesus. Marsha – are you sure about this?" Lucy asked, incredulous.

For a brief moment, Marsha hesitated. Scout held her breath—

anxious, hopeful. And then, "Yeah, Luce, I'm sure. I don't think we really have a choice. It's now or never. Let's do it."

WHEN THEY EMERGED from the cave this time, Scout was surprised to find that they stood not on the beach she had seen before, but in a deep forest glen. The ground beneath their feet was spongy with thick emerald moss. Trees, gnarled and ancient, extended in all directions around them; their branches forming a leafy green canopy high overhead. The light that filtered down through the boughs was muted, silvery, shifting with the soft breeze that stirred the leaves. Sara had joined them again. But this time, Scout didn't think she was there to guide her, but merely to provide her with companionship.

"*Do you know where you're going?*" Marsha asked, and Scout couldn't tell if the words came from within her mind, or from the room outside.

"No. Don't you?" she answered, feeling slightly puzzled by the question.

Marsha chuckled. "*Hey, this is your subconscious. I'm just visiting.*"

"Oh. Well, I think there's a path...that way." Scout gestured toward one part of the grove. Although there was nothing to mark it, she was certain a path wound its way through the trees just there. She felt an urgent need to follow it.

"*Well, sure. There're probably quite a few paths. We're looking for something that will take us back to the afternoon Lisa disappeared. Think that's the right one?*"

"Uh...yeah. Yeah, I do."

It didn't matter if it was the path they were looking for, or not. It sang to her. She had to follow it, had to find out where it led. She began moving forward, impatiently, drawn toward she knew not what. Conscious of a growing sense of anticipation...and wonder... and...heat.

Something was happening. The path she had been following—where was it, now? She could no longer see...much of anything. Her body was on fire. Blazing with a need that was raw, raging, sexual. So much heat, such fierce, desperate passion, that reason was swamped by it. She could think of nothing else but getting closer to the source.

*I want it. I want it now.* Her heart pounded, loud and insistent, as wave after wave of pure sensation rippled through her, and—*Oh. My. God*—suddenly, heat and pleasure were everywhere at once.

She shuddered with heat. She was hotter than she'd ever, *ever* been. At least, well she couldn't remember if she'd ever— but then again, she was having more than a little trouble trying to think, what with the way the blood was thundering and burning through her veins. Her breath kept catching in her throat, so that she had to release it in little whimpers and moans. So hard to breathe with all this heat, and – *omigod* – what was *that*?

But even as she thought it, another part of her mind supplied the answer: Nick. His hands, moving over her body left little trails of flame in their wake and his mouth— whatever he was doing, it felt so utterly, amazingly good— *Ohhh, yes*. Do that again. Right there. *Oh, please!* [1]

The pounding of her heart was so loud, though. Or maybe it Nick's heart? Whosever it was, it was loud. *Kind of distracting, actually.* And, come to think of it, wasn't it louder than a heart actually *could* beat?

She fought against the confusion that surrounded her. But, really, wasn't it? Way louder? Loud enough to almost be the sound of someone's fist pounding on the apartment's front door?

Abruptly, all the lovely sensations stopped, and the heat receded, and she felt Nick pull away from her with a muttered curse. Then he was off the couch and storming toward the door and, oh, God, where could he possibly be going? And what was taking him so long to get back? It had been...several seconds already, surely. But at least she could see again now that her eyes were open.

The room was dark, all the shades drawn. She could just make out the brown shag carpeting, the heavy dark, rustic furniture. Everything too dark and heavy, weighing her down. The coffee table. The bookcase. Not to mention the couch, which she could feel beneath her.

The couch was also dark brown, she remembered, smiling as the memories surfaced. Dark brown vinyl with rows of those stupid, little, thumbtack thingies, whose purpose she had never understood.

It was easier to breathe, now, too. Not that she was sure she actually wanted to. If she were given a choice, between feeling the way she had a moment ago, on the one hand, and breathing on the other? Well, after all, oxygen wasn't even the most exciting element on the periodic table, now was it? And she was ready to consign the entire contents of that, and any other table straight to hell, if only Nick would please come back and touch her again.

Except something was clearly wrong because, instead of doing that, he was putting his shirt back on. And unless she'd missed something really important during the confusion of those last few minutes, when she thought her heart might have beaten itself right out of her chest, that was not a good thing.

"Nick?"

"Sorry, babe." His face was grim and desperate, his voice even more so. And he couldn't even look her in the eyes as he said, "I have to get back to work."

"What? Not— Not *now*?"

*Was it her? Had she done something wrong? Had he learned her secret, somehow?*

What had she missed? She had to have missed something because he could not have meant— "You're leaving? *Now*? You-you can't..."

He groaned. "Tell me about it."

He sat back down on the couch. Not touching her, anywhere, but looking...looking and looking at her with an expression of such pure, naked lust on his face, that she could feel her blood begin to heat again, just from the thought of being wanted like that. *Yes, please. I want you, too.*

"Oh, God, Jen," he said, shuddering as he closed his eyes. "I can't — You gotta stop looking at me like that."

"But..."

"I know. I'm sorry. Believe me, this is the last thing I want to do right now. But I have no choice. I really do have to go."

Scout took a deep breath—it looked as though she'd have to settle for oxygen, after all, damn it—and blew it out again, before she could answer. "Okay. I guess...I understand."

"Next time, babe. I promise."

"Soon?"

"Yeah. Oh, God, yeah. Abso-fuckin-lutely," he said with a smile. And then he was gone. Without even one last kiss.

"*Oh, wow. I can see now what you meant, the other night. But...oh, my God, Scout. The next time— It really wasn't soon at all. Was it?*"

"No. It wasn't," Scout mumbled, inconsolable. And then it hit her. "Marsha? What the hell?" The room spun crazily, as she sat up and looked around. But there was nothing to see. Because it was all in her head, wasn't it? Or somewhere? *Where am I? Where is she?*

"*Whoa...calm down. Sorry. I didn't mean to intrude or anything, but I'm just tagging along, remember? This is your trip.*"

"Oh, shit. I can't believe this crap. I *knew* I was gonna hate this. God *damn* it. What now?"

"*Well...let's check in with how you're feeling. First off, are you sure this is the right day?*"

"Oh, yeah. Yeah, I'm sure, all right. I remember it as if it were... umm...right now, actually." Confusion rippled through her again. If the past was now the present, did that mean the future had become the past?

*Where am I? When am I?*

Marsha's chuckle reverberated through her mind. "*Yep. Welcome to the ever-present subconscious. Gotta love it. Okay. So, let's move on. Let's see where you can go from here.*"

Scout tried to leave. She really did. But knowing she would never be back, knowing how much she'd lost when Nick walked out that door, she couldn't make herself go. She wandered through the dark rooms of his apartment like a ghost. Eerily aware of the dog trailing along behind her – right there with her, and yet not there at all.

She looked around again, drank in the sight of all that thick brown carpeting, and she couldn't help but smile. It was so ugly, and yet, oh, God, what wouldn't she give, if she could only stay right here and look at it forever?

The same went for the wicker shelves in the bathroom, packed with so many intimate reminders of Nick, and of a time long gone. The carefully arranged spices in the kitchen cabinets tugged at her heartstrings. As did the chunky, gray and blue earthenware coffee mugs. The brown velour bedspread...

And those white satin sheets on his bed. The ones that she'd never, not even once, gotten the chance to lie between. [2]

*"Scout? I think we need to go now."*

"I can't Marsha. You don't know."

*"Scout, listen, to me. I understand what you're going through, but this is important. I really think—"*

"No!" The pain of having lost him then and having lost him again only – was it yesterday? – was too much for her. Pain slashed through her heart and mind, as her world tore apart.

She felt the now familiar rush of vertigo as the vast swirling cloud of darkness crashed into her, and through her, and over her again. And only the sensation of not being completely isolated in the icy blackness, of not having been thrust alone into the maelstrom of pain and regret and loneliness that flooded her consciousness—only that, could have saved her from total annihilation.

Still, her mind reeled in anguish, so hopelessly cold and empty did she feel.

*"It's okay, Scout."* Marsha's voice wrapped itself around her mind. *"It's okay; I've got you. You're not alone."*

Not alone. She heard the words and tried hard to hold on to them. But, oh, that's not how it felt. From some other corner of her mind, long denied – suppressed, but never quite extinguished – an unquenchable flood of loss was pouring itself over her. And it chanted, *alone, alone, alone,* much more loudly and with far greater clarity.

Scout felt herself losing the battle. In a moment, she knew it, she would disappear forever, sunk beneath the weight of all that horrible blackness. She would be swallowed up by the inky cold emptiness that surrounded her and filled her and had festered within her for years.

And then, her fingers closed on something. Something warm and furry and alive. She felt the unmistakable touch of a dog's tongue on her face. And warmth washed through her once again.

Scout clung to her dog with all the strength she could find, sighing with relief as the roiling storm at last began to recede. She felt herself relax, an almost infinitesimal degree, just enough to regain control. And she knew it was triggered by the love and concern she could sense emanating in waves from Marsha, and from Sara, as well.

*"I know it seems endless,"* she heard Marsha say. *"I know it does. It seems like it's forever, doesn't it? But it's not. I promise you, it's not. Time is an illusion. This too shall pass. It already has passed. You're okay."*

And somehow, Scout knew it was true. She would survive. It would hurt like hell, for a long, long time. Maybe forever. But she would live. Or at least...well, maybe 'live' wasn't quite the right word either.

*"Never mind the semantics. Let's get out of here. I know it's hard but try and think. Where did you go next?"*

Where had she gone? Scout tried, but thinking was still too painful. She forced herself to take every last shred of emotion she could feel and lock them all away in some dark, dark recess in the back of her mind. In a place where she could – she hoped – retrieve them again, someday, when this was all behind her.

Immediately, she felt clearer, stronger, calmer. *Okay, let's think Where* did *I go?*

*I was with you.* She remembered having told Nick that, just recently it seemed.

To which he'd replied, *right. And then you were with Glenn.*

But that was wrong, wasn't it?

*You knew I wasn't. The afternoon of the murder, the day that Lisa ran away? You knew I wasn't with Glenn.*

*But you did see him. Later that day.* Nick had been pretty insistent about it.

But had she been with Glenn? She couldn't remember anymore. What had she done that afternoon? Where had she gone? If she hadn't gone home like she'd told Nick she had...

Scout floated, for a moment in a haze of indecision. Everything around her grew foggy and dim. Shapes, vague and amorphous, seemed to hover on the edge of her ability to sense them. Colors and scents with no names passed like ghosts around her. It seemed as though her mind was reaching out, reaching through the swirling mist, searching for something. Or someone...

SLOWLY, the mist resolved itself. Scout's vision cleared once again. Had she been here before? Had she cut across this field? It seemed entirely possible. Everything around her seemed vaguely familiar. Had there always been this chill in the air? And had she felt it knife right through the thin T-shirt she wore over her running shorts?

The T shirt was damp with sweat, that was why it couldn't keep her warm, sweat that had come from running all the way here.

*Wait. Why am I running?*

It was mid-May, but still as cool as March, and she had run here...

*Why?*

But that was a ridiculous question to ask. Of course, she had run here. She was always running, wasn't she? Didn't she have to, to keep in shape? Didn't she have to train for...whatever she was in training for. What was it, again? She couldn't remember.

It had been so long ago. It had been no time at all...

She didn't look up at the buildings as she hurried over the grass, but she knew where she was now. She went to school here, didn't she? No. That wasn't right either. That had been someone else.

*Hurry past the buildings. Not supposed to be here. Quick now. Before someone looking out one of the windows sees me. Get out of sight. Stupid coming here. But this is where she said she'd be.*

In the woods. By the pond.

And wasn't it just like Lisa to think of something lame like that?

The sun glowed low in the sky. It was getting late. Later. Better hurry. Lisa would be waiting. And she *hated* to be kept waiting. Really, she could be such a bitch, sometimes. She'll be waiting in the woods. And there's something we need to talk about. Something important, she'd said. Something very important...

But what was so fucking important that it couldn't have waited for another time?

That was Lisa for you. Drama Queen. Everything that had to do with her was always so important. Ticked off about Scout again, most likely.

Although, how she could've found out about that – it was a mystery. It wasn't like either of them would have told her.

Goddamnit. I don't need this shit. *The wind's picked up. Getting really cold now. Running late.* Don't know what this is about, but it sure as hell had better be important. *So cold. Getting tired, now.* They had to do this quick. Not that anything was ever quick with Lisa.

*Lisa. Lisa. Lisa...*

The name echoed through Scout's mind, but it was getting hard to think again. Something was wrong. Something was very wrong. But there were too many voices in her head, and she couldn't sort through them all. Couldn't sort anything out. She heard Marsha saying something, but she couldn't pause to listen. She couldn't stay and talk. She had to get to Lisa.

She had to get to Lisa, *now!*

All at once, Scout found herself rushing through space, speeding through the swirling cloud of mist, faster than thought. When she opened her eyes again, she was deep in the woods. By the pond in the woods. Feeling as angry as she'd ever felt in her life. Angry, hurt, and frightened. *And damned if that sonofabitch wasn't late again. Always keeping me waiting. Always.*

She wished Lucy hadn't been right about the baby, but all the same, she knew that she was. *I can't keep the baby just to spite Scout and Glenn, because then...well, then I'll have to keep the baby, won't I?* And that – no, Lucy's right. I sure don't see myself doing that.

Still, it's not like the decision *not* to keep the baby was making her feel any better. That sucked, too. It hurt, damn it. And she didn't see why she had to be the only one hurting. That just wasn't fair. Not when there was so much blame to go around, so much pain to go around...

Which was *why* she was doing it. This would be good. This would help...a little. Knowing that she wasn't the only one hurting. Not the only one who was losing something precious, something that they'd really, *really* wanted.

That ought to make her feel a whole lot better; shouldn't it? Why should she be the only one to suffer, after all? And it's not like Scout didn't have it coming. Not after what she'd done...

The bees were back. Scout was vaguely confused by that. They seemed madder than ever, and big as...big as mice, from the feel and the sound of them. The thrumming drone of them. Filling her head with noise and pain and making it impossible to see or hear or to understand anything that was happening.

Too many people in her head. *Entirely* too many people, damn it. And all of them trying to talk at once. She couldn't concentrate, couldn't follow their thoughts. Not with all their emotions flying at her, so thick and fast. Emotions. That was the problem. Too many emotions, and not all of them hers. Too many voices, making too much noise. She couldn't concentrate like this—nobody could.

And she had to find a way. She had to concentrate now because it this was important. Because of Lisa.

She had to get back to Lisa. Had to tell her. Warn her. Save her. Because she'd be waiting in the woods, by the pond, where they'd arranged to meet and—

*Any minute now. It's gonna happen...*

But not the way she'd planned it. Not the way it was supposed to be.

*Wait. How do I know that? Whose memories are these? Whose mind am I reading this time?*

*It doesn't matter. It's not important.*

What *mattered* was that she already knew what came next. She knew about the fight they would have. Were having. Had already had. Both so angry, both so young. They were going to fight about the baby, and then—

There was no warning this time, either.

Just like last time, and the time before that, the torrent of emotions she'd been trying to suppress exploded through her. Only this time, they weren't just her own emotions, and she had no chance of stemming the flood.

Scout was on her feet and running for the door before either of the others had a chance to react. The circle was blasted to pieces. The candles guttered and went out, and the cats disappeared from the room in a flurry of screaming fur...

THROUGH THE OPEN FRENCH DOORS, Lucy could see Scout, already halfway across the lawn, headed for the trees. Adrenaline surged through her, pulling her to her feet, as well. She should go after her. She had to go after her. But wait—

Her glance went back to Marsha who was still lying on the floor. She hesitated. "Are you okay?"

"Yes." Marsha struggled to sit up; schooling her features to give nothing away. "Yes, I'm fine. Go! Go after her. She's headed for the pond."

As SOON AS Lucy sprinted out the door, Marsha collapsed on the floor again. The truth was, she was *not* fine. Her head was splitting and everywhere inside her violent energy churned and swirled.

*"This is why you must always release a circle properly upon concluding a ceremony."*

"I know that," Marsha moaned. Who was that speaking to her? Was that Celeste, or someone else? And did it even matter?

*"You shouldn't be alone right now. You need help."*

"I know that too."

But there'd only been Lucy here to help her. And, at the moment, Scout needed her more.

*God, I feel sick.* Marsha had caught just a glimpse of what Scout had seen, or sensed, at the very end there, but it had been enough. They had their answers.

She struggled to her feet and grabbed her bag from the daybed. They *were* going to need help; there was no question about that. She had just retrieved her cell phone when she felt the blow against the back of her head. Light exploded behind her eyes as she pitched forward into blackness.

---

1. Sorry to interrupt at this sensitive junction, but I would just like to interject for a moment. You see, this is the location of one of my favorite typos ever. A typo that, thanks to auto-correct, or the accept-all-changes command, or possibly simple user error, kept re-appearing in draft after draft after draft.

   I know it made it into print in at least one edition, but hopefully—fingers crossed—it's gone now.

   For the longest time, however, the phrase "His hands, moving over her body left little trails of flame in their wake" kept showing up as "little trails of *fame*" which, truth be told, I always found mildly hysterical.

   Anyway, that's all I had to say. I now return you to your regular program, already in progress.

2. I realize that this might be of no interest to anyone other than myself, but...

   The blue and gray earthenware mugs are based on a wedding present I received.

   The brown shag carpeting was installed in my boyfriend's (now husband) van.

   The faux leather couch belonged to my husband's cousin, who roomed with us for a while.

   And the white satin sheets are indeed a nod to the Moody Blues song. Feel free to imagine it playing while Scout continues to wander through her memory of Nick's apartment.

# 34

By the time Lucy caught up with her, Scout had reached the pond. She would have waded right into it if Lucy hadn't pulled her back.

"Let me go," Scout sobbed, fighting to get free. "She's in there. I have to get her out."

"Out of...the pond?" Lucy asked in disbelief. "What're—? *Who* are you talking about?"

"Lisa. Or Robyn? Maybe both. I don't know." Scout collapsed on the bank, sobbing in Lucy's arms. "I don't know, I don't know...I only know that they're dead. They're both dead. Lisa..."

"Who did it?" Lucy asked, barely resisting the urge to shake her. "Do you know? Tell me! Is it someone you know? Someone you recognized?"

"I saw it happen." Scout's eyes were wide and empty, as if her mind was far away. "She never went anywhere, Lucy. She's been here the whole time."

"What?" Slow waves of fear and denial began to wash through Lucy. She shook her head. "No. No, that's not possible; you've gotten it wrong. Listen to me, Scout. You're wrong, okay? Lisa ran away."

Scout looked at her, pityingly. "Oh, Lucy. No. She never did. She never even planned to." And then she was weeping again, lost in some private vision that Lucy could neither see nor, really, even believe in.

"Stop that," Lucy snapped. "That can't be how it happened. Remember the letter she sent me? She couldn't have mailed it if she were dead! I don't know what you think you saw, or found out, but whatever it is, it makes no sense."

"Oh, Lucy." Scout's voice sounded firmer now, her sobbing had stopped, and Lucy thought her eyes had regained something like their usual focus. But she still wasn't making any sense. "It really does. Lisa didn't mail *anything* to you. It wasn't her. She wrote that note while she was still in school. She was going to give it to you there, but she never saw you. Her killer found it in her backpack and used it as a...as a distraction. To make everyone believe she'd only gone away after...after she was already dead."

Lucy wanted to be compassionate. She really did. But her temper had always been far too short, and her nerves were already frayed by the day's events.

"I don't believe you," she said, her voice harsh, cracking, but still hardly more than a whisper. "You're just making this shit up because you don't want it to be your fault,"

Scout shook her head sadly. Her voice was just a whisper now, as well, filled with pain and sorrow and regret. "Of course, it's my fault—more than you know. More than I'd ever even realized. Not because I drove her away, but because I was the killer's alibi. And all this time—All this time, I thought he was mine."

"Y-you thought he was *yours*?" Lucy could barely get the word past her lips—probably because she wasn't even sure she wanted to hear the answer to that one. Something about the look in Scout's eyes, the anguish in her tone, was making her wish she'd never asked. Surely, she didn't mean...she couldn't mean that... "No. No! It's not true."

"My alibi," Scout said softly. Then she glanced up at Lucy and blinked. Her eyes refocused. An expression of horrified surprise transfixed her face. "What the hell, Lucy? What did you think I meant?"

"Never mind what I think," Lucy croaked. "Tell me who you're talking about."

"Well, Glenn, of course. Isn't it obvious?"

Obvious? No, it sure as hell wasn't. "You're saying Glenn killed Lisa?" Lucy knew an instant of confused relief, and then another voice rang out from several feet away, sending cold chills racing over her skin.

"I knew you'd figure it out. I always knew it. You were all so close. You were all so smart. That's why I knew I had to try and kill the rest of you, as well."

*Glenn? Oh, shit.* Lucy turned her head and saw him standing there. Breathing hard. The gun in his hand pointed at them both. *A gun? Perfect. And I didn't even think to bring a knife to this fight.*

"I tried to get Scout, but she tricked me—twice. I nearly succeeded with Marsha. And I would have gotten you years ago, Lucy. If that damned cousin of yours hadn't interfered," Glenn continued coldly. "But he's not here now, is he?"

Lucy knew she should be afraid. She stared at him, stared at the gun he held. Time slowed to a crawl as she took in every detail. The slight tremble in his hand. The choppiness of his breathing. The glassy blankness in his eyes. She knew she ought to be very, very afraid. Hell, anyone with a single grain of sense would be frightened at a time like this. But she'd already been through confusion and fear and horror and relief...

And then he had surprised her, sneaking up on them in the middle of the woods, and she hadn't *ever* liked surprises. They tended to make her angry, even at the best of times.

And this was not – not by any definition she could ever imagine – the best of times.

She got to her feet, only distantly aware of Scout, sinking back to the ground beside her, softly sobbing, once again. She stood and faced Glenn across a seemingly endless space littered with twigs and dead leaves.

Fury made her voice shake. "Glenn, you stupid asshole, you put that fucking gun away right the hell now, you hear me? Now. Before you hurt someone. If you think I need my cousin, or anyone else to help me kick your sorry ass, you can damn well think again." Reaching a hand down, she grabbed Scout's arm and hauled her to her feet. "Now, get out of my way. We're leaving."

For a fraction of a second, Scout felt Glenn waver. His gaze dropped to the gun in his hand, and he hesitated. She saw a dark, unfathomable expression pass across his face; there one instant, and just as quickly gone again.

"Oh. Yeah. That'll happen," he scoffed. "But you're right about one thing, Lucy. We *are* leaving. All of us. Now, get moving—both of you."

He was upset. Angry. Frightened. Scout could sense the panic that gripped him. It rolled off him in waves. A sticky, viscous substance, slimy and dense and oddly familiar. She could almost smell the guilt and desperation that clung to him. She tried to track down the vague sense memory that was tickling the back of her mind, but she was practically in sensory overload, just trying to catalog all the impressions that came at her from every direction. It was irritating. And confusing. And more than a little distracting.

The expanded vision she'd been experiencing ever since she'd first linked minds with Marsha, allowed her to see currents of energy flickering around each of them.

Interesting. Lucy's anger was neither murky nor dense, but bright and clear, just like last time. Only then, it had been Lisa who had been angry. And Glenn hadn't *really* meant to hurt her.

*How do I know that?* She couldn't possibly know it, but she did. Just as surely as if she had been there—

She shuddered, hearing that sound again. The sound of a skull striking rock. Lisa's skull. She saw her body jerk and fall still. Saw her blood as it seeped out onto the ground. And, oh, God, she was going to be sick. She felt his sickness, too. Felt his panic, which then became her panic. Felt his remorse, his horror. His disbelief. He hadn't meant for it to happen, no. But all the same, once it had—

Once again, the scene unfolded, and she had no choice but to watch—helpless to interfere—as Glenn weighted Lisa's clothes with rocks and rolled her into the water. *No!*

While Lisa's body sank beneath the cold, black surface, Glenn scuffed dirt and leaves over the bloody ground where her head had lain. Just as he was about to throw Lisa's bag, with all her books and papers into the pond after her, Scout heard the sound of footsteps hurrying along the path from the school. Footsteps coming his way. A flash of red hair through the trees. Ms. Burnett?

A tremor ran through Scout, an echo of the one that had run through Glenn at the time. She tasted his fear, sharp and bitter on her tongue, as he grabbed up the bag and tried to hide among the trees. But beneath the fear there was anger.

*This wasn't my fault; it was Lisa's. She made me do it! And I'm not gonna go to jail for her mistakes.*

He couldn't let anyone find him there. He knew what he had to do. And Scout knew it, as well. He'd kill again if he had to. Before he'd let anyone find out what he'd done, what he'd become, he'd kill again.

He really didn't have a choice. *It's not my fault!* In order to protect himself, to save himself, he'd have to kill. And kill. And kill again. Until he was safe.

Scout snapped back to the present. They were out of the woods now, heading back across the lawn toward the house. She was startled to see that it was still early in the afternoon and not almost sunset.

Everywhere she looked she saw an endless confusion of flickering energy. It came from everything around her –from the plants in the garden, from the cats prowling restlessly on the patio. And it was fascinating, but she had to force herself to pay attention. Why was Glenn taking them back toward the house? If Marsha saw them coming—

Her head throbbed suddenly, as though it were on the verge of exploding. Awareness flickered within her mind. She looked at Glenn and she *knew*. Marsha. Oh, God, no...

Ignoring the pain, and the flood of images that poured through her, ignoring the startled look on Lucy's face, she rounded angrily on Glenn. "She's not dead."

He didn't even ask who she meant. "Yes, she is," he insisted mulishly. "Damn it, this time she has to be! I thought I'd gotten rid of her once before, when I ran her car off the road. Like I tried to do to you. But the two of you've got more lives than a cat." He shivered violently. "I hate cats."

Scout shivered as well. *Oh, hell yes.* She knew exactly what he meant. *They were such nasty, evil, creeping beasts.* Except ... why was she thinking that? She didn't feel that way about cats, or about anything, really.

But the feelings were there, just the same; lodged somewhere deep inside her.

"What're you two talking about?" Lucy demanded. "Who's not dead?"

Scout sensed the rush of anger as it sizzled along Lucy's nerves, following the path of her fear. She knew she should be glad for it, but this wasn't the time. The danger to Lucy was suddenly too extreme.

"No one," Glenn growled at her. "Keep moving."

Scout could smell the guilt that rose like steam from his skin. She felt a moment of panic as all her senses went on the alert. No. Not now. Not yet. Not here. I can't...

"I'm not going anywhere, Glenn." Lucy continued to insist. "Not until you tell me—"

"Marsha, all right? And she is too dead. Now move it, Lucy. Or I swear you'll be next. I'll do you right here and—"

"Oh, yeah? Why don't you, then? You miserable sonofabitch!"

Scout grabbed for her arm. "Hey, Luce. He's a sonofabitch, for sure," she soothed. "But, right now, he's a sonofabitch with a gun. So why don't we just do what he says, okay?"

Lucy's eyes narrowed, but Scout was already turning away to deal with the bigger problem. "What's the plan, Glenn? Where are you taking us?" She was pretty sure she knew, but she needed to hear him say it, anyway. Needed to distract him, keep him talking, get his mind off Lucy and keep it off her—for as long as possible.

"We're just going for a little drive," he said, still training a wary eye on Lucy. "That's all. Out in one of the canyons."

*Just as I thought. Perfect.* "It won't work you know." Scout was amazed at how unafraid she was, but that was Lucy's doing. The moment she'd grabbed hold of her arm, Scout had felt Lucy's anger as it surged through both of them, making everything burn brighter and more clearly, blocking out the other emotions. All the pain and anxiety that still had the power to confuse her. *Good.* "My car's not here, and no one is going to believe I kidnapped Lucy if we take her car. Or yours, either, for that matter. So, why don't we just—"

"Scout, Scout, Scout," Glenn shook his head at her, a sorry little smile twisting up the corners of his mouth. "I'm way ahead of you, sweetheart. I always was. Of course, your car's here. I stopped by the garage on my way over and picked it up—just like you asked me to do. I even made sure to mention to the mechanic that you'd said you were gonna take a little trip out of town."

"You're leaving?" Lucy turned to frown at her. "When did you—?"

"I didn't!" Scout snapped. "Obviously."

Glenn shrugged. "My word against yours. Except you won't be here to set the record straight. Because right now, like I said, the three of us are going for a drive. And if you don't cooperate, or if you try anything funny, I'm gonna shoot your friend here, right in the head."

Well, Scout couldn't help but laugh at that! She really couldn't. She knew it wasn't the time or the place, but oh, dear. Poor Lucy! Scout read the outrage on Lucy's face, felt it flare to life within her.

"You *did* say things would end badly," she couldn't help but point out. "And now, it sure does look like you were right. Doesn't it?"

"Oh, go to hell, Scout," Lucy bristled.

But Scout merely laughed again. "No, thanks. Not just yet."

She'd been to hell. It was icy cold and left a taste in your mouth like ashes. She wasn't in any great hurry to get back there. And next time, she *definitely* wasn't going there alone. She felt such lovely stinging heat – Lucy's anger – it warmed her through and through.

"Oh, my God." Through the heat and the laughter, Scout could hear Lucy's voice, dripping with disgust. "Scout. Have you *always* been insane?"

"I don't think so." Scout thought about it. Maybe she had been. The amorphous plan forming in her head was almost certainly nothing a sane person would consider. Not unless she'd run out of other options. *Which we most definitely have.* "But, believe me, I'm working real hard on that angle."

NICK BURIED HIMSELF IN PAPERWORK. Anything to keep his mind off the depressing scene in his kitchen this morning. And the even more depressing prospect that he'd be returning home tonight to an empty apartment. By midafternoon, he felt as if he were making real progress. He could go for a whole ten minutes at a clip without thinking about Scout. Just as long as nothing happened in between times to remind him. He was about three minutes into one of these Halcyon periods when the phone on his desk rang.

"Uh, yeah..." an unfamiliar voice addressed him hesitantly. "This is Mike over at Village Auto Service? You asked me to, uh, you know... to let you know about *that car*. The one that came in earlier this week?"

Car? It took a moment, but he finally made the connection. This was about Scout's car. Great. Just what he needed. Another reminder.

"Yeah, Mike. Hi. What's up?"

"Yeah, well, uh...I guess the lady who dropped it off must be getting ready to leave town, or somethin'? 'Least that's what the guy who came in and got it said."

Leaving town? For a moment, Nick's mind went blank. Then it hit him. Rage exploded in his head. *She's leaving me. Again. Without even saying goodbye. Just like last time...*

Well, fine then. Just fine! Fuck it. Let her leave if that's what she wanted. The sooner the better. See if he cared. Just as well, really. One thing less for him to worry about.

Because as far as he knew no one *outside* of Oberon had any reason for wanting her dead.

"I would've called you sooner," Mike said, still stumbling a little over his words. "Like you said to, right? Except...well, I guess I was on my break when he picked it up. I only just found out about it. Sorry about that."

"No, that's okay, Mike. Not a problem. Thanks." Nick sighed, ready to hang up the phone and go back to his paperwork. Determined to put it all out of his mind. No reason to be surprised, was there? He'd already figured he'd be going home alone.

He just hadn't known he'd be *this much* alone. And, well, it *was* a surprise, come to think of it. She'd at least seemed committed to hanging around until they managed to track down Robyn. And her sister. And—

Finally, Nick's brain caught up with his ears. Adrenaline flooded through his system. "Wait! Hold on a minute, Mike. Who'd you say picked up that car?"

"HEY, there Marsha. Time to wake up, girlfriend." A familiar voice spoke softly in her ear, but Marsha couldn't see anything through the bright haze that surrounded her. Must be a white-out, she mused, her thoughts as foggy as the scene. Anyway, she didn't need to see. She'd recognize that voice anywhere.

"Lisa?" But no. That was impossible. It must be this headache that was making her so stupid. Still... "What are you doing here?"

"Uh, no, Marsh. Sorry to be the bearer of bad news, but I'm afraid it's the other way around. Again."

The other way—? "D'you mean that I'm...that I'm *dead*?" Damn, her head hurt. She couldn't make sense of anything, except— *I can't be dead. Can I?* It seemed unlikely, given the way her head was aching. Why did it have to hurt *so much*? And where the heck was Scout? She was supposed to be here, wasn't she? Somewhere?

"Yeah, well. As it happens, we need to talk about that," Lisa's voice came out of the haze again. "You dragging Scout back into this shit? Not a good idea, as it turns out. Matter of fact, as far as ideas go – this one sorta sucks."

"Tell me about it," Marsha groaned. The fog was beginning to lift a little, or maybe her eyes were just adjusting to the light, she couldn't be sure. But gradually the scene around her drifted into focus. She could see Lisa – looking not a day over seventeen – as beautiful as ever, still dressed in her school uniform, perched on the edge of a beige metal utility table in the corner of a large, sunny room. Her feet were planted on one of the half-dozen folding chairs that had been pulled up to the table. Her arms rested casually on her knees.

"Hey, there you are," Lisa said with her usual cool smile. "Yeah, it's good to see you, too. Why don't you grab a seat."

The room looked vaguely familiar. Marsha looked around her curiously. Along one wall, five tall, narrow windows framed a breath-taking view of the Bay. The other walls were covered by a brightly painted mural. The room was sparsely furnished. A couple of vintage sofas, in what looked to be about the same state of disrepair as the one in her office, were clustered in front of a rather large television set. A row of vending machines stood nearby, offering hot and cold drinks, snack foods, candy and cigarettes. A handful of mismatched end tables, two ancient, scarred coffee tables and an eclectic assort-ment of lamps pretty much rounded out the furnishings.

Marsha sank down on the nearest couch and tried to pin down the location. It was familiar, but she just couldn't quite— "Lisa, what is this place?"

"Senior lounge," Lisa muttered, her mouth pursed around the cigarette she was lighting. "More or less." [1]

"Oh, yeah." Marsha smiled reminiscently, "That's right. Jeez, I'd forgotten all about that." Then another thought struck her. "But, uh...why?"

"Ah, you know how it is." Lisa shrugged. She shook out the match, dropping it into an orange plastic ashtray that Marsha could have sworn had not been on the table a moment earlier, and glanced around the room. "It seemed like a cool idea at the time. I could change it, I suppose, but I've kinda gotten used to it, so why bother? Anyway. Getting back to Scout. You really got yourself in over your head on this one, girlfriend. You should have known better than to attempt a chakra link without first checking to make sure she was clear. All that energy should have been neutralized ahead of time!"

"I know." Marsha nodded, lips twisting into a rueful grimace. She should have thought of that sooner. She should have remembered something so basic. If only Celeste had been there to remind her.

Marsha sank back against the cushions of the couch and closed her eyes. She felt exhausted. Defeated. Weary from her struggle with Scout's mind, her heart battered by memories of the encounter. Memories of Celeste. Memories of all the other times she'd messed up like this. *Will I never learn?*

Lisa snorted in amusement. "Now there's a good question. I wish I had the answer to that, myself. I gotta tell you, we're looking at a whole lot of negative karma building up out there. This is *not* a stable situation you've created. You guys are gonna be *years* working this stuff out. And that's assuming you've even got that long because, frankly, things are not looking so good for Scout right now. Or for Lucy either, as a matter of fact. And as for you—"

"Oh, shit," Marsha sat up again, eyes wide, heart pounding, as the implications hit home. "Lisa...if they're in trouble, we need to do something. What can we do?"

Lisa frowned. "You know, Marsh, we did talk about this kind of thing the last time you were here. When was that, again?"

"The last time I saw you? That'd be about nineteen, twenty years ago, I think."

"Bullshit. Blink of an eye. You just gotta get the perspective right."

"Yeah, well," Marsha shrugged. "Whatever. I was in a coma at the time if you'll recall. And besides, a lot's happened since. You expect me to remember every little thing we talked about back then?"

"Well, if you don't, then I guess you'd better start paying attention, hadn't you? You know the drill. There are some entities here who feel you've been playing a little fast and loose with the rules again, if you wanna know the truth. They think that, for someone with your abilities, you've maybe been getting a little too *involved* in other people's business. You do know what I'm getting at, right? Free will and all that shit?"

"Sure, Lisa, I know what you're saying. But sometimes you just have to help people before they can help themselves."

"Uh-huh. I believe they call that a rationalization. And that's not the point. You know better."

"Maybe."

"A word to the wise, chica—clean up your act. 'Cause the next time you're up here, it could very well be the real deal."

"Fine. I'll try. Now, what are we gonna do about Lucy and Scout?"

"What makes you think we're gonna do anything?" Lisa asked peevishly, but Marsha could swear she saw a hint of something very like a smile lurking in her eyes. "Haven't you heard a word I've said?"

"Yes," Marsha answered evenly. "I heard you. But something tells me that you haven't exactly moved on." She looked around the room again and smiled. "I'd say you've still got some pretty strong ties to this lifetime."

Lisa's gaze traveled the room as well. She shrugged. "I suppose I have been known to take an interest, every now and again, in what you all are up to. But don't go getting all optimistic, or anything. You guys have been playing around with some serious shit. There's always gonna be a price to pay for that. Take it from me."

She stubbed out her cigarette and jumped off the table. "Now, you'd better get going. I got something I gotta do; and I believe *you* were about to make a phone call, weren't you? An important one? You don't want to put that off."

Marsha noticed that the light was getting brighter again. The room began to recede into the haze.

"And while you're at it," Lisa's voice continued to echo around her, even though Marsha could no longer see her. "You'd better call someone to come out there and take a look at your head. It seems to be leaking."

*Leaking?* Marsha, chuckled sleepily, as the bright haziness faded slowly back to black. Wasn't that just like Lisa? Always with the lame jokes. But...*ouch*...she might just have a point about the head thing.

Well, okay, she'd definitely get it checked out. And she'd try to remember about that other phone call she was supposed to be making, as well. The important one. She'd get to it soon. Real soon. Just as soon as she woke up, in fact. Whenever that happened to be. But what was the hurry? After all, time was an illusion. Perhaps an even greater illusion than death, itself.

So, this is what came of being selfish, Lucy thought, feeling very much aggrieved. She could have been camping right now. Tomorrow morning, she could have woken up to birdsong and sunshine and cool, fresh, pine-scented air.

And to Dan, climbing back into the sleeping bag they shared. His skin would be cool against her own, but his lips and his fingers as warm and as welcome as the dark, bitter coffee he would bring her. In her useless, blue spatterware mug. The one that burned her fingers and wouldn't keep the coffee hot for more than a minute. But which she always insisted on using anyway when they camped, because it seemed so authentically rustic.

But no, she'd chosen to be selfish. To stay at home. To take some time for self-care. And now?

Now, by tomorrow morning, she'd most likely be dead.

Dead! She thought about what that would mean. Thought of never seeing her kids again. Or Dan. And, oh, God, didn't she just want to weep at the unfairness of it all?

How the fuck had this happened? And how was it that *she* got to be the lucky one, forced to drive Scout's car – at gunpoint, yet – while Scout lounged in the backseat?

Not that there was a whole lot of room for lounging, or anything like it. Who'd even want a car like this, with a pointlessly small back-seat—oh, of course. Someone who was single and childless. But hey, at least in the back seat there was no one jabbing a gun into your ribcage.

And, while she was on the subject, what the hell was up with Scout, anyway? Lucy glanced in the rear-view mirror.

*Look at her. Just sitting there, damn it. Huddled in the corner, quiet as a tick. Just staring out the window. Shouldn't she be doing...something?*

She felt Glenn shift restlessly beside her, and she returned her gaze to the road. Shit. It wasn't that she didn't appreciate the way Scout was going along with everything in so unusually docile a manner. Especially as it was Lucy's head that was at risk of being blown off otherwise. It was actually... surprisingly considerate of her. But wasn't it just the teensiest bit out of character?

Not to mention downright stupid?

Shouldn't Scout be running for her life right now? Leaving Lucy to fend for herself?

*Okay, never mind that. Let's pretend I never thought that. Bad idea. Very bad idea. Better think of something else. Something like—*

"Glenn? Did you really kill Lisa? And...and Robyn, too?" She couldn't believe she was asking him that, but there had to be a more logical explanation for what was happening.

*Glenn, a killer? How could we all have missed seeing something like that?*

"Robyn was a mistake," Glenn muttered angrily. Lucy felt the gun dig a little deeper into her side. Not a good sign. "An accident. I never meant to...but she had *the dog* with her, damn it! Scout said *she* was going to walk the dog." He sent an angry glance her way, but if Scout heard him, she gave no sign of it. "But instead, she sent Robyn out with it. She tricked me."

He sounded pretty upset about that, Lucy thought. And she could relate. Scout did have a way of ticking a person off. "And Celeste? What did *she* ever do to you?"

Glenn's voice trembled, just a bit as he answered. "She knew too much. She could see things."

"Yeah, I know she can. But—"

"Lucy," he growled, suddenly impatient. "Did anyone ever tell you that you talk too much?"

Lucy lapsed promptly back into silence. So maybe she did talk too much, every once in a while. But nobody had ever said she couldn't take a hint.

But not talking left her with too much time to think. And what she kept thinking about was that goddamned gun. It had been better when she was talking. It had been better when she was just blind angry, too. Although, of course, she couldn't really think as clearly when she got that mad, but...no, actually. There was no *but* about it. That *was* the better part – the not thinking clearly. *Am I kidding? That was much better. In fact, I'd really like to get back to that again.*

So, if she wanted to go back to feeling angry, maybe she should try thinking about Scout. That usually did the trick. Come to think of it, she still could not believe the bitch had laughed when Glenn threatened to shoot her. Yeah, that was the Scout she'd always known and loathed, all right.

*You did say things would end badly...*

*Yeah, well, fuck you, too. I was right, wasn't I?*

Like she really needed Scout to tell her what she'd said. Funny, thing though.How did Scout even know she'd said it? It's not like she was there. Would Marsha have told her? Or maybe it was something she picked up while they were linked.?

But, oh God. What had happened to Marsha, anyway? Could she really be dead? Scout said she wasn't. Not that you could count on anything she said. But she would know, wouldn't she, if something had happened to Marsha? If the link had held. But had it?

Damn. If only Scout hadn't broken the circle. The powers they'd raised would have protected them, and they could have directed the energy where they wanted it to go. Glenn wouldn't have stood a chance against them then. But now? Who the hell knew where all that energy had gone, or what was going to happen now? Certainly, she didn't.

*Fey*. That was the word. Scout had been thinking and thinking and finally it clicked. Fey—that's how she was feeling right now. Which was maybe good, maybe not so good. It depended on your perspective, she guessed, but—

*What was my point, again?* Oh, right. Too much undirected energy. That was the problem here.

She turned her head and watched the scenery crawl by outside the window. It being Saturday, travel along the coast road was slow. Terrified tourists in their rental cars crawled around the curves at well below the speed limit, clogging the narrow lanes. She could tell it was making Glenn nervous, the way they had to keep slowing and stopping. It wasn't doing Lucy's nerves any good either.

*God, I love this road.*

Not that she was a huge fan of traffic jams, of course. But normally, when it wasn't so crowded, she loved the views, the twists and turns, the sweeping curves...

Focus!

It was important that she keep her mind on the subject at hand, but it wasn't easy. *How the hell does Marsha do this, anyway?* She'd ask, but somehow, she had the feeling that Marsha wasn't quite with her at the moment. Not dead, she didn't think — although she was by no means as certain of that now as she had been earlier — but not being real helpful, either.

Still, even without Marsha's help, she ought to be able to do something with all these extra senses, and all this mindless energy that was currently swirling around her, and through her.

All of that *should* be useful, but at the moment, it was merely annoying.

The road curved again, and the ocean swung back into view. *Now, that's a sight. Lots of sailboats out there today. Looks like some good wind, too. I always wanted one of those. Too bad...*

Focus.

Yeah, that was the trick, all right. Hadn't she been having a hard enough time, these last couple of days, just keeping her own emotions in check? Now she had Marsha's to deal with, as well. And occasionally Lucy's.

And most of Glenn's, too, just to top it all off. And she *really* could have done without those.

Sure, it was a good thing, in a way, that she was able to tap into his mind and know what he was thinking. But, oh, she'd so much rather *not* be subjected to all his thoughts and memories.

Her heart constricted in pain as the images began to form once again in her head. She saw the shock on Robyn's face, bright in the headlights, just before the car struck her down and sent her flying. She felt Celeste struggle – actually felt the pounding of her pulse in her own hands – as Glenn squeezed her throat. She felt her strength begin to wane, felt her go heavy and limp. And then she watched Marsha fall, as well. Saw her sprawled face down on the daybed, blood trickling down the back of her neck.

Scout shivered in anguish, and tried once more to turn the pictures off, but her mind was a twisted wreck, and she could not make it behave the way she wanted it to. Over and over again she heard the screech of metal, the squeal of tires as first her father's car, then Marsha's, and then her own were struck from behind. And over and over again she heard the echo of Lisa's head striking rock, until she thought she'd go insane.

416

Desperate, she forced herself to back away. To view Glenn with dispassion. Jeez, wasn't he a trip, though? Cats! What was he thinking? And all those accidents he'd arranged for her? The car. The stove. The basement stairs. She should have known right away that something was wrong. Caroline would never have let the house fall into disrepair like that. And...had he really thought she'd go to bed with him again? After all of *that*? Who'd have guessed that he was such a total psycho?

Although, she supposed it could be he was just your average jerk, with twenty years' worth of guilt, and fear, and craziness taking its toll on his brain. She knew what that could do to a person, all right.

*Yes, I do.*

Too bad. She quashed the faint trace of empathy as it tried to surface. She didn't care if that was the case. A savage anger burned within her – in that part of her mind that ached with loss, with pain, with remorse – and crazy or not, guilty or not, jerk or not, she was taking him down.

She was a woman on a mission. A mission, maybe, but with no clue how to accomplish it. No real plan, either.

But fuck that. Here's a plan: If worse came to worse, she could simply go down with him. Kamikaze his ass straight into hell. Gladly. No problem. She knew just how to get them there.

*Not like I'd be much of a loss to anyone...*

But that was just self-pity talking, and she didn't have time for that either right now.

*Must stay focused.*

She took a deep, deep breath. The biggest problem was how to keep her mind from continually drifting off like this. The second biggest problem was how to keep Lucy from getting caught in the middle of whatever went down. Which wouldn't be easy. Lucy took being difficult to a whole new level of complicated.

They had turned off into the canyon by now. *We're almost there. Not much longer.* Anticipation prickled her skin. She knew just where he'd want to do it...

*Ah, damn. Of all places...*

Scout felt her mind stretch out and flow into everything around her. Felt it flow into the hard, yellow sandstone and the pungent gray-green sage. Into the live oaks with their hidden caches of mistletoe, and the rolling, grass covered hills.

It was almost impossible to maintain any kind of focus when everything within her was striving to reach out and merge with the life-force she could sense pulsating in every rock and tree and bush and blade of grass. Everything was so beautiful, so perfect.

*But why, oh, why does it have to end here?*

On the other hand, she had to die somewhere, didn't she? It could be worse. At least she had fond memories of the place.

She really had to hand it to Glenn. This was not such a bad plan. As far as spur-of-the-moment homicidal psycho plans went; it didn't suck. If things worked the way he expected them to – and it was a little hard to see why they wouldn't – everybody would assume she'd killed Robyn, and the others, in a fit of insanity. And that she'd been attempting to kidnap Lucy when she'd, somehow, lost control of her car and run the two of them off the road.

Of course, it only made sense if you bought into the scenario that she was crazy, but that was the real beauty of the plan. All week long, Lucy had been telling everyone who'd listen that Robyn had been afraid of her for exactly that reason. Hell, she'd even told the police about it!

Of course, that was just Nick, and he probably wouldn't believe it. Except, maybe he would, if something happened to Lucy. And, oh, God, the guilt would just about kill him.

*No. No way. I can't let that happen...*

Scout took several deep breaths and tried to calm down. She'd just have to make sure Lucy didn't get hurt, that's all. No matter what else happened, she had to save Lucy's ass. For Nick's sake, if nothing else.

One thing she could try was to keep Lucy very angry. She'd had a nice protective anger going back at the house. It shouldn't be too hard for Scout to keep that stoked. She was a master at getting under

Lucy's skin and making her mad, with years of practice under her belt.

They were almost there now. The canyon had never looked so lovely. Everything green and gold under the hard, blue, limitless sky. No wildflowers though. Not that there would be at this time of the year.

*Not like the first time.*

She was a little sorry about that, because she really would have liked to have seen them one last time...

---

1. I did model this after the senior lounge in my high school. Funny thing, after spending three years wallowing in FOMO, I don't recall spending any time there at all during senior year. Anyway, in the real senior lounge there was no smoking, no cigarette vending machine, and no killer view. Other than that, I think Lisa did a pretty good job of replicating it. Or I did. Yeah, that was definitely me. lol

# 35

"Well?" Heather asked, as Ginny shook her head as she slowly replaced the phone. "Marsha's not at the hospital. She hasn't been since yesterday. She hasn't even called."

"Did you try the teashop, again?"

"Heather, what do you think? Of course, I did." Ginny sat down on her stool, behind the bookstore's counter and clasped her hands together in her lap. "All anybody there seems to know is that neither she nor Lucy are expected in today. She's not answering her cell phone. And there's no answer at Lucy's house, either."

"Did you check at—"

"The nursery? Yes. They're not there either."

"You know, I'm beginning to wonder whether Lucy might not have had a point, last week," Heather said, idly flipping the cover of the book she'd been attempting to reading. "Have you noticed how, ever since Scout came to town, things have really gone to hell around here?"

"Oh, yes," Ginny answered, grimly. "I certainly have. And considering she's the last person we know for sure was with Marsha yesterday— Do you think you can keep an eye on things here, if I—"

"Oh, no you don't." Heather slammed her book down on the

counter and got to her feet. "If you're going somewhere, I'm coming with you. I don't know what all this is about, yet. But we're not taking any chances." [1]

"OKAY. This is good. Pull over here." Glenn's voice broke the silence, startling Lucy and making her jump. She twisted the wheel a little too much, and the car rumbled off the pavement before jerking to a halt, hard up against the dusty, scraggly coyote brush that grew at the base of the cliff. "Hey! Watch what you're doing," he growled. "Don't you know how to drive?"

"Well, excuse the hell outta me," Lucy muttered through clenched teeth. Her anger, that warm sustaining flame, flared up again, brighter than ever. *What does he want from me?* She glared at him. "Do you really think I give a shit about how I parked the fucking car, Glenn?"

"Get out," he said, but so quietly she couldn't hear him over the loud pulsing of blood in her ears.

"What?"

"Get. Out."

*Out?* She stared at him blankly.

"Get-out-of-the-car, Lucy. *Now!*"

Scout watched the others as they exited the car – both of them from the driver's side door. First Lucy, face screwed up in a frown, her aura pulsing with anger and fear. And then Glenn. His aura was all but non-existent. Dark. Muddy. And his movements were sluggish and imprecise as he struggled to manipulate his bulky frame over the console, without loosening his grip on the gun. Unable to use the passenger door because of the way Lucy had all but skidded into the side of the hill.

*Way to go, Luce,* Scout thought, as she pushed the driver's seat forward and unfolded her legs. Lucy's attitude had Glenn thoroughly rattled. If Scout could've afforded another emotion right now, she might almost have pitied him. But she had to stay focused, remember what she was doing. The keys dangled in the ignition. She removed them almost without thinking, pocketing them even as she braced her other hand on the doorframe and levered herself out of the car.

Stepping out of the air-conditioned interior of her Mustang into the warm, spicy air of the canyon was like walking into a wall. Scout felt the impact with all of her senses. She took several breaths of the heady, chaparral scented air in an effort to regain some measure of control. She stiffened. Somewhere in the back of her mind, she heard a faint howling.

It seemed to grow louder as she listened. She could scent the anguish that lay just beneath Glenn's anger now. She could almost taste it...like blood in the water, she thought, slightly startled at the image. It aroused sensations she couldn't ever remember feeling before – primal, vicious, cold. She knew an insane desire to sink her teeth into his jugular, and tamped it down, impatiently.

*Stop that!*

Once again, Scout let her eyes sweep over Lucy and Glenn, taking in every detail of the energy that surrounded them. Perhaps it was time to turn up the heat a little more.

"Shit Lucy," she drawled, noting with approval the effect of her voice on Glenn's already raw nerves. "Park a little closer to that bush next time, why don't you. I just had the car fixed, now you've scratched the shit out of it, all over again."

Lucy's eyes snapped closed for just an instant. Her aura vibrated like a tuning fork that had just been struck. "You are such an asshole. *Next time?* What the hell are you thinking? There's not going to *be* a next time—haven't you figured that out, yet? Also, I'd like to see *you* try driving while some maniac holds a gun on you. You really think you'd do better?"

"Ha. No contest." Smiling, she turned to Glenn. "You know, Glenn, I've been thinking. If your plan was to kill her, you really should've done it back at the house. No one's ever gonna believe I'd want to kidnap her. And now, you've got her fingerprints all over the steering wheel. How'd you plan on explaining that away?"

"Why are you even talking to him," Lucy seethed. "He's not gonna listen."

"I'm just pointing out the obvious, Luce." She shrugged. "I'm sure he can see that I'm making sense. You agree with me, Glenn, don't you? It's never gonna work this way. She's not gonna cooperate. And I tell you, her cousin's not gonna play ball with you, either. He's got a real bad temper. And you know how fond he is of her. He's gonna be real ticked off if she gets killed. You might want to reconsider."

"You can't even hear yourself, can you?" Lucy shook her head in disbelief. "No wonder Nick ran out on you this morning."

Scout winced as the disgust in Lucy's voice whipped right through her defenses and slapped down, hard and fast, on something already painful and raw. A cascade of fiery energy crackled through her. For a moment she saw nothing but blood-red rage.

But in its wake came another sensation. An alien, unfamiliar energy washed into her. Scout's brain reeled at the impact. She felt her consciousness shoved abruptly aside. Pushed to the outer edges of her own mind, where she could only observe what was happening, as if from a great distance.

"How about you both just shut the fuck up," Glenn growled, as his nerves hit the skids.

"Or what, Glory, honey?" Scout heard herself purr, in a voice she barely recognized. She walked towards him; her movements awkward, at first, as whosever spirit had possessed her learned how to use her body. *So weird. How does this work again?* "Are you gonna hurt me, Glenn? You don't really want to do that, do you?"

"Back off Scout. I got no choice," he spoke fiercely, but his hands were trembling.

She crowded in closer, chuckling softly. "Oh, sure you do, baby. You always had a choice. No one ever made you do anything you didn't want to do, Glenn, honey. It was always a matter of your own free will."

She was right in front of him now. So close that she could feel his breath, see the sweat shining on his face, taste the turmoil seething just beneath the surface. The thrum of blood through his veins—

*Oh God, I've missed this. It's been too long. I want it back.*

Scout felt her lips move as they were forced into a smile that probably looked as fake as it felt; a smile that seemed all wrong for the shape of her face. "You don't really want to kill me, again, do you? After all we meant to each other. I know you remember what it was like. What we had once. What we could still have."

Glenn shook his head. "That won't work, now. It's too late. Lucy'll talk."

"Shh, not to worry. Let her talk. It'll be her word against ours, after all. Who's gonna believe her?"

For a moment, a long, tense moment, they stared into each other's eyes. She read desire and indecision in the glassy blueness that stared back at her. She read hope there. And disbelief. And, finally, confused recognition.

"But you..." Glenn frowned; his tongue swiped nervously over his lips. "You're not...? Lisa?" His voice was a cracked and broken whisper. "Is it really you?"

Scout's lips stretched wider. "Hey, baby. Long time no see, huh?"

"I— I'm sorry. I never wanted it to be like this."

"I know, baby," she soothed. "I know."

He blinked and shook his head. "I'm sorry," he said again, as he swung the gun up – right into the side of her head. *Shit. Sorry sis. So close...*

*...Guess it's all up to you, now Luce.* The alien thought skittered across Lucy's mind, feather-light and fleeting. She watched, with an eerie sense of detachment, as Scout crumpled to the ground.

Glenn stood motionless, as well. For a long, long moment they neither spoke nor moved. At last, he raised his eyes to her, raised the gun in his hand and motioned her back towards the car.

"Is she dead?" Lucy asked, her voice sounded surprisingly steady and dull.

"Who—Lisa?" Glenn blinked at her in surprise.

"What? No! I'm talking about Scout."

"Oh." Glenn's eyes traveled back to the body at his feet. "No. I don't think so." And then he refocused on Lucy. He reached out and grabbed her arm. "Quit stalling. Let's go."

Lucy was aware of the tension vibrating in him, but she still couldn't quite get a grasp on her own emotions. She seemed to have gone somewhere beyond both fear and anger, and beyond rational thought, as well. "What are we doing here, anyway?" she asked, feeling stupid. Like she was missing the point of this whole exercise.

"I'm going to put you in the trunk," Glenn explained, with surprising patience. "And then I'm gonna put her in the front seat, put the car in gear, and roll the whole friggin' package over that cliff out there."

Lucy swallowed hard as the reality of her predicament finally sank in. She was going to die. No question about it. She was definitely going to die.

She was kind of surprised she hadn't figured that out until now.

"Oh," she heard herself replying, faintly. "I guess that could work."

"Try the bell again," Heather suggested.

Ginny shook her head impatiently. "No. The door's not locked. I'm goin' in."

"Jeez. *I'm goin' in?* Aren't you supposed to say something like *cover me,* first?" Heather muttered sarcastically, but Ginny wasn't listening. She pushed the door open and cautiously stepped into the hall. She paused, listening to the silence. Dust motes swirled lazily in the still air.

"Do you hear anything?" she asked in a loud whisper.

"Besides us, you mean? No. Why are you whispering?"

"I'm not sure." Ginny glanced around. "It just seemed like the right thing to do, you know?"

Heather shook her head in disgust. "And you have the nerve to say that I read too many thrillers? Ha! I don't think so. Come on, we better get moving."

Heather looked briefly into the living room, and the small powder room near the front door. "We'd better hurry. There's no telling how long we have before the axe-wielding maniac shows up. Where'd you think we should look first?"

Ginny gave a shaky giggle and pointed down the hallway. "Well, the cat seems to want us to follow her. And I must say, I do think you've picked the wrong genre, dear. This is clearly a tale of supernatural suspense. The danger will undoubtedly take on a much more esoteric form. Nothing so mundane as an axe-wielding maniac."

You're probably right," Heather agreed "More'n likely it'll take the form of a shape shifting-cat-demon-from-hell. But what the fuck? Let's follow her anyway."

"Oh, please. A shape shifting cat? That's just ridi— wait. Be quiet a minute. Did you hear something, just now? Like...like someone groaning?"

Heather glowered. "Oh, for fuck's sake, Ginny. Quit fooling around. That's not funny."

"I'm not— Listen. There it is again."

"Holy shit," Heather groaned, feeling the blood drain from her face. I don't believe this. Come on, she's gotta be back here somewhere."

"So...uh, where're the keys?" Glenn asked, staring stupidly into the car.

Lucy rolled her eyes. *Yeah, this is some great plan, all right. First the trunk's locked, and now the keys have gone missing...*

"Gee, I dunno Glenn, but it's Scout's car. So, maybe she would know. Too bad you can't ask her about it since she's fucking dead now!" Her voice rose into a shriek as shock morphed back into the edgy irritation she'd been feeling earlier.

"She's not dead. At least, I don't think she is," Glenn muttered uncertainly.

Lucy glared at him. "Oh, well, that's a relief. You wouldn't want her *dead* already, would you? Not if you're gonna *kill her!*"

"Shut up," Glenn growled, waving the gun at her. "I need you to go and check her pockets. Now."

Lucy balked at the suggestion. "N'uh! Not if she's dead, I'm not."

"She's not dead," Glenn insisted. "I didn't hit her that hard. She's just— oh, never mind, I'll do it myself. But first...you are definitely going into that trunk. Right the fuck now."

THERE WERE TOO MANY VOICES. They echoed in the darkness, all of them talking at once. And Marsha couldn't make sense of anything that was being said, although the words seemed to bounce around in her brain like rubber balls. Pinging and ponging in a most unpleasant manner.

There was something familiar – about the words as well as the voices. But the way they bounded and rebounded in the emptiness was excruciating, aggravating the pain in her head, which already felt as if it had been split into several pieces.

She closed her eyes more tightly, but the voices refused to recede. She opened her mouth, determined to tell them all to shut up and go away. But the words that came out sounded different than those she'd planned to use. In fact, they sounded rather incongruously like: "*Domingo Canyon. Hurry—send help!*" At least, that's how she thought they sounded. But perhaps she was mistaken.

The darkness increased. The voices faded into oblivion. Somewhere in the distance, she could hear the faint barking of a dog. Then, a blessed silence swept her away and her soul once again took flight...

THE BLOOD POUNDED in Lucy's ears, so loud she could hardly think above the din. She was conscious of the gun trembling in Glenn's hand, once again, as he reached back inside the car to pop the trunk. She was aware of his labored breathing and her own heart's panicked racing and the tremors that afflicted her whole body, making movement of any kind extremely difficult.

Glenn pulled her around to the back of the car. Fear narrowed her vision until the only thing she could see was the trunk, looming in front of her.

*That trunk is gonna be my coffin.*

The thought terrified her and she gulped for breath. It was hard to focus, hard to think. It took several seconds before she even noticed that her hands had closed, of their own volition, around the tire iron.

She barely felt the weight of it as her arms swung the heavy metal bar around in a vicious arc. Almost failed to register the way it connected with a solid, satisfying impact, glancing off Glenn's rib cage, landing dead in the center of his chest. Before he even hit the ground, she was sprinting back towards the spot where Scout lay, still as death, on the dusty ground.

NICK SWORE SAVAGELY as he swerved around yet another car, and then spun through the next curve. His car shuddered violently as two of the wheels left the pavement and bounced over the loose scree of the shoulder.

*I'm never going to make it.*

He knew it with icy certainty. There was no way he could get there in time. If they were counting on him to save them, they were shit out of luck. They'd both be dead before he even got close. If they weren't dead already.

He had been stupid. So amazingly, abysmally, irredeemably stupid that he couldn't – even now – grasp the enormity of his mistake. How could he possibly have been so blind?

If Scout had not been with Glenn the day of the murder, then she didn't have an alibi—but neither did he. Why hadn't he realized that sooner?

He should have seen it last night – as soon as she told him. And if he hadn't been consumed with jealousy, he was sure he would have, too.

Now she would die – because of him. Because he'd been jealous and blind, and too stubborn to believe her, to accept her at her word, he would lose her forever.

His eyes barely registered any of the familiar landmarks as he flew past them. His every thought was focused on the turnoff for the canyon, still several miles away. He didn't even recognize the thirst for murder building in his blood. The wailing of the siren drowned out every thought but one. *I'm already too late.*

SCOUT WAS CONSCIOUS. Sitting up finally, one hand clutching the side of her head, a dazed, angry expression on her face.

Lucy crouched in the dirt by her side. "C'mon," she urged. "Get up. Let's go! We haven't much time." But she wasn't even sure the words were getting through. There was no change of expression on

Scout's face—just that odd, abstracted look. As if she was looking at, or listening to, something beyond what Lucy could see or hear.

"*Scout!*" Lucy shouted angrily.

Scout turned to look at her. "Lucy, where's the gun?"

Oh shit. She'd forgotten all about that. She gazed in horror at the Mustang. She could sense motion from the other side, where Glenn had fallen. "No time. We gotta get out of here. We gotta—"

Too late. Glenn was back on his feet now. He was coming after them again. God damn it, why hadn't she thought to take the gun? Anger brought her surging to her feet. She took a step forward, placing herself just in front of Scout. Her eyes locked with Glenn's, determined to stare him down with her last breath.

"No. Lucy, wait!" she barely heard Scout speak, neither understood nor cared about the sudden urgency in her voice. She continued to glare at Glenn as he approached, his gait unsteady, his face a ghastly mask of desperation. Scout had gotten to her feet as well, now. Lucy felt her clutching at her arm, breathing hard. Taking long, slow, deep breaths...

Until, suddenly, there was a strange pulsing of electric blue energy everywhere in the atmosphere around them. As if a storm were rolling down off the mountain. Everything grew muffled, indistinct. A fitful wind rose, seemingly right out of the canyon floor, and gusted over the road, kicking up so much dust she could hardly see.

Lucy's lungs strained. She felt as if she were trying to breathe through heavy layers of grayish yellow cotton candy. Through the confusion that swamped her senses she heard an odd, keening sound. It seemed to hang like a mist in the air. She watched the gun in Glenn's hand rise slowly. His hand shook so violently, he could barely aim it. Not that it would matter. At this close a distance, it would be impossible for him to miss.

And then Scout was speaking, cool and implacable, infinitely regretful. In a voice that sounded eerily like Marsha's...and yet...not quite.

"It's over now, Glenn."

"No," he pleaded. "No, it can't be. Not like this."

"Yes. It is. Listen to me. You think I don't know what it's been like for you all these years? It was like being caught in a bear trap, wasn't it? With no way out. No way to stop the pain. The stench of death always there, always with you. And cold. Jesus. So cold. Colder even than it must have been for Lisa, don't you think? Down there under all that water. So dark. So murky. Way down at the bottom of the pond where you put her. Lost in all that darkness. The soft sucking mud grabbing at her flesh. And the weeds. And the fish...

"What was that like, do you think? Fish nibbling away at you constantly until there's nothing left."

Lucy shivered as the images formed in her head. She tried to push the thoughts away as they arose, but Scout's voice went on and on, forcing her to think about it. Forcing her to see what she wanted her to see, and to feel—

"I bet it's gonna be like that in prison, too, Glory. Cold and dark and endless and dank and—"

"No!" Glenn protested again, but his voice sounded hollow and uncertain. "No. Stop it. Stop talking. Stop!"

"Or maybe they'll kill you. Maybe attach electrodes to your skin and make you fry."

"No. Stop it," Glenn protested. "I didn't mean to hurt her. It was an accident. I—"

"I know," Scout continued softly. "You really want to believe that, don't you? You want to forget how it really went down. But do you honestly think that's going to matter? Think it'll change anything? Listen...do you hear that? You do, don't you? You know what it means? It's over, Glenn. You know it's true. Even if you kill me, it's not gonna matter. It won't be enough to save you. You've gone too far. Nothing can save you anymore. Nothing."

Scout, or whoever it was that inhabited Scout's body, kept talking. Her voice grew stronger, deeper. It echoed in the heavy air; almost like multiple voices were speaking at once. Lucy could see the anguish on Glenn's face. She could almost feel the tightness in his chest as he struggled for breath. Her own breathing had become more labored as well. The air around her was thick and dark, almost syrupy.

Then the light began to die, as though she were on the verge of losing consciousness.

"It's over. Glenn. It's all over. You've lost everything. *Everything*. It's gone, now. All of it. Gone."

"No. Please," he begged, his eyes locked with Scout's.

She shook her head. "I can't help you, Glory. Not now. No one can. You've gone too far."

The screaming pressure in Lucy's head grew louder and more insistent. But was it just inside her head? Or did it fill the air around her? It was the sound of lost souls, she thought. The hounds of hell, thirsting for blood. It was the sound of death itself.

Lucy made one final effort to move, but then Scout spoke for the very last time. Her voice—crackling with power, relentless as stone—swept through the air on an invisible current of energy. It robbed Lucy of breath; even as it seemed to smash through Glenn's defenses. Like a sonic boom striking a wall of glass, it hit them with a shattering, stunning force.

*"It's over."*

*"No!"* Glenn screamed as his arm swung up in a sudden movement, bringing the gun to his temple even as he squeezed the trigger.

At the last moment Lucy turned her head away, closing her eyes against the destruction. Her hands rose instinctively, palms outward in a warding gesture of shielding and rejection. But she could tell that Scout, rigid beside her, had not so much as blinked. She stood firm, even against the backwash of energy as it crashed over them. She held Glenn's eyes, and his attention, until the very end.

The echoes of the report had not even begun to die away before the screaming in the air resolved itself into the familiar sound of sirens. And then, in a blur of speed and motion a car exploded around the turn in the road, shrieking to a stop just a few feet from Glenn's body.

Scout still hadn't moved. She seemed barely even to be breathing, while Lucy's lungs heaved, taking in great, gulping breaths.

Lucy watched as the car door opened and Nick got out, slow and shaky, like everything around her seemed to be – as if time itself was winding down.

The three of them stood there. Staring at each other. Caught in a frozen tableau that seemed to last forever; or took no time at all.

There was no sense of relief, or even repugnance. No room anywhere for joy or anger or guilt, or even grief. There was only a vast consciousness of emptiness. And of loss. And an invisible, inaudible, roiling in the atmosphere, as the cloud of energy that had surrounded them with power, dissipated away into nothingness.

---

1. Back when I was first drafting this book, when I still thought I was writing a cozy mystery. I assumed that Heather and Ginny would feature more prominently in the series.

   I thought having access to all those books would be instrumental in solving whatever puzzle cropped up. And the fact that they were reading all the time meant they'd know things that would prove useful.

   Things didn't work out that way, but I still would like to craft them a novella someday.

   By the way, the name of their bookstore, Digressions, comes from the following Laurence Sterne quote from Tristram Shandy:

   "Digressions, incontestably, are the sunshine; — they are the life, the soul of reading; —take them out of this book for instance, —you might as well take the book along with them."

# 36

*It's over.* Lucy sat in the car, her keys in her hand, her eyes on the house she and Marsha had only just left. She could still hear that single sentence, spoken with such deadly intent, repeating itself endlessly in her mind. She wondered at the many levels of meaning that could be encompassed in two short words.

*It's over.* The horrible sense of finality that Scout had invested in those words, the vision of desolation she'd used them to evoke—

Lucy shuddered. How had she known to say those things? What had she seen while entranced to give her such awful power over him?

*What have we done?* Together, the three of them had summoned up enormous, primal energies, tapped into ancient forces that were both great and terrible. And Scout had used them ruthlessly. Channeling them in some manner that Lucy still did not understand. She'd flung them at Glenn and, by doing so, had probably saved both their lives.

*But at what cost?* Lucy shoved the thought aside. It was justice, of a sort. And there had been no other choice. Still, she couldn't help but wonder at the price they'd have to pay for their actions. Or when the bill would come due.

*It's over.* Jesus, she needed to get a grip on herself. It *is* over, damn it! There was nothing to worry about any longer. Everything should be fine now, right? But she knew it wouldn't be.

It had been such a relief to get back to the house and to know for certain that Marsha was okay. Even though both Scout and Nick had assured her she was, Lucy needed to see for herself.

The reaction was really hitting her then, she was barely conscious of the ebb and flow of people around her. It was so damn cold, too. She hadn't thought it possible it could be that cold. But, until she'd drunk at least three cups of that vile tea Marsha kept urging on her, she hadn't even been able to think.

Heather and Ginny had left by then, as had the paramedics. The police were the last to go. All except for Nick, of course, he was still there, even now. His eyes, when he'd looked at her, and even more so when they fell on Scout, were as dead as anything Lucy had ever seen. She couldn't shake off the sense of weariness that just looking at him caused her. But she knew she had to try. She needed to pull herself together, figure out what to do next.

What should she use to clear the energies in the house this time? Which incense could she burn to lift the despair that seemed to radiate from every surface?

Lucy was fairly certain that the problem lay *not* in the house itself, but in its occupants. And she wasn't sure she could do anything at all about them.

She'd agreed to spend the night with Marsha, as much because of the possibility of concussion, as for her own emotional turmoil. And the need – which was building but had not yet reached viability – to talk about what had happened. To talk it through with someone who wouldn't think her crazy.

She wanted, desperately, to be away from here. And yet—

"You'll see that she eats something?" she'd heard Marsha say to Nick, just before they left. Heard his terse assent – in a tone of voice she knew well and dreaded hearing again. It was as though that single sentence, still reverberating in her mind, was also emanating from within some shredded chamber of his broken heart.

*It's over.*

"Listen. I can't stand this," she said as she turned to Marsha. "We've got to *do* something. They're so miserable it's breaking *my* heart. And she still insists she's leaving town."

"I know." Marsha frowned, her own gaze returning to the house, as well. "I'll come back tomorrow and try to talk to her again, see if I can't change her mind. But I don't know how much good it will do."

"Well, she can't, that's all! We can't let her go. And Nick is... Shit, I don't know what's wrong with him. Why's he acting like this? We should do a— I don't know, a love spell, or something. Or maybe a common-sense spell. Is there any such a thing?"

"Lucy, please. My head is hurting enough as it is, without thinking about trying anything like that. I just want to go to bed. Maybe with a nice cup of tea. Besides, we *can't*. All right? We just...*can't*...keep doing that kind of thing."

"Are you kidding? After what we did today? Of course, we can. Shit, woman, we can do *anything*! How hard could it be? A couple candles. A couple prayers. A few of the right herbs. Just, you know, a little nudge in the right direction. It'll be easy."

Marsha sighed. "It would be manipulative. I think, maybe I've finally learned that particular lesson. They haven't asked for our help. We have to let them handle it on their own."

"Well, of course they haven't asked for help! Have you met either of them? But what does that matter? You know it's what they want. They love each other!"

"Well, yes, I can see *that*."

"And they're perfect for each other. Much as I hate to admit it."

"I know."

"Okay, so, look, if you don't want to do a spell, then fine. How about I just go back in there and talk some sense into them?"

"Lucy. I think you're getting a little hyper here. Probably still too much adrenaline in your system. You really should have had more tea. Don't you think you've done enough already? You left enough rose and jasmine incense burning to set off every smoke alarm in the neighborhood."

"Obviously, that's an exaggeration. What if—"

"No! Just leave them alone!"

"Why's that, Marsha, huh? So they can both be miserable for the *next* twenty years, too? Do you have any idea how annoying that's gonna be? For us, I mean? No, you don't know. But I do.

"I've been through this once already with Nick. And I'm telling you, I *cannot* go through that shit again. I mean it, Marsh. I really can't. Especially not now. Because now— Ah, shit, you know I'm gonna be worried about both of them now, don't you?"

"I know. But, if things are going to work out, they should be able to do it on their own."

Lucy glared. "Oh, that is *such* a cop out. And what if they don't?"

"Well, then, when they're crying on our shoulders, we can tell them they're idiots. But they probably still won't believe us, even then."

She shook her head. "I don't know. Do you think I should have used the honeysuckle and sunflower incense instead? You know to give their brain cells a little boost? Or maybe the lilac?"

"Okay, look." Marsha frowned thoughtfully. "Maybe...it's just barely possible, I suppose...that they're under some kind of hex, which would already be manipulative. And not our fault. So, if we maybe just concentrate on removing any obstacles that shouldn't have been there in the first place? That wouldn't count as interference. Would it?"

"No." Lucy shook her head emphatically. "No way. Are you kidding? Absolutely not."

"Well, why don't you focus on that, then? You can make some of your rosemary focaccia—one for each of them. And maybe slip in a little rue, while you're at it. And I can fix them up with a little clover tea to, you know, go with it. But tomorrow, okay? After my head stops throbbing? Please?"

"Okay," Lucy sighed. "I guess I can live with that. As long as I can feel like I'm doing *something* to help them I won't feel so frustrated. But...do you think it will be enough? You're sure we can't just do something a little more, you know, pro-active?" she asked, as she started the car.

Marsha rolled her eyes. "Yes. I'm sure."

"I don't know. It doesn't feel like enough. I don't like it."

"Lucy," Marsha smiled fondly, "you never do. Now, let's go home."

THEY WERE ALONE, finally. But they couldn't even look at each other, and the silence between them had grown so oppressive that neither knew how to break through it.

Nick was the first to try. "I thought I told you to stay away from here, today?" he asked, and he thought his voice sounded almost normal.

"You said I shouldn't be here alone," Scout replied, a fragile smile almost forming, and almost as instantly dissolving from her lips. "And I wasn't."

She huddled in an old leather armchair next to the fireplace. But given the cold, pinched look on her face, he didn't think the flame's warmth was doing her a bit of good. "Yeah, well. A fat lot of good it did you to have those two as company."

He leaned his head against the back of the couch. "I swear, if I had any idea you would try some crazy scheme like this, I would have taken you down to the station with me this morning and locked you up."

"Well, you could have tried. But you know Lucy; I'm pretty sure she'd have found a way to spring me, just the same."

She was pleased when that surprised a weak laugh from him. It made her bold enough to risk taking a peek at him. His eyes were closed, and he was sprawled on the couch looking every bit as tired as she felt.

It had been a long day. A dreadful day. She supposed she should let him go. She should send him home now, so he could get some sleep. But, God help her, she just couldn't do it. She was going to have to leave him soon enough. She didn't know when –

or even if – she'd ever see him again. How could she send him away?

"You were nearly killed." Nick's voice was barely a whisper. "The whole way out there, I knew I would be too late to save you. I still don't understand what happened. How did you—"

"Shhh. Don't. I can't talk about that right now." Scout closed her own eyes then, but that didn't shut anything out. She knew exactly what had happened out there in the canyon. She didn't think she'd ever forget any of it. But she didn't know if she'd ever be able to talk about it, either.

"I'm supposed to make sure you eat something," he said, rousing himself a little. "I suppose it's too much to hope that you actually have any food here?"

"Oh, sure I do," she answered, glad for the change of subject. "There's soup. And...and I don't know. But I'm sure there's all sorts of stuff in the cupboards."

"Yeah, I've seen what's in your cupboards. That's not food. We could always go back to my apartment and—"

Scout felt her heart lurch. She shook her head. "No." *No. I couldn't bear it. I'd never want to leave.*

"No," he agreed, sighing heavily, "of course not."


BUT WHY? He wondered, watching as her face turned hard and cold. "You know, I never realized it was that bad of a place."

"It's not!" She looked startled. "It's not that. I just..."

"It's not because you don't like my cooking, is it?"

She smiled, her cheeks coloring as she dropped her gaze, shaking her head a little sadly as she said, "No. Of course not. You— You can cook for me anytime, Nick."

"I just might have to take you up on that," he warned.

She didn't answer, but the smile drifted away from her lips. His eyes roamed greedily over her face, taking in every detail. The old bruises fading along one side of it, the new ones – and they were going to be beauties, he could tell – swelling and distorting the other.

439

Even now, banged up as she was, she was the most beautiful, desirable creature he'd ever known.

"I guess, now that this is all over, you'll be leaving Oberon?" he couldn't help asking.

Scout shrugged. "I guess."

"I uh, don't suppose you're planning on coming back any time soon?"

"No."

"Right."

*It's over.* Nick closed his eyes again, wearily. So. This was it. She was everything he'd ever wanted, and now she was just going to walk out of his life again.

For years he'd survived on dreams and memories. On the strength of all the lies he'd let himself believe about her. Now, and for the rest of his life, all he'd have was the truth.

And right now, the truth was more than he could handle.

When he spoke again, his voice was hardly more than a whisper, "Come here."

She knew he'd only break her heart again, but Scout could no more refuse the appeal in his voice, than she could refuse to breathe. She went. She melted into his arms, when every instinct for survival she possessed was telling her to flee.

He began to kiss her. Soft, tender kisses that only made her want more. Just one more. Just one. More.

"Do something for me," Nick said, breaking off their kiss to whisper urgently against her ear. "Please."

Scout was conscious of the passion and need radiating from him, felt it flowing into her, as well. "Anything."

"Just for tonight." His voice was low, shaking. "Lie to me. Just one more time. Tell me you care. Say you'll stay. I need you so much right now. I just— Oh, God, Jen, I need to hear you say it, even if it isn't true. I swear it doesn't matter that you don't mean it. I've always been willing to believe whatever lies you tell me."

"What?" Startled, Scout pulled away so she could see his face. He looked more dangerous than ever. His eyes glittered madly and his face was taut with exhaustion and strain. With her senses still heightened from this afternoon's experience, she could feel such dark waves of pain and anguish welling up inside him, it made her weep.

"What do you want me to say?" she asked, the tears in her eyes almost blinding her.

"Say you love me. Say you'll stay."

"But I do," she murmured between kisses, "I will. Always. Always!"

Why he should think she was lying she didn't understand, but there was no time for questions or explanations. The heat and the need and the darkness were too demanding. She went into it with him willingly. Not caring if it was for a minute, or forever. Giving herself up entirely to his need of her, and her own need for him. To have him one more time. Just once. Again. Just one more time. No matter what the consequence. No matter what the cost.

THIS TIME, Nick had no thought of stopping. He had no thoughts at all. There was just hunger and the need to have it filled. Just desire and a need to quench the pain. Somewhere, far away in the back of his mind, he knew it was partly the reaction from the day's events, from lack of sleep, from years of longing, but he didn't care. He was conscious of her voice, and couldn't tell what she was saying, didn't care that she was lying, only prayed she wouldn't stop.

THE HEAT and the darkness claimed them. Together they moved into a place from which they both knew they could not escape unscathed. But they were too far gone to stop. Scout was aware of his hands, hot against her skin, and the need for more inflamed her. Nick felt her body writhe beneath his and could not resist the urge to sink deeper, deeper, deeper into her. The climax, when it came – and afterwards, neither would ever remember who'd broken first – only caused them to cling even more tightly to each other. So that when it was over, they were locked together with neither the strength nor the will to separate.

NICK KNEW that he was probably holding her too tightly, but he couldn't bring himself to let her go. He lay still, his eyes closed, his hands tight on her, praying that they could stay that way forever, or at least for a little while longer. Praying for the strength to let her go. Praying for he knew not what.

"Why did you ask me to lie to you?" she asked.

She lay so still against him, so soft and unresisting in his arms. As if she knew that she belonged there, as though she'd never pull away from him again. *Liar*. And her voice was soft, as well. Soft and sweet and sorry. *Sorry for me*, Nick supposed. Well, he was sorry, too. Sorry that he couldn't have been stronger for her. That he couldn't have hidden his pain a while longer. That he hadn't been able to let her go without—

"Nick?"

He sighed and closed his eyes even tighter. "It doesn't matter. I just wish things were different, that's all. I wish..."

"Yes?"

"Nothing. Never mind." His hands stroked down the length of her back, wanting to remember all of it. The curve of her waist, the flare of her hips, the sweet weight of her, as she lay on top of him, so warm and solid and real. How her head fit so perfectly, tucked beneath his chin. The way it felt – right now – as she moved her foot a little and it brushed against his calf. Oh, why couldn't they just stop talking? And let him pretend for a little while longer, that she'd ever been his, or ever could be.

"You asked me to lie. To tell you I'd stay. But—"

He opened his eyes at that. "Don't do this to me. Please. I know what I asked you to say. I know you didn't mean it. But please don't—"

"It wasn't a lie! I mean…I don't *want* to leave you, Nick. I thought… I thought that's what *you* wanted. Isn't it?"

"What *I* wanted?" He looked her full in the face then, saw the questions, the doubt in her eyes, and was astonished. "What are you thinking? Don't you know—? My God, Jen, I have loved you since that very first night, when you jumped into my car. All those years you were gone – did you really think there was ever a moment when I didn't want you, and long for you, and dream of someday having you back in my arms? How could you think I'd want you to leave? I don't *ever* want to be without you—not ever again!" [1]

SHE COLLAPSED AGAINST HIM THEN, and he held her close, his hands caressing her bare skin, not seeming to mind the hot tears she shed against his neck.

"That horrible day at your school, when I learned the truth, when I knew I couldn't have you— oh, man, I thought I would lose it for sure. But you were so cool and calm, facing everybody down, and then staring through me, like I wasn't even there. And all I kept thinking was, 'my car is right outside. If I move fast enough, I can grab her and be gone before anyone can stop us.'"

His arms tightened around her. "But I couldn't figure out how far we'd be able to get before they caught up with us." He laughed, mirthlessly. "I tell you what though, I almost didn't care. I think I would have driven us straight into hell, for the chance of keeping you with me."

Scout shivered, remembering.

"You're cold." Nick grabbed his shirt from the floor to cover her. "There, is that better?" he asked, so tenderly that she could only nod her head, knowing she could never tell him it wasn't the lack of clothes that made her shiver.

443

"So...you're staying?" Nick asked again, a long time later, still not quite daring to believe it. They hadn't moved from the couch, which suited him fine. He didn't particularly care if they never moved again.

"Yes. Yes, I'm staying. Oh, Nick, you knew, didn't you? You had to know that I never wanted to leave in the first place. After everything I did to keep from losing you, whatever made you think I didn't care?"

He chuckled a little, not bothered by any of it anymore. All the pain was in the past now. It could stay there. "Oh, well, you mean beside the little things like your staying gone for twenty years? Not to mention having the incredibly bad taste to fall for a serial killer while you had me head over heels in love with you?"

Scout glared at him indignantly. "I did *not* fall for Glenn. I always thought he was a jerk. Although..." she fell silent for an instant, he felt a small shudder pass through her. "I don't think anyone realized how unhinged he was."

"No. You're right about that. Unfortunately."

"The only reason I slept with him was so I wouldn't lose *you*."

"How's that?" he asked on a yawn. He looked down at her curiously.

She sighed. "I know, I know...it was really dumb, okay? But I thought that if you ever found out that I was still a virgin, you'd figure out that maybe I wasn't quite as old as you thought I was. And the way we were going, I figured you'd realize it soon enough. I had to do something."

She paused and sighed again before continuing. "And there was Glenn. Even though he was seeing Lisa, I knew he was available. We all knew he'd screw anything. And at the time...oh, at the time I was pissed off at Lisa anyway, so— Nick? Are you *laughing* at me?"

"I'm sorry," he gasped, trying without success to stop the convulsions that had seized him. "So, okay. Let me see if I've got this straight. What you're saying is...you did it for me?"

"In a weird way...yeah. I guess, you could say that."

"Wow. That is just – you know, Scout, I really want to say that's the nicest thing anyone has ever done for me, but...well, hon, it's gotta be about the dumbest thing I ever heard of."

She nodded. "Yep, I kind of figured that out, pretty quick myself. So, can we please, please never talk about this again?"

"My pleasure. Just answer me one more question."

"Oh God," Scout groaned, dropping her head against his shoulder. "What is it now?"

He tipped her chin up so he could see her face. "Let's be serious for a minute. Are you sure about this? You're not going to change your mind and disappear on me again? I mean, we talked about this the other day. I know you have a whole life somewhere else, and it's no secret that you're not too fond of Oberon."

Now it was her turn to look surprised. "What does that have to do with anything? I thought I'd lost you *forever*! What was the point in coming back? And as for my having another life, well, you do too, don't you?"

"I suppose."

"You—?" She pushed away from him and sat up. "My God, Nick, you have so much more of a life than I ever had. You have a home and a family. People who love you. Your life is so full. I didn't know if there was any room in it, for me. I thought probably there wasn't. That was why I couldn't stand being in your apartment, you know?"

"How's that?"

"The whole time I was there, I couldn't stop thinking about what it would be like, having a life with you. I knew if I spent too much time there, if I let myself get comfortable, it would only hurt that much more when I had to give it all up again."

NICK LAUGHED WEAKLY as he pulled her back down to him. "Oh, God. Honey, you have no idea how much I wanted you to be comfortable, or—" He broke off and buried his face against her neck; inhaling her fragrance and her warmth, remembering the night before, the way she had looked asleep in his bed.

"Okay," he said, reaching a decision. "You really want to know what living with me is gonna be like? Come on, get dressed."

"What? But why?" Scout whined. "Where are we going *now*?"

"My place." He rolled off the couch and hauled her to her feet. "I'm making you dinner."

"Dinner? Isn't it going to be a little late for that?"

"Yeah, it is. And we still have to find a grocery store that hasn't closed yet, and then the sauce has to cook. So, hurry up."

"All right, all right." Scout sighed, and began pulling on her clothes. "So, what are we having, anyway?"

"Meatballs."

"*Meatballs?*" She sat back down on the couch and started to laugh.

Nick looked at her in surprise. "Spaghetti and meatballs. Yeah. It's my specialty. What's so funny?"

She shook her head. "I'm sorry. It's just that you cook all these wonderful meals and tell me they're nothing fancy, or they're just something you threw together. And then your special dish is, well, *meatballs*? It's surprising, is all."

"Oh, I see. You think just 'cause it's meatballs, it isn't special enough, is that it?"

"Well, yeah. Now that you mention it."

"Ah," he said as he pulled her towards the door, a glint in his eyes. "You just think that because you haven't tried mine."

"WELL?" Nick's eyes sparkled in the candlelight, and Scout wanted to laugh at the smug satisfaction in his voice.

She took another bite. She took her time chewing slowly and thoughtfully, before she finally answered. "It's good."

"Just good?"

Nick's eyebrows rose as she nodded her head in grudging approval. And then she smiled. "I'm kidding. It's *very* good. Delicious, in fact. I could definitely get used to this."

"Told you so." He reached across the table and took hold of her hand. He held it very tightly. As if he had no plans to ever let it go.

"But," she said, unable to resist teasing, "we don't *always* have to wait until three in the morning before we eat them, do we?"

"No." Nick frowned, sounded ever so slightly scandalized at the thought. "Of course not. Don't be silly. They're very good for breakfast, too." [2]

---

1. That last scene has always, always been one of my favorites. I love everything about it. Yes, even all the head-hopping.
2. You know who else's specialty is meatballs? This girl right here! My father thought his were the best (of course) and they were pretty good. But mine are better. That's my story and I'm sticking to it.

## 37

*S*o, it looks like they were able to work things out after all," Marsha observed as she peered out the kitchen window at the two figures bundled together on Lucy's porch swing.

Lucy looked up from the special Fourth of July dessert she was preparing – raspberries and blueberries layered with a rich mixture of whipped cream and mascarpone cheese, carefully arranged over a base of Chambord-soaked ladyfingers – and rolled her eyes. "I know. Sickening, isn't it?"

Marsha looked amused. "You're just *never* happy, are you?"

Dan laughed. He sneaked another piece of strawberry out of Lucy's dessert and fed it to her. "Ah, she's a real romantic this one. Don't let her fool you, Marsha. It's her aunt she's thinking about. But like I keep telling her, if those two aren't worried, why should she be?"

"That's the problem," Lucy grumbled. "Those two aren't worried about *anything* right now." She shot an exasperated look at her husband as he popped a blueberry into his own mouth. "Although, I suppose, worrying can't be all that easy for them, what with all the sleep they're obviously *not* getting. Which, by the way, some people here might want to take note of."

Dan grinned. "Hmph. I can see I've got my work cut out for me, all right." He leaned in close, just barely brushing his lips against hers in a mere whisper of a kiss. Pulling away with a wicked, tantalizing smile, just as she'd begun to move in closer, he whispered in her ear, "Just wait and see how much sleep *you* get tonight."

"I've been thinking," Marsha mused, as Dan left the room. "About Celeste's share of the store."

"Huh? What'd you say?" Lucy shook her head, as comprehension hit. "Oh, no. Why do I get the feeling I don't want to hear this?"

"Well, I thought it would make a nice wedding present."

"A what? Oh, God, Marsha. Please tell me you're joking. No, never mind, don't tell me anything. I don't even want to hear about this."

"Well, I always did like the idea of having three of us involved in the business. You know, because of the whole Triple Goddess thing? But if you have someone else in mind?"

"No," Lucy sighed. "I don't. And I suppose it fits. Anyway, Celeste left it to you, along with everything else. So, it's your call Marsha. Whatever you want to do is fine with me. It's just...shit, I'm never going to be finished with this particular karmic lesson, am I?"

Marsha shook her head. "Probably not in this lifetime. But, come on, Lucy. It's not really *that bad*, is it?'

She shrugged. "It could be worse. At least, I guess it could be worse. Somehow."

"Oh, yeah. It could definitely be worse."

"Still. It's a hell of a way to organize a universe, that's all I can say."

"You got that right." Marsha leaned against the counter and regarded her friend fondly. "By the way, are we actually going to eat that dessert any time tonight?"

Lucy nodded. "Yeah, yeah, I'm almost done. Just let me make the coffee."

"Little late for coffee, don't you think?"

"Nah," Lucy chuckled, "The way my life is going? I got a feeling I'm gonna need all the caffeine I can get, just to see me through it."

FIREWORKS BLOSSOMED in the sky above their heads as she and Nick sat together on Lucy's porch. Scout basked in the unfamiliar feeling of being surrounded by a family.

From the house came the pungent aroma of espresso brewing, and the sibilant hissing, bubbling sound of milk being steamed for cappuccino.

"She's taking this pretty well," Scout murmured quietly.

Nick smiled back. "I told you she might surprise you."

"Oh, you have no idea!" she said, laughing as she snuggled closer. "Of course, she doesn't know everything, yet. Do you really think I'll make an okay stepmother?"

"I think you'll be a wonderful stepmother. And if not, you know what to do, right?"

She glanced up at him, puzzled. "No, what's that?"

"What you always do. Lie to me."

"Huh!" For a moment, Scout was speechless. "You know, it would serve you right if I did." She sighed. "I bet Caroline would have loved the idea that I'd grow up to become somebody's stepmother."

"Sure, she would. She loved you."

"I still can't believe it. All those years I thought she hated me, and the whole time— She really *was* afraid that someone was after me." She shook her head sadly.

"Well, she was right. And the way I kept showing up on her doorstep looking for you probably only made her more afraid." Then he sighed, as well. "Who knows? If I'd kept away, she might have stopped worrying. She might have allowed you to come back, maybe years sooner."

"You came looking for me? I never knew that."

Nick wrapped both arms around her then and pressed his lips against her head. "Of course, I did. How many times do I have to tell you? I was going out of my mind without you. I kept hoping that—

And, jeez, I don't know how many times I tried to ask Lucy if she'd heard from you."

"Oh, is that right?" Scout's lips curled into a little grin. "Because I distinctly remember your telling me that my name had not come up in any conversation you'd had with your cousin."

"Well, they weren't conversations. Not exactly. And anyway, seeing as you two are getting along so well, I don't know that we should be talking about anything she might have said back then."

Scout laughed. "Oh, I think I can pretty much guess. I've heard her views on the subject a few times myself. It's all right, you know. She was only trying to protect you. She just didn't understand, is all."

"What is it she didn't understand?"

"That I loved you, of course."

"Oh. I see." Nick looked at her curiously. "You do know, don't you, that this is the first time you've ever actually said the words?"

"Said what? That I loved you? No! Is it?" Scout stared at him in amazement. "Really?"

"Yes. And...tell me something. Is there any *particular* reason you're only using the past tense when you *do* say it?"

"Well, what's the difference?" she asked, with a smile. "Past. Present. Future. Take your pick. It's all the same, you know. And it's all true. I love you. I've always loved you, Nick. And I always will."

"Oh, well, in that case. How about I pick...all of the above?"

The smile she gave him then was everything he could have ever asked for. "Mm. Good answer."

THANK you so much for reading this book. If you enjoyed it, I hope you'll consider leaving a review. Now, read on to learn about the rest of the series, which will be returning soon.

# COMING SOON TO OBERON

A Sight to Dream Of
Oberon 2.0

Sam Sterling is a man with problems. Including a partner who is trying to kill him, and a nosy reporter, who's just turned up dead! It's going to take a miracle to save him. Or, better yet, an angel.

Marsha Quinn is used to being called a witch. After all, her abilities as a psychic make a lot of people uncomfortable. But no one has ever called her an angel before!

Falling in love was not a possibility she'd ever envisioned, until Sam the skeptic arrives in Oberon, and teaches her to see past the scars she carries, and the lies he's told her, to the love that lies within their hearts and minds.

Release Date: October 24, 2023
Now Available for Pre-Order
https://books2read.com/SightDream

## Sound of a Voice That is Still
### Oberon 3.0

Some wounds take a long time to heal, others never do. Four months after being wounded in the line of duty, Ryan Henderson is beginning to fear that his is of the latter variety. He's a patient man, but a poor patient. As winter drags interminably on, he's growing desperate for distraction—anything that might take his mind off his injury, and his fears for the future.

Siobhan Quinn could give the injured officer a lesson or two in living with pain. It's been ten years since her life was changed and her heart critically wounded as a result of the tragic accident that robbed her of her family. She knows firsthand how grief can cripple a soul and drive a sane mind over the edge.

Sometimes it seems like Spring will never come again. Sometimes, the only alternative to living in inner darkness, is death. Your own, or someone else's. In the depths of winter, Ryan and Siobhan will have to make a choice: to help each other heal, or die trying.

Release Date: November 21, 2023
Now Available for Pre-Order
https://books2read.com/SoundVoice

# ABOUT THE AUTHOR

PG Forte inhabits a world only slightly less strange than the ones she creates; filled with serendipity, coincidence, love at first sight and dreams come true. Originally a Jersey Girl and forever a California Girl at heart, PG currently makes her home in the beautiful Texas Hill Country.

Learn more about PG and her books at www.PGForte.com

To stay up to date on new releases, access free reads, ARCs and more, please consider joining PG's reader group on Facebook at: https://www.facebook.com/groups/TheCronesNest

Or sign up for her newsletter: https://www.pgforte.com/newsletter

**Join PG Forte Online**

# EVEN MORE OBERON

Click the following links to learn more about:

The Oberon Series
The Oberon Novellas
The Oberon Christmas stories
The Oberon/LA Love Lessons Crossover Novellas

There's something magical about the little coast town of Oberon, California. Anything could happen here and all too often it does. It's a place filled with mystery, intrigue, mysticism and romance and while the location is fictional, the people populating it can seem all-too real.

The Oberon series is currently undergoing a re-boot. But you can read the prequel novella, *Such Fleeting Pleasures* now! Join my Facebook group, The Crone's Nest, for access to your free download!

Or learn even more about the series at any of these links:

Who's Who in Oberon
Oberon Chamber of Commerce

## Going Back to Oberon
### (*A __very__ short story*)

This story started out as a feature on Cabin Goddess's "Fourth Wall Friday" blog; in which authors were invited to put themselves into a scene where they interacted with their characters.

I had a great deal of fun imagining myself returning to the scene of my very first series. It started me thinking about all the Oberon stories I hadn't told yet. And it really motivated me to start getting some of those ideas out there.

You can download a copy HERE. Enjoy!

# THE LA LOVE LESSONS SERIES

An aspiring actress searches for her leading man; an amnesiac heiress seeks clues to her true identity; and a tarnished movie star finds love and acceptance in the last place she ever expected. Love like this could only happen in LA.

### *Waiting for the Big One*

*Aspiring actress Gabby Browne refuses to consider her best friend, and personal trainer, Derek Novello for the role of soul mate fearing sex will ruin their beautiful friendship. When she meets Zach, she's convinced that he could be The One. Too bad Derek isn't willing to share-leaving Gabby forced to choose between two sexy co-stars.*

*An early morning earthquake provides Gabby with the impetus she needs to stop waiting for the stars to align and finally cast her leading man.*

### *Going to the Chapel*
An Oberon/LA Love Lessons Crossover Book

*Gabby and Derek went from friends to lovers. Now, they're waiting for* their "big day". But will it be the wedding of their dreams? Or a bride's worst nightmare?

A quick trip to Gabby's hometown turns into the wedding from hell when Gabby and Derek are plagued by hailstorms, lost reservations, voracious goats, angry bees and enough family drama to fill a barn.

Can the happy couple hold it all together, or will their Big Day turn into a Big Mess?

***A different version of this book was previously released as part of the Sapphire Falls Kindle World program***

### Love, From A To Z

Zach Harris is sure the girl he'd picked up last night had said her name was Angel. Too bad she didn't tell him anything more about herself, because, this morning, it's not just him she can't remember, she doesn't even know her own name!

What April views as a problem, Zach sees as a once-in-a-lifetime opportunity; a chance for her to discover who she really is. Not her name or her address, but the important stuff. Her personality. Her likes and dislikes. Her preferences—in and out of bed.

### Let Me Count the Ways

As the owner of The Body Electric, LA's hottest new exercise studio, sexy, former film star Claire Calhoun has her pick of studly young men eager to do her bidding. Small wonder she's used to calling the shots, both in and out of bed. But everything changes the night the actress-turned-entrepreneur has one mojito too many at a party and decides it would be fun to pick up her accountant, Mike Sherman. She's thinking fling. He's thinking forever.

Claire has been Mike's fantasy since the first time he saw her bare it all for the camera. Now, she's in his bed and he'll do whatever's necessary to keep her there.

## RELEASING LATER THIS YEAR

### Christmasing With You
An LA Love Lessons/Ugly Christmas Sweater Story

*The sweater was just the beginning...*

Mike's been a very good boy this year and Santa Claire has the perfect present picked out for him—one that's both naughty and nice!

*One more disaster could be the end...*

Mike and Claire were hoping their first Christmas together would be unforgettable. But when their sexy, adult-film-themed weekend abruptly veers into low-budget, chiller-diller territory, they're left to worry that this Christmas will turn out to be memorable in all the worst ways.

An isolated cabin, a winter storm, a hungry cougar—what could possibly go wrong? In a word: everything.

This Ugly Christmas Sweater short story features the characters Mike and Claire from Let Me Count the Ways (LA Love Lessons, book 3).

COMING SOON

### Last Room at the Inn
An LA Love Lessons/Ugly Christmas Sweater Story

All April and Zach had planned for Christmas was a quiet getaway...but even the best plans can go awry. Especially at Christmas time.

This Ugly Christmas Sweater short story features the characters April and Zach from Love from A to Z (LA Love Lessons, book 2).

### Going up the Country
An Oberon/LA Love Lessons Crossover Novella

*How far would you go for the love of your life?*

Pro-wrestler Wyatt Novello never believed in love at first sight—until he attended his brother's wedding and met a girl who made him go weak in the knees.

Arielle Browne knows a bad boy when she sees him. Her weakness for the type has already landed her in trouble a time or two. It didn't take more than one look to convince her that Wyatt was everything she wanted in a man--and everything she needs to stay far, far away from. Both for her own sake, and that of her two impressionable sons.

But Wyatt's determined to go the distance. Either he'll find a way to convince Arielle that she's wrong—about him, and their chances of achieving their own Happily Ever After—or he'll die trying.

They're each convinced they've chosen the right path. But how do you know when you've gone too far?

# THE GAMES WE PLAY SERIES

**The Games We Play/Wild Geese trilogy**

A quirky, family-owned resort on the Jersey Shore is the setting for this erotic, lightly paranormal series. Cousins Brenda, Luke and Gwyn are determined to turn their failing hotel business around. They have no time for love. They're in no mood for games. But it's not going to matter. Not when they're up against a handful of ghosts, a mischievous boggart, a family curse, and destinies written in stone.

Truth or Dare
Games We Play 1.0

After their drunken menage goes wrong, Gwyn wants nothing to do with Berke and Cam—until seven years later, when they show up at her family's hotel with a tempting proposition she just can't resist.

Never Have I Ever
Games We Play 2.0

After having been friend-zoned by Kristy when they were kids,

Luke had mostly resigned himself to being "just friends" with her, but working together, night after night, is shredding his self control.

Two Truths and A Lie
Games We Play 3.0

Brenda's relationship with Max is a sexy sham designed to keep her cousins from learning of her plans to sell their family's inn. Falling in love for real? That was not supposed to happen.

**The Games We Play/DiLuca Brothers Duology**

The Atlas Beach  Chamber of Commerce's innovative mentoring program—partnering successful  business owners with some of the newer start-ups—has just what food truck owner Carly Meyers and baker Stephanie Sands needed to get their businesses off the ground: The Delectable DiLuca Brothers.

These Jersey Boys might be cocky, but cooking's not their only talent, and the kitchen's not the only place where they'll be turning up the heat.

The Name Game

Tino DiLuca knows exactly what's hurting Carly's business and —exactly how to fix it. But his number one solution, changing the name of her signature sandwich, is the one thing she's not prepared to do.

Funnel of Love

Baker Rocco DiLuca is *not* a happy camper. He's just found out that his baby sister is getting married—to his former best friend— and he's not invited. But that's not even the worst part. They've hired *someone else* to make their wedding cake!

*The Games We Play Series*

Releasing in 2024

**The Games We Play/Coffee House Collection**

Includes the novellas *Put a Ring Around the Rosie*, *The White Elephant Gift Exchange*, and *Whole Latte Love*

Put a Ring Around the Rosie

*February 14th is just another day...until it's not.*

They say timing is everything, and that certainly has always been the case where Alex and I are concerned. We met nearly two years ago when he was hired to work at Cup of Joe, the coffee shop where I was already an old timer. It was lust at first sight, at least on my part, but I had a boyfriend then, and so did he. By the time we were both single and I'd worked out that he was bi, things between us had become complicated in so many other ways that it seemed much simpler and safer to just stay friends.

We were work spouses for a while, and then we weren't. And when we reconnected with each other last month it was after a prolonged period of hurt feelings and miscommunication during which we barely spoke to each other at all.

Now, even though our friendship's caught fire, so to speak, I feel like we're both still recovering from that last, disconnected phase. Heaping a bunch of unrealistic expectations, or a need for chocolate hearts, plush toys, or rose colored anything on top of that seems like a little too much added pressure.

Now Available for Pre-Order

SCENT OF THE ROSES
*Oberon: Book 1*

**20th Anniversary Edition**
**Copyright © 2023 by PG Forte**
All rights reserved.
Cover Artist: PG Forte
digital ISBN: 978-1-880370-45-2
print ISBN: 978-1-880370-49-0
Published in the United States of America
Chapultepec Press

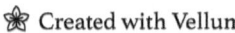 Created with Vellum

www.ingramcontent.com/pod-product-compliance
Lightning Source LLC
Chambersburg PA
CBHW020629020726
47494CB00001B/109